FOSSIL COVE PRESS

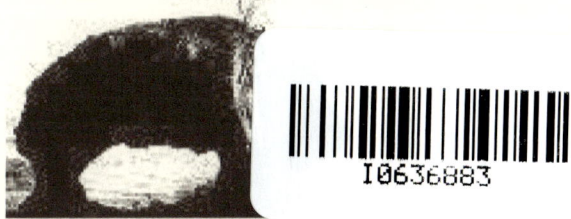

I0636883

BENNY THE ANTICHRIST

And Other Stories

by

Scott Ellis

BENNY THE ANTICHRIST and other stories
By Scott Ellis

FOSSIL COVE PRESS, Winnipeg, Manitoba

Fossil Cove Publishing
1301 - 90 Garry Street
Wpg, Man, Canada, R3C 4J4

Cover by Dawn Dominique, based on short story, Saccade

Issued in print, electronic and audio formats
ISBN: 978-1-7778108-1-8 (ebook)
ISBN: 978-1-990860-43-0 (print)
ISBN:978-1-990860-32-4 (audio)

Dedication

None of this work would have been possible without the constant care, organizing ability and many heroisms, large and small, of my wife Anna, who for years has done far more than her fair share to keep our household together and healthy. Anna, I can never thank you enough.

The Ellis mob, including exes and semi-Ellises, past and present, and their associated crime families also had roles in producing all this: Don, Pat, Brian, Matt, Jen, Charlotte, Leon, Margaret, Miles, Robin, Rory, Ian, Ava, Juliette, Freya, another Matt, Davis, Karen, Nancy, Jim, David, Greg and a bunch of others: There would be no me without all of you.

Friends: To Herb F., a skeptic's skeptic, an utterly decent person who makes nerd a title of honor. To Laura, who is far more competent and better company than she realizes. Peter D., gifted explainer, whose sheer intellectual stamina leaves me awestruck. To Al R., an inexhaustible source of ideas, and a constant reminder that words are only one way to make a world. Joanne H., who animates the phrases "fighting the good fight" and "keep on keeping on" and makes them more than clichés. To Patrick L., who, without pretension, can always be relied upon to bring out the moral dimension in all actions. Phyllis and Larry C., boon companions and guides to what's behind the scenes in everyday events.

And a host of others, role models, horrible examples, troublesome heroes, gifted kvetchers, conspiracy theorists and inspired goofballs, who gave me more than I will ever completely understand.

BENNY THE ANTICHRIST
And Other Stories
Table of Contents

BENNY THE ANTICHRIST

I'm kind of used to Frank, actually. This is good, because there is not a lot I can do about him. Frank is an enforcer for one Benny the Antichrist, a local shylock not half so pleasant as his name might suggest. Local meaning I'm pretty sure Benny's from somewhere within a few parsecs and has been here, controlling everything within those parsecs since at least the fall of Rome. So he and Frank aren't problems I can wish away, much as I'd like to.

Presently Frank is looming over me, something he could probably do lying down, and even though I have the window open, the air in my third storey walk-up office feels kind of close. I call him Frank because if I called him what everyone else does, Large Francis, I might start to giggle. Frank is a tolerant person, but there are limits.

More importantly, he is a person, barring a few trifling augmentations. The last of Benny's emissaries who graced these premises wafted in on a cloud of methane and proceeded to do troubling things with an ovipositor. I'm still finding larvae in odd places.

For some reason I feel Frank's presence in my office is Benny's effort to spare my feelings, though imagining kindness on the Antichrist's part is like looking for the bright side of Ebola. But in my position, into Benny for sixty large, one doesn't question things. Frank has just explained to me that his employer and said employer's business associates wish to savor the pleasure of my company, post-haste.

He declines to elucidate further. I object that I am paying off the vig, have even made a slight dent in the principal and that our next appointment is three days hence. Frank compliments me on my prudence, and allows as how the Antichrist has commented on my unexpected financial resources. At this I have a certain sinking feeling. The only way to keep on the good side of the Bennies of this nebula, I reflect, is to avoid all of their sides. You can't even do right by doing right. Meanwhile, Frank is explaining that his boss would like certain favors done and is willing, Intergalactic Bank-like, to re-schedule my payments in exchange. I am still not enthusiastic, for much the same reason that bunnies do not go calling on bobcats.

"Understand, Arnie, it isn't as though I don't sympathize with your position. But my employer has backed your financial endeavors, and, sad to say, though normally the soul of prudence and acumen, Arnie, you do keep betting on the Cubs. Now, may we go? I got a dentist's appointment." He leans over me and my office like a melancholy mountain. Is he getting a touch of gray at the temples, I wonder, or just snow on his summit?

It really is not difficult for Frank to dominate me and my place of work, and not just because he is large. I had taken note of this the first and last time I hit him, aiming for a couple of places where nobody is big and tough. All I did was hurt my foot and annoy him. It is difficult to defy someone after an episode like that.

Nor is my office impressive. Just a little third-storey, one window joint above a store, off Wacker. A desk, a receptionist, a phone with four lines, and an open window with a view of the alley. As for my business, well, it's a little of this, some more of that, and a lot of the other. I do a lot of, shall we say, freelance shipping and receiving and a little consulting on the side. It can be fairly lucrative, if you move often, and there is not a lot of overhead. In fact the biggest expense, my receptionist Bernice, has been on coffee for the last hour. Prudence rubs off quickly in this business.

"I realize that you are right, Frank," I temporize. "I don't really have a choice. By the way, what's wrong with your teeth?"

"I cracked a molar on a guy's tiepin. Shall we go?"

"I know an orthodontist who ain't fussy what you pay him with."

"I will keep this in mind. After you."

"Frank, for as long as I have known you, I never asked for a favor."

He frowns. "That's true."

"--and believe me, I don't like asking you for one now. How-somever-"

Frank scowls, looking like a large, destructive weather system. "Don't," he says.

"Don't?"

Benny the Antichrist, Page 3

"Diacopes." He waves a huge paw in front of his face as though brushing off a pesky fighter plane, "What-person-soever. New-by-God-York. Absogoddamlutely. Shoddy, inflationary discourse. An incontinence of emphasis."

"Why Frank, I had no idea that you were such a dyed-in-the-Italian-tailored-wool rhetorician."

Frank looks even more unhappy, something that genuinely alarms me. "I know, I know. You hate tmesis to pieces."

"Sometimes, Arnie, I think our discussions are jinxed."

"You're not just whistling Dixie."

"The request, Arnie, the request!"

"Frank, in all our dealings, have I ever caused you any trouble? I mean, saving our initial acquaintance, I have always behaved appropriately, am I right? And now for all my propriety and following the rules, you have come to take me to your boss and his business associates, somewhere you know I really don't want to go. So what I want to do, this one time, is hit you."

"Hit me?"

"One punch. On the chin."

"Arnie, the last time you hit me you hurt yourself. I didn't even have to retaliate. Just collect you."

"That's true, Frank, but this is a matter of my self respect. Besides, I think I can get better torque this time."

Frank considers, looking like Vesuvius on a calm day. A tiny breeze finally makes it through the window. "All right," he says. "One, on the chin."

"Frank, I'm touched by your fairness and trust."

"I wouldn't wish you to feel that you had not exhausted every possible avenue of escape at your disposal, Arnie. Besides, you have seen examples of my handiwork. I feel confident that you would not do anything that would seriously upset me." He positions his chin within easy striking distance. "Ready?"

It's like aiming at Ayer's Rock. I stand up, loosen my shoulders, plant my feet, measure the distance, clench my fist, wind up and dive through the window.

This is not as rash it may seem. Directly below my office, on the first floor, must be the only working clothesline in downtown Chicago. I have often wondered why no civic officials have been by to declare it a historic landmark. I believe the residents hang apparel out there in order to originate and market the Corroded Look, a vogue they hope will sweep the planet.

I hit the lines painfully, but not fatally, then manage to let myself down, pursued by battalions of ripped t-shirts, headbands and one corset of heroic dimensions. But not by Frank. He just sticks his head out of my window and observes "I would have believed better of you, Arnold."

"Well, Francis, I guess I'm smarter than the average goon."

So saying, I race rightward up the alley to my aircar. Like everything else I've done so far, this is a mistake.

Standing in front of my Ford Fruitfly is one of the associates Frank spoke of, Rudolph "Rudy the Razor" Canetoad and his torpedoes, Charles "Dick" and Richard "Chuck", the Bltzfk Twins. I turn in consternation, but there isn't a Stage Left for me to exit to. To one side of me is Etienne "Stevie Fingers" Kwakwakuong, Guiseppe "Nunchaka Joe" Yeeurghz, and Howard "Howard" Schwartz. To the other is Lance "Plague of Boils" A-27 and his underlings Raymond the Juggernaut and Paul "Generic" Janeiro. Rounding it all out, behind me, is Benny the Antichrist, who today has donned human guise like an expensive but badly tailored suit.

"Howard" snickers. Rudy looks as if he'd like to know just what my peritoneum looks like. Raymond rubs his wings together and glances at my ribs, no doubt wondering how many he can smash at a punch. The twins glower at me for reasons I doubt I will ever have time to explain. "Let's do something excruciating to him," says one, though it could be the other. And Benny smiles, a phenomenon I would spend a lot of time and money to avoid witnessing.

By way of chitchat, I offer "This must be some sort of convention. I never saw so many wiseguys together in my life. I thought the Star Cops thinned a few of you out." I am babbling, I know, but these are surely extenuating circumstances.

Benny's smile broadens. He motions the Juggernaut forward. Raymond looks eager, his mandibles stridulating in anticipation, then disappointed when Benny indicates that all he wants him to do is put me in a sleeper hold. Just before everything goes black, Benny catches my eye and leans forward. He says "I'll do the thinnin', around here."

** *

People always say it's a pleasure watching a real craftsman at his work. I don't know for sure, but they're probably not referring to

Benny the Antichrist, Page 5

instances where the job he's doing uses your face as raw material, getting rawer with every punch, tentacle sting or mandibular pinch. Not that I'm complaining, mind you.

I'm also bound to report, that, as these things go, Raymond the Juggernaut is showing a certain amount of restraint, administering a beating that probably counts as a polite introduction around here. Bruises, not fractures. The merest hint of contusion. It's a whack job with all the p's and q's.

Since my escape from Large Francis and subsequent cornering, these gentlecreatures have escorted me to a nearby packing plant. I'm getting the benefit of what Bernice would call a learning experience in one of the coolers. It's half full of hanging cadavers of various provenance. There are also empty hooks just waiting for a carcass. Eyeing one, I wait for the next morsel of pain. Things could be worse. They will undoubtedly get worse.

In between bouts of Raymond's impromptu plastic surgery, Benny calls out to me, "I'll be with you in a bit, Arnie. Just gotta call one of my local guys," much as if I had someplace else I was going to go, should these proceedings grow wearisome.

In these homey environs Benny has reverted to his native aspect. Imagine Napoleon crossed with Jabba the Hutt. Then deck the hybrid with pseudopods, flagellae and organs describable only with recourse to some special, criminal xeno-zoology. Seeing him thus, I am reminded that he is a "Benny" only because the last human who tried to accurately pronounce his name shattered his own jaw and blew his ganglia out his ears. Keeping one eye swiveled toward me, Benny grips a strangely shaped phone with one appendage or another and has the following conversation:

"Shelly, my man! Ernie. How're Glenda and the kids? Good, good. Katya's fine. Well, she knows, but she don't, y'understand what I'm talkin' about? Yeah, it's a lock. Prenuptual. I got Kuwait, the Great Barrier Reef and whatsisface, that little twink singer, total rights to everything he even dreams. Yeah. Everybody laughs, I say that, but it's true.

"Anyway, reason I'm callin' is the Gaia deal. Shelly, we gotta get on the good foot here. How's your guy? Good. Listen, we got no problem, the plate tectonics clauses, that's cool. But the genotypes we gotta have.

"Uh huh. Uh huh. Listen, Shel.... Shel.... Shel. Shel. Shel. SHELDON!!! Look, I'm gonna explain somethin', you should know

Benny the Antichrist, Page 6

already, OK? And once I'm done, you better tell your guy, ya hear me talkin' to ya?

"Look, Sheldon, who you think you're dealin' with here? Don't kid yourself: We are the OPPRESSORS. That's right. And I'ma tell ya something else: We're very comfortable with that. I gotta therapist, comes in once a week, helps me integrate that. Yeah, Marcia. Well she does have her degree. Yeah, the headlights help. Should see her in a bustier.

"Now, like I'm sayin', Shel, once in a while we spot a new prospect, like your guy, comin' along. And nearly always, dude's got a little "Let My People Go" action on the side. Hey, you're only young once, 'less you buy into the right product, am I right? Actually, it's kind of a giggle, you know? Rapin' and pillagin' gets to be nine to five, like everything else.

"But don't kid yourself. Let's get our priorities straight. You're messin' around with some heavy suppliers, here. No! I don't have to name 'em, and you know that, Shel. Look, guy, let me make it simple for you: Here's our opening position: SCREW YOU. Here's our fallback: AND ANYONE WHO LOOKS LIKE YOU. You got that?"

'Cause if you don't--I hear you got some plans for Tierra del Fuego, with the cobalt an' that? Never mind how I know. How'd you like a big earthquake down there, like tomorrow, huh? You know me, Shel--I deliver. Yeah, you tell him…."

"OK, OK, let's go through it. Norway, check. Novaya Zemlya, check. Australia, check. Sudan, check. The Dinka mythology? You never know--I like to keep things covered. I got more things in my line than you'll ever know about, Shel. OK, OK, you're right, ya bandit. Tell you the truth, it's my niece Drambuie. Yeah, eighteen and cute as a button. Radcliffe. Anyway, she's got this anthro course and they gotta analyse some belief structure. An' all the easy stuff, Eastern Orthodox, Yanamamo, that's all been done to death. So I'm scoutin' around, ya know, playin' the market--and I check into the Creed Exchange. Well, the Dinkas got a brand-new offering--pastoral pantheists--that kinda stuff. Kind of like the Watusi--tribe of basketball players. Oh sure, they can do their rituals an' like that. 'Cept now they'll have to pay Drambuie a royalty every time.

"OK, Belgium, check. Ireland--no, Ireland can wait. Gambia and Cameroons, good. Togo--Togo? You're shittin' me, right? No, no, nothin' wrong with it. It's just--I thought everybody knew that story.

Benny the Antichrist, Page 7

"Oh, no. Some other time. Let's just--OK, alright, you're twistin' my cilia, Shel. This was just towards the end of, the-hell war was it? Last century, or maybe the one before. Maybe this one. Jeez, time flies. Anyway, there's a buncha the usual guys, hackin' around Europe somewhere, just off one of the battlefields, some chateau or other.

"We hadda lot on our plate, what with all the colonies an' that. So we decide, get the easy stuff outa the way first, you know, divvy up Africa an' get some shut-eye. So that's what we do.

"Well, turns out Africa ain't as easy as all that, what with everyone wanting to hold on to the goodies and leave all the tribes at each others' throats. Gets to three A.M. Everybody's dog-tired, what with looting and shooting all day, and we decide to take a break, have a snack. But the servants are all gone, or maybe we hadda kill 'em--I don't remember. So we gotta order out. I'm on the horn and--oh, come on Shel, we always had that, way before Alexander-Haggis-Face-Bell--Jeez, you young guys--anyway, like I'm sayin'--I'm callin' out. And I really gotta yell, 'counta the shellbursts an' that.

"Meantime, some of the guys are talkin', standin' around the map. You know how it is. One of the flunkies, Metternich or Mountbatten or somebody, he's been worryin' about some little corner around the Equator that nobody's bothered with yet. I'm on the line, shouting, for the umpteenth time 'I said, 'I want this all TO GO!!!'" And the guy--he's so fried--he writes it down! On the map!

"Well, we all had a good laugh. But you know, it sounded about right, considerin', an' we had bigger fish to fry. So now ya know. Remind me to tell you about porky Burkina sometime...."

All the while he's talking Benny is watching Raymond work, much as a housewife watches a mover reposition furniture around a room, save the items being shuffled are elements of my physiognomy. When he's satisfied with the arrangement, he nods to Raymond, who stops, looking a little disappointed, knowing he hasn't been allowed to really show his capabilities. Nunchaka Joe steps forward like he's next in the batting order, but the Antichrist frowns and he steps back hastily. Rudy the Razor cocks his head like a guy giving a haul-away junker the once-over. The Bltzfk twins just giggle.

Ending his phone call, Benny winks and explains "Local talent. Kind of pushy, but you gotta love the ambition." Extruding a hospitable pseudopod, he holds out an elaborately bejeweled and nasty cigarette case. "Smoke?" he offers.

Benny the Antichrist, Page 8

I take one. It never hurts to be mannerly, Mom always said, though the requisite etiquette in a situation such as this was probably not what she had in mind. It does hurt less, I think, for the time being.

I am not reassured when Benny himself gives me a light, using not matches, but an organ of his own, evolved, no doubt, for much worse purposes. Not that it matters what I think, but if Benny must needs know of my existence, I'd prefer his usual impersonal malevolence. You want to stick to the predictable, in my position.

"You know, Arnie," Benny the Antichrist says conversationally, drawing on a cigarette inserted in an orifice whose puckery similarities I'm trying not to dwell upon, "you and I got something in common."

Off the top of my head, I can't think of what that might be. Maybe that we're both vertebrates, except, probably, for him. But I'm thinking that this is likely not what he means, so I clam up.

"What I'm talking, Arnie, is you're in business. Me, I'm in business too. I'm in business to do business. I do business with the people I do business with. I don't, and I wanna stress this, I don't do business with the people I don't do business with. The people I do business with, they hear I'm doin' business with the people I don't do business with, well then, they make it their business to give me the business and bada boom, bada bing, I can't do business no more."

He fixes me with a stare both multi-faceted and bloodshot.

"It's tricky, this business thing." He pauses, like he expects me to leap in with some audience participation.

Me, if this is the section of the evening's entertainment between getting homogenized and having to do whatever abominable thing Benny's got in mind, I'm just as happy to savor the moment. I stay doggo, using my tongue only to test a loose tooth.

Benny sighs, which normally would alarm me, like anything else he does. Right now, I'm content to wait and surmise the nature of entities whose disapproval would worry the Antichrist. I don't speculate about it too hard. I know I'm due to find out for sure, and sooner than I'd like.

"So, Arnie," he finally says, "here's where you come in. What I need here is a neutral, whadyacallit, a guy who ain't associated with me, an emissary, if you get me." He pauses. "You get me?"

Maybe, I'm thinking, maybe I can wiggle out of this by shameless, groveling flattery. "Jeez, Benny," I whine, "you really think you need a

Benny the Antichrist, Page 9

mook like me? I mean, a made guy like you, Gotti, Attila the Hun, Krongor the Magnificent ain't fit to carry your krzugl strap. You got galactic dictators and gods lining up to kiss your tush. You got more muscle, packing more heat, than the Vnjnilliar Horde. You own the electroweak force and several dimensions. What could a schlubb like me possibly help you out with, you couldn't handle on your own?"

Another sigh. This sighing thing, in my opinion, is not a felicitous omen. "There are Powers, Arnie," the Antichrist says, "Dominions, Thrones and Principalities. Kingdoms in the Shadows, know what I'm talkin' about?"

I take this as my cue to nod sagely, not that I've got clue one.

"Good." He seems relieved, almost embarrassed. In an odd way, it's like I'm in control here. Overlooking, of course, small details of the setting, the legions of thugs in his employ, the threats of several varieties of death and worse, etc. "All those things you were saying, Arnie," Benny allows, munching ruminatively on the skull of some beast which, despite its surroundings, doesn't seem quite deceased, "they're all true. Whatever goes down, from a space armada conquering a constellation, to a three card monte grifter rooking a tourist, I get a cut. Guys who ain't born yet are gonna pay me vig with their first allowances. I put a contract on a guy and ba bing, three stars go supernova, just to flush him out. I collect royalties whenever a plant uses photosynthesis. The entire Crab Nebula pays me protection gelt. I am the Greatest, the Supreme Made Guy in this and several other universes. I got Existence by the short and curlies.

"And yet, and yet, it's begun to, how ya put it, to pall. The other day I had a guy, a guy who used to give me trouble, and I was giving him a choice between being digested alive by a Sluuphenian slime snake or having his children, and their children, hunted down by meteor piranhas. The kind of thing that used to make me feel all warm and fuzzy. And I was thinking: maybe I should just whack the guy. Worse, I was thinking: maybe I'll let him go. I was the larva who dismembered everybody in his nursery brood. How could it come to this?

"So I'm thinkin' about this when I got my weekly with my therapist, Marcia. And she says I'm jaded and I gotta get back to my first principles, to find my joy, my real desire. And I don't mind tellin' ya, Arnie," he says, sucking fluids from the still squealing skull, "this gives me pause.

"Since when do I got principles? What would they be? It's a regular, howyacallit, enigma. And I'm thinkin' and thinkin' and I ain't getting nowhere. I'm getting' kinda frustrated. You know, the kind of mood where you could just exterminate every single sentient being in the Magellanic Cloud, you're so honked off. And I'm thinking: maybe I'll do just that, when Large Francis comes in with your latest payment."

"Where is Frank, by the way?" I ask, not looking forward to another visit.

"Well, Arnie, he let you get away, if only temporarily. I hadda have his left foot chopped off, ground up and fed to him. He'll be fine, with some reconstruction and a couple years physio. You see what I mean? This crisis of meaning shit's turned me into a big softie!

"Anyways Frank comes in with your payment and you've made your vig and even put a dent in the principle, ahead of time. It occurs to me that I wish every one of my guys was like you. You know: business-like. And it hits me: Business. That's what I always wanted to do. And what's the first principle of business? Easy. Service to the customer.

"Now I know what you're thinkin'. Murder, drugs, whores, assault, fraud, arson, bribery, extortion, destruction of star systems: Benny, you're thinkin', you run a full-service shop. And it's true I try to cover all the bases, best I can," he says, looking humble as is possible for a three metre sack of malevolent slime. "But in recent millennia," he continues, "I have lost contact with my customer base. And frankly," he says sotto voce, swiveling a stalked, multifaceted eye back at his goons, who are cheerfully dismembering a senior citizen and laying bets on her projected time of demise, "I may not be associating with the nicest people.

"I need a change, is what I'm tryin' to tell ya. So I'm turning to you, Arnie, to help me get past this, how ya wanna put it, existential mishegas. What do you say? Are ya up for it?"

I'm being offered a choice between doing whatever stupefyingly horrible thing he's got planned and suffering torture right down to the subatomic level. I nod.

Inexplicably Benny seems reassured. He touches a pseudopod to my shoulder in a gesture no doubt intended to convey manly solidarity. It stings, as if he's inserted something there. "Good," he says. "Here's what I want you to do..."

* * *

Benny the Antichrist, Page 11

So this is how I find myself, after numerous circuitous rides and switchbacks, quietly slipping out of my Ford Fruitfly and schlepping up a sidewalk to a house in a place I'd really rather not know about.

Everything about this locale puts my back up. It's got all this... space. Everything's all... green, with grass and trees sprouting up everywhere you look. It's creepy. You don't know where to put your eyes. I try to watch the house, both to save myself when whatever horrible Being Benny has sent me to visit makes an appearance and to shut out the terror of all this leafiness.

Something hisses and I scream when I feel a cold touch on my neck. I spin and slam up against the house, stiletto at the ready. It seems to be something mechanical, which for some reason is rhythmically spitting streams of cold water on the grass.

Just then I hear the door open. I close my eyes and swallow. Then open them again and take a cautious peek at the Entity Benny wants me to approach, ready to run or grovel as needed.

She's wearing a tailored pink silk pantsuit. Her hair is waved and frosted. Her nails have little hearts painted on them. She's got a silver tray in front of her. "I just baked some chocolate chip cookies," she says. "Would you like some?"

A moment later I am seated in large, well-appointed but unused-looking kitchen at table that seems far too cute and delicate for chow with the likes of me. I am cautiously munching my cookie and sipping coffee that seems to be half candy, weighing the pros and cons of my situation.

On the one hand my hostess is setting up a large, multi-tiered, hologram-enhanced display from out of an impossibly thin pink attache case, no doubt diagramming some scheme involving pain, humiliation and danger on my part.

On the other, there seem to be no massive, brutal creatures here to hurt me, at present. But can anyone Benny wants to meet be trusted not to do horrible things? Contrariwise, he did say he wanted to change his life. Besides, what choice do I have?

My panicked ditherings are interrupted by the Pink Lady, who ascertains my name, informs me that I am to call her Lindy and advises me that someone with my seasonal coloring (I am a Spring, evidently) ought to wear more greens and soft earth tones. She would also like to know how I found out about TerraWay.

As per my instructions, I tell her I heard about the organization through a friend whose name escapes me at the moment. At this

Benny the Antichrist, Page 12

lapse of memory a tiny moue crosses her face, hitherto completely cherubic. I brace myself for some painful persuasion and attempt to conceal my trepidation, reaching for another chocolate chip cookie. For some reason this lightens the mood. Lindy garners my hasty agreement that the cookies are scrumptious and informs me proudly that they are Self-bakin' Li'l Chocky Chunkytones (tm). At this, the cookies all begin to sing:

We're chunky, we're sweet, we're so good to eat,
We're low in trans-fats and won't hurt your pecs,
We bake without a sheet and keep your kitchen neat,
We're Li'l Chocky Chunkytones and better than sex.

Their voices are high and clear, their harmony perfect, though the one I've half eaten and, startled, dropped on the floor, tends to slur a bit.

The tribulations of my day all catch up with me at this point. Thus far I've held up, in cringing, hangdog fashion, through threats, beatings and intimations of unutterably worse to come, but the cookie chorale undoes me. I begin, I'm sorry to say, to sob. I'd call for my Mommy if she hadn't blackmailed me last time I saw her.

Lindy, prepared for all contingencies, passes me a box of tissues to assuage my grief. This is a comfort till I find that each fluffy sheet is stroking me gently, whispering "awww" and "there, there, you poor thing" and notice that they are Li'l Tear-Activated Cuddles (tm). Somehow this dries me up quickly.

Again my hostess is way ahead of me. Quickly, she dowses me liberally with a kiwi-fruit scented mist she later informs me is Granny's Transcendent HappySpray (tm). This makes me feel (a) so much better that (b) I want to shout "Glory Halleluiah!" and (c) go shopping.

Lindy then activates a hologram of a radiantly happy, healthy, handsome family whose racial and species characteristics change depending on the angle and asks "Why are you here?" The family looks alert, expectant.

Before I can formulate an answer, she has one: "You are here because you want, you need, to join our Family, the TerraWay family of Health, Happiness and Hygiene. And in your need, dear, sweet, suffering Arnie, you have made the right choice, the only choice. For as our Beloved Founder, Gaia P. Johnson, has wisely said: TerraWay is the Way and the Light, Wholesomeness and Refreshingness. None shall come to the Kingdom of Joy, Perkiness and Eat-Off-The-Floor

Cleanliness but through TerraWay. TerraWay is the Yumminess and the Glamour, the Alpha and Omega…." I'm not sure how long all this goes on; the details are kind of hazy. Suffice it to say that I testify many times to the Healing and Deep-Cleaning Power of TerraWay, dance with the TerraWay holo-family, sing corporate hymns along with the Chunkytones and accept many Free Gifts of the Spirit, including Rose of Sharon Toilet Sanitizer, Circe's Facial Cream with Rejuvenating Nanobots and Low Probability Jojoba Bath Crystals.

At points during these and other travails too numerous and humiliating to mention, it occurs to me that I ought to deke out the back door and catch the first fast spacer to the nearest Black Hole. But then there's another Free Gift (Self-Cleaning Shiatsu Massaging Toenail Clippers) and another uplifting hymn(Shave Me Closer, Lordy) to sing. . .

Finally it's time, time to receive my own pink case and become an official TerraWay Dealer. There is a solemn hush in the air, save for the cookies, gravely humming churchly chords in the background. My head is bowed, as I remember my promise to bear this prize back to Benny and wonder if there is any chance I will survive that last encounter. Intoning some words of mystic beauty and sanitizing import, Lindy passes a pristine pink carrying case into my trembling hands.

The moment my fingers touch that rosy Naugahyde a pulse runs through my shoulder and I realize that the sting I felt previously was Benny planting some sort of transmitter to alert him at just this juncture. The doorbell rings. The plan was for me to bear the case to him in secrecy, but it seems he just couldn't hold himself back. Before I can warn her, my hostess excuses herself to open the door. I watch, paralyzed, as the door swings open and there stands my employer, three metres of miasmic, pseudopodded malificence, Benny the Antichrist. "Hiya Lindy," he says. "Long time, no see." Watching Lindy's face I see, not fear and horror, but the glowing satisfaction of a consummation devoutly to be wished. In the first seconds of watching her form melt and change to resemble Benny's and his to match hers, listening to and breathing the abominable sounds and smells of their conversation, I realize that this, finally, is my chance to scoot. Discreetly stomping the Chunkytones before they can raise the alarm, I absquatulate out the back door, leaving all my Free Gifts of the Spirit behind.

Benny the Antichrist, Page 14

As I race toward the nearest spaceport, it comes to me that on first meeting Lindy, I had felt deep pity for her, so soon to be an associate of Benny's. Later, somewhere into my TerraWay indoctrination, I had conceived, hard though it may be to credit, sympathy for Benny. Now I'm just sorry for the rest of us....

Comment

"Benny" started out as an entry to a contest run by long-dead Toronto magazine, a sort of elaboration of the Exquisite Corpse game. where the last line of the former issue's story became the first line of the new piece. From there it slowly accreted new features and directions, jokes I stole and (I hope) improved, a set piece I wrote for Talk.Bizarre, an 80s and 90s listserv, and a third act.

I wrote this piece in dribs and drabs, mostly as the jokes occurred to me, (or were stolen and embellished) but it all came from same impulse. Think of the result as a kind of bastard child, a mashup of S.J. Perelman, E.E. "Doc" Smith and Damon Runyon, with an unhealthy predilection for elaborately donnish puns, spike it with a little William Gibson, shake it to a light froth and see what poured out.

The End

BROWNOUT

An enterprising soul has somehow carved the words "THE BROWNOUT IS HERE" into the Trust Sector walkway, in dark, infected letters.

Glistening nanophages work to eradicate the grafitto, but it clings like a bad cough. Part of me may have seen this before: I page Tokyo for a reference.

The sun is shining. I smile - the mild irony of enjoying a public resource. The air twitters and shimmers with data. Tiny, engineered mites on my perfect skin secrete UV blockers. I am already at the meeting I am walking to, astral voices osmoting through the stubborn creatureness of the dura mater, making decisions, hiring, firing, expanding, contracting, electro-digital pseudopods and cilia waving here and gone.

My second-in-command says I needn't be there fleshly; she can handle it. But sometimes they need to see that power has a body when it needs one.

The buildings, the walks, the sky all mercury, self-organizing geysers from debentured sockets and I flow with them, smooth, silver. Small blue windflowers chirrup pleasingly, among the shifting, Persian carpet patterns of the soft, multicoloured grass.

They're taking the trees away. A part of me, somewhere, maybe in Swaziland, had them do that. I don't know why, but everything can be replaced.

The walkway skims a shiny bench wave along with me, in case I should fain lie a-doon, cool my o'er-fevered brow, but I smile and motion it on, no thank you, you're too kind...

My second-in-command on my visual cortex, smiling the nervous smile I gave her, giving me an executive summary of negotiations. I notify Berne to monitor her neural account.

Benny the Antichrist, Page 16

A white, fluffy terrier romps among the muted geometrics of the boulevard. "Mister, mister," it barks at me.

I crook my head slightly to the left. Something flashes under the dog, cooking it where it stands, singeing the paisley grass. A small lawnbot rushes over to repair the damage. And stops. There is a piece missing and I realize, suddenly, that the anemones have broken their gentle song.

Up ahead of me, something is slowly pushing its way up through the turf, grunting with effort as the grass loses its Trust Sector nutrient connections, goes matterdull.

I try to notify Security, but no one answers and the air is full of dust. There are no frequencies. An old word comes to me: alone. I try to turn and walk away, but my feet have sunk into the walkway and the sodden metal is crystalizing around my ankles.

I look at the hump in the grass and see that it's a woman, rank, matted hair falling into her eyes, rotted teeth endlessly gnawing a scabbed lip. She's gaunt, but her belly is swollen and I remember another old word: pregnant. She's looking at me, as though she means to say something.

She looks down toward the long, notched knife in her hand. She bends down to hack at the sod that still holds her feet back. Now she can move and she comes at me, a determined stumble. She opens her mouth.

Sweet Jesus, the smell!

The End

THE REASON OF SLEEP

Sunday night Callie dreamed she was logged into the Bioco MUD, one of the big virtual offices where she temped. Somehow she could see everyone, not just their online personas, but the real people as they sat at home at their keyboards or using rentaterms at the JobMall. They were at terminals in places all over the world and off it, in tiny prefab downtown apartments just like hers, in lo-grav condos in the Sea of Tranquility, in thatched huts outside Mumbai, but they were also sitting, row upon row, in a gigantic office.

Everyone was frozen in place, staring at terminals or stopped in mid-word. Her friend Raelene, another temp, pregnant and still in her nightdress, was pouring herself some coffee. The brown arc and splash hung in the air. She could hear someone coming, someone with jarring, uneven footfalls. It was like Gator Day at one of the places she temped, when a green alligator image crawled the virch-office at random intervals, picking off low producers, but worse. She needed to run.

She saw her husband Gareth sitting crosslegged at a desk beside hers, eyes closed. Somehow she knew he was watching her, that he was logged on even if he wasn't in his virch-chair, that he could help her. If he would only wake up. The footsteps were getting closer. The virch-office was beginning to smell like an alcoholic's sour sweat. A glint of eyes hung somewhere over Gareth's shoulder. She reached out to him and he revolved smoothly at her touch, as if his spine were the axis of a turntable. The lights started to flicker, their muffled hum turning to whispers. Gareth turned like food in a microwave, his sleeping face always aimed her way. It wasn't one face, she realized, but thousands, each splitting off from the last almost too quickly to see, then fading into the next like water soaked up by a towel. The air was hot and foul. She could hear the door groaning open. At least she thought it was the door. How could there be a door to a virch-office? Where was the groan coming from? Where could she run?

The alarm went off at 5:45 and for once she welcomed it, drifting to consciousness while a cheery-voiced newsreader bubbled about "drought-stricken France, where crowds rioted when they were given e-credit coupons instead of the food they expected". The newscaster managed to make the rioters sound ludicrously naïve.

Gareth had plugged into the brokerage and was already in his surfer crouch, twitching and gesticulating, hands grasping and shuffling virtual data-blocks, feet locked into his skimmer pedals, patrolling Thieu-Armstrong's cyber-periphery wrapped in the womb of his virch-chair. To reach her terminal, she had to walk around him, careful not to trip over the wires to his visor and gloves.

The first thing she saw when she powered up her screen was an e-mail from Gareth. Before she read it, Callie remembered the little lovenotes they used to leave each other on the pillows. "Please think about it," the message said.

There were three other e-calls waiting for her onscreen. One was her usual from Kelly OnLine, asking if she was available for work that day, with a list of jobs she was entitled to bid on. After checking her latest BankAmerica Registered Dataflow/Error rating (still fine, but not as good as three weeks ago - Callie wondered if she should start taking hormone regulators again) she highlighted a stint with XTek, following up on one of their credit sweeps. She hated listening to people beg for just a little more time, but there was enough piecework to pay next month's rent, if she got her rate back up. The pay scale average looked low. She'd heard that XTek was using bots to pull their costs down. Illegal, of course, but there wasn't anything she could do about it. She decided to put in a bid at her normal rates.

While she waited for XTec's reply, she read her other mail. One was a message from a RanChek, certifying that she was not a bot, as of 1:48 A.M. this morning. Callie supposed she ought to feel grateful: The last time they'd mis-identified her she couldn't work for a week while they handled her appeal. Idly, she checked the balance in the joint account she shared with Gareth: 17,825,000 Reformed New Dollars. That wouldn't even get them to a sub-orbital loop, let alone up to the asteroid belt.

The last message, a vid, was from Raelene, who was sitting in bed nursing her baby. "Callie, say hello to Zorah." Raelene's smile was deep and satisfied. "She got born eleven o'clock last night. Four kilos, and she didn't put her Mama through but an hour of labour. Did you, honey?" The baby, unruffled, suckled on. "Beau says hi, but that man been workin' so much overtime lately, he asleep before he get done with dinner." Raelene's brown hand suddenly blocked out the camera and the screen tilted.

When it cleared there was Beau, a heavy-shouldered man with a scarred, gentle face. He was sprawled in an armchair, just waking up. He waved, vaguely, and said "Hey, Callie."

"Beau must've worked three days straight, fixin' up the cutest little nursery for the baby. You should come over and see it, Callie. Man a genius with a hammer and saw. Paints, too, just like some of them old paintings in a museum." Beau smiled shyly, stony face suddenly boyish.

"He gonna get plenty of rest soon, though. Soon as we get Eunice's citizenship all straightened out, we going home to St. Kitts for a while, see the folks. I just wanted to say so long." She frowned. "Oh, and Beau say he saw your sister round Washington Square. Said Sonya with the Revenants now and she don't look too healthy."

As soon as she closed up Raelene's vid Callie did a search on the Revenants, mentally chiding herself for not keeping up with the news. There were way too many hits to view systematically, as usual. Most seemed to be propaganda sites, for and against. One blogger said President Conley--was she the third or fourth president this year?-- was relying on them for public medical coverage, though a spokesman denied it, so maybe not. People called them the Dreamers or the Ghosts, though their official name was the Church of the Risen, which explained some things she'd seen on chatlines. A Recombo singer, Moll the Dragon, had recently had a run-in with them, which was now being settled in court. There was a clip of a tiny, nearly nude person who'd probably started out as a woman but was now an emerald and scarlet apparition of scales, horns and wings, growling something about "hypnocratic fascists". Callie made a mental note to look those words up. Then X-Tec called back and it was time to go to work,

* * *

That night, she woke up at midnight to find Gareth sitting by the bed, frowning, watching her sleep. She reached for him. His hands were cold.

Benny the Antichrist, Page 20

"They want to give it to me. A twenty minute operation and I'm on the partnership track," he said. "They will, as soon as I have a LERT-chip."

"Honey..."

"I don't understand why you want me to spend my life, a third of my life, like this. What can you have against me getting the operation? We could climb out of the Gravity Well, put down a stake in one of the asteroid colonies, where it's clean, where you don't have to worry about some crazy spraying the block with penetration rounds. Breathe air that doesn't make you sick. You could have a baby."

"Gareth, please, I'm so tired. Let's talk about it tomorrow."

"I guess you want to sleep on it. That's how you work, isn't it? Sleeping on your decisions."

"Do it, then. You obviously don't care about what it does to you. Or us. Make yourself like Sanders and Dvorak and all the rest of the zombies. Stay virched up with a neural tap. Never sleep or dream for the rest of your life."

"Here we go again. Sanders and Dvorak, World Without End. Look, those were two unlucky guys who got the early implants. The new chips are nothing like that. You can turn them off anytime you want."

"Everybody always says that. Let me ask you though, how come nobody ever does? Why can't you turn on the TV without hearing about some exec going on a rampage because they were 'under a lot of pressure'? Isn't that the code phrase? Like that woman in Delaware who killed her kids. Did you see them taking her away? She had one of those new wireless chips, so she was probably virched up while she was cutting up her little girls. I remember she was wearing an Armani worth two years of your salary. Soaked with blood. Her face all clawed up and hair pulled out so you could see her scalp. She'd done that herself, they said. Laughing at the cops, calling them sleepyheads. And talking with that little giggly voice, just like Sanders, only ten years after he cracked up."

"Some people can't handle the pressure. Of course there'll be burnouts. But, Callie, this is what I'm really good at. I've got the best investment returns for six months running. In two years I could be running the Ganymede branch. Addison practically promised me."

She grimaced, thinking of Carter Addison, Gareth's supervisor, a tall, sleek, asexually predatory man. "Like they promised Tom Chao?"

"What's that supposed to mean? Tom had personal reasons for dropping out. Anyway, he's doing fine."

"Fine? Gareth, he practically jumps out of his skin every time someone talks to him. He's on anti-compulsives just to keep him from clawing himself raw. Raelene says they're canning him next week."

"Oh, so this is where you're getting all this stuff. Jesus, I should have known it'd be Raelene. She lasts--what?--three weeks there. Bails out like the loser she is and all of the sudden she's an expert on Shunt Syndrome."

"At least she isn't jacked in 24 hours a day, working for people who 'practically promise' things and throw you out like a rag when you're all used up. She's going back to the island with her baby. I wouldn't mind trading places with her sometimes."

"Oh you wouldn't, huh? Well ask yourself this: How are Beau and she paying the fare on his odd jobs and what she makes temping? Plus that new place they have. Lot of phone work for a pair of tickets that I couldn't afford, last time I looked."

"I don't know. They make sacrifices, I guess."

"Yeah, well, last time I saw Raelene, she was living large. She kept having to hit the Ladies every time her pager rang. Flashed some big time cash too. Wish I had that kind of walking around money, on what she makes."

"Stop it. You're just saying that."

"You need to open your eyes, Callie. Look, all I'm saying is there isn't an easy way up. Don't you see? I want what you want. I want a family. I want out of this mouse hole." He gestured around their tiny apartment. "I want to go for a walk without armor and a gas mask. And I'm asking you to let me take our best chance."

"I just don't see why you have to have a neural feed to the markets 24 hours a day. They've got computers for that."

"Honey, Cerberus duty is just being a watchdog. Remember the crash of '15? And in '18 when everyone's programs started selling at once? Half the world's brokerage houses went bankrupt. There's people who hit the bricks ten years ago and still haven't gotten back on-market. Just staying up-to-speed takes all your energy and computer power. Every time your heart beats, Thieu-Armstrong does 2,000 transactions. And we're not even that big. Multiply that by a forty million investment programs, any one of which could start a major trend. The firm needs a round-the-clocker looking out for their interests, making sure our systems are optimal and secure. Yesterday I saved us eighty bil when Indnet went down."

"I still don't see why it has to be just you."

"Oh, they're bringing Jocelyn along, too. You remember her, from the party?" They'd been to a Thieu-Armstrong staff party a few months ago, a loud, joyless affair at a trendy new Russian restaurant. Jocelyn Niarchos had been at their table, a tiny woman with a dancer's figure, huge, hard eyes and a wounding, flirtatious manner. She'd left with Addison, though the vibe between them seemed like something scarier and harder than sex. "She's chipped up already and hot on my heels," Gareth was saying. "Count on that. And that's why I have to take it. You either run ahead or get trampled. We've got to go for it. Do you want to end up like your sister?"

From there things had deteriorated to a shouting match, until one of the neighbors pounded on the wall.

***

"In other news, a majority decision handed down by the U.S. Circuit Court of Appeal has blocked the families of Thomas W. Sanders and other alleged victims of so-called Shunt Syndrome from suing Cerebella, makers of the Limbo-Encephalic Redistributive Transcoordinator or LERT chip. A company spokesperson said Cerebella was completely vindicated in its contention that there was no plausible connection between an early version of their product and a so-called syndrome, cobbled together from a mass of unrelated symptoms and causes. He also pointed out that the latest generation, wireless Mark 7 model is completely shielded against microwave leakage and rigorously failsafed against sleep-deprivation psychosis. Round-the-clockers in government and non-sleep industries have hailed the decision.

"On the international front, millions are racing to evacuate the region surrounding China's Three Gorges Dam. Unconfirmed reports allege that officials used funds slated for repairs to play the stock market for days on end and that Lee Xiang, chairman of Three Gorges Inc., has been known to appear nude on-site and threaten safety inspectors with a sword."

Monday was Gareth's day off and they slept in. Callie woke up at ten, feeling like she'd gotten enough sleep for once. Her mind drifted back to last night's argument, but this morning was brilliantly sunny, Gareth's arm was draped over her shoulder and somehow she couldn't hold a grudge. A pigeon cooed outside the window. Gareth

Benny the Antichrist, Page 23

didn't like them, but Callie had grown up on a Northern California kelp farm and they reminded her a little of the birds back home. She found herself idly tracing the muscles in Gareth's forearm. He stirred against her back, then touched her the way he had when they first made love, very lightly, his fingertips barely tracing the swells and hollows of her body. She shivered, her body a string bowed by a faint, insinuating breeze, then finally moaned, turning and opening to him in one movement.

She was hungry when she woke up the second time, at 12:30. The sky had clouded over a bit, but it still looked like a nice day to have a leisurely brunch at the Farmer's Market and do some open-air shopping. She hoped Gareth would come. Lately he'd been saying the Market was too dirty and dangerous and you could get better prices on the Net anyway. It had become a point of friction, as if they needed another one. When she tried to get him up this time, though, he didn't argue, just smiled and rolled over.

"This poor working man's gotta get himself some rest," he groaned into the pillow. "You're gonna have to squeeze them tomatoes and knock on them watermelons all on your lonesome, li'l podner."

"Oh, you poor sagging boy. I'll just have to perk you up, then."

"Woman, are you trying to kill me?"

"Now I know for a fact that's just the way you'd want to go. But actually, I meant that I'll make you an omelet when I get home, because I hate to see you so weak and pitiful. You just rest your weary bones, darlin'."

* * *

The weather had definitely turned by the time she got into the street. A stiff wind was blowing from an ash gray sky. She decided to grab a quick bite and do her shopping before the storm blew in. The market wasn't as crowded as usual, though there was the usual straggly line of dealers hawking everything from weed to speed to lyght. Staring past the bony, scarred man in green leather pants who thrust a grubby-nailed handful of blue lyght capsules at her, Callie glimpsed a figure in Revenant colors, a long, pale blue dress and pink shawl, drifting toward the busker's corner. The ever-so-slight limp and slender back said "Sonya" from a hundred paces. Callie shouldered past the lyght pusher and rushed between stalls, calling her sister's name. The shaven-headed woman didn't stop until Callie laid her hand on her shoulder. When she turned Callie almost didn't recognize her. Sonya's round cheeks were sunken and marked with swollen keloid scars in an angular spiraling pattern. Her big hazel eyes were covered with mirrored lenses and rimmed with brown grime. Her breath had the acetone stink of malnutrition. She trembled slightly, as if flickering in a tiny breeze.

"Sohnny? Is that you?"

"Callie... The Master said today I would struggle with my Illusion Life... I was afraid, but now I'm glad... to see you."

Callie stepped back from her sister, feeling, as always, impossibly big and clumsy. Sonya was almost six inches shorter than she, light-boned and thin where she was heavy-hipped and muscular. "Why have you got those horrible lenses on, Sonya?"

"Oh, Callie, I've died and it's so wonderful... Sometimes I have to come out here, to the Pain Clock Time, but not for long. Come with me. We can go to the True Light together and dream God's Dream. It's so..."

"Sonya," Callie, helpless, gathered the slight form in her arms. More than anything else, Sonya's tremor worried her. Lyght sometimes damaged your nerves like that. "When was the last time you ate?"

"I don't know. Maybe a couple of days ago." She held up a crockery bowl between two hands. "If you give me some money, I could buy something to eat."

"If I give you money, it'll go back to your master, won't it?"

Sonya didn't deny it, just held up the bowl, waiting, smiling.

"Can't you see that--no, never mind. Will you eat with me, if I buy you a meal?"

They went to an open-air vegan place on the edge of the market. Sonya wouldn't leave the vicinity. Callie ordered nut and bean loaf for both of them but Sonya seemed uninterested in the food. As she watched her sister pick at her slice, Callie wished she could somehow make Sonya care more about herself. It was as if the slight figure were ready to float away at any moment. Callie tried everything she could think of to reach her sister. She asked Sonya about her friends in Fine Arts, the paintings and performances she'd been working on so feverishly before she dropped out of school, the prof she'd with whom she'd had a fling, to their mother's shock and disapproval. Nothing elicited more than a brilliant, vacant smile, a few words of mumbled dismissal. It was as if she were talking to a translucent shell, a cast-off cicada's husk of the woman who had been her sister.

Benny the Antichrist, Page 25

The closest she got to reaching Sonya was when she steeled herself and asked if she was doing lyght. A tiny, evasive frown flitted over her sister's blank face. "Not much, any more. The Master says the enlightened shine with their own light."

"Do you shine with that light, Sohnny?" She'd read somewhere that high-level Revenants had their thymuses retrofitted to synthesize lyght. Her only answer was a dreamy smile.

Looking past Sonya she could see the ragged lyght pusher sometimes glancing their way, though he never approached the café. Sonya never looked back but somehow she seemed as aware of him as she was of anything else around her. It was hard to tell how much she could see of her surroundings. Callie remembered hearing somewhere that the mirrored lenses Revenants wore were almost completely opaque. Sonya didn't squint when the sun broke free of the gloom and blazed down on their table. But she adroitly caught the saltshaker Callie knocked off the table waving her arms during a story about their mother. She did it as she did everything else, in a manner that was cheerfully absent.

After a while, Callie needed to use the restroom. She told her sister to stay there, that she wanted to come to their temple and make a donation. She hurried into the Ladies, trying to remember a news story about a local company that specialized in deprogramming, wondering if she could bring herself to do that.

When she came out, Sonya was gone and it had started to rain, not hard, but steadily. Tossing some money on their table, Cindy raced out into the market, calling her sister's name. She couldn't see her anywhere. The lyght pusher was gone too.

Three hours later she trudged home, wet and muddy. She'd searched the market. She'd asked every Revenant she'd seen if they knew Sonya. The ones who hadn't ignored her completely had shaken their heads, smiling wanly. She'd walked through a Revenant street clinic, peering through doorways, and over partitions till two Healers and a security man made her leave.

Then she got the idea to hike over several blocks to where she remembered passing a Revenant ashram several months ago.

It took her a while to find it. The ashram was set back from the street and screened off with bio-boosted lilac bushes, the kind that grew two inches a day and were supposed to be good at de-toxifying the air. It was like other Dreamer dens she'd seen on the Web, a soft bulbous shape, the lines of the original brick tenement block faintly

Benny the Antichrist, Page 26

visible through pale pink translucent plaz-foam. Rounded freeform blobs and ledges gave it the air of a somewhat grimy cumulous cloud inexplicably settled to earth.

They hadn't covered over the second and third floors yet, which was why she'd missed it behind the ten-foot lilacs that hadn't been here when last she was this way. She stood across the street, peering up but couldn't see any activity through dusty windows, some broken, some boarded over. She crossed over, called, yelled and finally pounded on the plaz-foam, denting it slightly with her fist, to no avail.

It took her two circuits round the building, picking her way nervously through the weed-choked yard and the junk and rubble between the ashram and blocks on either side, to find the entrance. On her second trip two young men, boys really, emerged from a ramshackle frame house across the alley. They were both thin, ragged and they moved as if the air were thick syrup and their bones only slightly more solid. The Chinese-looking one had an open sore, shaped like a lightning slash, on his cheek. They watched her silently, gazes slow, vapid. The red-haired one trembled slightly but constantly.

Callie turned away, clutching a mace scream canister. If they were lyt up they were probably harmless, though there were stories. While she was in school a girl in her dorm tripping on lyght had supposedly ripped a toilet out of the floor.

She saw it then, a faint path up the left side of the ashram, leading to a hole almost obscured behind thick goutweed, lined with dirty pink plaz-foam. She thought of crawling down there and mentally quailed.

She turned back, wanting to see where the boys were now. They were back to back, crooked elbows linked, slowly swinging each other down the cracked and scarred length of the alley away from her, a weirdly graceful pushme-pullyou creature.

She faced the Dreamer den. It was getting dark, the pink plaz-foam starting to glow phosphorescently. At least the rain had stopped. She realized she'd have to do this quickly if she wanted to do it at all. She strode up the path and dropped to her knees.

She didn't want to go down the hole head-first but didn't know if there would be room to turn once she was down there. With a muttered "Goddamn it, Sohnny," she crawled in.

Benny the Antichrist, Page 27

It wasn't totally dark in the hole; the phosphorescent plaz-foam glowed dimly through grime and soil. It smelled of unwashed bodies and was slick, yet tacky to the touch, like styrofoam packing. There was gritty soil under her hands and knees and small things that felt sharper than pebbles. It was a tight squeeze through the foamed-over hole in the basement wall and she was having trouble breathing when she came to the plug.

It wasn't a door, at least she couldn't see any hinges or feel them. Just a roughly circular convex plug of plaz-foam, darker red than the rest, but still glowing. There was just enough room to squat or turn around in front of it and the floor was original concrete and fairly level. She peered and felt along the wall, calling but there didn't seem to be any way of announcing her presence. She pressed her ear to it and thought she heard a cadence like far-away chanting, but it could have been the wind passing through the cracked panes of the upper storeys.

Suddenly furious, Callie pulled a jackknife out of her purse and jabbed it into the plug, prepared to hack her way through it if she had to.

A squeak and clatter of tiny claws in some unseen chamber brought her to her senses. She had no idea if there was anyone up there or if so, who it would be. She grimaced and turned, shouldering her way as quickly as possible back up the narrow, stinking hole.

She stood up and stretched when she got out, then bent and dusted off her jeans. It was dusk but the full moon was out and the sky clear for once. Her left knee was glowing, not pink like the ashram, crouching over her like some mute and formless ghost, but blue like crushed lyght capsules. The grit pressed into her palms glittered slightly, as if full of tiny slivers of wire and silicon.

Something was still jabbing her. Reaching down to her calf, Callie pulled out a shard of plastic, end dark and wet with her blood. It glowed blue and silver in the dark. Pinstripes. It was a sliver of slashed credit card, the Shanghai Bank Special rappers flashed in videos but you rarely saw. Addison had one.

* * *

Gareth was gone when she got home. He'd left a note on the fridge. Gone for a walk. In spite of her worry over Sonya, Callie felt a little better. For months he'd done nothing but telecommute and report bi-weekly to the office. She'd begun to think he was agoraphobic. Maybe getting out for a bit would clear his head.

Benny the Antichrist, Page 28

Callie decided not to do any web-searching on the Revenants until she calmed down a bit and could think clearly about Sonya. She might have logged in at BIOCO or another office MUD and gotten in a few hours, but she decided the apartment needed a cleaning. A place as small as theirs got cluttered and dirty quickly during the week, given all the hours they logged. She was scrubbing Gareth's virch-chair, grimy with hours of logged-on sweat, when the phone rang.

A glance at the display told her that her mother was calling. She clipped on her headset and pressed talk, her expression a mixture of annoyance and concern.

"Hi, Mom."

There was pause as her signal travelled up to the Aristarchus Crater and her mother's came back. At least this time she'd called when the Moon wasn't on the other side of the Earth.

"Callie? Have you seen the news? SinoRus is having a seat sale. Half price to the Belt if you sign two years in advance."

"Gareth and I don't have that kind of money yet, Mom. Besides, SinoRus has a terrible safety rating." She frowned as she came to a lump in one of the back cushions. There was something beneath, stuck to the frame of the chair.

"Always some kind of excuse with you. You could have it if you wanted. Gareth knows it and you should, too. Lucas says he'd be happy to help you climb out of the Well." Lucas was her mother's third husband, a retired PharmCo salesman she'd met at a casino at the Mare Orientale. He was a confirmed Selenian and would talk your ear off about the virtues of lo-grav living.

"I saw Sohnny today," she said, heading off the lecture.

The pause that followed was more than the signal delay. "How is she?" her mother finally asked.

"I don't know, Mom. She's joined the Revenants. She's too thin, but she seems happier than I've seen her in a long time."

"The Revenants. Aren't they the lyght dealers? My God, that girl was born for trouble."

"I don't think Sonya's a lyght dealer, Mom. Not after what she's been through."

"Wake up, Callie. Once an addict, always an addict. Where do you think the Dreamers find their converts? I saw it on a news holo. Thank God there are none of them up here. Lola Benson--you met her when you visited us last, remember? In 16-G?--Lola says her

Benny the Antichrist, Page 29

nephew in New Shanghai took lyght once and now he's hooked for life."

"Lola Benson?" She grimaced, partly because she remembered her mother's garrulous, panicky neighbor and partly because she'd finally winkled the lump out from beneath the cushion. It was a benzedrine capsule. Gareth had told her he wasn't going to use uppers again. "Oh please, Mom, I took lyght once--"

"Callie! You didn't!"

"I did, Mom. When I was 17. You and Dad never knew. I took it at a club, then got up and went to school the next day."

For the second time today her mother seemed lost for words, a thing that seldom happened. In the silence that followed Callie thought about her lyght trip while she walked over to the kitchen sink. She couldn't remember much about it, really, but she did recall the brilliant streamers linking everything she saw to everything else. Her only strong memory was coming home still tripping and seeing her face in her bedroom mirror, tied by strands of undulating light to a picture of her grandmother, who was at that time slowly dying in a palliative ward. It had seemed to her that she could feel a faint arrhythmia in her heartbeat, could tell which joints would stiffen and fail her first, where cancer would fist its way out through her flesh. It had frightened her enough that she'd never tried it again. She washed the benzedrine capsule down the drain while she waited for her mother to compose herself.

Finally her mother said "Well, that was you. Sonya's a different matter."

Sonya had always been a different matter, according to her mother. Even though she'd thought herself about getting Sonya deprogrammed, Callie found herself, as usual, defending her sister. Some things never seemed to change. She wondered if all children of aging parents had these conversations that followed the inevitable steps of a recurring dream.

Gareth rescued her, swaggering through the door whistling an old club anthem. How long had it been since she'd heard him whistling? He'd gotten his hair spiked and dyed in black and scarlet streaks, the way he'd worn it when they first met. He also had on a new earring, an iridescent stone that seemed to flash something she could almost recognize when it caught the light.

By the time he got there Callie and her mother were lost in their usual maze of accusations and denials and had abandoned any politesse. Callie had angry tears running down her cheeks when Gareth plucked her headset off while her mother ran down a long and well-rehearsed list of the ways her daughters had disappointed her. Finger to his lips, he winked and blew her a kiss, head still bobbing to silent music.

Though she knew she ought to be angry at his high-handedness, Callie couldn't help but smiling as he grinned and mugged through the tirade. At length her mother must have paused for breath and Gareth said "Hello Clara." Everyone else was required to call her by her second name, Martine, but Gareth had always known how handle Mom. From there on he applied his usual mixture of charm and briskness and in ten minutes had her mother mollified and off the line.

He was in such a good mood, so expansive and funny, that she couldn't bring herself to bring up the benzedrine. Maybe it was an old stash he'd forgotten about she thought as she listened to him imitating one of their cranky neighbors.

They ate out that night, something they'd solemnly sworn they wouldn't, except for birthdays. Somehow it just felt right and Callie thought The asteroid belt will still be there even if we're a few days late.

They came home and made love again. This time it was a brisk, high-spirited gallop, fun, but over just a little too soon. She usually liked to lie in Gareth's arms after, talking, maybe even smoking a little weed. But he was too charged up tonight to lie still, talking a blue jag with the snap and energy that had drawn her to him, Thieu-Armstrong office politics, some asteroid belt blogs he was following, the plot of a web-novel he'd been trying to write since she'd met him. Finally he strapped himself into his virch chair, blowing her a kiss before he logged in. She lay for a while, watching him work, his arms moving in a kata of data manipulation, she wondered how long it had been since they'd done that twice in one day. It had been since before he started working at Thieu-Armstrong, she thought. Maybe things are changing.

She woke late that night to find Gareth in bed beside her, his body trembling and jerking. He'd thrown off his half of the quilt, but as she tried to cover him up, his skin was hot and drenched with sweat. "Baby," she said softly, laying her palm on his cheek, "are you having a nightmare?"

He opened his eyes immediately and his gaze wasn't the slow, wandering focus of a man clambering up from a dream. It was cool and, somewhere far back, amused.

"No," he said. "I'm fine. Go back to sleep, Callie."

***

Time passed quickly in the next few months. Callie had as much work as she could handle, more even, though she hadn't lowered her rates or her error average. In fact she gave herself a raise. It didn't seem to matter. She got almost any job she bid on and new offers arrived daily. On the jobchat lines other people complained about being squeezed out by bots or lowballed by multiplexed-virchers working out of Mumbai grindhouses, but people were always complaining about something.

She left messages for Raelene but their schedules never seemed to mesh. The one time they got to talk Raelene was in an all-night joint between shifts, the kind of place Callie hadn't been in since school, with dim biolume walls and thudding trancelok music. When she asked Raelene where she was working her friend rattled out a couple of names she hadn't heard before. Crappy work, but the shift premiums made it worthwhile, Raelene said.

Another time she called and got Beau, who was usually polite but taciturn in her presence. Raelene had told her Beau could fix machines effortlessly, but never got through middle school and couldn't really read. Most of the time, she said, he only really talked to her.

But when she called this time he was downright bubbly. "I been painting Zorah's room," he said, cradling the baby who snoozed contentedly in the crook of his arm, looking impossibly tiny. "Wanna see?"

When she said yes he practically bounded into the nursery. He was so eager to show her his creations on the walls she had to ask him to slow down and start again. It was an alphabet of found materials, cut into intricate, fantastic shapes, glued and nailed on the wall in layers and painted in brilliant, but subtle colors. "A" was a craggy mountain, bejeweled with meadows. "B" was pair of curled-up monkeys, one above the other on a branch. The edge of light from the moon eclipsing the sun formed a "C".

Looking at them, Callie had the sudden sense, overwhelming though brief, that there was a way out for her and Gareth, just the way Beau had found a way beyond the letters that imprisoned him. In the midst of her exclamations Beau suddenly stopped smiling.

"You seen Raelene?" he wanted to know. "She ain't been home in two days."

***

When she had the energy Callie tried to research the Revenants, but sifting through the mass of pro- and con- websites was slow going. A doctor's organization issued a warning against Dreamer cures, saying they used untried and unapproved methods and drugs. But a lot of commentators said the government wasn't doing the job, so why not give the Revenants a try?

She found an old, unedited 2D TV newsclip on a blog she sometimes followed. It started out slowly. There was a tall, vaguely familiar TV reporter in a Kevlar-lined blazer, fussing with his hair while he stood with his back to an open field where people in diaphanous pink and pale blue robes were swaying slowly in what looked like an enormous dance. There was a throbbing, humming sound that sounded like singing in the background. The reporter wasn't paying much attention, except to ask someone off-screen how long this had been going on. He got back an inaudible answer and whistled under his breath. There was a faint "Take one," and he suddenly seemed taller, his face more defined, eyes more intelligent.

"I'm standing at the site of a mass worship session, billed as a Planetary Consciousness-Raising by The Church of the Risen. Founded in 2007 by Reverend Awnee-... Ownee-... by a Nigerian missionary, the members of the Church, also known as Dreamers or Revenants, believe they can save the world when mankind begins to... to do something they call Dreaming the Dreams of God....

Jeez, Bert, isn't there any way we can sex this up? They all look like they're on heavy tranks out there." Someone spoke off-camera and he rolled his eyes, bored. "Yeah, yeah, man of mystery, ties to the great and mighty, drugs, blah, blah... OK, let's get this sucker shot and in the can." The newscaster shrugged, then straightened and jutted his jaw, preparing his on-camera persona. "I'm standing at the site--"

At that point the camera suddenly wandered off to the reporter's side, where a small, very fat black man was gliding toward the news crew, the long train of his sky-blue robe borne up by half a dozen statuesque young girls in pink gowns that left very little to the imagination. For some reason the camera operator seemed shaken by this appearance and the picture blurred and shifted several times before coming to rest on the man's dark, beatifically smiling face. There was nothing remarkable about the Reverend Ibrahim's features. He had a round, jowly face, bald except for a fringe of gray hair behind his ears. The only thing that drew and repelled you were the eyes. They were sewn shut with bright green thread.

The newscaster leaned into the frame, obviously agitated and winging it. "Ladies and gentlemen, we've just been joined by... for the first time in five years, the Rev--"

"Children, it is time." Onyema Ibrahim's voice was a feathery, startlingly youthful tenor that climbed thrillingly, then swooped to a rich, raspy basso, crooning and rumbling seismically in the space of that short sentence. "Time to lay aside the distractions, all the things that have kept you so busy, so tense, so unhappy. Time to Dream the Dream of God. The Time beyond--"

"What about the allegations," the reporter broke in, struggling to regain control of the news spot. "What about the allegations that the Dreamers have been tied to major lyght manufacturing and distribution--" He stopped, as though he'd lost track of his thoughts. The camera panned slowly back to show the Reverend's round, chestnut brown hand resting gently on the reporter's cheek. The reporter's eyes were closed. His mouth opened once, then relaxed into a slack smile. His head rolled like a baby as it nods into its mother's hand before drifting into sleep. Abruptly he fell to his knees, flinging his arms around the Reverend Onyema Ibrahim's broad hips. Callie heard muffled sobbing before the feed cut out.

* * *

That night at dinner she finally told Gareth she was pregnant. He looked at her blankly. He had been doing that more and more lately, looking without seeing, as if there were something between him and wherever his gaze pointed. He said it was because of the big merger deal at work. With a new chain of command and new board, the axes were being sharpened. Everyone was looking to optimize their returns. He'd already caught Niarchos trying to poach one of his accounts. He had to be on his guard.

"Gareth, I said we're going to have a baby."

A pause. "I thought we agreed... uh, that's... Callie, listen, I can't think about this now. I'm right in the middle of--"

"You're eating supper. At least that's what you look like you're doing, to me. I've waited all day to tell you this. All week, really. I'm due in October."

"God, this couldn't come at a... I'm just... Didn't we say, I'm sure we said, we were going to wait until we got out of the Well? On top of everything else."

On top of what else? she wondered. "I've been looking into about that. According to some people, lo-grav babies have a lot of heart and respiratory problems later on."

"Which people?"

"Well, Doctor Wozniak, for one."

"That talk show bitch? Well, I guess it must be true then."

"You don't want this baby."

"Of course I want a baby. Haven't I always said I want children? I want children with someone I can trust."

"I didn't mean to!"

"I don't know, Callie. We've always been really careful, at least I have."

"No, don't you do this, don't lay this all on me, like you always do! I've been careful too. It just--"

"Look, Callie, I want kids, OK? I said it and I meant it. When the time is right. But now..."

"It'll take us two more years, Gareth, with what we've been putting away, to get to the Belt. What's another year, more or less?"

"God damn it, Callie, you don't know..." He paused, fighting for self-control, hands on either side of his head. He was fiddling with his opalescent earring, a new tic of his. "I need some time... I just can't, can't do this now. I'm up to my neck in... I've got to work now." Avoiding her eyes, he put on his gloves and visor and virched up.

Callie glared at him while he worked, watching him shuffle and realign data blocks, swaying metronomically, hands pushing, pulling, moving top to bottom and back again, fingers writhing on independent virtual keyboards, labelling, deleting, calling into being. Taking no care to be quiet, she piled dishes into the sink, shouldering past him on her way out the door. He took the noise and the bump without reaction.

* * *

As she had for the last few weeks, she roved the Farmers Market, looking for Sonya.

Benny the Antichrist, Page 35

When she got home, Gareth's dinner was still half-eaten and he was still jacked in. She noticed how pale he was, how thin. He'd been talking about the merger for weeks now. Sometimes she thought she knew the personalities involved, the factions, the tactics and stratagems better than she knew her own life. The merger had certainly taken over Gareth's. He's like a ghost, she thought, and so am I. We eat and sleep in these little closets, afraid to go out in the midday sun, but where we live is a phantom world, everywhere and nowhere at once, ruled by powers that summon and dismiss us at a whim, haunted by dreams we'll never touch. She was suddenly desperate. Without a word she gently took Gareth's visor and gloves off. Like a blind man he let her lead him to bed.

He lay quietly for a while, then began to stir beside her. Exhausted, she let him do as he would. It didn't take long. He efficiently brought her to orgasm just before he came, silent except for a hissing exhalation at his climax. He rolled off and was still for a minute. Then his limbs began to move, gathering and sorting virtual data in his sleep.

* * *

She woke, or thought she did, in the silent darkness alone. She reached over and felt only Gareth's pillow and his side of the bed, cool as if he'd never been there. She tried to call out, but somehow her voice wouldn't come. She kicked her covers off and swung her legs over to stand up. The bottom dropped out of her stomach when she found herself drifting away from the bed. Only a mad scrabbling at the mattress kept her from floating away in space. Space. That's where she was, suddenly seeing the cold blaze of the stars around her, under her feet and above her head. They never sleep, she thought. Just keep watching while everything that isn't big enough to have its own gravity drifts apart or is finally crushed. At that the mattress drifted free of the bed. She watched the bed dwindle and finally disappear in the distance, wondering if it would travel forever or fall into the atmosphere of some planet or star, a brief dart of flame.

* * *

Gareth seemed to have resolved something in his own mind, though he didn't talk about it. He said having the baby now was fine, that they could wait to emigrate, but never seemed interested in planning beyond that. He said things were too up in the air right now to tell what was going to happen. He still worked longer hours than

Benny the Antichrist, Page 36

she did, but he took time off to sleep. He never seemed to sleep deeply these days, but then he seldom did, and at least he'd stopped snoring. She told him so and he said he'd learned an exercise for the soft palate. He said he'd find the website he'd gotten it from, but somehow he never did.

She finally worked up the nerve to ask him why he didn't talk about getting a LERT-chip any more. For a moment he stared blankly, as if he weren't sure where her voice had come from. He did that occasionally these days, but Gareth had always been able to concentrate. Then he smiled. "They decided to try a new bot on Cerberus watch. So far it seems to be working out."

"And aren't you glad you waited?" she couldn't help saying, "No chips in your head and we're doing just fine."

"Yeah, I guess we are." He smiled back, but she could tell his mind was back at work on something.

One day she took a break for lunch and climbed out of the luxy new virch-chair Gareth had gotten cheap at Thieu-Armstrong. Gareth's chair was empty. He wasn't in the apartment. For a moment she panicked. It wasn't like him to leave without telling her when she was virching. In fact she was surprised he was able to do it at all. She had always been the one who was more alert to outside stimuli, who heard the fire alarm or the doorbell, who smelled dinner burning in the oven. But that was before she'd gotten pregnant. These days she often felt as if there were a gauzy veil between herself and the world. When she wasn't getting sick to her stomach.

Idly she noticed that Gareth had gotten a new virch interface. How long has he had that? she wondered. It didn't look all that different from hers but somehow it seemed cooler, more sophisticated. She wondered vaguely why she thought that but didn't pursue it. What drew her attention right now was a thick crusty stain on the microfibre-covered headrest of Gareth's virch-chair. Lately he'd become kind of a slob, a real change for him. Gareth had always been like a cat, the kind of man who could keep himself neat and clean in the midst of utter chaos and filth. But sometimes these days she'd find him bleary-eyed and snot-nosed, smelling of sour old sweat.

She managed to scrape away some the crust with her fingernail. It came off as a gritty, rust-coloured powder. Without thinking, she stuck her finger in her mouth: the unmistakeable salt tang of blood.

In that moment she felt very cold and off-balance, as if the tiny thing in her belly were a heavy, slowly-swinging stone weight.

Feeling faint, she made herself sit down at their small kitchen table.

Callie wasn't sure how long she'd been sitting there, staring at nothing, when she noticed a pile of something in a dim corner cut off by Gareth's virch chair. Reluctantly she shoved the chair out of the way and bent to inspect the pile.

It was just some snail-mail bills, flyers and other commercial stuff. She fastened on them almost gratefully, happy to sink into the routine of sorting, checking figures and settling accounts. The bank statement was what she expected, a few more hundred thousand closer to the asteroid belt. She sighed.

Then she came on the second statement. Ripping it open, she scanned down the paper. Stopped. Looked again and really read it, took in the figure this time. Gareth had opened a new account three weeks ago and it had 52 million Reformed New Dollars in it.

She stared unseeingly at Gareth's virch chair. Her thoughts were halting, as if she were mentally pushing through something dark and sludgy. Finally her eyes focused on his virch unit. It was finished in gray-violet titanium and had the cool, unanswerable poise of high-end electronic design, but there was something wrong with it. Her eyes flicked back and forth from her own unit to his. The connector socket. Gareth's unit didn't have a jack outlet in front.

Front jacks were legally required in any standard virch unit, a last fail-safe against data overload. They had to be easily pulled out, so end-users could terminate connection instantly if they felt the onset of a seizure. A lot of people illegally clamped theirs in, because it was a hassle rebooting if you happened to make a sudden movement, but every virch unit Callie had ever seen had a small circular hole somewhere on its front surface. Except this one.

Her eyes travelled down the length of the wire leading from his visor, looking for the Integrator box into which it and his virch gloves should be plugged. There wasn't one. The jacks of all three units lay uselessly on the floor, taped neatly to umbilical cord of wires leading to the virch unit. He didn't need them. He was jacked in all the time.

Callie began to pace. She couldn't seem to focus on this. She'd try to decide what she was going to say, to do, and found herself feeling how her feet were swollen, how her bra straps were digging into her shoulders.

She sat down at her chair, slipped her gloves and visor on and virched up. Fly-by ads raced by her. Bioco was having a data-flow sweepstakes for a full body makeover. A taller, chestier Callie in a shimmering gown slouched alluringly in the lower left corner of her viewscreen till she deployed a sweeper bot to get rid of it.

She called up full financial profiles for both of them, something she hadn't done in months. Sure enough, there was the new account package. She stared at the new black attaché case floating beside the one for her and Gareth's joint account, her mouth working silently. She paused the screen and pulled off her visor and gloves.

The battered pedestal lamp by their bed had a screw-on plate in its base. She and Gareth had put a little piece of paper in it, a list of all their various passwords, when they first rented this apartment, just in case. She held her breath while she unscrewed it.

Her husband was a creature of habit. There was the password, a string of random numbers and letters, in fresh ink at the bottom of the list. She copied it and went back to her virch chair.

There was 63 million in the account now, easily enough to get them both to the asteroid belt. It was registered only to Gareth.

Abruptly she stood up, yanked out her jack, shut off her virch unit and grabbed the bank statement and the code list, shoving them in her pocket. She didn't know where she was going. She had some idea of taking the subway down to Thieu-Armstrong's offices and confronting Gareth there, but even as she opened the front door it was starting to fade. How did she know he'd gone there? Suppose he had and was in the office still. Could she even get in? Gareth had told her about iris scans, bi-weekly password changes and vigilant security staff. Suppose she managed to convince someone to let her enter. What then? Did she really want to have a fight in front of his co-workers? Where it would get back to Addison?

She wandered irresolutely down the dim hall to the elevator, nostrils twitching as always at the compound of out-gassing insulation and carpeting, a thousand over-spiced, hastily-cooked meals, smoke and stale sweat. She was relieved be alone, probably safe in the mid-day lull. What if, she thought while she waited for the elevator, what if Gareth and Mom and everybody else are right? He's making good money, the money that could finally get us out of this giant stack of hamster cages, this air like pus, this noise so constant that silence shocks like cold water, away from the stalkers, the beggars, the druggies, the people who'd kill you because God said to or for no reason at all.

The elevator door opened and it was empty for once. She was about push the ground floor button when she noticed a smear of blood on the panel. She looked down. There was a little trail of red splashes, almost obscured by dusty shoeprints. She tried to peer into the hall to see if the trail led from there, but the doors were closing, the elevator heading down.

She checked for more splashes on the ground floor but the janitor had made one of his infrequent passes with a mop and the floor was clean.

Outside, the steps down to street level were clean or at least free of recent blood. She stopped on the sidewalk, undecided about what to do next, an islet in the stream of lunch hour sidewalk traffic. *Maybe I'm getting all knotted up for no reason. He could have had a nosebleed a long time back and missed a spot when he was cleaning up. I don't even know that the blood in the elevator was his. And if it was, so what? Maybe he cut himself shaving.*

Somebody jostled her and she turned. An anonymous man, masked and filtered against the UV and smog, hurrying somewhere. She probably should go back, or at least buy a mask. She turned to scan the street again and saw a tall woman turning away, with cornrows spilling out of a slouchy hat. She was sure it was Raelene.

Without thinking about it much, she started walking, trying to catch up with Raelene. She needed someone to talk to and Raelene was always levelheaded. It had just rained, so the air was pretty clean and she could breathe without difficulty, a small mercy. But the street was filling up and she couldn't seem to catch up to Raelene, who was walking briskly toward the Farmers Market.

Callie wondered what could be so important to her friend that she'd leave her baby to walk in the streets. Then she shook her head in self-dismay. *Silly,* she thought. *Maybe she just needs a break.* But Raelene's hurrying gait didn't look like anyone out for a stroll.

Then Raelene turned left at Harcourt, when the Farmer's Market was on the right. Maybe she had an actual desk job in the financial district, though Callie thought news like that would be big enough to send in an e-mail. Hurrying to catch up, she rounded the corner in time to see Raelene turn right down Severn Avenue. And on the other side of the intersection she saw Addison, also turning down

Severn. She couldn't tell if he'd seen her. If he had he didn't seem to be paying any mind, which would be odd in itself. Addison had made a point of favoring her with his bland, faintly menacing attention every time they'd met.

She'd lost sight of Raelene and was feeling lost in general. She had never come this way. The farther she went up Severn, the rougher it got. She passed a grafter bar called Eely's just as the door opened and three recombos spilled out, two men and a woman. The guys were laughing and feinting at each other. Their movements were quick but sloppy, as if they'd taken stims and something that blurred their focus. The tall one with the scarlet pompadour had his knees reversed and his feet re-engineered like a chicken's, with a gamecock's fighting spur. The other's thickened skin was lumped in scaly gray plates down his bare shoulders and chest. He had a stubby horn between his little piggy eyes.

She sped up her pace but the men got on either side of her, still sparring, using her as a moving barrier, giggling loopily when she shrank away from punches and kicks to either side of her. "Guys," she said, trying to defuse things, "I wonder if you can help me. I'm looking for my little sister." Her answer was a chorus of deep grunts from Rhino-boy and a triumphal crow from the rooster. She gasped, then bit down on a cry when one of his talons raked her side.

Fighting to keep her voice steady, she said "No really, I've got her picture right here." She shoved her hand into her purse.

Just as Callie's hand closed on the Mace-screamer, the grafter woman yelled "We got no time for this, Cocky. Leave the norm alone, fuck." She reached down the back of his pantaloons and hauled him back.

Cocky was indignant. "Fuckin' leggo me, Louisa. I'll fuckin'--" That was as far as he got when she backhanded him.

"Am I askin' you, Cocky? Do you hear me askin' what you wanna do? No? Nothin' to say? Good. Now let's go before you fuck up this deal too." Cocky blushed furiously, opened his gap-toothed mouth, thought better of it and fell into step, shooting a glare at Callie.

Without his buddy to back him up, Rhino-boy lost interest. He drifted back to his friends, looking like a chubby boy in ugly pajamas.

Callie started to thank the recombo woman, but stopped at her warning glare. Louisa yawned hugely, showing three rows of translucent, back-swept fangs. Callie stopped and let them get far ahead of her.

Benny the Antichrist, Page 41

She couldn't see Raelene or Addison anywhere. By this time it was just past noon and the white fist of the sun had flattened every shadow.

She really needed to get inside. She was risking heat stroke or serious UV damage, not to mention air-poisoning. Her side ached. She was probably bleeding, but didn't want to examine herself out on the street. The pain felt like a gash over her ribs. At least he probably hadn't reached her belly, she thought. She had a sudden image of a claw slashing a baby's face and almost vomited.

She looked around. The only place that looked remotely open was Eely's. The impossibly thin fish-woman on the old-fashioned painted sign beckoned her and she could hear a band inside playing an Atav version of an old Aryan anthem, but Callie really didn't want to go in there. She decided to head back as quickly as she could.

Then she heard the chanting. Or rather, she realized she'd been hearing it for some time but had only just become aware of it. She couldn't make out any words, but it seemed to be coming from up the street. The chant was a hypnotic call and response, a slow, rolling basso invocation, answered by a humming melodic phrase that changed subtly with each iteration. She found herself walking toward it.

She rounded a corner and found the source, a Revenant ashram, the biggest she'd ever seen in person. A long time ago she could see it had started life as a Gothic-style church, adding on more buildings over the years. She could still make out some of the chiseled inscriptions through the pink plaz-foam that swirled, arched and bulged over the old gray stone like some huge child's idea of a coral reef.

Over it all swarmed the dreamers. In rosy pink and baby blue robes they sat in the curving sill of the rose window, they stood on and straddled pink extrusions of plaz-foam. Arms linked, they covered the sharply pitched roof, facing up to the sky, some of them dangling heads down over the drop, as if glued there by faith alone. The pink steeple and other, smaller peaks were ringed with chains of them, seemingly held up only by the strength of their hand-in-hand grips.

And they sang. The three-deep ranks surrounding the ashram would let loose a short, forceful basso phrase, answered by a buzzing, trebly response by a pink and blue line of them snaking up a buttress, which in turn got a thuddingly deep reply those who ringed the lower

Benny the Antichrist, Page 42

part of the steeple, over and over, the chant flowing through and around the pink and blue-clad masses like some great current dancing its way through an inscrutable pattern. Sometimes they'd fall silent, save for one trilling from the top of the strangely floral structure through which she could see a gray stone cross. Other times the whole building would erupt in a great, ear-splitting chord, giving way suddenly to quiet, intricate counterpoint.

On and on it went. Callie couldn't make out the words clearly, although she thought she heard "God", "dream", "death and "birth" a number of times. It was intoxicating. She forgot herself, forgot her pain, thirst and anger while she followed the shimmering, interwoven strands of the great hymn.

Then one, two, six more singers launched themselves from one of the pink plaz-foam minarets, 80 feet up. Three of them actually dove. The others just fell, two hitting the sides of the ashram as they tumbled, taking other worshippers with them. They hit the trampled grass with ragged thuds.

The chant rolled on, unabated. Holding her side, which suddenly ached furiously, Callie stared at the bodies lying like scraps thrown aside by some enormous, negligent child. As she watched, wondering abstractedly why she couldn't scream, four of them, bleeding and moving brokenly, actually got up and haltingly began to climb the pink walls of the temple again. The rest just lay there.

It came to her with the force of a physical blow that Sonya could be up there, might be readying herself to leap. She gasped, then fought down retching by main force of will. She stared up, squinting, but the sun was in her eyes and they were all parts of the same pink-and-blue-robed, faceless ecstatic creature. She thought of trying to push her way closer, but even if she could manage it with her side throbbing, what good could she do? Even healthy and rested, Callie couldn't climb a stepladder without feeling dizzy. Clambering up the side was out of the question.

She shook her head, then stoppered her ears, trying to think. She decided she needed to get inside. Maybe someone would tell her if Sonya was there or she'd find her. And if her sister was outside with the other singers, there had to be ways up the structure that didn't involve scaling the outside. She could get someone to look at her wound. Even their detractors conceded that the Revenants had amazing healing skills and medicines.

Benny the Antichrist, Page 43

Holding her side, now wet with blood, she circled the building slowly, watching for any place people might be going in.

It wasn't hard to find. They'd added on a spiraling plaz-foam passageway that ended in where the church's front door used to be. The ceiling dipped low and she had to duck to get in, but at least she didn't have to crawl or burrow.

When she'd straightened up inside Callie gasped, her pain momentarily forgotten. They'd taken down all the structurally inessential walls, creating one huge, vaulting space that echoed, hummed and chimed sympathetically with cascading voices of the singers outside. The pews were gone, replaced by mats and the occasional pillow or hassock. The room swarmed with sun, beaming down from the skylights they'd cut in the roof, glowing on the blissful faces of the Revenants, darting and playing on the streamers and ribbons that festooned the heights above. Some of them were faint, gauzy lace so attenuated it was more a notion of pattern than substance. Others were twisted, knotted arches of velvet so thick and deep it seemed to muscle into the air. Satiny, leathery, nubby, matte, the eye lingered on them like a seamstress's fingers. And the colors! Maroon dark as starved blood scalloped with shimmering aquamarine, salmon iridescing with palest green, blue-black with orange hound's-tooth, bruised ruby shot with café au lait slivers, a thousand shades and patterns, somehow harmonious beyond any notion of taste, they swayed gently in a faint, incense-freighted breeze.

A small circle of blue-robed Dreamers sat in front of the doorway, all in lotus position, facing each other. With no apparent signal one rose smoothly, letting the torque of his straightening legs turn him around to face her. He was tall and could have been anywhere from his twenties to forties. His head was shaven and his pale blue eyes matched his robe. His smile didn't change as he gazed slowly at Callie. Silently, he extended his right hand, palm up.

As soon as her hand touched his, Callie began to feel better. Her breathing slowed and the ache in her side was a stain gradually fading in lapping water as they walked slowly toward the apse. They passed small groups of Revenants chanting or stretching or cleaning the mats, thoroughly and without haste. A trio of blindfolded children played catch with a small ball they caught as often as they dropped. Her legs felt good, as if she'd had a long sleep and a good stretch. A slow, warm surge of energy rolled up her spine. When she came to

Benny the Antichrist, Page 44

the stairs leading up to the altar, she almost hopped up them two at a time.

The woman sitting on a hassock facing the stairs was old, probably. It was hard to tell because she had no hair, not even eyebrows. She didn't have eyelashes because she had no eyes. The space under her brows was smooth, as if there had never been anything there. She smiled and pointed toward a foam pallet on the floor. "Welcome," she said in a resonant contralto.

She lay down and the woman knelt beside her, her hands hovering above Callie's face, then moving down and around her body. A friend of a friend once did raki for her. This felt a little like that, but not much. For one thing the Healer touched her occasionally, once even squeezing Callie's calf quite forcefully. For another, she talked while she worked. "Just a scratch on the ribs," she said. "No poisons I can detect. Nothing the grafters usually use, anyway. Everything inside seems safe." Callie wondered how she knew all that but somehow the words to ask never came. "You came looking for something," the Revenant said. "What is it you seek?"

"I'm looking for--" Callie answered. And stopped. She came because she was chasing her husband, to say she didn't know what to him, then saw her friend and followed her, then got hurt, then worried about her sister. What was the answer? What did she want? Was her purpose nothing more than flotsam, tossed on the currents of other people's wills? It was hard to think about it. She felt tired but warm and comfortable. What could she want more than this? Something. It was big, but it circled in the shadows, just out of sight.

"Why do you have all those streamers and colors in here, when so many of you are blind?" It was as if the adult part of her was away working on something, leaving behind an inquisitive six year old.

"Ah... I made and hung three of them, one for each time I gave up my outer eyes. The last one I wove myself, out of silk and jute. It was my favorite. Pink grapefruit pink that darkened to umber, with gold embroidery. I had to get special dispensation for the gold. Can you see it?"

Callie had a hard time opening her eyes. She looked at the hanging forest of cloth but couldn't make out anything matching that description. Before she could say no, the Revenant woman said "No matter. There are a thousand as beautiful."

"But--"

"We strive to see with the eyes of the spirit in the Dream of God. Every one of us who dreams the True Dream brings the world closer to where it is going, beyond the Pain Clock time. We give up our eyes to see, then get them back to know what's beyond seeing and that we must let them go again."

"And the singing? And the jumping off?"

"There are different paths beyond the Pain Clock."

They talked of those things and others for a time. Callie thought vaguely that she ought to ask about Sonya, but it didn't seem all that important. She was just awake enough to feel a warm, viscous, mildly burning liquid being rubbed into her wounded side. It was whitish and smelled like seawater. The Healer seemed to be exuding it from her fingertips, but it was hard to tell.

* * *

In her dream she, Sonya and Gareth were living on an asteroid together, which was also their apartment, where they had a farm that they plowed leaving red gouges and grew corn, except its ears were filled with rows of lyght capsules. The sun shone all the time and they never stopped singing, not even her little boy, who played with his dog in the craters. His name was Carty and he looked like Addison.

* * *

Callie awoke alone on the pallet. She was naked, though she didn't remember getting undressed. She couldn't tell how long she'd slept. The space was still full of light, so probably not long, she thought. The gouge on her side was covered with something translucent, smooth and a bit stiff. Underneath it was a little sore, but nothing she couldn't handle. She could remember very little of her conversation with the Healer, but knew that she had been charged with a task: To find that which she sought. And that meant deciding what she wanted.

She got up, wrapping a sheet around her. She felt a little shaky, but her balance came back with a few steps. Her clothes were neatly folded on a pad beside the pallet, except for her blouse, which had been soaked with blood. It had been replaced by a loose, Revenant blue top. Not her style, but at least more opaque than some of the robes. No one seemed to be paying any particular attention to her. She thought of asking someone about Sonya but when she looked over toward the portal, the blue-robed circle was gone and there didn't seem to be anybody else around who looked in charge of things. She remembered her plan of getting up by some interior

Benny the Antichrist, Page 46

route, but quickly gave it up after scanning her surroundings. There could be a door to a passageway anywhere or nowhere. She could search for hours and still end up having to ask someone to let her in. And why would they, since her only plausible purpose for going up would be to interfere with the singers? Assuming that Sonya was up there, that she was even at this Ashram and Callie could find a way to reach her.

She needed a plan. She needed to get out of this chiming, echoing hive so she could hear herself think.

Out in the yard surrounding the Temple she noticed some police cordoning off a parking lot. They didn't seem to be coming onto the grounds, just keeping an eye on a few dispirited demonstrators who trooped around in a little circle, holding up placards and chanting something it was hard to hear over the singing from the Ashram. One of the signs read "Matthew 4:7". The man wielding it was talking to a reporter, who looked half asleep. Others had set up their sightlines so the Ashram was their camera background. The dignified sobriety they strove for was made difficult by having to shout over the singers, the protesters and other reporters. She heard one of them say something like "funeral celebration".

She approached a cop, a big, 40-ish woman who looked Chicano. She was dressed in riot gear, but had her visor up. She eyed Callie warily as she drew closer. "Could you help me," Callie said, shouting over the din. "I'm looking for my sister."

"She one of the spooks?"

"Excuse me?"

"Ghosts. Howyacallem. Reva..."

"Revenants? Yes, she is, but she's--"

"She sign up of her own free will?"

"Yes, well probably, but she wasn't---"

"If she joined voluntarily, lady, I can't do nothing for you."

"But she could--" Abruptly the great choir fell silent, the echoes of their last thundering chord echoing faintly in the distance. It was as if the air was suddenly lighter, more breathable. "She could kill herself," she continued quietly. "Isn't there a law against suicide any more?"

"Law? 'Course there's a law. Thing is, we got laws, they got lawyers. Good enough lawyer can make you believe up is down and shit is icecream. Make a judge believe, anyway."

"But--"

"Look, lady, I can't help you here. Talk to your elected representatives. Send a letter." She glanced around and her expression softened a bit. "You didn't hear it from me, but I'd hire me one of those deprogrammers, I was you. These guys," she nodded at the Ashram, "these guys got protection from on high, ya know what I'm talkin'?"

"But I'm here now. I just want to see if she's all right, at least."

She sighed. "Yeah, I hear you. Look." She pointed off to the left, towards the church complex. "One of those buildings is their administrative centre. The brown one, I think, maybe. They might be able to help you out there."

She looked in the direction the cop was pointing. There was a commotion off to the side. A large black man was having a heated conversation with one of the officers, who had his billyclub ready. The man was heavily muscled and half a head taller than the cop, who looked like he was ready to call for help and start swinging. With a start she realized it was Beau. She opened her mouth to call him, then closed it. If she wanted to move freely around here, would it be wise to link herself with someone who was getting himself in the police's bad books? Not to mention calling attention to herself, should anyone from the Revenants' hierarchy be watching. Feeling like a traitor, she turned away.

"Thanks for your help," she said to the policewoman, as she turned toward the complex.

"No prob. And lady?"

"Yes?"

"The reason we're down here is these Risen types have some kind of big wingding planned, 'counta their grand poobah, that Nigerian guy? He just died. Just so you know. Only reason I'm telling you is when the spooks party, it's never just dining and dancing. Always some kinda trouble, but you didn't hear that here. You get a chance, grab your sister and get out quick, is what I'm saying."

"Thanks again. Muchos gracias."

"De nada."

None of the buildings had any obvious signs to indicate their functions. The nearest door on the brown two-storey one the policeman had indicated was closed. When she went around to the other side, she found a small, Japanese-looking Revenant man methodically spraying it with pink plaz-foam. His smile was vapidly beatific, but at least his eyes were open and not covered with

Benny the Antichrist, Page 48

mirrored lenses. They were dark and looked like they might be his originals too.

At that moment the singers started up again, even louder than before, a burst of soprano and tenor arpeggios against a swell of alto and basso that counterpointed the upper range singers with their own warbling harmonics. "Excuse me," she said, trying to match his smile, "I'm looking for the administrative center."

His head bobbed up and down happily. She wondered if he'd really understood what she'd said. But he turned and indicated the building behind him, plaz-foam sculpted already into the shape of a broad thunderhead anvil. "Arrigato" she said, drawing from some forgotten store of linguistic knowledge. He smiled even more broadly and turned back to his work.

The building had two different entrances that she could see. As she watched, a woman in a navy blue, discreetly Kevlar-padded pantsuit walked in the right door. Callie followed her.

The door opened onto concrete stairs lit with LEDs. Callie could hear the woman's heels clicking in front of her, then a blast of loud music, a strange choral cover of an old Dungeon-beat hit, as a door opened and shut. She was probably in the wrong place, but decided to check it out anyway. You could never tell around here.

She walked down one flight, then two more. As she got lower the gray concrete walls were specked, then regularly patterned, then completely covered with little rectangles of cardboard and plastic. Business cards.

She was sure it wasn't the administration center when she opened the door and smelled smoke, tobacco, pot and a few other things. The sound here was deafening, the same kind of kaleidoscopic chorale she'd heard at the Ashram in a setting of wailing synths and harsh guitars, grounded by a throbbing, polyrhythmic beat and bone-jarring bass. The light was dim except for the strobe-lit dance floor, where people were dancing in a way that looked both athletic and deliberately spasmodic. There was a jarring pattern to their movements, but she couldn't pick it out. It was as if she were watching the mating ritual of some strange new species, one that only superficially resembled business-garbed lawyers, consultants, brokers and robed Revenants.

She was about to turn and leave when she saw Addison. Finding him gyrating among the Dreamers left her so nonplussed that it took her a moment to realize he was dancing with Jocelyn Niarchos. By

Benny the Antichrist, Page 49

this time Addison had seen her. "Oh Gareth," he said. Who turned and wove his way leisurely from the back of dance floor to face her. Whose blank eyes didn't change when he said "Hello, Callie."

For Callie, a day that had been careening out of control abruptly slowed to a ponderous stagger. She stared at Gareth and at the place in which she'd found him. She wanted to scream, to run, to shake him till he gasped. And all the while some meticulous part of her was quietly insisting that she see, hear and remember everything. See the faint unsteadiness of her husband's gait as he led her to an empty table in a slightly quieter corridor in the back, the scratches on the side of his head, where he'd pulled his hair out. Hear the giggly undertone of his voice as he started to talk to her, to justify, to explain. And most of all, remember Addison saying "Oh Gareth." There was something about that. Something that made all the difference.

Gareth was talking. "... really quite impressed with you, finding me here and--"

"I wasn't looking for you."

"You weren't? But then how... oh, yeah, Sonya. Well, she's probably around here somewhere."

"I know that. I even understand why, a little. The thing I don't understand is why you're here. Why you lied to me about getting the LERT chip."

"Callie..." He sighed. "All those things you want, a safe home with clean air and space to raise a kid, you think they just give them to people like us? I figured it out once. At the rate we were saving it would have taken us eight years to get off-planet. Eight years. Assuming neither one of us got hurt, that fares or rents or food didn't go up. Assuming that we both kept our jobs. Assuming we had jobs waiting when we got to the Belt. Assuming no pregnancies."

"I didn't... You should have talked to me."

"I tried, Callie. When did you ever want to talk about it? When did we ever have time?"

"We could have worked it out."

"I did work it out. I saw our chance and I took it. I made that sacrifice."

"Sacrifice." She looked around her. Across from them two business-suited men gasped and moaned buy and sell orders while masturbating each other under the table. Three tables down two buxom young girls in diaphanous pink teddies and a bald man whose

Benny the Antichrist, Page 50

clothing consisted entirely of chains and steel mesh did something
that looked painful involving tongs, needles and a small pump.

"Oh this," Gareth waved dismissively. "This is just R and R. The
Church of the Risen's one of our clients. They get top-drawer
treatment. We get to dream."

"I don't, I don't understand any of this, Gareth. When were you
planning on telling me about this? What about our plans to get out?"

"Oh come on, Callie. You knew. You wouldn't let yourself think
about it, but you knew all the time."

"I didn't--"

"Where do you think all your jobs have come from? You're not
any better or faster than you were, but you're getting virch temp jobs
left, right and center, while other people, people with better rates, are
begging for work. I'm on the partnership track, Callie. I'm in the club
and membership has its privileges. Like deciding who works and who
doesn't. Think about that next time you feel like sneering at Thieu-
Armstrong. Or any other company with round-the-clockers working
for them, for that matter. We feed all you sleepyheads. We make the
decisions that run your dozy little lives."

"Is that your dream, Gareth? To run my life? I always thought it
was to raise a family with me in the Asteroid Belt. I guess I've been a
fool for believing you'd want something like that."

"We're already in the Asteroid Belt, if you only knew."

"Now I know you've lost your mind."

"Not at all. See this?" He tapped at the earring he'd worn since
the day of the operation and now she could clearly see the stylized
TA that was Thieu-Armstrong's logo winking at her from within the
opal. "Cache memory and a few other things. Lets me select a key
indicator datum and track it, so I can get a heads-up on any trend
coming down the pike. Remember that insurance policy we took out
a year ago? Couple weeks ago, just for laughs, I decided to break it
out, see who was trading on it. Turns out the Belt Consortium has
invested heavily in indemnities, including ours. They own a bit of our
future, Callie, and we own some of theirs. You and all your daytimer
friends just blunder along, dreaming your itty-bitty dreams, thinking
you're in control of your separate little lives. But we're each of us all
over the world and out into space. Every time you touch a keyboard
something happens in China, on the Moon, out on the Belt. And
round-the-clockers like I can see where it's going, can manage it."

Benny the Antichrist, Page 51

As he talked, Callie suddenly knew what had bothered her about Addison announcing her presence to Gareth. The way he had said "Oh Gareth" was an imitation of her own breathy voice, her cry at the height of making love.

Without a word she turned away. The tiny life barely swelling her stomach now felt like an iceberg. The room blurred and she blundered off, only knowing that she wanted to be somewhere, anywhere, else.

And came to a quiet, brightly lit room where people with little take-a-number tickets waited in rows of chairs, till they were called up to the front counter, where they waited again till their wads and pocketfuls of street cash were tallied up twice, then given a little bag of lyght capsules and a receipt. And sitting in a chair, waiting with the others, was Raelene.

She was trembling as she sat there, one hand clenching and unclenching, over and over. She dug furiously in her purse, finally winkling out a light capsule and popping it triumphantly. The tremor got a little better. Callie wanted to say something, to run over there. What stopped her was what she hadn't seen from out in the street, the little belted pouch slung over Raelene's shoulder. She had her baby here. She was nursing.

Raelene could have seen Callie at any time, if she'd looked up. She didn't look up.

Callie felt a tap on her shoulder. She turned. It was Gareth. "Told you," he said.

She strode past him, searching for the door. Indifferently she caught a glimpse of his face, his mouth hanging open, as if he'd never been ignored before. Then he turned to follow her. His mouth worked a few seconds before anything came out, as if he had too much and not enough to say. "What are you going to do, Callie? Gonna tell someone? Don't you think they know already, huh? Everybody knows, except a few dozy daytimer sleepyheads. All these people down here, they're the people who run everything, government, business, law enforcement, everything. They've all got the chip because you need to be on your toes 24-7 if you want to get anywhere. And all that stuff about not dreaming, what do you think the lyght does for us? Who do you think Raelene's customers are mostly? Your LERT-chipped boss and his boss, that's who. They come down here to take the edge off. To dream. I've got a dream on now. And you know what? We even dream better than daytimers, because we know where our dreams are going." He caught her shoulder. "We know where they're going and how to make them work for us."

She twisted out of his grip. She was at the door and about to step through, when she turned to face him. "Fine. I'm a dozy little sleepyhead and you don't care about me or what we planned. What I can't understand is not caring about yourself. Look at you. You're shaking like a leaf. Your head's all scratched up and your skin's gray. How can you and Raelene do that to yourselves, is what I don't get. How can she do that to her baby?"

"Don't worry about that. Lyght doesn't get in mother's milk."

"You're sure about that. You'd swear to it."

"Callie, there are studies--"

"Paid for by who?"

"Relax. You're making it bigger than... Look, it's covered. Say, just hypothetically, that I sustain a bit of nerve damage, some symptoms. I'm due for my checkup in a couple of weeks anyway. If, and I say if, there are any problems, then I've got three weeks full-pay down time written into my contract, with an optional Cerebella full neural regeneration package. It's all good."

"What about Raelene?"

"Who the fuck... If Raelene needs a treatment, I guess she can get one too."

"How much does it cost?"

"I don't know. A lot, I suppose. I could find out."

"Don't bother. Just get yourself looked at. Then do whatever you need to do, is my advice to you." She turned and walked out the door.

She heard the door open again before she'd gotten halfway up the first flight of stairs. "So that's it, huh?" Gareth said. "You're storming out, full of righteous indignation. Little Miss Purity, Miss Holy Denial. You're flouncing off because I committed the sin of telling you all the things you knew already but didn't want to hear. Look at me, you hypocrite. Look at me!" He grabbed her wrist, then fell back when she turned and raked him across the face with her nails.

"Bitch!"

"Yes, Gareth, I guess I am a bitch. Or something too small and silly, no, dozy to live in your world. And maybe I knew and was lying to myself all the time. I don't know, I really don't. But one thing I do know is that you never had the right to turn me, us, into a dirty joke for that sleazy reptile you call your boss. Now goodbye, Gareth."

She turned again and walked up the stairs. She had the outside door open when she heard her name bellowed like a curse, like a scream for help, from down in the depths. She stepped out without looking back.

Outside, her eyes and ears told her something was going to happen. Everyone else knew too. The protesters had stopped marching. The police weren't watching the spectators. All eyes turned toward the Temple, where the perching, clinging choir was building to a crescendo in a series of ascending, jagged arpeggios, egged on by a swaggering basso chorus. The music throbbed and swelled, throbbed and swelled, paused, gathered itself... and erupted in one apocalyptic chord.

Then all the singers fell.

A few dived, graceful as falcons. Many just toppled over. Others were pulled off by their falling neighbours, or jarred into space by bodies crashing down from above. They were silent, mostly, while they fell. The screams came from the spectators and those who had hit the ground.

In the midst of everything she saw Sonya. Sonya letting go and falling. Sonya hitting the mass of those who'd already jumped.

Forgetting everything, she ran toward the pile of dead and injured. The police were already moving to form a cordon, but she burst through. A hand reached for her shoulder but she twisted away.

They couldn't touch her then. It was bedlam, a scrum of broken, groaning bodies heaved together higgledy-piggledy, some drizzled, others soaked by blood, piss and tears. Heedless of who or what she stepped on, Callie threw herself into the mass, tossing bodies aside with a madwoman's strength, until she came on a pair of legs she recognized. She rolled a man twice her size off to the side, while he spasmed and gurgled.

Sonya was very still, but didn't seem to be bleeding. Not on the surface anyway. Bending down, one foot on the ground, the other on someone's back, Callie gathered her up by main strength. She turned and staggered away from the pile, listening for her sister's heartbeat, looking for a way out.

By this time the police had cordoned off the jumpers. They were keeping reporters and protesters out, but they also kept ambulatory Revenants in. They seemed to be waiting for something. It was hard to hear or think, with the protesters chanting and reporters barking questions. She caught a glimpse of a little line of blue robed Dreamers, most of them older, heading towards the pile. Her Healer was one of them. She wondered whether she should just stay and let the Healers do what they could for her sister.

Then Sonya opened her eyes. She'd lost one of her mirrored contact lenses and seemed to have trouble focusing. She was crying. "You came for me, Callie." Then: "Oh, Callie, it hurts."

"Hang on, Sohnny," Callie said. "We're going to get you some help."

"It hurts, Sis. I never knew it could hurt so much." She was quiet after that.

Looking around, Callie spotted a row of ambulances in the parking lot. She started for them. Blocking her way were two police, the Chicano woman she'd talked to and a younger, taller man with a big blonde mustache.

Mustache said "Whoa, lady. I can't let you out. Why don't you just wait here for the nice people to come and help you." He nodded toward the line of Healers.

"I don't need any help. This is my sister. She needs medical attention."

"And that's what coming. Medical attention." He looked to be only in his late twenties, but well on his way to baldness.

"If I leave her here, they'll have her on that building again as soon as she can walk. They'll have her jumping till it kills her."

"Not my problem, lady. My orders are to keep people inside in and people outside out."

"But it's suicide." She looked in appeal to the Chicano officer, who shrugged and glanced away.

Mustache sighed, then spoke in a monotone, as though reciting, "According to my captain, it's religious freedom. As long as your sister joined voluntarily, we got no beef here."

"She asked for my help. She doesn't want to die."

"I don't know about that. And I got my orders."

Finally the Chicano cop couldn't take it any more. "Her sister asked her for help, Kendrick. Let the lady through."

"Captain said--"

"Fuck a whole bunch of that noise. You want to piss and moan, kiss McCormick's ass and put the whole thing on me? Fine. Now let her through."

Benny the Antichrist, Page 55

Mustache reddened. He opened his mouth to say something, then shrugged and got out of Callie's way.

They were halfway to the parking lot when a TV reporter spotted them. Grabbing a cameraman, she hustled over and stuck a microphone in Callie's face. "We're talking now to a woman who has managed to break through the police line carrying... is she a relative of yours? Can you tell us what is going on now within the Cathedral of the Church of the Risen?"

Callie smiled and shook her head. She tried to sidestep the reporter, who matched her step for step. "Miss, could we have your name please? Miss, how do you feel--"

"Ain't it obvious she don't want to talk to you?" Callie looked over her shoulder. There was Beau, standing with his thumbs hooked into his belt.

"And you would be?"

"Someone else who don't want to chat. Look, the lady's trying to get her sister to the ambulance, " he said, gently but firmly pushing the reporter aside. "Are you too damn rude and stupid to get that?"

"So you know her. And how is it that she and only she--hey!" Beau had simultaneously grabbed her mike and the videocam. He smashed them together. The cameraman dispassionately reached in his bag. He was pulling out a spare videocam when Beau's stare halted him.

"That be the end of this interview."

"You can't--this is a free--our lawyers are gonna strip the flesh off your bones." The reporter was sputtering.

"They gotta find me first. Now maybe you transmitted enough to do that. You got one of those facial recognition programs, it prolly ain't that hard. Maybe I'm screwed already, huh? So it don't matter now if I yield to temptation, kick me some media ass." He looked down at the cameraman, then the reporter. "A whole lot of ass." As they scuttled off, he yelled "I got me some buttkicker friends too. Just so you know."

"Thanks Beau."

"Hey, no problem, Callie. You want me to carry her? She might be the one who's hurt and all, but you've looked better."

"I'd take you up on that any other time, big guy. But I feel like I've got to do this."

"I'm down with that, I guess. You seen Raelene?"

"I did. Beau... she's..."

Benny the Antichrist, Page 56

"Yeah, I figured. Is Zorah OK, at least?"

"As far as I know. Maybe you should go get her, while the Ashram is wide open."

"Tried it. They sicced some little guy on me. Told me I got to go. I tried to push him aside and damn if I didn't wake up out here half an hour later with two cops standing over me while they checked my priors. They said the Dreamers had swore out a restraining order on me. Told me if I showed up again, that'd be cause, what with Raelene doing shit and all, take our baby away."

By this time they'd gotten to the parking lot and the music started up again. Sonya was beginning to stir in her arms as Callie approached one of the ambulances. The logo on the side said St. Joseph's, a big public hospital. The attendants were leaning up against the side, watching the show. "My sister needs to get to a hospital," she said.

One of the attendants, a long-faced mixed race man with red freckles, gave her the once over. "She covered?" he wanted to know.

"Covered? I think so. My husband works for Thieu-Armstrong. We've got medical."

"Two what?"

"Sorry. Thieu-Armstrong? It's a brokerage. We've got full medical." Callie wasn't sure of this at all, but if Gareth had been promoted it seemed like a good bet. Sonya was definitely starting to squirm in her arms. Eyes closed, she writhed like someone in the grip of a nightmare. "Rest easy, honey," Callie crooned. "We're nearly there." Her words seemed to have no effect and finally she had to say "Beau, I can't hold her any longer." He took Sonya in his arms and she quieted a bit. She looked like a tiny, malnourished child against his thick torso.

The attendant asked "You got a medical card?"

"I--" Callie realized she'd left the apartment in such a hurry she hadn't even picked up her purse. She had a wallet and couple of credit cards in her pocket and that was it.

"Look," said Beau. "She married to a big-time stock broker. Her sister covered, OK? Now put her in the damn ambulance."

"Holy shit," the other attendant said. They turned to see what he was looking at. The choir had fallen silent, save for a low drone. A young man had climbed the steeple and, precariously balanced at the top, was singing a solo. Even at this distance it was easy to tell he was badly injured. His face was streaked with blood, one arm hung useless

Benny the Antichrist, Page 57

and his hip cocked at a strange angle. But he sang in a clear countertenor, a strange, sweet melody that never resolved because he pitched over in the middle of what sounded like the final bar. The choir waited for a few measures, then started up a chorus that sounded, to Callie, obscenely jolly.

All through this Sonya became increasingly agitated, writhing and bucking in Beau's arms. Her eyes were still closed, but she began to sing along. Her voice was amazingly loud and full, coming from that wasted, battered frame. Callie couldn't understand the words and she realized from the swelling on the side of her face that Sonya's jaw was broken. She started kicking and flailing her arms and Beau said "I got to put her down."

As he did Callie moved to help him and glared at the mulatto attendant. "Can't you give her something?"

He looked at his partner, a stocky, Mediterranean-looking guy, who nodded. "Hold her steady, man," freckle-face said to Beau. "I gotta get something." He jumped into the back of the ambulance.

"I'm trying, but I'm afraid I'm going to hurt--Yo, Zorba? You want to give us some help, like you 'sposed to do?"

"I'm not allowed to, unless they're covered. I could lose--Aw, shit." He moved in to grab a spasming leg. The three of them tried desperately to hold on without hurting Sonya, while she bucked and bellowed. "Hurry up with that trank, Milt!"

Milt reappeared at that moment with a huge hypodermic. "Hold her ass!" he yelled. They managed to press Sonya's hips down long enough for him to jab the needle in her left buttock. The plunger was halfway in before she quieted, too late to save Callie a headbutt to the forehead that left her dizzy and weak.

They laid Sonya down on a small patch of grass bordering the parking lot, then collapsed themselves. Callie could feel blood trickling down her side where her wound had reopened. Sonya began to hiccup and finally to snore.

Zorba had gotten an elbow to the windpipe. When he could finally speak he looked across at Callie. "Here's the deal," he said. "Unless you can show me a medical card, I can't take her. Even if I did, and I tried this once, they wouldn't let her in ER."

"But we're covered. If I showed you some ID, couldn't you cross-reference it and look up my husband's policy?"

Benny the Antichrist, Page 58

"Ma'am, even if, by some miracle, our lines were clear enough and my dispatcher had the smarts and would take time to do it, how do we know it'd cover your sister for this?"

"But--"

"You ever read an insurance policy looking for something specific? Trust me, we don't have time."

"Man, this is bullshit!" Beau roared.

"You get no argument from me."

"But what am I supposed to do?" Callie wailed. "She'll die if she takes another fall!" Sonya groaned and started muttering something.

"Lookit," Zorba said. He had a broad, heavy-jawed face with soft brown eyes under a thick uni-brow. "We don't have a lot of time here. I seen these wackos, no offence ma'am, take twice what Milt give her, wake up in five minutes and go toddling off when they should have been dead, by all rights. What ever they fill 'em full of at the spook house there, it makes them damn near impervious to things that'd flatten you and me. Even if we could take your sister to ER, they'd have to chain her to her bed in a locked ward. And I heard some of them get out anyway."

"Oh God. Why are you here, anyway, if you're not going to pick anyone up?"

"We're looking for one kid. Dad's a senator. He heard his boy was down here."

"But he was too busy to come himself, right? Let me guess. He's got a LERT chip. Stays awake day and night, playing the market and generally being master of the universe. But he's too busy to come and get his boy back. So he uses his juice to send an ambulance, from what we used to think was a public hospital. Only it's just to pick up his kid, nobody else. Am I close?"

"Well, we can help other people, long as they're covered. But you got everything else right."

By this time Sonya was starting to rock from side to side. She kept trying to get up and falling back. Her eyes opened and she looked around wildly with her strange one-lens, blue and silver stare. "Callie? I'm not supposed to be here, Callie. This is the Pain Clock time. I'm supposed to be with the Master. Not here. Not here."

"Oh, Sohnny..."

Sonya shrieked, a sound so loud and harsh Callie's gut knotted just to hear it. Then she began, slowly and painfully, to get up.

Benny the Antichrist, Page 59

"We got maybe a minute," Zorba said. "Milt can hit her up one more time before we go. Or..."

"Or what?"

"Or you can let her go. They'll fix her up at the Ashram. Some of the stuff they can do there is amazing. Don't let any doctor tell you different."

"But she'll die!"

"Everybody dies, ma'am." Callie looked at his quiet, heavy face and knew this wasn't a truism, coming from him. It was what he saw every day. "Besides," he continued, "looks like the shindig is done for now." And it was true: The singers were climbing down off the pink walls, the healthy and the lame, looking like workers at the end of a long shift. A few rays from the setting sun managed to dodge clear of the skyscrapers.

"They don't all die right away," said Milt. "Some of them become Healers, right? You gotta last a while to learn all that stuff." He glanced professionally at Callie. He nodded toward her side, where blood was slowly darkening the blue cloth. "I could bandage that up, you want."

By this time Sonya was on her feet, straightening out. She favored Callie with a dazzling, lopsided smile and turned toward the Ashram, singing.

"Beau?"

"I'll help her back, Callie. If you want. Maybe they let me in to see if Raelene still there."

"You sure?"

"Can't be sure of nothing. Just doing what I can." Sonya started limping away and he followed, stooping to give her a shoulder to lean on. She beamed up at him and didn't protest when he scooped her up finally to carry her back.

Callie untucked the Revenant top and unzipped her jeans to let Milt bandage her side. He'd just cleaned off the cracked coating the Healer had laid on, when a thought occurred to Callie. "Hey, Beau!" she yelled. She looked at Milt. "One minute." He nodded.

She ran painfully after them. Beau stopped and let Sonya down when he saw her coming. Her sister limped on, singing, her voice cracking with weariness, but soaring and happy.

"You want to go to the Asteroid Belt, Beau? The air's clean and nobody shoots at you. We could work a claim, grow our own food. Come with me, Beau."

Benny the Antichrist, Page 60

"Callie, I don't--What am I gonna do up there?"

"I don't know. You're smart. You'll figure something out. Raelene always said you were smart."

"Raelene think she smart too, and look what happen."

"Yeah, but you can fix things. There's always work for a guy who can fix things."

"Callie, look. My woman and my baby are here. No matter how fucked up they are, they here. That's where I gotta be. They on the Moon, in the Asteroid Belt, I'd be there. Maybe I even finally figure out how to use a keyboard, if I got to. But they here. And if all I can do is wait till Raelene bring my baby home, then that's what I'm going to do."

"You're a damn good man, Beau." She hugged him, then ran to waylay Sonya before she got to the Ashram door. Her side ached fiercely but she didn't care. She wrapped her arms around her sister, halting her briefly. "Goodbye, Sohnny." She kissed her and let her go.

The tears rolled down Callie's face but she held it together as Milt bandaged her side. Zorba was talking on a cellphone, reporting no sighting and booking off the shift. "Catch a ride home with you guys?" she asked. Zorba said sure and she climbed into the back seat. They let her use the computer terminal back there. She dug the code list out of her pocket and called up her account information. Before they dropped her off she'd opened up a new account and transferred everything from Gareth's and her joint account and his secret one into it. In two hours she was packed. In a day she was off-planet, heading for the Asteroid Belt.

Comment

One of the nifty things about writing fiction is that it can reveal concerns that you had heretofore only vaguely suspected were of any importance to you. This one pretty much sprang into being fully formed and until it did, I wouldn't have said I gave sleep, and our society's ambivalent relationship to it, much thought at all.

I've spent much of my life working in outbound call centers, and I'd commend a spell of such employment to anyone who wants to know how management really works. Which is to say interviewer's scripts are confessions of sorts, their ungrammatical, overlong, logically shoddy sentences testifying to the arrogance and intellectual poverty of the buck-passing class, be they corporate or governmental.

Once a script has passed the committee phase, which is to say, diddled by a group who will never have to read aloud words cribbed from other surveys, in the service of clients who have a vastly inflated idea of their pet topic's importance and the general public's interest and tolerance for smug cant, it goes to the programmers, working, as best they can, with software purchased by managers who will never have to use it, either in development or with a respondent on the line.

Scripts are recited by phoners, a group made up of students, recent immigrants, second-jobbers, academic and professional misfits, underpaid, sleep-deprived, many of dubious literacy, and all pushed by middle managers to produce at any cost.

I have been a phoner for more years than I care to admit. While the work has allowed me to first support myself, barely, and later to contribute to my household, it hasn't been good for me in a number of ways. When the words of some rabbit-brained sociology grad without even a first language make me sound like a fool, well, long term, icy resentment is not good for the soul.

Which is not to say the job doesn't have its pleasures. I've enjoyed, often for twisted reasons, different interviewers' techniques and their juxtapositions. I've been privileged to listen to the maternally sweet tones of June (all names changed to protect the guilty), who at one point inspired a Carolina fisherman to exclaim "I don't really know what you're talkin' about, ma'am. But I sure do need a woman." June sat right across from Griselde, a hollow-eyed, damaged-looking woman whose style was pure, cold, bureaucratic bullying. I once heard her tell a respondent that they would now "undergo" the survey. Then there was Nenet, a doctrinaire Marxist who dressed like a pool shark, with hair from "Planet of the Apes". Getting a call from Nenet was like being interviewed by an unctuous Bond villain. Before you even asked, he would purringly assure you that the call was strictly confidential and would never, no, never ever, be used for nefarious purposes. Absolutely no black helicopters would show up at your house. Contrast him with Mort, with a radio announcer's voice and the quick wit of a practiced debater. Many's the time I heard him argue some recalcitrant farmer into a logical corner, to the amusement of everyone around him, but without the slightest success, because formal rationality counts for almost nothing in such situations.

There was Eva, whose cigarette baritone was like bastard file on your eardrums, and Robbie, a metalhead whose main strength was that he wouldn't hang up, no matter what abuse you screamed at him, and who seemed to draw all the most florid nutjobs, the Moldavian nazi, the woman who couldn't get a job because the man who lived inside of her wouldn't allow it, the guy who had to consult his dog about each answer.

But the creme de la creme, so far as I was concerned, was Tino.

Tino's English was, put kindly, laborious. But he showed up early every day, did his work, and never complained. I mean he Never Complained. Tino would take the most badly written, misspelled, ungrammatical script and read all of it,

Benny the Antichrist, Page 62

from pompous, off-putting opening, through self-evident intros, wordy, logically flawed questions, and half-assed outro, right to the bitter end. He read in a pleasant, but somewhat baffling Filipino accent, every time, never varying his approach, no matter who he had on the other end, no matter what they said. To Tino, the script was The Script, and you followed it as the word of God. If you had given him a piece of paper covered only with tire tracks from the parking lot, it wouldn't have mattered. He was selfless, a human automaton, a saint of the mass information capture system.

Callie, the heroine of "The Reason of Sleep", is not such a saint. She's like most of us, trying to get by in a world very slightly further along in various directions towards which it is currently sliding.

The End

JOB INTERVIEW

Listen, sorry it's taken so long to get to you, but we had a couple of things come up. Jeez, I'm starving. Tell you what, we'll do this over at the submarine place over at the mall. I'm buying.

Pastrami and peppers. Lotsa peppers. You? OK, make it two.

You really want this job? Yeah? OK, here's, lemme see, four quarters. Take 'em. You ever played Tetris? Good. What you're gonna do is you're gonna play that Tetris game inna corner over there. Yeah, it's old. Maybe the last arcade Tetris in the city. But anyway: You get to round, lessee, I got, what, a dime, a nickel and four pennies left, to round 19 and you got the job. No, I'm not kiddin'. But you gotta start at the 'Difficult' level. No sense fartin' around, eh?

OK, the name of the game is top-down management, exactly how the Company is run. Don't let nobody tell you any different, all that 'employee incentive' crapola. See, all those little shapes you gotta fit together? You don't get any say in what's comin' at ya - ya just gotta do it. Makes sense that Tetris was invented in the Soviet Union before Glasznost. Central Planning, if you wanna call it that. Lesson one.

Lesson two. What happens when you fit a row together, like that there? Right, it disappears. Same over here. Don't expect no gratitude, no perks. We only deal in 'What have you done for me lately?' It's called motivatin' the workforce.

OK, the shapes are comin' down the screen, like they're fallin', but does that matter? I mean to say, they could be goin' sideways or up, am I right? Right. Gravity don't have anything to do with it. 'Spite of the way it looks. Lesson three: We got our own brand of physics here.

Benny the Antichrist, Page 64

Just because it don't seem to make any sense, well, that don't concern you. Thing is, somebody, some Einstein, at Head Office decided this is the way it is and as far as you're concerned, when the word comes down, shit starts fallin' up, right?

Right?

Right.

Now you're at level 12 and you're down to two quarters. You fucked up twice, but you got to keep playin', 'cause you slipped them quarters in before anybody noticed. That's what you gotta do. Cover up and do it fast. Might even give yourself a little breather, if you do it right, all that shit don't come at you so fast for a while. Like with here. Lesson four.

Uh oh! Down to one. Really gonna have to hustle now. And you got all that shit comin' up under your feet, makin' it hard to concentrate. There's your lesson five. You start where we're gonna put you - well, it's borin' but you know what's what, right?

But an ambitious guy like you - you *are* an ambitious guy, right? Good. Like I was sayin'… an ambitious guy like you, soon as you start climbin' up the old corporate ladder, you notice that the ground starts gettin' all shaky and weird. Right under your feet. And it's only going to get worse, the higher you go. God, I love this country!

Y'know, eh, some women love this game. Addicted, like. Someone did a study and they found out that these broads, whenever they play Tetris,they get like a shot of estrogen in their blood. It's a high, for them. Not shittin' ya. Now why would that be? I figure it's an evolutionary response to sexism.

That's right. For centuries guys have been comin' home from work, huntin' mastodons, whatever, and layin' everything on the old lady. He's had a lousy day - she's gonna hear all about it. AND he expects her to make it right. While she's gettin' him dinner and keepin' the kids out his hair. Plus, if he's got any energy left, maybe he'll give her another baby to look after, when the football game's over. So I figure women have evolved to where they get a high out of solvin' these problems, takin' all this shit and makin' it work. Lesson six: Somebody's always going to be better at this stuff than you, because they're wired different.

Excuse me. Man, I shouldn't be piggin' down the peppers. Not good for my digestion. Put it over to the side! Not that side - ya missed it! Hard to concentrate when I'm right up in your face, talkin', burpin' and like that, eh? The shit's comin' at ya and some higher-up

Benny the Antichrist, Page 65

is lookin' over your fuckin' shoulder, backseat drivin', why aren't you doin' this an' that, eh? Lesson seven - expect lots more of this.

See that Cossack in the gun tower, dancin'? If you're not gettin' that faux balalaika music, he pulls out a Kalashnikov and starts blasting. Believe it.

Well, Holy Moly, ya did it.

Thought you were goin' to wuss out there, but you came through. Here, lemme get you a coke - you just sit down there, get your breathin' back to normal, eh? So, the job's yours, ya want it. Uh huh, you'll think about it.

Thought you might say that.

Don't take too long....

The End

FAE-DAR

Watching the troll reaching down for him and feeling himself alone, pinned by inhuman eyes and deadly trapping glamours, Todd knew the night had gone terribly wrong because of what his ex, Moira, would have called his usual cluelessness.

It all started earlier in the evening with a little happiness, his first in months. Somehow all the psychobabble they hawked in his severance package therapy group, "giving myself permission" and "connecting with my inner whatever", seemed to make sense tonight. He felt like a man boldly facing into the winds of change, not just a 40-something pushed out of his job at Policico by the younger boss who'd stolen his wife from him.

When the session ended he caught his reflection in the night-darkened conference room window. Fleetingly he saw himself as that Dark Elf Prince the National Enquirer had spotted recently, visage all angles and hollows where Todd was open-faced and a bit jowly. He shook his head, smiling ruefully. Moira was the one who was gaga about what the media called Supers. He looked back and saw a man who'd slimmed down by bicycling to work in the mornings, staring back at him coolly, gleaming eyes hooded in shadow. Not a legendary creature, but not to be trifled with. I like your chances, he thought.

Energized and slightly frustrated that Judy from Accounting wasn't in the session tonight, he decided to cycle all the way home from the Policico office instead of taking his bike on the commuter train, even though the later part of the rush hour was a peak mortality time. Todd Vauxall, Super-Actuary, taking life by the horns and braving traffic all the way to Lewis Corners on his Costco mountain bike.

He had a close call just before he got to the bike trail beside the freeway. As he was waiting, signalling a left turn, he was almost clipped by by one of those new BMW Troikas with lines meant to suggest a fairy war chariot. Suddenly angrier than he'd been in months, he yelled "Hey!" and flipped the driver the bird. He was answered by a hand making one of those hex signs you saw Warlock rappers using in videos. Freddy Kowalchuk could probably tell him what it meant.

Of course he didn't call himself that now. Now Todd's soon-to-be-ex-boss went by Eowaaian Gilhjalgalion, which was only an approximation of his true, High Elven name, revealed to him, he said, by the Sidhe soothsayer who told him he had the blood of Fae royalty in his veins. Most of the people in the office believed, or played along with his story, and the capes, ruffled shirts and jodhpurs Freddy affected instead of suits and ties. Management seemed to think the man could do no wrong.

Todd went along too, til he'd caught Moira and Freddy together. By then it was too late. He'd been expertly eased out of the way and no one he talked to seemed to wonder why a magical being with an unpronounceable name would be working in an insurance office.

Maybe there was something uncanny about the way his co-workers accepted what Freddie said, even when he told them most of the cleaning staff were goblins. Moira had certainly bought in all the way.

But if it hadn't been Freddy, it would have been some other guy with a line about the Magic Kingdom. When the media broke the news about the Sidhe, the stability Todd offered began to seem like a trap to her. She was fascinated by the Supers and couldn't understand why he wasn't. The last straw came when Todd said he'd worry about pixies, silkies, ogres, rusalkas, trolls and all the rest when they started buying insurance.

Everyone seemed crazy about Supers except he and a few other sticks in the mud. Might as well get used to it. But he couldn't help chuckling when he saw the Troika pulled over by a black-and-white underneath a billboard splashed with USA Today's latest ultraviolet spycam shot of a Centaur in the subway, reading USA Today.

Todd was so intent on watching Mr. Wannabe Super explain himself to the cop that he nearly hit a derelict lurching towards him on the bike path. At least he thought it was a derelict, though whatever the fellow snarled at him didn't sound like any language

Benny the Antichrist, Page 68

he'd heard before and he seemed too broad at the shoulders by half. You were never sure these days, ever since that news photographer took some remarkable telephoto shots with an ultraviolet camera, revealing quite ordinary-looking people to be strange creatures of legend. Sixty Minutes managed to interview some down-at-the-heels Pixies and Ogres and the story was out.

Experts couldn't agree on much, but they all said elves, spirits, gods and giants lived among humans, hidden by powerful cloaking spells. You could stand right next to one, touch and talk to him and never know. The spells would even fool most cameras, if the Super knew they were there. It was only in this age of multiple concealed spycams, ultraviolet and polarized lenses that the news media caught an occasional glimpse of a Super with his guard down.

But all the pundits said there weren't many and most kept to themselves. And that's what Todd never got Moira to understand. Why obsess about these creatures when you were never likely to meet one? It was like running your life around the chance that you'd be struck by lightning.

He arrived in Lewis Corners pleasantly dazed with endorphins and absurdly pleased that he'd beaten the 7:14 train by three minutes. He told himself he'd do this more often, then remembered tomorrow was his last day. Freddy and Moira had said they wanted to make the transition as smooth as possible, but over was over.

Todd decided he needed to break the rules, kick over the traces and mainly he needed a drink. He was about to head to the Stilton, the local bar, when he stopped abruptly. Suddenly the idea of drinking with software salesmen, personal assistants and insurance underwriters like himself seemed like settling back into his life's usual stultifying routine. What sealed it was the slim figure he saw disappearing round the corner, the final flip of long hair like a crooked finger drawing him in.

Pedaling round the turn, he glimpsed her just as she disappeared into a bar down the street. It was a place he'd never heard of, which was odd. There wasn't a lot to Lewis Corners, an uneasy blend of housing development, besieged farming community and half-hearted gentrification. Maybe the name, "Sam Hayne's", should have alerted him. Perhaps he should have twigged when a dragon tattoo gave him a wink from the bare shoulder of a prolifically pierced and inked young thing in full dominatrix regalia stumbling out the door as he walked in.

Benny the Antichrist, Page 69

But he really should have caught a clue when he walked in through the elaborately carved oaken doorway and everything went vague. Not misty, mind you, although there was plenty of smoke in the air. Todd wondered faintly how they got around the local anti-smoking ordinance. But that thought was like everything else in Sam Hayne's. He couldn't focus on it, couldn't keep the details in mind.

Moira always said he had lousy Fae-dar. But really, what was a Super bar doing in Lewis Corners, where the biggest excitement lately had been a Target store's Grand Opening in nearby Charlesmont?

So he walked in, sat down and ordered a beer. Perhaps the atmosphere cooled as all the various nixies, pixies, pookas, seelies, elves, goblins, incubi, adhene, norns and rusalkas noticed the human in their midst. Perhaps the bartender, a heavy-set fellow with a curly black beard and an odd capering gait, glowered and muttered something before he passed over the glass. Todd never noticed. He'd lost sight of the girl but that was all right: The night was young. He decided to update his Blackberry. He had an interview at 10:30 tomorrow. Maybe he'd call Judy and they'd go for lunch at that new Laotian place.

The beer was odd but tasty, definitely not Budweiser. He scanned his surroundings with a cheerful, preoccupied gaze, not really registering that the place was far bigger than it looked from the outside and that many among its shadows were not particularly human-looking. What a colorful crowd. Who'd have guessed you could find such a motley crew in Lewis Corners? Life was a rich pageant.

Then a ragged drunk lurched over to Todd's table, muttering incomprehensibly to himself in a gravel truck basso. He was nearly seven feet tall and thickly built, with a lumpy bald head and tiny black eyes under a heavy retrograde brow. His skin was gray, whether with pallor or dust Todd couldn't say. He reeked of grease, spices and something long dead. Ignoring Todd, he thudded down on the groaning chair across the table and swiveled it around to face the bar.

The drunk glared at a woman hunched over the bar. At least Todd thought it was a woman, maybe the one he'd seen outside. All he could really see was a cascade of wavy red hair reaching almost to the ground. "Well, fack me blind," his tablemate growled. "If it ain't me favorite screamer. Oy, Siobhan, open up that pretty mouth of yours for us. I'll give you something to stop it up."

Benny the Antichrist, Page 70

The woman gave no sign she'd heard, which seemed to provoke the huge man more. "Too good for the likes of me now? Maybe ye'd rather forget how ye'll slink and sidle around anything in pants when you're in heat. Would that be the way of it, Siobhan?"

This was only going to get uglier, Todd decided. He didn't know what to do. He cleared his throat, a nervous habit that always annoyed Moira.

This fellow didn't take it any better. Turning his massive body laboriously around, he glared stonily down at Todd. "Lookin' at someone, Morty?" he asked in an ominously quiet voice.

Perhaps the bartender had slipped a foolhardiness potion into his drink. Or three after-work sessions of assertiveness training had warped his judgment. Or maybe Todd had had a lifetime to get tired of doing the prudent thing. Whatever it was, what he said, in a voice much smaller than he would have liked, was: "Leave her alone."

Someone snickered. Out of the corner of his eye Todd saw the bartender grin sourly and make a complicated hand gesture. Suddenly things sprang into clarity and he saw he was alone among a crowd of creatures, some winged, or sporting animal parts, or green-skinned, tiny or huge. Biggest of all was the drunk, whom he finally saw was a troll, nearer ten feet tall than seven, a mass of malevolent, animated stone.

Off to one side Todd saw a naked, wild-haired man painted in blue runes hold up a fifty dollar bill and two fingers. A sparkling winged figure who looked like Tinkerbell's evil twin held up one finger and nodded. The first did an uncanny mimesis of a head being twisted off. The bad fairy grinned, shook her glittery little head and made a squashing motion. The troll gave a seismic snort and started to rise.

"Let him be, Carraig. Trust you to make bad enough worse." The woman at the bar had turned around on her stool. She was tall and delicately beautiful the way only redheads can be, with huge, piercingly green eyes matched by her green suede jumpsuit, but her croaking voice was like something scraped raw and boiled in acid.

"At last her bleedin' majesty deigns to speak. Sussin' out a new bedmate, Siobhan? Fancy Morty here?" A great, blunt-fingered mitt groped toward Todd, who'd slipped off his stool and was trying to gather up his fanny pack and bike helmet. When his grip closed on nothing, Carraig lurched into the path to the door.

"How about it, Morty? Up for a shag with a beanie?"

Benny the Antichrist, Page 71

"Black Annis's hairy tit, Carraig," rasped Siobhan. "I can smell the ribs on you from here. But that doesn't give you leave to play the fool."

"Fool, is it? We'll see what young Morty--"

"My name's not Morty."

Of all the things Todd could have said, that was probably the dumbest. His answer was a backhanded swipe that would have taken his head clean off, if he hadn't stumbled over a chair leg.

The troll roared, a sound Todd felt in his bones more than heard, and flung the heavy wooden table aside, where it crashed into the fireplace and scattered sparks among a table of drowsy-looking folks who were something between Irish peasants and seals. One moustachioed geezer spat out a large fishtail, cursed in an oddly musical language and flung a china pitcher that shattered on Carraig's ugly knob of a nose. The troll started, then turned heavily and glowered that way before the crowd's clamor reminded him of his main quarry.

Todd lay there stunned for a moment, when he felt a poke in his ribs. He looked over to see a green, pointed shoe, attached to a little fellow just as green and pointed. "Are ye just goin' to lay there like a dim mooncalf and let him tear you limb from limb?" the leprechaun wanted to know. "Where's the sport in that?"

Todd nodded and rolled to one side, barely in time to dodge a massive square boot thundering down where he'd been. With a grace he'd never suspected in himself he gained his feet in the same movement. He was about to race to the door when the same thrust-out green shoe tripped him. He stumbled and would have fallen flat, if he hadn't slammed up against Carraig's stony left shin.

The troll hooted and reached down, just missing when Todd managed to scuttle around back of his leg. Carraig slowly bent at the knees and waist, his great, gray paws getting nearer and nearer...

Todd blinked and shook his head, rasping his ear on Carraig's scabrous flesh under the thin wool of ragged trousers. Close up the reek of garlic, chilies and carrion was overpowering. All he could hear was the crowd, silkies, brownies, hags, nymphs, harpies and beings he couldn't name, roaring their bloodlust. He was going to die here because he'd been oblivious, just like Moira always said. He deserved to lose her to Freddy.

The troll was taking his time, just brushing the top of Todd's head with huge stony fingers. Todd saw they were surrounded by glowing, misty green bands undulating slowly between him and the gloating Supers. Trapping glamours, he thought. He'd read about them in Readers Digest. There was nowhere he could run. Carraig reached down and Todd figured the blue painted man was going to win his bet.

He saw Siobhan, hand over her mouth as if to stifle a scream. When he caught her eye she turned away, shame-faced. And suddenly the whole monumental unfairness of the moment, the evening, his whole life, enraged him. He hunched down, just out of Carraig's grasp, clinging grimly to the troll's calf with arms and legs. He even tried to bite, though it was like gnawing granite. He'd be damned if he'd make this easy.

Gradually the troll got more and more frustrated. He just couldn't bend far enough to reach his troublesome prey. Worse yet, some of the crowd's ferocity had turned to catcalls and laughter. When he felt the mortal's teeth on his leg he straightened and kicked like a man trying to shed a sticky clod of mud.

At the apex of Carraig's kick Todd unwrapped his legs and got his feet under him. Using every part of his back and legs, he got his shoulder under that stony ankle and pushed up.

The troll was even heavier than he looked. It felt like he was made out of solid iron ore. But he was thrown off by the unexpectedness of the resistance and he stumbled a bit. And when Carraig wavered Todd heaved up with all his strength, feeling something give in his back, driving up, up, heedless of the pain, the tears in his eyes and roaring in his ears.

Carraig flapped his huge arms like a boy teetering on a fence, then started slowly to topple. He slammed down with a force that cracked several floorboards, tipped over a few pitchers of ale and knocked a gigantic black spider off its web and onto its back in the middle of the pool table, where it lay cursing til a dryad flipped it over with a cue.

Slowly Todd straightened up. He'd pulled something lumbar and was definitely going to need some massage therapy. The room was deathly still. The trapping glamours still ringed him, weaving oozily.

Someone cheered shrilly. A bull-headed man let off a great bellow. The silkies clapped like seals en masse. The evil Tinkerbell blew him a kiss that, somehow, he felt. Kobolds and hobgoblins raised glasses and started singing something wild and triumphant. The trapping glamours faded and flew apart.

Benny the Antichrist, Page 73

Then the troll started to get up.

As quickly as it started the cheering faded. Carraig nodded to Todd and grinned when he was halfway to his feet. His teeth were like jagged pieces of obsidian. He reached out...

And there was the big bartender, grabbing the troll's huge thumb with both hands. He twisted and Carraig's eyes bulged. A tiny squeak came from the troll's thick throat. "You had your chance, Carraig," the bartender said in a silky baritone. "Now you need to go sleep it off."

"Ye've got no call to come between me and that mortal shite, Stavros." Carraig rasped. "Yer callin' down the troll doom on you and yours."

"I got curse coverage up the ying-yang, you dumb Mick, and I keep up with the payments," Stavros grunted, forcing the troll toward the door. "You need to shut up before your mouth buys you something your ass can't cover." He manhandled the troll through the rapidly parting crowd, then literally kicked him out the door with what Todd finally realized wasn't a boot but a cloven hoof. "Show up again tonight and I'm callin' your Mama," he yelled through the swinging doors.

Todd was trying to limp toward the exit when someone pressed a pint glass into his hand. Several hands, some hairy, some ethereal and one with far too many fingers whacked him on his aching back and pressed him down into a chair. In no time the tabletop was crowded with drinks sent over by many strange strangers. What the hell, he thought, I'll have one for the road. Some dimly-heard actuarial part of him was clamoring famous last words, but he brought a faintly green pint up to his lips anyway...

Only to have it gently pushed aside by a white, scarlet-nailed hand. "That one will be delicious," Siobhan said hoarsely, "but you should only drink it if you plan to put down roots here. Also branches and leaves."

Todd had never been the world's smoothest talker and Siobhan close up would take any hetero man's breath away. She had a pale, heart-shaped face dominated by huge, long-lashed green eyes and a full, red cupid's bow mouth, framed by masses of wavy, deep red hair. The kelly-green suede jumpsuit she wore managed to say almost everything about the hourglass figure beneath without vulgarity. Without waiting for Todd to reply she turned and barked at the

Benny the Antichrist, Page 74

barkeep. "Oh, and Stavros, thanks ever so much for jumping in right away."

The bartender called over his shoulder "Hey Siobhan, what can I say? Guy's a whatchamacallit, a champion. Standin' up for his lady fair. Takin' on the forces of, like, darkness. This crowd, they eat that Beowulf shit up."

"Cuchulain's brass balls, Stavros! Does he look Beowulf to you?"

"Honey, I was there and this guy makes a better Beowulf than the original."

"And how would that be?"

"Well, he's just cute as a button." He winked at Todd and blew him a kiss.

Just then a muscular, heavily bearded fellow, not quite five feet in every direction, shouldered his way through the front door and up to the bar. "Dude, I hope I'm not, you know, harshing anyone's trip here," he said nasally, "but there's a troll totally lurking across the street and it's kind of, like, creeping me out. Conflict gives me hives."

Siobhan caught Stavros's eye and nodded significantly toward a small platform in the back that looked like a bandstand. The barkeep lifted both hands and grimaced. "That'll be the third time this month," he carped. "My bill is gonna be through the roof. And for a mortal!"

"Stavros..."

"OK, OK, but I don't gotta like it." He sighed heavily, then turned to Todd. "Where do you live, Morty?"

"Eight thirty-five Leland Cre--" Todd caught himself. Moira had gotten the house. She and Freddy were selling it and moving into a luxury condo on Bayview street. "Apartment D, one thirty-three Carter Street. My name's Todd."

"At least it's close. OK, Todd, up on the stage. You too, Siobhan. He's your project."

"Stavros, you know I hate Sending."

"Someone's gotta hold his hand or he's not goin'. I'm not having anybody faint in there again and I gotta get a repair mage to come and suck him out with a hose. So get up there."

Siobhan made a face, then nodded at Todd. She stepped up on the stage.

Todd wasn't sure about any of this. "I've got my bike locked up outside. Couldn't someone just come out with me till I unlock it?"

Stavros sighed again. Todd wished he'd stop doing that. "Lookit, Todd," the bartender said, "you shamed a troll here, in front of a lot of people who are going to talk. Trolls are real touchy about stuff like that and where there's one, there's ten close by. And that particular individual, Carraig O'Meara, just happens to be the only son of the local Queen troll. If you think sonny-boy's a nasty piece of work when he's on a toot, wait til you meet Mom. That's on one of her good days, which, as of now, this is not. So no, nobody's goin' out there with you to get your bike. We're tryin' to save your dumb mortal ass and send you home through the back door, so to speak. You've even got your own beanie Girl Guide to keep you out of trouble. So get on the platform."

Todd stepped up. He was worried about what was going to happen next, but mainly preoccupied with not staring at or standing too close to Siobhan. Not that he would have minded getting very close indeed. She smelled wonderful, like ginger and some flower he couldn't identify. He wondered how anyone could smell like that after spending time in a smoky bar.

Meanwhile, the bar's ambience seemed to have drifted back to normal, whatever that meant here. Two baggy-jeaned hobgoblins were doing the rap dozens, dissing each other's copious bling while a small dragon provided the inhuman beatbox rhythm track. A gnarled, white-haired fellow in flowing blue robes and a pointed cap was hitting on a sleepy-looking faun. Three hags were piling up Scratch and Win tickets while kvetching about the inflationary prices of potion ingredients. No one seemed to be paying much attention to the doings on the stage. Todd wondered if things like this happened often.

Stavros busied himself trying to get a large embroidered tapestry of a griffin off the wall. It was high and hard to reach til he got help from a very tall, greenish-gray fellow who seemed to be covered in nothing but bark. When he had the cloth gathered in his arms he glanced over at the platform and grinned crookedly. "Get closer, you two. I pay for this by volume." Todd sidled nervously closer to Siobhan, who sighed and leaned his way. "No, no. I mean really close. C'mon Todd, put your arms around her. She won't bite unless you ask her to."

Todd did as ordered. She felt even better than she smelled. "Sorry," he whispered.

"It's all right," Siobhan croaked softly back.

Benny the Antichrist, Page 76

Just then Stavros flung the cloth over their heads, chanting something that sounded suspiciously like "Do you know the muffin man?" There was a flash of light that somehow Todd could feel right up his spine and the sensation of being turned at right angles to himself.

He found himself standing on the steps of his cruddy apartment block, body tingling, his arms still around Siobhan. He cleared his throat and disengaged. Was it just his imagination, or did she look a bit disappointed? The sky had gone dark and she was lovely in the moonlight. "Well, um, thanks for... If you don't mind my asking, what's a beanie?"

For some reason Siobhan found this funny. Her laugh was unexpectedly light and silvery.

"Ah, Todd, Todd. What with all the papparazzi and reporters doggin' our steps, I forget there are mortals who don't know much about us at all. You just go on about your life, don't you? Good man.

"Beanie is Fae slang for Bean Sidhe. I'm a Banshee." She watched his face closely as she said this.

"So, um, you're a Banshee. I'm sorry but I don't know too much-"

"They call me a screamer and it'd be well for you if you never heard me do that. Because when you hear the scream you know someone's going to die. Could be it's you."

"Not that it's any of my business, but how did you get into--"

"It's a long tale involving names well forgotten and curses better left unsaid. It's my doom. Listen, I should be--"

"What a terrible thing to have to do."

She stared at him and the desolation in her eyes struck him like a physical blow. Then she smiled and touched his cheek. "You've already made my lot a bit better Todd, muirni. And now I need to--"

"Listen, would you like a cup of coffee before you go? I've got--"

The rest was cut off by Siobhan's long pale hand over his mouth.

"Whisht! Have you no more sense than to dive into bad luck? You don't invite the Banshee into your..." She glanced up at the dirty gray brick apartment block and then back at him, appraisingly. "This isn't really your home, is it Todd? Not yet, at any rate. If you're lucky, not ever. You're a vagabond, just like me."

Somehow, being called a vagabond suited Todd just fine. He had a brief, absurd vision of himself wearing comfortably ragged clothes, striding through a flowering field with a beautiful red-haired girl by his side. He reached up and clasped Siobhan's hand, drawing it down

Benny the Antichrist, Page 77

from his lips. "So that means it's OK for you to come up for coffee, right?"

The loneliness on Siobhan's face was so naked he almost turned away. "Todd, peg 'o' my heart, I can't--"

"So that's where you are." A massive hand thudded onto his shoulder. He only had time to see the troll looming behind him in the dark when Siobhan screamed, shriller and more terrible than anything he could have imagined and his consciousness shattered like glass.

* * *

To say the next several hours were a blur would not be strictly accurate. Much of it he didn't remember well, how he'd managed to climb the stairs to his apartment, for example. But he had a very clear recollection of how it felt to lean on Siobhan while she rummaged through his pockets for the key, the feel of her lips on his, her nails faintly scratching as she tore his clothes off, the exquisite weight of her breast, the churning heat of her centre and smoothness of her heels on his shoulders, the way they lay facing each other on their sides, fondling each other, one arm each stretched out toward the headboard like the smart kids in the class, ask me, ask me, I know the answer...

Those memories made it easier not to think about things like the terrible words he could almost understand in the Banshee's wail, and that he might have heard his own death sentence.

That's what he tried to do when he woke up alone, magnificently sore at noon, look at the positive side of things, the way they always talked about in therapy. It came to him with no particular urgency that he'd missed his job interview. Well, fuck 'em if they couldn't take a joke. He wondered if that was being positive.

He probably should have phoned with an apology and an excuse, but couldn't be bothered. He suddenly realized that tired and chafed as he was, one thing that didn't hurt was his back. His throat felt a bit swollen, but he'd been wavering on the edge of a cold for the last few days. Bad luck, my ass, he thought.

He found a note on the kitchen table, scrawled in her oddly childish hand. "Dearest Todd," it said, "My doom calls and I must go. Don't look for me and pray we never meet again." There were three strange runes at the bottom that must have been her signature.

He frowned, then brightened. Of course she was pessimistic. Ages of wailing death prophesies would do that to anyone. But this was 21st-century Lewis Corners, not prehistoric Ireland. Supers were just another constituency. There had to be a treatment for whatever ailed her. He tucked the note in his pocket.

He checked his phone and saw he was supposed to show up at the house later to gather up the last of his possessions. He still had a key and decided he'd go now. Moira had been making noises about keeping some things he wanted, in particular a recliner she said Todd didn't have room for. He'd be damned if that chair was going to comfort Freddy's bony, quasi-Elven ass.

He'd just let himself in when he saw they'd already gotten the chair in a box, leather upholstery peeking out the top. Without pausing, he towed the box to the front door and was about to haul it out when Moira and Freddy hurried in from the back. They were flushed and Freddy's velvet shirttail was out. They'd knocked off a quickie in the bedroom, he realized.

Moira said "Todd, I thought we agreed that chair was too big for your place."

"No Moira, as usual you just made your mind up and assumed I'd fall into line. I'm taking the chair."

Freddy took a step closer and put his hand on the box, beaming his usual supercilious smile down at Todd. "Have a care, mortal. Anger not--"

In all his life, Todd could never have imagined making the sound that came out of his own mouth next. It was more than a scream, it was an utter breaking with the world as it was and a sealed doom of the one to come. It had words he didn't know but whose ghastly portent hung like an icy blade. It was wrenching. It felt terrifyingly great.

Freddy and Moira were sprawled like cast-off puppets on the floor. Moira was going to have a nasty bruise on her jaw and Freddy had broken his nose.

Tough luck. None of this seemed quite real to him. When he was sure they were both breathing, he hauled the chair out to his car. Moving like a sleepwalker, he made several trips for things, then spent some time searching for a favorite sweater and a vase his mother had given him. He considered taking their keys and combing the condo for it, but discarded the notion.

They were starting to come to. Moira was clutching herself as if she were freezing and Freddy was mewling like a frightened child when Todd left.

Benny the Antichrist, Page 79

He drove halfway back to his apartment in a daze, then pulled in behind a service station, got out and threw up his breakfast.

What was happening to him? At least his throat didn't feel so sore any more, though why that should be he couldn't imagine. The sounds he had made weren't just scary, they didn't seem human. He needed some information quickly, but the only thing he could come up with was going back to Sam Hayne's, though that filled him with dread.

He cruised the area several times, searching for red-haired women or looming gray figures. Not only did he not spot Siobhan or the troll, he couldn't see any evidence of anything supernatural. In the four o'clock sunshine Sam Hayne's was just another dusty, unpromising bar in a neighborhood going to seed.

His bike was still locked to a signpost halfway down the block. Telling himself he'd just grab it and take a fast peek in, he stopped and put a dime in the parking meter. He quickly unlocked the bike and manhandled it into the back seat. He locked up, then strode quickly on the edge of the sidewalk toward the bar, eyes alert for shadows between cars and down alleys.

At the door to Sam Hayne's he turned to face the street, squinting at every imaginable hiding place.

His bladder almost let loose when he felt the great hard hand onto his shoulder. He ducked away, intending to run, then turned, realizing his car was the other way. Carraig had somehow materialized out of the side of the building. He was smiling.

Abruptly furious beyond measure, Todd charged him, tackling his left leg again. "Why can't you let me alone?" he shouted. "What did I ever do to you?"

It didn't go the way he'd hoped. The troll's balance was better or he was ready for this tactic.

At least Todd wasn't being pulverized just yet. Slowly he realized that Carraig was saying something in quiet, reasonable tones. "Todd, I wish ye'd quit makin' a spectacle of yerself. Ye embarrassed me last night, which I bloody well deserved, but now yer mortifyin' the both of us, which is a shame, because yer a better fellow than that."

Todd looked up. "I am?"

"Sure ye are." Carraig looked downright benevolent. In fact Todd noticed that he smelled good today, well-washed and discreetly cologned. He was dressed in a gigantic, but well-tailored blue suit with a matching floral tie and hankie. Even his skin was healthier shade of gray. "I just wanted to make things right with you, after all the unpleasantness. At least let me stand you a jar and explain meself. My sponsor'll be the death of me if I don't at least try."

"You're sure? No tricks?"

Carraig held up two gigantic fingers. "Troll's honor."

Not entirely sure this was a guarantee he could trust, Todd nevertheless followed Carraig into the bar. Apparently everything had been smoothed over. Stavros nodded at Carraig, who held up two fingers again and said "Yer best". ` Todd was just about to slide into the booth opposite Carraig when he stopped. "Hey wait a minute. You've got a sponsor? Are you sure a bar is the place you should be, Carraig? Because isn't this how you got in trouble in the first place?"

Carraig's face underwent a slow evolution from incomprehension, to dawning realization and sudden mirth. He loosed a booming gust of laughter and pounded the table alarmingly. "Todd, Todd," he said when he finally got his breath back, "I'm not in AA. I'm a troll. I'm an Irish troll. I could drink this bar dry, River Dance my Hibernian butt over to the next bar and do it again, over and over, with nary a stumble. But yes, I do have a sponsor. I guess you'd say I'm in BRA." He roared again with laughter.

"BRA?"

"Barbecued ribs knock me right off me chump. Yer tomato and chili pepper, ye'll recall from history class, are New World vegetables, not to be found in the Ould Sod til very recently. Turns out some trolls, being strictly Eurasian in origin, have a bit of a problem with them metabolically, particularly in combination. Mix in pork, which, not to put too fine a point on it, is the closest thing to man-meat, and you've got yourself a spot of bother.

"Which doesn't excuse my behavior last night, for which I'm profoundly sorry. I hope, and me ma hopes, that you'll accept my apologies." He held out an enormous gray paw.

The troll's grip was almost dainty, given the flinty hardness of his skin. Shaking his hand was like moving a delicately balanced boulder. "May I ask you something?" Todd said. "If you know barbecue ribs are bad for you, why do you eat them?"

"Todd, if ye knew how bland and awful me ma's cookin' is, ye wouldn't ask. Plus bein' a vegetarian cuts down on me culinary choices somethin' awful. There be times when I think if I see another turnip I'll do meself a mischief.

Benny the Antichrist, Page 81

"I was comin' home late from the job site--I'm a construction engineer, by trade--and I passed a rib joint. I'd been pullin' a double shift and sure I was hungry. It smelled so good and I thought to meself, just one can't hurt. Ten minutes later I was on a toot like ye saw. Lucky ye kept yer wits about ye and they got ye out of there before me sponsor arrived. Me ma was in a killin' mood and not particular about who."

"Your sponsor came to the bar with your mother?"

"Me sponsor is me mother. Also Queen Troll, hereabouts. She's a caution when she's crossed, is ma. Matriarchy," he added darkly, "It's a bitch."

" So how did you find us, when they magicked us back to my place?"

"Trolls have really good noses and I'd got a snootful of you. You only live a few blocks off, so I just followed the breeze. Plus I'd know Siobhan's scent from halfway round the world."

"How did she drive you off?"

"Screamed me death doom, didn't she? She's done it before, when I was gettin' obnoxious. I know all about it, the place, the time, the little prick who's going to strut round like a big hero after he's done me in."

"You seem pretty calm about it."

"Well, it's not for a few centuries yet. But it's still upsetting to hear it again, in detail, from someone whose specialty is bad news. Like a blade twisted round yer guts, it is. I ran off home to sleep it off."

"Listen, about that, I need to know--"

"Don't take this wrong, Todd, I'd love to share a few jars and while away the afternoon. But I'll need to be going shortly. My temple's hostin' a delegation from the Dalai Lama tonight."

"You're a Buddhist?"

"Oh, aye. Converted centuries ago, didn't I? Eatin' villagers and hangin' about under bridges, well it's fine when yer young an' that, but it wears thin.

"Most Fae still follow the old ways, but there's a fair number of converts. That lass," he jerked a huge thumb at a willowy, raven-tressed woman talking with a huge black cat, "she's a Methodist. Polyphemus'll talk yer ear off about Scientology. Got Tom Cruise's autograph and all. 'Course, old Polly's not the swiftest--'Noman did this to me,'--I ask you. Though truth be told, he's more typical than

Benny the Antichrist, Page 82

I'd care to admit." He nodded his head toward a couple of brawny, ram-headed warrior types talking loudly and accentuating conversational points with headbutts. "Not exactly a brain trust in here."

"Um, about the screaming--I need to ask you something."

"Oh sorry, me mouth's run off with me again. What do you need to know, young Todd?"

"Well, I need to find Siobhan--"

"Lovestruck, are ye? Todd, if I never speak another word of sense, believe me in this. Take yer night with the Banshee and pack it away in yer memories. Because there can be no repeat performance. If ye ever, and pray ye don't, meet her again, it'll be in professional capacity and that'll be the sad and painful end of you."

"There's got to be a way."

"Trust me, boyo, there's not any good one."

"But she's got to cure me." And he described what had happened with Moira and Freddy, the cuckolding, the loss of his job at Policico and the scream.

Carraig's brow furrowed as he listened and he was silent for a while at the end. Finally he asked "Is there any prophesy in your family, Todd?"

"What kind of question is that? My family's from Flatbush, for God's Sake."

"It's just that I've heard of beanies occasionally passin' it on, in the way of an STD, but usually the victim's got some kind of family predisposition."

"Well, my Aunt Tildy was a bit cuckoo..."

"Could be, could be. Tell me, how did you feel just before you started cursin' them?"

"Strange. My throat was really tight. It hurt."

"That'd be the doom-sayin' swelling up in you. Did you feel better, once you finished?

"Yes, God help me, I did."

"How do you feel now?"

"My throat's a little bit swollen, but--"

Carraig dug in his pocket and fished out a little vial. With amazing deftness, he unscrewed the lid and took out two little white pills. "Here. Wash them down now."

Todd eyed them suspiciously. "What are they?"

"Aspirin. To control the swelling."

Benny the Antichrist, Page 83

"That'll work?"

"For the time being. Do you happen to remember what it was you were sayin', during the curse?"

The strange thing was that he did, even though he didn't know the language he was speaking. He closed his eyes and repeated the words, quietly, he thought.

When he opened them again the bar had gone silent and a number of patrons were pointedly not staring at him. A couple of pixies hurriedly settled their bill and everyone within earshot looked sombre.

All except Carraig, who was rocking with suppressed laughter. "Ah Todd, if ye ever decide to take up the dark arts, let me know and I'll see ye get a good coach. Ye've a real talent for malediction, boyo. I've never heard the Old Tongue put to use describing embezzlement and SEC investigations, but ye've done a grand job of it."

Todd felt a huge weight lift off his chest. "You mean it's not about some horrible death?"

"Well it won't be any picnic for Moira and whats-his-face, but no, you've just got a slight case of prophesy. So far. You could work on it, either way. Have another aspirin. I can hear your voice tightening up. You might go back and have done for the lovebirds, but I'd leave it, if I were you. They'll not trifle with you again."

"I never wanted to hurt anyone--"

"Todd, me lad, we both know that's not true. But you're a rare thing around here, a talented mortal with a good business head and some modulation."

"Modulation?"

"Most cursing is too all or nothing to be really useful. Eternal fire, plagues of adders, blah blah blah. Or just plain outdated. What we've got here is a bunch of folks who've never really modernized. You know that little green shite who pushed you into me? That's the lad who done Jack with the magic beans. He'll tell you so himself, over and over again. Hasn't learned a new trick in centuries. If ye ever went into business ye'd clean his clock. Speakin' of which..." He groped in his pocket and pulled out a cell phone and a stylus, which he used to dial quite quickly, considering the size of his huge blunt fingers.

"Chaim? Carraig. Grand, just grand. Listen, I want to sell Policico short. What are they at now? Yeah, I'll wait... Eight dollars? Let's bite them for twenty thousand shares." He softly mumbled part of Todd's curse to himself, nodding. "Keep going till they hit two dollars, then call me. Aye, it's a lock. Let's just say some new talent's said some disparagin' things about them. No, sure, the more the merrier. Yeah, thanks. Love to the missus. Bye." He winked at Todd. "Hell of a broker and a nice lad, for a dybbuk. You're in for twenty percent commission on anything I make, by the bye."

Todd gaped.

"Strictly risk free, boyo. Don't look so gobstruck. A cursing gift like yours is as close to a sure thing as there is in this world. And I'm just makin' sure I'm on the right side of the new gun in town. Oh and I think you've just found your first customer."

Stavros was standing by their table, looking a bit embarrassed, but determined. Nodding at Carraig, he cleared his throat. "Listen Todd, you wanna make some coin? I got a health inspector who's been givin' me nothing but grief..."

Comment

Here's something on the lighter side, about the kind of bar you've never been able to get into, and what happens when you do.

There's a piece of Black American English I like: "signifying". Someone who signifies a lot is faking it till they make it, or in a holding pattern till "it" is passe and some other "it" is in the ascendant. Most of us do it, at some point in our lives.

Todd, protagonist of Fae-Dar, is someone who can't or won't signify, even if it costs him dearly. By training and temperament he knows what he knows, and what he doesn't know. More importantly, he won't stop asking reasonable questions about the Cool New Thing, questions that no one else wants to hear.

His story is what happens when a modest, honest person confronts the Uncanny without any real intention of so doing. To his surprise, he finds this new realm has more to do with him, and he with it, than anyone could have guessed.

The End

BY THE COURTHOUSE

Please, tell me you can see me. It's so cold here at night, the gray marble slabs between my bones. My blood running slow between their tight straight cracks.

Mister, give me a quarter so I can go to Ithaca Club and drink my black coffee sweet, sweet. The people here don't stop. Cars minnowing, gulls shrieking. How long since I hauled in a heavy net? My wife back home, weaving.

When I left the island I bought a beret and a leather jacket, so they will know I am a man of affairs. I have a deal in development, any day now.

In the Men's Shelter, they turn to beasts in the night. It's safe here, but so cold, so hard to leave. The sun is small, here. Yesterday, it rained and I could not see myself, too thin even to go milky, like ouzo. The stone draws me. Only a pair of gnarled hands, reaching from the gray wall.

Give me a quarter and tell them you saw me, but not like this.

The End

IN THE SHAFT

I open my eyes and I'm in the long, black, hole I've dreamed of every night in my room far away. Outside, nattering afternoon crowds jostle, skate and drive over sun-softened asphalt. But here in the catacomb dimness, the world's sounds only worm their way in, lost among the low moan of electric motors.

I wonder, while I lie on top of the elevator rushing down through the dark, fossil air of the Carmichael building's elevator shaft, if the two suits in the car I'm riding can hear Stair's boombox blaring out Death Rock from beside the hoist motors in the roof, thin, poisonous skronk seeping into Prozac elevator music. The elevators have metal grid false ceilings over their fluorescent lights, fans and wiring, so we keep the maintenance hatch on top open a little and check out the citizens.

Jeffers, Lee and Culhane has the whole 33rd floor, where these two got on, and I try to catch whatever real lawyers talk about when they've got no one else to bullshit. After all, I could be articling there in a few years.

They just stand staring down at their wingtips. Then, just as they're about to get off, one gives the other a little squeeze on the butt.

I turn away and watch Stair race through the huge, dim vault of the elevator shaft, lit only by what seeps through the cracks between the sliding doors. He seems to glow in the dark, lit by an invisible green spotlight. He wears a leather jacket with our high school's basketball team decals. The way he moves would set my stomach to flip-flops, even if I weren't feeling leftover queasiness from the plane trip in. Deking, juking, head-faking, dribbling an imaginary ball between his long legs, Stair skips lightly, down, up and way down,

Benny the Antichrist, Page 88

across the tops of three cars as they pass each other around the 23rd floor, surfing effortlessly.

Kim took me to the beach once and we watched the surfers. I saw one guy disappear into a monstrous breaker, right into the tube, only to pop out like a magician's coin, shiny and grinning in the sun. I can't swim and I'd never get on a surfboard. But when you time your moves in the shaft just right, dipsy-doodle down the swaying line of cars, it's like being in that roaring blue tunnel. You forget about about the cruising sharks, the cold drowning deeps, the rocks beneath.

Then Stair comes up, a phosphorescent deep-sea carnivore rising to feed, arm hooked around a cable pulling a counterweight smoothly up the wall-mounted trestle as its car goes down to the main floor. He's got one sneaker braced on the iron counterweight, the other dangling out over empty space. At the last moment, he jumps six feet down and three across, onto my car. As always, he hits perfectly, avoiding the two-inch metal lip sticking up around the car's edge, landing quiet and flexed. You'd never guess he weighs 210.

I shiver. Maybe I shouldn't have come today. My folks wondered why I was in such a rush to go downtown on my first day home. But I just had to get down here.

"Wool-gathering again, dude? Swear-to-God, Pudge, you could be doin' it with some fine Stanford babe and you'd be worrying about your grade point average, or some dumb thing."

I smile and hunch my shoulders. Was it always this cold and damp? Ever since I got off the plane, I can't seem to get warm. And there's something in the air, a sweetish reek, every now and then. "Shows what you know. We Californians can multitask."

"Is that what they call fretting?"

"Ah, Stair, my boy, if only you knew... Compared to here, Stanford is Chick Central."

"Yeah, well, only if you've got the nerve to talk to one. Seriously, how you doin' out there? You a long way from home, boy."

I sigh. "You got that right. Stanford's huge, Stair. I got intro classes as big as our whole school."

"You gonna get into Law, like you wanted?"

"Well, my grades are good enough, I think. If you think I'm a keener, you should see some of the kids there. They don't do anything but study. They'd hook themselves up to an IV, so they wouldn't have to stop to eat."

Benny the Antichrist, Page 89

Stair glances at my gut. How does the guy do it? Eats like a horse, sits on his butt all day driving forklift at the Plant, goes through a six or so every day between quitting time and bed. And look at him--lean and quick as a rattlesnake. His long, pale face almost gaunt over jutting bones, glowing, like he's lit from within. Standing hipshot, thumbs hooked on his wide belt, fingers trailing down to the heavy crotch of his tight jeans. Hasn't changed a bit since last time I saw him here.

"How's Chrissy and the kid?"

Stair gets a distant look. "Bobby's good. Regular little hellraiser. And Chrissy--well, you know. Same old same old. How 'bout you? Gettin' any?"

"Well, there is someone."

"Hey, awright! The Pudge is comin' along! And not just any old girl, but 'someone'. What's her name?"

"Kim."

"Kim, huh? Maybe I'll come get some sunshine and scope out what my buddy's into." He winks. "Show her what she's missing."

I dig in my pocket for a tissue to clean my glasses. They say California's polluted, but it doesn't come close to here for dust. And the chill--how can Stair stand it, just that tight, thin tee under his open jacket? "That'd be great, Stair."

"Well, pretty soon I ain't gonna have nothin' but time. Layoffs comin' down."

"Aw shit, man. What are you going to do?"

"Don't you worry about old Stair. I got something coming up. Gonna take care of business.

"But you know, Pudge, you did the right thing, gettin' out. This whole town is dyin', man. Plant's shutting down, all the farms going bankrupt. Even this place--Fatcat HQ--half empty. It's all goin' down and takin' us with it."

"Hell, Stair. Why don't you move? Guy like you can land a job somewhere else."

"What? And leave all this?" Sweeping his hand out to encompass the dark catacomb, elevators rising and falling in the shadows.

"Believe it or not, there are other office buildings in other cities. Some even taller, with more elevators."

He yanks me up close, up on my toes. "Don't you talk down to me, you little dickweed."

Can't breathe--cold and that putrid reek, worse than ever. "C'mon, Stair... "

Then, just as abruptly, Stair relaxes. A cockeyed grin. "Aw, man, you're just bullshittin' to make me feel good."

"No really, you could get out of here. Find yourself a place with a future."

Momentarily, he looks as tired and sorrowful as I've ever seen him. "Pudge, you know all my future's in the past."

"Jeez, Stair, don't talk that way. You and me, we put our heads together, we can figure out how to get you out of this burg. You wait and see. We'll be together. Just like old times."

Then it's back: the secret, dark glow in his eyes. "I'll consider it, buddy. But until I get this business cleared up, it's the Carmichael for me."

We sit, legs dangling off the back of the car, watching the elevators on the other side of the shaft rise and fall. The Carmichael Building is the newest, tallest office tower in town, 35 stories up. It's got eight elevators, two rows of four, back to back in a central shaft. Even though it's only four years old, there's mouse shit on top of some of the cars, which pleases me somehow.

And that stink I smell every so often. Like when we shot a badger and the dog dug it up two days later. Did the place always smell like this? Poor venting, I decide.

Stair lights up and passes me a jay. Sinsemilla cut with angel dust, like old times. Long afternoons, Stair's old man sawing logs on the couch, home from one of his caretaking jobs, which is how Stair got the elevator keys. We'd be sitting out on his front porch steps, the overgrown lilac hedge half-hiding us from the street, sneak-passing a joint or a mickey, talking about the big things we'd do when we got out of this town. Stair was going to get a basketball scholarship to UCLA as their star small forward. I was going to be a famous writer in California. Sometimes they'd talk about the girls in town, Greta Markowitz with the 40-Ds, skanky Suzy Muller who'd do it for cigarette money. Or, really, Stair would talk. I just made wisecracks and tried not to let my ignorance show.

Then we'd go elevator surfing at the Carmichael, Stair's favorite. He explained it once. "See, in the classroom, I'm not that hot. I have to work like a dog to get B's, and it bores me stiff. And B-ball is great, but coach is always on my butt. Says I'm not a team player. Says I got too much playground attitude. Even on the playground, there's guys

Benny the Antichrist, Page 91

who're stronger than me, guys who shoot better. But come here and I'm the Man. All these citizens, watchin' the floors go by, late for their appointments, worryin' about their jobs. And me swingin' storey to storey, Tarzan of the Shaft. I'm the King."

Sometimes Jerry Gooch or Paul Blaschuk came, but usually we were alone. Something about Stair scared most people off. We always brought along the boombox with some metal or old school rap. The best time to get there was just before the offices let out, so you could catch an empty car. Then up through the trapdoor and wait till they all started moving, taking workers and execs down to the lobby, evening shifters up to work. Stair'd race over passing cars, jumping and whirling. He even talked about getting a couple of basketball hoops and mounting them at the top of the shaft in opposite corners. It would be an all-elevator league, one that played at rush hour with the cars hurtling up and down. When I laughed, Stair told me it was the only chance I'd ever have to dunk, which was the God's own truth.

You could prop up the maintenance hatches open a little and listen in to the citizens. The high-rise was full of salesmen and they always talked sports, sex and business. They'd be bitching about the tightwads in Accounting and I'd say, just loud enough to be heard: "Hung like a hamster."

Or bragging about a secretary they were porking, and Stair'd whisper"in your dreams". There'd be a tiny pause. Then they'd decide they couldn't have really heard that and off they'd go again.

I used to have a snack and eavesdrop on a group of secretaries in the building cafeteria. Every so often, they'd get going on how the building was haunted. Lorilene, a mousy Cracker who worked on the eighth floor, told stories about weird sounds and things that went on when you weren't looking. Things out of place, things missing.

Stair loved it. He brought a cassette of old organ pieces, real spooky horror movie stuff and played the Toccata and Fugue till the boombox ate the tape. Stair'd turn it down till they were passing eight, then crank it up max, aimed at the wall in front of where Lorilene was a dentist's receptionist. Once, when he knew she was in the car, he stood on top and howled her name like some Georgia banshee. I laughed, but was sure someone would finally twig and call Security.

Out at Stanford, somebody sent me a clipping from the local paper, dated a few months after I left. In a silly-season piece about

Benny the Antichrist, Page 92

the Carmichael Building, the reporter sneered for five paragraphs at the "haunting". It was dressed up in I'm-a-worldly-journalism-grad cynicism, but underneath there was real anxiety, a feeling that somehow this was connected to how the city was being gutted and left behind. I must have read it a thousand times.

Of course, anything's funny when you've done enough sinsy. That last time, Stair started joking about getting Chrissy McBain knocked up and having to work at the Plant, though I thought there wasn't much to laugh about.

Stair didn't even like Chrissy much. She had a whiny voice and a mill town girl's squinty, suspicious face, like someone had played a joke on her that she'd never understood or forgiven. I couldn't imagine having sex with her, let alone living with her.

Sometimes I find myself reminiscing, when I should be writing a paper or studying. If I could have frozen time, just put the brake on my life, I'd be wrestling on Stair's dryrotted old front steps forever, high on sinsy, laughing like a fool. Those steps gave him his name. Partly, anyway. Stair hated his small, stuffy room. And his old man and he couldn't share breathing space without fighting, so the living room was out. So he always held court on the front steps. Plus, his given name was William Harold Astaire, which settled it. He never liked Billy. And he'd kill you if you call him Fred. Any guy who'll croon and tapdance wearing evening dress was a fag, according to Stair.

I kind of like those old musicals. I even told Stair so once. We didn't talk about it.

Things changed once Stair got Chrissy pregnant. He quit school and started working at the Plant. They got married and moved into an apartment in Barrington. I went there once, for the housewarming. It was a shabby, sad little place.

After that, I got busy studying and sent applications to every good school I could think of, so long as it wasn't within 500 miles. The acceptance from Stanford had just come through when I ran into Stair downtown that last time.

Stair nudges me and I shiver. What a time to catch a cold, on summer vacation. "Hear that?" he says.

"I don't hear nothing."

"Pree-cisely my point. We just lost our soundtrack. Can't have a bash without the thrash." Stair has what my English prof would call a strong sense of ritual.

Benny the Antichrist, Page 93

So do I, I guess. "I'll go flip the tape." I climb to my feet.

Bad move. That grass must've hit me harder than I thought. And I never could handle angel dust. My head aches and spins, like someone's clamped it in a paint can shaker. I have a sudden vision of the unfinished sub-basement, way down below, the damp concrete floor, the rebars sticking out of the wall, twisted, jagged with dark red rust. I take an unsteady step backward.

"Oh man," says Stair, grabbing my shoulder. "You'd better sit down."

For some reason I feel colder than ever, especially where he's touched me. I've got to be coming down with something. "Yeah. Shit, I think you're right." I sit.

"You gonna be OK? You look a little spooked."

"Sure. Just shouldn't smoke on an empty stomach, I guess. That'll teach me."

"I got just the thing for that. Just give me a sec, and--" He pauses to let an elevator draw within jumping distance, then leaps effortlessly, catty-cornered, over to the car where he left his duffle bag. As the car rises past, he digs inside, then tosses out a bag of Cheetohs and a can of Coke from two stories up. I manage to catch them both before they hit the roof.

Then my car goes down to the main floor and his continues up. So I've got the Coke halfway finished and a mouthful of corn chips when we pass again. "Got a surprise for you, Pudge my man." He holds up the duffle bag. Something long and thin is sticking out. "But it needs the right theme music." He's holding up a cassette. I can't read the label from here. Then he turns and starts working his way toward the steel ladder mounted in the corner of the shaft, where he left the boombox.

My car stops on the main floor and I jump over to next car, which is just starting to rise, trying to shake off my jitters. There's a knack to doing it so you don't hit the lip or get tangled in the power lines. I peer through the slightly open maintenance hatch. There's a couple on this one. She looks like she dips herself in corporate shellac every morning and gets buffed on the way to work. Dark blue Power Outfit. Consultant, I figure, or upper exec. He looks awkward in his suit, like he can't figure out what to do with his hands. Big. Bit of dandruff around his sunburned bald spot. I decide he's a construction foreman.

They're standing together, not talking. Got to be going to the marriage councillor on 22. Or maybe up to 33, to fight over child custody. You can almost see the lines of force knotting and crackling between them, like wizards in a comic having some mystical slugfest. I can see their faces in the elevator's mirrored walls. She's got that blank Conglomerate Calm, like she was born with teams of top attorneys to back her up every time she steals someone else's credit or fudges an expense account. He's already getting red and they haven't even started up on him yet. He's going to get his bones picked.

Then she smiles at him. A real smile, not one of those calibrated things they flip you to keep you moving down the line. And Mr. Construction smiles back. Puts his arms around her. And I want to say to him: Listen, man, tell her about these places. She thinks she knows because she works in an office, doing meetings, writing memos. But she doesn't. You know. You've put them up. Tell her that every one of them has a big, dark, empty space in the middle, all the way up, behind all the offices with the expensive carpeting and veneer and investment art on the wall. And if a bomb were to hit this place tomorrow, that's what would be left: the elevator shaft, full of nothing but shadow, echoing in the wind.

They get off at 17 and I try to remember what's on that floor. Maybe a cancer clinic.

I scramble onto a counterweight as it slides up its track on the wall. I grab the cable tight, remembering. Of course that's why I jump on, too. Both hands clenching the cable, standing on the stacked iron, ass to the void, shooting up to 35. Somebody must be going to the basement. I never go to the basement.

Stair is sitting between a couple of hoist motors, doing something to one of his sneakers. He's just finished changing tapes when I crane my neck around and yell "Yo!" This is the first time I've ever had the balls to ride a counterweight. He smiles, makes a pistol with his hand and shoots me, winking. It's his highest compliment.

Then he spins, grabs one of the motor mounts and casually lowers himself, like he's starting in on a set of chin-ups. He catches hold of the counterweight cable, sets his foot against it and rides it down, a fireman on a pole. All of this lickety-split. The guy has brass balls. And I'm sweating till my counterweight starts sliding down and I can get my ass onto the relative safety of an elevator roof.

But that's how Stair's always been. At school they thought we were an odd couple, Stair all whipcord muscle and tattoos, me the

Benny the Antichrist, Page 95

round-faced bookworm. Some thought we're fags. But it wasn't that--nothing like that. We were just poor kids in a school where people got brand new cars for their birthdays. Stair's smarter than anyone gives him credit for. And I've got a few tricks.

Nodding, smiling, I stumble. Catch my balance, disoriented, on the edge of a dark drop. Look down and see Stair almost at the basement, tiny, glowing, a live coal falling in an endless pit. My nostrils full of musty-sweet reek. A dead rat in the air vent or something? An icy nausea grips me. Then my car goes down and his rises.

Going down to the main floor, it hits me that something funny's going on. It's the music. Stair's playing something weird, at least for him. Instead of the usual metal or rap, he's got on old big band stuff with one of those smooth singers he always used to hate. It sounds strange with the cheap boombox speakers distorting, cranked up to max, echoing down the shaft and off the randomly moving elevators, like some Forties ballroom in Hell.

When we pass Stair is on the far elevator, slantwise to me, digging in his duffle bag, doing something to his shoes. "What're you going to do, when you're a lawyer?" he calls out over his shoulder, as he glides up past me.

"Oh, I guess I'll go into public advocacy." I try to toss this off, like it doesn't matter. Most of my classmates roll their eyes when I talk this way. "So many fatcats screwing the public. Somebody's gotta put a crimp in their plans."

"Yeah, well, that all sounds well and good. You sure you're not going to wind up chasing ambulances, suing someone's ass off because your client was too dumb to look before he leaped?"

I stare down and I can see it, the body stabbed through with rebars, ripped open with its own hurtling weight, twisted and broken in the angle between the rough wall and the cold, gray floor. The dark bloodtide rolling. My stomach does a tight, sick lurch. "I guess it's all a matter of interpretation," is all I can manage.

"Interpretation." He sniffs. "Yeah, I know all about that."

He gets too far away to talk and I wonder if I shouldn't call it a day. Just go home. I'm feeling sick and this isn't working out like I hoped.

Then my car goes up, all the way up to the 35th floor. You'd think it'd be warmer up here. And that dead smell--How do the office workers stand it? Stair is up there, long legs crossed, leaning on what

Benny the Antichrist, Page 96

looks like a walking stick. He's got something black, flat and shiny in his hand. Then he flicks his wrist and it springs out, snapping into place. It's one of those collapsible top hats. Opera hats, I think you call them. He puts it on, tilting it down towards so it leaves his face in shadow. All I can see are the glint of eyes. He says "What do you think?"

"I'm speechless."

He grins. "Wait till you see this." He whirls and stamps, heel and toe, with a clicking sound. Then somehow there's more light, coming from him. He's dressed in tails and low cut dancing shoes. Shirt and tie so white it hurts to look, diamond studs glittering. And in his hand an ebony walking stick, silver-headed. He whirls it, a black blur. Then he spins, bucks and wings, slides and cakewalks, feet beating out triplets and paradiddles, all in counterpoint to the jaunty, jazzy rhythms of the tuxedo-clad dance band, dim in the shadows behind him.

Stair slides by the bandstand and the trombonist stands for a solo. It's Kim, short hair greased back, pushing the long slide in and out, leering and winking. They lock gazes, two tall, pale figures, leaning toward each other. I can't look.

But then the sound changes, thinner, harsher. I turn back and Stair's alone, luminescent in the heavy dark, leather jacket tied around his hips, his sneakers clicking and scratching the roof of the elevator. And it comes to me: tacks. He was shoving tacks into the soles of his sneakers. The cranked-up boombox squalls and roars like a mad thing, down the black corridor.

My car starts to go down before the song is finished. It's almost two floors away when Stair leaps down and over, his arms spread, the cane outstretched, Captain Blood in hightop sneakers. He hits the raised lip at the edge. He's tottering backward, his arms windmilling over the drop. His wide eyes are locked on mine. My mouth shapes a silent, anguished howl. I'm frozen in place.

Then some part of me notices that his arms are moving exactly in rhythm to the song. He's laughing. He spins, still on top of the narrow lip, still on the beat, then dances to my side, finishing off the song with a flurry of tap-dance, shave-and-a-haircut, two bits. He hips me, just a little, toward the edge.

God, I'm cold. Dizzy. Like I'm standing on an ice floe, choking in a carrion-smelling fog. Down below, in the dark, the twisted, stabbing

Benny the Antichrist, Page 97

horns. "Oh man," I gasp, when I get my voice under control. "Don't ever do that to me again."

He grins at me, leaning on that black stick. "Got your butt all loose and watery, did I? Well, don't worry. Never again."

"Stair, if someone asked me what's the last thing you'd ever do, what I just saw would be close."

"Yeah, I'm just full of surprises."

"I know, but tap-dancing?

"Well, you know, as time goes on, you take the longer view. A while before I saw you last time, I was just hangin' around the apartment one night and Chrissy had on the late show. I was half cut, like usual, so I sat through one of those old movies you like. Daddy Longlegs, I think it was. And ol' uncle Fred, he was pretty cool. Made out with Leslie Caron too, so I guess he was all right. Next day I went and rented a bunch of his movies.

"I got to thinking. I mean, look at this place. My Kingdom. And what's a King for, if he don't do cool things in his own Kingdom?"

"I guess that makes me the Prime Minister."

"You got the training. What kind of law are you going into, anyway?"

"Well, I'd like to do both criminal and administrative. And a little corporate and - "

He waves a hand impatiently. "Only one kind of law really matters. And this is it." And smashes me in the side with his cane.

I'm staggering back, hand on ribs. All I can think is: He's broken one for sure. A jabbing in my lung. What has he hit me with?

"Stair, why--"

Two-handed, a batter hitting a low ball homer, he sends it hurtling into my kneecap. Feel it snap. Unreal. I simply can't make myself believe this. As though it were happening to someone else. I watch myself kneel.

"That's it, you little cocksucker. On your knees, where you belong."

"What--"

"You think I didn't know? You think I don't know why you let me drop, you faggot? Chrissy knew. Knew you hated her 'cause she stole me away." Waving the length of rebar. Twisted, dark, almost black with old blood. A wrathful King with his sceptre.

And in that moment, I remember. Remember Stair jumping from one car to the other, the one I was standing on. Remember him

Benny the Antichrist, Page 98

hitting the lip, reeling, tottering. And me, frozen. Panicked. Watching as he tumbled, end over end, down the dark shaft. Screaming. Oh God, I'm cold.

"Stair, I never--"

"Over you go, Buddy." And he rams me with the rebar, down into the shaft.

Scrabbling. I'm scrabbling. I manage to get hold of the lip. The rough metal edge, cutting into my fingers. Stair watches, grimly amused.

"Tell me about your 'girlfriend', Pudge. You think I don't know that Kim's a man's name too?"

"I was going to tell--"

"Yeah, like you told me about everything else, huh? Your fuckin' literature and your history and everything but what a greasy little queer you are--"

"Please, Stair--"

"You hung out with me so nobody'd smash your cocksucking little mouth in. Got your kicks from me. Old stupid Stair. Climb on him, up and out. Leave him to die. Ain't that right? You think I'm that stupid?" He raises the rebar, ready to smash it down on my head.

"Stair, listen. You're right. I wanted out. I'd have used anyone, left anyone, to get out of here. Including you." My eyes filling with tears.

He grins, skull-faced. He lays the rebar on my cheek, cold, rasping. I can't stop shaking.

"And?" he says.

I take a deep, pained breath. "And I am gay." My fingers shrieking with strain. "But you have to believe me--I never let you drop. I loved you, Stair."

"Fuck this." He pulls the rebar back, shifts his grip. Now he holds it like a harpoon. He's going to skewer me like a seal. My guts twist and heave.

"No, Stair! Wait!"

"Talk fast, asshole buddy. Then it's the long drop. You're finally goin' down the way you should've."

How could I have taken him for a living being? In the dark he glows with rot, a dead thing. Gasping, trying to gather myself. My side afire, fingers knotting and slipping. The shaft's cold, carrion-stinking air playing over my belly. "Kim and I, we like to go to parties. Dress up. Like in the old movies."

"So?"

Benny the Antichrist, Page 99

"So," I lick my dry lips, "could you please let me have that hat, your hat, before you send me down?" I nod toward the top hat, which has fallen a couple of feet from my head.

He grimaces, disgusted, the waxy skin crinkling.

"It would mean so much to me, Stair."

He laughs, a hissing, scraping sound. "Sure, faggot." He nudges it toward me with his foot.

It's all I need. I snatch his cold ankle, pull. A shriek and he's on his back, eyes wide with shock. He's dropped the rebar. With one convulsive motion, I hoist myself up and grab for it.

He bats it away. We grapple--me, clutching, desperate--Stair, cold, heavy fists and elbows smashing me again and again, the miasma of his rot choking me. He breaks my hold and slams my head against the raised steel lip. Dazed, eyes full of blood, I feel him gather himself to kick me over, down the dark shaft. And I do the only thing I can.

I kiss him. Full, long and deep. Kiss the dry, twisted lips, willing them sweet and pliant. Stir his tongue's dull, cracked weight with my own. Wrap myself around his skeletal length.

He stiffens, whipped taut as lightning. Then, all at once, he yields. In that moment I can feel his longing for softness, peace. For cleansing. He rests, quiet in my arms. I draw him in, to a deeper embrace, eyes about to close for sweetness.

Till I see his hand inching toward the rebar. I see this and I clench him, right at his rancid core, by what I once wanted so much. I twist and I pummel and I rip them, the rotten, pulpy things, while he screeches, thin and weak.

Then I reach and grip the rebar. Raise it. And beat him beat him beat him, while he spasms, howls, splinters.

Stop. Snarl. Glare into the frozen eyes. And ram it home, black blood blinding me.

Pass out, feet dangling over the void.

And when I can see again, there's nothing there. No Stair. No rebar. No boombox screeching into the emptiness. Just me and the old, dry dust on top of the elevator. I crawl to the centre of the roof and weep, as I never wept before, in spasms and shame. Then hang my head over the edge and vomit, puking fear and pain down into the shaft. Then weep some more.

Finally, I open the maintenance hatch. Lift up the section of false ceiling. Two women in there, secretaries. One of them, I suddenly

Benny the Antichrist, Page 100

realize, is Lorilene. They stare in shock, shrinking back as I half climb, half drop down. Standing on my good leg, I push the button for the main floor. The women are silent, unwilling to move until I get off. I try to smile at them, blood oozing from my side, puke on my breath, hands black with old grime. "I'm one of you," I say. "I'm going down. Down and home."

Comment

Two guys go elevator surfing. What could go wrong?

The End

SACCADE

"You might have been supportive, for once," Lilith said, glaring at him through dark ringlets while she dug in her gigantic hemp-cloth purse for some herbal placebo or other. Privately Julian noted, not for the first time, that people who allowed hair to block their vision were not inclined to look at things clearly. He also promised himself that after tonight he would confine himsef to affairs with women who used the word "supportive" only when describing girders or beams. Someone like Tatyana, for example, the strawberry blonde engineer he'd chatted up at cocktails yesterday.

Dinner was not going well, which was to say it was going very well indeed. Lilith (Nee Debbi Dempster actually: He'd paid an investigator to have a look at her birth certificate) was in an ugly mood, had nearly gotten into fisticuffs with another woman in his condo's garage over the latter's alleged inability to park or drive properly. More than alleged really, she'd cut him off, beetling her 10 year old Chevy inches by his bumper in her rush to snare the last visitor's parking spot, or perhaps for the sheer small pleasure of being a little closer to the door and beating out a Jaguar. As befit his regretful, noble and firm persona of the evening, Julian had merely smiled ruefully and parked quietly in his assigned space.

"Yes, my sweet," he said, consolingly, knowing this particular endearment always irritated her, as she suspected, rightfully, that she was being mocked. "But had I added my voice to your chorus of complaint, what then? What was done was done."

"Aren't you the little tin saint tonight," Lilith said in a low, dangerous voice, her contact-lens green eyes flashing, "What have you got up your sleeve there, Juju?"

Smiling while he put on a CD of Scarlatti harpsichord concertos (forestalling Lilith's usual Sonic Youth, Wagner or Gregorian Chants) he reflected that he'd miss her occasional moments of insight somewhat, coming as they did as sunny beams through storm clouds of estrogen. Not to mention that splendid chassis, heaving quietly now, but just waiting to jump into high Drama Queen gear, replete with rage, sex and tears. Fine, it was time. With luck he'd have this break-up over in time to play a little serious on-line chess.

"Oh shut up, Lily. You've been on a tear ever since I picked you up after your Coven meeting or Sabbath or Hootenanny or whatever. It really isn't any of my doing that a pack of ditzy, delusional grad students who mumble spells rather than thinking has you browned off. Frankly I'm fed up with the whole dilettante lot of them, their herbariums, their hocus-pocus and especially the way they maunder on about holistic this and holistic that.

"Now here's your choice," he said, knowing that demanding Lilith face binary alternatives was a sure way to drive her into a rage. "You may consume this splendid dinner I've prepared and we can have a civilized evening. Or I'll give you cab fare and you can go stir your cauldron or sacrifice a goat or whatever your little Wiccan heart desires. What's it to be?"

To his surprise, the Debster, as often he thought of her, beamed at him. "You're right, dear. I've been silly this evening. Let me freshen up and we'll have a nice meal." Without a hint of petulance, she strode off to the bathroom.

This was going to be harder than expected. Julian found amicable break-ups draining and awkward. They dragged on and on, one messy emotional stage after another, and the sex wasn't any good. Better to end on a bitter low note with Lilith, as had so many others, shouting recriminations at his rapidly receding back. A real Sturm und Drang parting was wonderfully invigorating.

He'd met Lilith at a party given by one of the Cryptum partners, on the bounce from Annette, a chemist, who, upon ascertaining that he was giving her the toss, had herself hurled a vial of acid at him. Just missed, too.

Newly un-Annetted and feeling frisky, he'd surveyed the deck like a stallion scouting out a herd of brood mares and potential rivals. As usual, a knot of nebbish-nerds milled by the barbecue pit, all untrimmed nose hair, etiolated, acned skin and unfortunate clothes, declaiming bits of mathematical trivia in loud adenoidal voices and scribbling on napkins. One or two of the more adventurous had cut some hapless secretaries from the herd and were trying to pitch woo with sweet nothings about Venn diagrams, superstring theory and pentahedral quark structures.

Benny the Antichrist, Page 103

Then there were the spies, mostly NSA and CIA, sprinkled with FBI and corporate types and anyone else who might have an interest in quantum cryptography, Cryptum's specialty. Interchangeably gray, dyspeptic men in their forties and fifties, they downed free drinks at an alarming rate, treated the nerds like plague vectors and reminisced in low voices about their salad days as coup instigators and torturers.

Most of these affairs had a leavening of artistic types and exotics, courtesy Pickering's wife, a former actress, painter and dedicated dabbler. Unfortunately, they seemed scarce at this do. He might have to content himself with a secretary or with Linda the tech writer, dim and with bad skin, but frantically available.

The partners, Pickering and Tsu, were a level up in the topiary garden with a view of San Francisco Bay, where they'd cornered a couple of possible investors. He could tell Tsu was trying to catch his eye. It was ever thus; he was far and away the most presentable of their employees.

He was about to climb the cedar stairs en route to launching into his usual song and dance when he caught sight of her, a vision of lush, dark womanliness against a backdrop of pale, flabby geek-and-spookdom. The men were intimidated by all those raven tresses, heavy, shapely face dominated by huge green eyes and wide scarlet mouth, prowlike chest barely contained by a low-cut embroidered blouse, arms a-clash with bracelets, white hands freighted with rings, bare leg peeking out of a long silk gored skirt. The women darted glances of open hatred.

She wasn't really his style at all. In general he preferred modelish or professional types who complimented his own fair, lean Waspish good looks. If they came colour-coordinated in blonde or auburn, so much the better.

But for something this magnificent he decided he'd make an exception. He approached her as if delivering bad news. "I believe there's been a mistake made," he said, smiling sadly. "This party is only open to people wearing nasty clothing, who can recite the Lord's Prayer in Klingon verbatim."

Smiling, she eyed him top to bottom, taking in his chiseled, tanned features (Say what you like about Mayflower descendants, they weren't hard to look at), the Saville Row tailored seersucker jacket over linen polo shirt and trousers. "How'd you manage to sneak in?"

"Oh I'm terribly nerdy in my own way. I just manage to conceal it somewhat."

"Really. And what do you do, Mr Secretly Nerdy?"

He'd leaned in then, locking her green eyes with his pale gray ones. "My specialty is something called the Kagawa-Van Dyke Hypothesis. Don't bother remembering the name. It's a cryptography problem involving math so complex, counter-intuitive and obscure that a ten minute lecture in the field will drive a class of ordinary mathematics students hopelessly insane. Twenty minutes and they're in irreversible comas. Our clients pay me absurd sums of money on the strict condition that I never, ever explain what it is I do."

He might have added that his trust fund helped too, but Mother had warned him about gold diggers when he started at Groton and again at Harvard, Oxford, the Sorbonne and Caltech.

She'd laughed and he knew he had her. Ten minutes later they were in his vintage, V-12 Jaguar E-Type, tooling down the coastal highway.

Sex with Lilith was a wonderful tonic. Julian's usual run of girls had three modes of lovemaking. The models were utterly passive unless they were lit on coke, in which case they were needy and oblivious. The managerial types tended to attack sex as a problem to be solved within a definite timeline. Being in bed with Lilith was like floating in a sportive, unpredictable ocean current, a smooth, powerful flow that suddenly turned into a maelstrom, flung him to the surface and tumbled him into a tsunami.

It would have been perfect, if not for her incessant New Age yammering. She was always after him to scarf down some health food nostrum, ginseng, St John's wort, royal jelly, devil's claw, manatee earwax, the whole worthless pseudo-pharmacy. Then he'd have to sit through a zealously vague lecture replete with gobbledy-gook about Gaia, chi, tarot, feng shui, chakras and, God help us all, wholeness ueber alles. He once interrupted one of these newage sewage perorations with the mild observation that while she found it terribly important to emote vaguely about everything, he was paid very well to think quite precisely about almost nothing. She didn't find this amusing.

They'd held together much longer than his affairs tended to last because Lilith, for all of her dark moods and unpredictability, was in many ways the sweetest, most affectionate person he'd ever met. She loved him, God knew why. Confronted with true generosity of spirit, Julian was like an accountant faced with the great Horn of Plenty, awed by an inexhaustible asset, worried about future tax problems, but hostage to its inexplicable power.

But even this would have been bearable for the sake of the sex, had it not been for the Coven. The Debster fancied herself a witch and ran with a pack of women, many of them fellow staffers where she worked as a university librarian. At first he imagined them as a circle of dark, mustachioed Mediterranean types who were quick to throw the Evil Eye and tried to keep you from counting their teeth. But she'd pointed out a gaggle of them, pallid, unkempt, lumpen academics with the vague looks and implacable, placeless malice of the witless and shitless.

She was always full of their doings and feuds, the curses and spells they'd thrown, what so-and-so had said to what's-her-face at the Vernal Equinox festival and how whosis had heard about it and now there'd be Hecate to pay. It was mostly due to the tiresomeness of it all, her dark moods, rages and worries stemming from a group of perfectly superfluous airheads, that Julian had decided she'd have to go.

Dinner, as he'd promised, was wonderful. The Coquilles Anisette were sumptuous, the Kobe Beef Wellington done to perfection, the Nuits St. Georges and Chambertin perfect compliments to the food. And yet he enjoyed none of it. Try as he might, he couldn't get under Lilith's skin. He tried the genteel gross-out, describing in loving detail how the Kobe cattle were hand raised on a diet of barley gruel and beer massages, the minutiae of force-feeding the geese for the foie gras stuffing. He tried pedantic provocation, explaining at length how the Scarlatti they were listening to was in fact discrete bits of sound data sampled hundreds of times a second, tricking their credulous brains into reconstituting it as music. He tried snide comments about Barb and Liz, her best friends in the Coven.

Through it all Lilith smiled at him, not exactly sunnily, more like with dark enjoyment at his predicament. With perfect equanimity she avoided all of his snares and affronts.

At length he excused himself, partly for the toilet, but more to nerve himself up to announce his intentions without benefit of conflict. Looking into the mirror critically for once, he damned himself for a coward, resolving to straighten his spine and get it over with. But in truth he was a bit afraid of her. As silly as some of her talk was, there was something about Lilith that was not to be taken lightly.

Benny the Antichrist, Page 106

A few months ago the Coven had met at his place, since it was Lilith's turn to host and she had pretty well moved in. He didn't mind being exiled; it was Thursday night, which he habitually spent at his club. Beyond innocently asking if he should pick up some toad's blood on the way home, he gave the matter no mind.

He returned to find them mostly gone but for a few stragglers, among whom was Noelle, a grad student working part time at the library. She was a cut above the usual wicca wannabe, with good skin and some wit to her. Noelle was ash blonde, tall and good-looking. Not a patch on Lilith really, but more in his usual run of girls. Also very confident: Noelle flirted pretty brazenly with him, heedless of Lilith's increasingly dark scowls.

What tore it was when she showed up at the condo the next evening, when Lilith was working late, in a minidress that showed a mile of long, tanned leg. She said she'd left a scarf behind. It was one of those clammy North Pacific evenings and he invited her in for coffee. Taking her coat he noticed a long blue silk scarf with a note pinned to it, hanging on the coatrack. It proved to be Noelle's and the writing on the note, equal parts grace and childish force, was Lilith's, though he didn't read it.

She did though, and he thought she paled a bit. Then she turned to him, smiled lazily, ran her hand through her wheaten hair and said, "Got anything stronger than tea?"

At that point the phone rang. It was Lilith, whose message was simple. "Tell her I'll be there in ten minutes." She hung up before he could object or dissemble.

He relayed the message and Noelle shrugged, still smiling. "Another time, perhaps," she purred, reaching into her purse and coming up with a gold pen and paper, on which she wrote out her number. She tucked it into his breast pocket and flicked her tongue to the tip of his nose. Then she tossed the scarf around her neck and sauntered out into the night. In thirty seconds she was gone, swallowed up in the fog.

As promised, Lilith was there in ten minutes, her face stony. Barely acknowledging Julian, she plucked the note from his breast pocket without a word, though it hadn't been visible, and stalked into the spare bedroom she'd claimed as her study.

Through the closed door he heard her low chanting and what sounded like peremptory orders, though there was no phone in her room and she loathed cells. At length she emerged, her face even more bleak, trailing a whiff of something sharp and burnt. She took a step toward him then stopped, trembling, her face crumpling, tears streaming down her cheeks. She sobbed, turned and raced back into her room, slamming the door.

By this time he was quite concerned and knocked on her door, hesitantly at first, then with increasing force and urgency. She never acknowledged his calls, nor did the door yield when he tried to open it. All he could here was her weeping and what sounded like entreaties in some language he couldn't make out. He was just about to try kicking the door down when she opened it. She rushed into his arms, still sobbing, holding him tightly, crying so hard he was afraid she'd choke.

During a small lull he asked if she'd like a glass of water and she wordlessly nodded. From the kitchen, as he reached for a glass, he heard the front door close. He rushed into the hall, then downstairs and out the block's front door, but she'd gone. He combed the area around the block, calling for her, to no avail.

Two hours later, having fruitlessly called all of her friends, he was about to go to bed when she walked in, still mournful, but quiet. He was so relieved to see her that he didn't think to ask her where she'd been till much later. She huddled in his arms like a little girl and they slept.

The story dribbled in for the next few days from friends and campus gossip. Noelle had been found by an alert security guard, hung by her scarf from the branch of a campus sycamore tree. He managed to cut her down just in time to save her life. The general verdict was that it was a suicide attempt; there were no signs of a struggle and the only footprints leading up to the tree were hers. Lilith had been her first visitor in the hospital. She told the nurses that she had had a premonition and they seemed to believe her unquestioningly. So did the police, oddly.

Over the next few weeks the news was mostly good. Noelle had sustained some brain damage but was making remarkable progress, though she'd never be as quick as she once had been. The nurses were full of praise for Lilith's devotion. He and Lilith never spoke of the matter and what with the demands of his work, he'd mostly forgotten about it till now.

When he returned she'd cleared the table and mixed them a couple of tall drinks. The Debster was no end of surprises, he thought and caught himself regretting the necessity of what he had to do.

He took a sip to fortify his nerves. It was delicious, in an odd way. He could identify traces of yellow chartreuse, gin and curacao from his own liquor cabinet. But there was something underneath, earthy and piquant, which might be unpleasant on its own.

Enough, he thought. To the business at hand. He turned to her, but before he could speak, she smiled and said "You want to break up."

"Well, I... that is... it seems for the best..." He felt more than a bit odd. It was if his body were linked by lines of tangible force with her and into the great spinning night of the World beyond. It gave him a terrible headache.

"Poor Julian," she cooed, "flitting like a moth through his fragmentary life, hiding from the splendour and terror of the Cosmos with his clever little theorems, his expensive toys and heuristics. You want to break up? Fine. I make you that gift."

She steepled her fingers, waving them slowly, ceremonially, like a priest with a censer, mumbling something in a hoarse, deep voice. Trying to remember later, he thought he heard the words "Omnium separatum," but he couldn't be sure. She drew her hands apart, but somehow her fingers stayed linked, as if they had grown into each other, to form a white cage that expanded as she slowly extended her arms until they were stretched out full on either side. His eyes were blurring with tears but he could see something moving within the darkness of the cage, something bloody, trying to be born.

Then a great shudder passed through her and the cage burst apart into a million bright faceted shards, flying in all directions. His last memory was her kiss on his throbbing forehead

* **

He woke up naked, but alone and in his own bed, feeling fit and full of energy. He tossed off the covers and stretched in the clear morning light, enjoying the articulated cracking of his joints, the shiftinnals under the tight skin of his belly.

He frowned suddenly and padded into the dining room, half expecting to see the teak-paneled walls pierced with the glittering shards of Lilith's hands. They were unscathed. The glasses had even been washed, which wasn't Lilith's usual style at all. What had she slipped him last night? No matter. She was gone and not too untidily either, all things considered. If all went well maybe he'd give Tatyana a call later on.

Work went well. Better than well, in fact, splendidly. He'd been working for a number of months on the Kagawa-Van Dyke Hypothesis, a decryption conundrum that, if it could be solved, would vault Cryptum years ahead of the nearest competition. This morning the proof, yesterday tangled in dark, thorny thickets of numbers and unresolved propositions, suddenly slipped clear, a brilliant, faceted gem surrounded by a glittering diadem of corollaries. He found himself gasping at the brilliance of it. There were at least four basic patents there, as near as he could tell. The partners were going to be ecstatic.

If he told them. Maybe it was time to set off on his own, he thought, deal with the highest bidder, be they NSA, CIA, some conglomerate or Al Qaida. The partners had, of course, had him sign a non-competition agreement. He resolved to have an intellectual property lawyer take a good look at that.

At six he abruptly realized he hadn't eaten all day. He consulted his I-Phone and messaged Tatyana, wondering if she'd like a bite at a new Cambodian place near Nob Hill. Five minutes later she replied, saying she'd love to, but was unfortunately tied up writing a proposal. Could they make it another day? He messaged back that he'd call her tomorrow, but decided that was contingent on what San Francisco had in store for him tonight. He set out for the restaurant on foot, leaving the Jag in the firm's garage.

Dinner was a mixed blessing. The crab was fresh but they skimped on the lemongrass, the coconut milk was approaching its "Use Before" date and they were too liberal with the fish sauce. The bar was undistinguished and full of some tour group from the Midwest. He caught himself staring at a beefy housewife in an "I Heart Wichita" tee shirt, counting hairs growing out of the mole on her left cheek.

He shook his head and decided he needed to sweat some tension out. Fortunately his club was but a few blocks away.

Julian could tolerate tennis, if only for business reasons. Badminton was a farce, squash bored him and racketball unspeakable. His game was rackets, the game for which squash had originally been a beginner's toothless practice. Played with an India rubber ball, rackets was pure speed and savagery, a dizzying duel of volleys where

Benny the Antichrist, Page 110

ball velocities routinely topped 200 klicks an hour. His main problem was finding someone who knew the game and was worthy of playing.

He was in luck. The club's pro, a bantamweight's worth of fast-twitch muscle named Jimmy Rodrigues, was in and not booked up. Julian had given him a run for his money before, but had never beaten him. He decided that was going to change tonight.

In rackets concentration and lightning intuition of vectors were everything. The best players started their swings before they even saw exactly where the ball was. There simply wasn't time to think or plan.

Or at least that's what it used to feel like. After "Care for a game of rackets, Jimmy?" he lost himself in the game, leisurely tracking the ball's progress as it rocketed down the long, narrow court, skittering crazily from wall to wall. Perfectly balanced, he eased himself into optimum position, effortlessly outflanking Jimmy and savouring the interplay of dorsal, lumbar, gluteus and quadricep muscles as he backhanded and smashed unreturnable shot after shot. After a time even the game vanished and there was nothing but him and the ball, a demon leaping, racing faster and still faster, bouncing maniacally with top- and bottom-spin and always under his complete control. The world was an oblong, echoing room and he its all-powerful deity...

Until he felt a hand on his shoulder and looked around to see Jimmy, his face set with awe and concern. "Closing time, Mr. Severn," Jimmy was saying. The words seemed to crawl out of his mouth, as if the air between them had turned to thick glue.

Looking up Julian saw the gallery full of the same stricken, amazed looks. They had been watching him for two hours, long after Rodrigues had slipped out of the court, playing one long, speed-blurred, perfect volley like some insanely faultless automaton. The floor was slick with sweat. He felt suddenly as if every single muscle in his body was going limp.

Of how he'd made it back to the firm and driven the Jaguar home Julian had no recollection. He'd done it without showering; the sheets reeked cheesily of old sweat. Upon waking he was stiff and sore from head to toe. He'd bitten his tongue badly in his sleep and his head felt like someone had played rackets with it. All he could remember of the night was a fragment of a nightmare: a huge snake tearing itself to pieces.

Pivoting his aching skull with infinite gentleness, he muzzily focused on the alarm clock and groaned. Almost five o'clock. The partners were throwing another investor-luring party, this time at a swank Egyptian eatery and Tsu had all but commanded his attendance.

Holding himself like a precious artifact bound together with ancient, rotten string, he limped slowly into the shower. He almost screamed when the water hit him. It wasn't so much that the spray was cold, it was the way he could feel each individual pore contract, every single hair spring erect and flatten again under each discrete, frigid jet of water.

He frantically turned the hot water on as scalding as he could bear it. It helped a little, but now he felt encrusted with grime, his body swathed in layers of greasy, gritty filth. He shampooed three times and scrubbed till he was sore. Reluctantly he gave up, emerging from the shower knuckling his eyes, feeling, insanely, that there were tiny feet clambering slowly up and down his eyelashes.

Two stiff shots of vodka, a thick emergency joint and a couple of extra-strength aspirins later he felt not precisely well, but at least as if he could manage the drive to work without shattering into a thousand shrieking fragments. If he kept his eyelids at half-mast the misty North Pacific sunlight was just bearable and somehow he found the hydrocarbon miasma of a San Franciscan traffic jam obscurely comforting, like some urban tribal sweat lodge.

He knew he was in trouble though, as soon as he entered the club. The air was spicy with hashish, incense and cinnamon. A flashing disco ball randomly illumined corners best left hidden. Her back to him, a belly dancer shimmied and bumped on a raised stage, coin-embroidered bra clashing and her zill, tiny cymbals, a pair in either hand, clicking. The party was in full swing, and somehow there was peace tonight among the tense and distrustful tribes. Nerds, spooks and office staff mingled all conjoined, one happy mass of shouted equations, bad hair, bad clothing and even bad dancing to the wailing of oboes and violins and circular beat of the drums.

His people. It was sickening. Get away from each other, he wanted to shout. You cretins barely know each other, which is good, because if you did you'd shrink back in horror. Every one of you is a barely cooperating mass of cells, organized differently and utterly unmixable with the mass of cells standing next to you. You speak different languages, those of you who have any language at all, and only utter chuckleheadedness lets you believe you ever communicate with each other. It's a wonder you can interbreed. Press a few

Benny the Antichrist, Page 112

Pavlovian buttons and you'd be at each others' throats in a second. Which would probably be best for all concerned.

Pickering and Tsu were at the back of the club, drinking cognac and smoking Davidoffs with some suits. His arm draped over the shoulder of a stocky figure in a dark Armani and white cowboy hat, Tsu beckoned him over enthusiastically.

Julian nodded, then paused to compose himself before threading his way through the press of bodies in his path. His brow was beaded with cold sweat. Feet, hands and head felt curiously distant from each other and he still couldn't shake the sensation of tiny claws pitoning their laborious way through his eyelashes. On stage the belly dancer pranced and shook her moneymaker, one eye flashing as she peeked over her shoulder through dark ringlets. A snatch of an old pop song came to him: "World moves on a woman's hips." One of her zill was pitched higher than the other, and somehow the tiny crash of it carried irritatingly over the hubbub of voices, drone of oboes, pulse of drums and dark melodies of the oud. He was not at all well.

Tsu was ebullient when Julian finally got to the table. Shifting a Cuban Corona to the side of his mouth, he gestured at him broadly. "Herr Kleinschmidt, I'd like you to meet Julian Severn, our man who's going to solve the Kagawa-Van Dyke Hypothesis and make Cryptum a blue chip stock. Julian, say hello to Otto Kleinschmidt." He nodded at the sixty-ish man on his right, ten gallon hat askew, very pink and eyes slightly crossed with drink. "Otto here's got controlling interest in Daimler Chrysler and a few other bad boys. He's in the market for some serious crypto."

The performing monkey part of the evening had arrived. Julian extended his hand, tried not to shudder at the German's wet, flabby grip, flashed his broadest, falsest grin and said "Pleased to make your acquaintance, Herr Kleinschmidt. May I ask, sir, are you primarily interested in encryption, decryption or both?" Meaning: Are you a tax cheat or an eavesdropper, or just an all-round bad egg?

Julian barely listened to the plutocrat's answer or any of the subsequent conversation. That belly dancer's mistuned zill was driving him crazy.

His inattention made no difference, as Otto was far more intent on groping the harem-pantsed waitress than quantum encryption. The cowboy hat had slipped further to one side of the bald pink scalp, revealing a nickel-sized melanoma. Julian couldn't stop glancing at it, couldn't compel himself to stop counting the burst blood vessels. The cacophonous clack of the zill made him want to scream.

Tsu was trying to get his attention. Over the pounding music, dull roar of voices, the hellish racket of the zill, he was saying "So Julian, what do you think of Otto's proposition?" He and the investor were staring at him. Even Pickering seemed to have surfaced from the depths of his stock negotiations with another German to watch Julian. Perhaps Tsu had said it more than once.

He struggled to recall what the suit could possibly have suggested, as the violin, oud and oboes were whipped by the drums to a moaning climax. There was a final flourish, a sudden lull and he glanced over at the belly dancer.

To find himself staring into piercing green eyes over a dark veil and heaving, heavy chest encased in golden coins. She lifted her left arm, clashed the zill..

and

abruptly

everything

changed.

The club broke into tiny shards in front of his eyes, yet somehow no one else noticed the explosion. His eyes were filled with a skin cancer, then the toe of someone's brown shoe, a spilled drink, a bead of sweat on the end of his own nose, a green eye, a patch of cushion, a belt buckle, the glowing end of a cigar, a tooth smeared with red lipstick, a napkin scribbled with figures, a cowboy hat, each image flashing briefly till the next one obliterated it. Balance deserted him. He felt in his inner ear, rather than saw the carpet rushing up to meet him, his eyes still racing madly from detail to detail, brain scrambling futilely to catch up, to integrate.

The muffled thud of his head bouncing on the floor was a relief. The spasms that shook him were distracting and painful, though. He managed to close his eyes, feeling precisely where the capillary had broken in his right nostril, sensing the path of the blood as it trickled through his nose and down his throat. Limp briefly, he let them hoist and carry him before he started spasming again, kicking out and biting his already sore tongue. The one on the right was Pickering. On the left was a new employee. Baker? Barker. He never thought he'd noticed much about even the people who'd been there for years, but he could tell it was Barker by how he walked on his heels and the eucalyptus mints on his breath. By the grip on his arm Julian could

Benny the Antichrist, Page 114

tell that Barker's left fingerprints were all arches, except for the ring finger, which had loops. He wondered if Barker would be interested.

It was hard to figure out what was happening after that. There was a lot of noise in many frequencies and wave shapes and some bright lights with different spectra, though Julian kept his eyelids tightly shut. His body kept jerking around and they all but dropped him somewhere. He kept hitting things. He could tell he was bleeding in more places. There were sounds that were probably voices. It was hard to say. Then there was poke in his left bicep. As the world darkened and grew quieter, as his body unclenched, he thought that's better. Now maybe someone will get the bugs out of my eyes.

* * *

He woke gradually, the muffled sounds of a hospital coming to him as if from a great distance. He opened his eyes cautiously. The chair, the flowers and the charts on the opposite wall had a halo, but they were whole and they didn't jerk around. Every so often he could finally see the bugs in his eyelashes, tiny squat things clambering around with infinite slowness, but somehow they didn't bother him much. There was a padded restraint in his mouth. His arms and legs were strapped down and his hands seemed to be wrapped in thick gauze. They felt kind of sweaty.

A head hove into view, long and bald but for a patch of graying red thatch behind each ear. "How ya doin', champ?" it wanted to know.

When no answer was forthcoming the face frowned, then cleared. Hands, presumably connected to the head, pulled the restraint out of his mouth and undid the straps restraining his hands and feet.

"How do you feel?"

"Fine. A bit sore and weak. Where am I?"

The head didn't answer, but backed away slightly, where Julian could see it was atop a tall, slightly stooped man in his forties, clad in expensively casual, but unkempt clothes. He wrote a few notes on a clipboard, then ran distractedly through the usual doctor's routines, the bright light in the eye, the little rubber reflex hammer, while Julian waited with mounting impatience. Several times he would have given the fellow a blast, but for the disconcerting way the doctor kept morphing into a series of random parts, an ear, an oversized, nicotine-stained hand, a sneaker lace, a gold pen. He held his peace.

At length the man finished his notes and seemed to belatedly notice that there was a human being in front of him. "You're in the

Benny the Antichrist, Page 115

Epstein clinic, specializing in neurological disorders. I'm Dr. Golding, usually of the Mayo clinic, but brought here through the combined string-pulling of your Mom and your firm. Plus, I have to say, a certain professional interest. You've broken every record I know for prolonged Grand Mal seizure. I've never seen encephalograms like yours. By rights, you should be dead or in a vegetative coma."

This fellow's bedside manner, Julian thought, could stand a bit of polishing. He also wished this Golding would settle down and stay in standard human form, without these distracting Picasso interludes.

"So I'm epileptic?"

"Well, that's the thing. None of your encephalograms read like epilepsy. Plus we've done some MRI and CT scans. It looks like you're growing new cells in there.

"Cancer?"

"Not so much, no. Wanna see?" He reached over to a table across the room, riffled through a stack of papers and drew out something shiny and brightly coloured. He was about to hand it across, but then said "Oops, sorry..." and busied himself pulling off the tape and gauze that bound Julian's hands.

When this was done he passed over something that proved to be a Magnetic Resonance Imaging scan of the top of the head. Julian's arms felt weak and sore, but he managed to grasp it. He didn't need to bring as near as usual to see it. He wondered if somehow his vision had improved.

"Now lookit over there, those areas on your pre-frontal lobe? And there and there? Those are new cells, but if they were cancerous they'd be blue or purple. They look completely normal, according to this. And they show pretty normal neuron and glia activity on your encephalograms. It's weird."

"How so?"

"Normal adult brains don't grow bunches of healthy new brain cells. Quite the opposite. And their activity, it reminded me of something, so I had a look. It's kind of unfocused, I guess you would put it. All over the place. Kind of like the activity you'd see in a newborn's brain. Babies have all kinds of neuronal connections that die out as we get older and more focused. If you're, say, a quantum researcher, you're going to have heavy left brain neuronal and glial activity and not so much in areas a poet or musician would use. These new cells seem to have all their sensory connections intact. And that activity seems to be spreading."

Benny the Antichrist, Page 116

"But that can't be right. You're telling me I should be making new mental connections. And I can't connect anything."

"How do you mean?"

"Right now I'm seeing this room as a series of random details, a tulip, your wristwatch, part of my sheet, the fluorescent light. It's like being inside a cubist painting, except the details flash by me one by one. Am I making any sense? I hope these are words I'm speaking. I can't really tell. Can you?"

He spoke this last in a rising panic. Everything seemed to be splintering into rainbow shards. He heard his voice as a jumble of different waves. The tiny bugs in his eyelashes were the one thing he could sometimes see clearly. They seemed to be dancing.

After a time, how long he couldn't tell, the room slowly settled, gathered itself into recognizable shapes of table, chair, flowers, Golding, a nurse. From the slight sting in his arm he realized they'd injected him with something.

Golding, looking concerned, was saying "...need to get some sleep now, Mr. Severn. I'll see you--"

With a supreme effort, Julian managed to grab the doctor's arm as he turned. Golding's forearm felt bristly and warm. There were tiny bugs on it. He drew his own hand back, quickly. "Dr. Golding, do you know what's happening to me?"

"Well, there are a number of tests we need to run."

"You've never seen anything like it, have you?" When there was no answer, he added, "And it's getting worse, not better, isn't that right? My God, how long have I been here?"

"Come tomorrow, it'll have been a couple of weeks. We just managed to get you to stop spasming a few days ago. Massive doses of thorazine and a few other things. It's amazing you're conscious. But then it's pretty astonishing you're alive at all. You're one weird-ass case." He sounded like an entomology student enthusing over some new bug he'd found.

"Glad to have provided some novelty. Have I had any visitors?"

"Well the folks from Cryptum have been dropping in when they can, but they're pretty busy people, with a lot on the go. By the way, Mr. Tsu told me to tell you, if you ever woke up, that your proof is going to put the company on the map. And your mother, but right about now she says you know she always goes to the spa in Switzerland. Oh, and there's that girl, Doris, Daisy? Something with a D. She's been coming here every day. In fact she just left a few minutes ago to get some air. She says you're not together, but if I were you I'd change that in a hurry. That chick is hot."

Julian had not the faintest idea of whom he could be speaking. Perhaps Cryptum had assigned some junior secretary to monitor his case personally.

"While it's gratifying that I'm being bedsat by someone attractive, doctor, I really would like to know what is wrong with me."

"You say you see all these separate details, one after another?"

"Yes, all these things everybody barely notices, that I never noticed, except as part of the whole picture. Do you really have any idea of what's happening to me?"

"Well I have an idea..."

"Tell me."

Golding hesitated, then seemed to come to some decision. "Have you ever heard of saccade?"

"Isn't that when a violinist bows more than one string at once?"

"Maybe that's what it is in music, but in neurology it means the way your eyes constantly shift in direction and focus, several times a second, all day long. At any given time you only see a tiny fragment of what you're looking at. It's your brain that remembers and integrates all the discrete visual details into one three-dimensional whole. Your brain does that for all your other senses as well. At least, most people's brains do. Yours seems to be noticing more and integrating less."

"Noticing more... Doctor, do you see bugs on my eyelashes?"

"No, I don't see them, but I know they're there."

"They are?"

"Sure. Eyelash mites. Everybody's got 'em. They're related, of course, to the mites all over our bodies, but they're a separate species, found only on eyelashes."

"Fascinating. And how big are they?"

"Oh, they're microscopic little critters."

"Then how do you account for the fact that I'm watching a pair of them mating as we speak?"

"That's not possible."

"Would you like me to describe what it looks like?"

"You couldn't be... " Golding grabbed the MRI print and studied it intensely. "It could just be..."

"What?"

"Well, bearing in mind that we have only the roughest map of the specific perceptual areas of the brain and that every individual's makeup is different--"

"Yes, yes. What?"

"It looks like your cell growth is in areas that we think are directly involved in sensory perception. Most of it. Some of these places we don't have any good handle on."

"But it's not an infinite process, right? I will learn how to handle this eventually, won't I?

"Um, sure. Probably, I think. The thing is..." He flipped through a stack of electroencephalograms, "I don't see any rise in activity in what we'd call broadly the integrative parts of your brain. To the contrary, they're... Could be just a phase, of course. It's fascinating..."

Julian was about to comment on the scant difference between medical specialists and ghouls, when the door to his room opened and a woman stepped in.

She was dressed in a pink pantsuit and her short hair was in a conservative cut. It took Julian a few seconds until the huge hemp-cloth purse cued him.

"Lilith, hello."

"Omigod, Julian. You're awake. Julian, I'm so sorry. How long have you been awake?"

"I don't know. Lilith, it's good..."

"Debbi. Call me Debbi. I'll never be Lilith again. A few minutes? An hour? How long have you been awake, Julian?" Her brown eyes were frantic and filling with tears.

"A while I guess--"

"Oh God, I needed to be here when you woke up for the counter-spell to work. Before your mind started to... Julian I never meant to do... Oh Astarte, I beseech thee--" She dug frantically in her purse, chanting something, choking down sobs.

Golding cleared his throat. "Um, Debbi, I know you feel responsible, but really there's no way you could have caused Mr. Severn's condition." He started forward, consoling arm ready to wrap around her quivering shoulders. "Julian needs his rest now, so why don't we--"

Barely glancing at the approaching doctor, Debbi muttered something under her breath and flicked something from a tiny bluish vial at him. Golding stopped dead, his mouth still working at words that never came.

Benny the Antichrist, Page 119

To Julian it was hard to keep track of what happened, what with everything flying to smithereens and what was probably his body flopping around so distractingly. There was a woman's face, wet with tears and sounds that probably came from her, then a broken vase and flowers, water all mixed with blood, some charts and papers scattering through the air, a button, a tooth, the swell of a pink-bloused breast, a shadowed area of linoleum. It was all very upsetting and tiring. The only ones that weren't upset were the bugs in his eyes. They hardly noticed all the hubbub. And the even tinier bugs on top of them never even looked up. "And so on and so on, ad infinitum" he remembered from somewhere, whatever that meant. It hurt to think. Pretty much everything hurt.

He closed his eyes, which took some doing, considering all the muscles involved. That was better. He was proud of himself, whatever that self was...

After, or perhaps before, an indeterminate time, there were some sound waves, probably voices. And there it was again, a thin, hollow shaft of metal pushing into an arm, presumably his. He sensed the same molecules coming out of it as last time, but somehow he doubted they'd do the trick again. Funny old things, molecules...

* * *

These days, if you know whom to ask and where to go, you can visit the world's pre-eminent quantum cryptologist in his private ward. There are always fresh flowers and a big corkboard with clippings detailing breakthroughs since the Kagawa-Van Dyke Hypothesis has been solved. He occasionally has visitors, most often a dark-haired woman who reads and talks to him as if he were answering. Sometimes she cries.

The walls have signs asking you to be quiet, but it doesn't really matter. The world's pre-eminent quantum cryptologist is busy listening to the mutter of the Big Bang, watching the dance of DNA in his cells and those of his many, ordinary parasites and feeling neutrinos from light-years away as they whip through the vast spaces between and within the atoms of a body, presumably his.

Comment

It seems to me that the ideal of mindfulness is a lot more dangerous than most people think. What happens when you can't turn it off?

Benny the Antichrist, Page 120

I've worn glasses since I was six. Which is to say, my vision anywhere past a few metres has always depended on two little, precisely ground lenses, held in a wire and plastic framework.

Not being athletic, and switching schools often, I was also the kind of kid who was always reading. Reading what? Basically whatever was to hand, which in my family meant many things, including whatever encyclopedia we had currently, as well as the ones at the library. So from an early age I knew about infrared, ultraviolet, radio waves and x-rays. I was also the kind of little know-it-all who would lecture you about protozoa, bacteria and viruses, as well as dinosaurs. Oh especially dinosaurs, who had the virtues of being bizarre, huge, scarier than any adult, and, conveniently, gone. Except they weren't, not really. I knew we breathed the same air they did, that the ground under our feet was made of their skin and flesh. No matter where we lived, I was pretty sure I could find their bones close to hand, if I only knew where to look.

Not very likely, you might say, in the various suburban yards in which I grew up. But my world was both bigger and smaller in those days. Nevertheless, it was a world similar in many ways to the one I find myself in now, full of levels and layers beyond the boundaries of immediate sensory apprehension. The only things that have changed, beyond most of a century's worth of scientific discoveries, is how much I know I don't, and can't, know.

So I grew up having a fraught relationship with those who were sure that seeing was believing. On the one hand I envied the certainty of unreflective people, the ease with which they did things that involved complex, unconscious feats of calculation and coordination. On the other, whenever they talked about anything more complicated and less immediate than say, snagging a fly ball, I suspected that most of their intuitions were just convenient prejudice and pretty ramshackle at that.

In other words, I was a dreamy, clumsy kid with a head full of facts nobody wanted to hear, full of the arrogance of the very shy and unpredictable, free-floating anger. Add to this the normal pains of adolescence, erratic social skills and you had a real piece of work.

"Saccade" is a story about another piece of work, a man whose job is to know a lot about very little and what happens when his world both shrinks and swells at the same time.

The End

TRANSUBSTANTIATION

Out in the harbour the sun hangs, flypapered, at two AM. Fat, white beluga whales whistle and chug through galaxies of capelin, tiny, innumerable fish, sparkling in the cold, green syrup of Hudson's Bay. Up on the bridge, Mahmood Sukarno, Joe Oomiak and I are talking metaphysics while we smoke elephant grass, drink Dutch beer, munch Gado Gado and raw sealmeat.

Once in a while we glance at Sukarno's German porn tape, blond people doing competent, heavily consonanted sex. Joe's two boys, Micah and Zeph,have a boombox set up on poop deck, blunt Inuit bodies turning Crip and Bloodhand jive into minimalist, Arctic semaphore while Schooly D shouts.

Sukarno has thought it all through. He's boatswain on this Indonesian freighter, the Star of Malacca, here to pick up wheat bound for Reykjavik. "What I eat becomes me and, to some extent, I become it."

Joe looks up from the walrus vertebra he's been tilting back and forth, wondering where to put the eyes and teeth that will make its spinal passage into the mouth of the Terrible Sea Mother he's been carving.

"So now part of you is under the ice twenty miles from here, waiting for me to go away, so you can take your first breath of air in an hour. Except I huck a harpoon into you, pull you up and club the shit out of you."

He grins at Mahmood with his six remaining teeth. On the screen snowy bodies collide in synch with an ambient soundtrack. Micah is doing gymnastics on the rail, 20 metres above the maindeck. Mahmood grins back with betel-blackened teeth.

Benny the Antichrist, Page 122

"Exactly. Just as part of you is in the soya bean roots on a flooded, terraced hill, sucking food out of murky water while a beautiful farm girl spreads water buffalo shit, and her family's, on top of you."

Inga, Inga, says one of the blond guys.

Zeph is pulling himself up on the ship's main smokestack. Both boys are still twisting and thrusting in time with the rap.

I look in toward the loading dock, at the belts relaying all the way back to the elevator, where grain cars from all over the prairies are being rocked empty in enormous steel cradles. I look out to sea: The gulls are momentarily quiet and there's a berg drifting in, glowing green blue in the twilight.

I can dimly see a polar bear, padding along its edge, about to swim into shore and walk to the town dump, where it will eat and mate.

For some reason, Micah and Zeph start to scream and laugh.

The End

MAGIC PHONE

Introduction

One of the embarrassments and dangers of setting stories set in the present and near future is the way technology and social change constantly upset and rewrite the references a writer can assume to have currency and resonance. I read an interview with William Gibson where he discussed the opening line to Neuromancer: "The sky above the port was the color of television, tuned to a dead channel." He pointed out that for someone with no memory of pre-digital video, this evocative description makes no sense. For someone born close to or after 2000 there are no "dead channels", filled with gray static. If the data stream is interrupted, usually the image freezes, or you might have a screen filled with a brilliant cerulean blue or just black. It's quite a difference, emotively.

This isn't a trap I have avoided very well myself. In "Benny the Antichrist" I make a series of jokes that only make sense if you have some familiarity with Hanna-Barbera cartoons of the 50s and 60s. Alert readers can no doubt find dated references in some of my other pieces.

"Magic Phone" is set in a time not very long ago, but with a key technological difference so radical as to seem science fictional to younger readers. Imagine a time when virtually all telephones were landlines. You didn't usually own a phone, but rented it from the phone company, of which there was one, and one only, in your area, or even in your country. Phones had no visual or computational capabilities. You could only move most of them around as far as the wire to the plug would let you. Many, such as the ones in numerous phone booths, were wall mounted and lacked even that capacity. You called the people you knew or those whose numbers you found in phone books and yellow pages, printed maybe twice a year. There was no texting, so there were no free-floating conversations, over a number of days, mutating into multiple threads, available through your phone or tablet or laptop.

Benny the Antichrist, Page 124

That's the time in which I grew up. Of course, even then, there was change, erosion and possibility around the edges. "Magic Phone" is about a guy who's at some of his own personal extremities, and what happens when he comes upon a small chink in the technological and social norms of his time.

MAGIC PHONE

Scene: Lights down. DWAYNE'S bachelor apartment. A narrow bed, a kitchen table, a cupboard, a chair, a small fridge and a cordless phone on a nightstand. Football posters and pennants on the wall, a Canadian and a Confederate flag, as well as electronic circuit diagrams and a Spanish bullfight poster. There are various items, a large calibre Glock pistol, a helmet, a football, a woman's comb and underwear, a dumbell, strewn about the place. As he talks, DWAYNE will examine and play with them at times. He will also get cans of beer out of the fridge, as well as a bottle of Jim Beam from the cupboard, from which he drinks all through the play. With lights down, DWAYNE stumbles drunkenly into the apartment, boisterously singing "Corinna, Corinna" and pulling off his pants, shoes and socks as he goes. As he gets his last sock off, he falls backward into bed, which he mostly misses, yelling "shit" in a Southern accent. He crawls into bed and stays there for 30 seconds, then says "Hell's Bells", gets up and turns the light on. He is a big, athletic young man, with a gauze bandage on one side of his face and one knee wrapped in a tensor bandage. He wears a dress shirt, loosened tie and jockey shorts. He picks up the phone and dials it. (note: Until DWAYNE turns on the phone's hands-free feature, all of MARAN's lines are unheard by the audience.) Also note that all female voices, save that of the YOUNG WOMAN near the end, (done by the actor playing DWAYNE) will be done by the actress

Benny the Antichrist, Page 125

playing MARAN.

DWAYNE: Hey, sugarlump.

MARAN: Dwayne? Where have you been? I was worried about you.

DWAYNE: Yeah, Maran, I'm sorry 'bout your worryin'. It was just--I was gonna break something if I stayed at your sister's place a minute longer. So I went downtown, found myself a bar and got good and cut.

MARAN: You didn't get in a fight, did you?

DWAYNE: A fight? Now that you mention it--coupla drunks started making fun of my accent, callin' me a sem-eye-- *(While he's talking, DWAYNE gets a beer out of the fridge, still holding the phone. Meanwhile, he's also unwrapping the tensor bandage and massaging his knee, grimacing. He tucks the beer under his arm, then of course finds that he can't drink from it, which he solves by turning on the hands free feature with his elbow. From here on, the audience can hear MARAN's half of the conversation.)*

MARAN: What happened? Oh Jesus, Dwayne, are you all right?

DWAYNE: Yeah, I'm OK. Nothing happened.

MARAN: Oh no, not "nothing" again. Define "nothing".

DWAYNE: "Nothing" means they jumped me in the parking lot.

MARAN: Oh, Christ. Are you sure you're not hurt?

DWAYNE: I took a good hard right to the jaw. It was great.

MARAN: Great?! What the hell's going on with you tonight? You come to dinner with a huge chip on your shoulder, then storm out halfway through. When I finally hear from you, you've fallen off the wagon and gotten in a brawl. I still don't know if you're hurt or not. Do I at least get to find out why?

DWAYNE: You know, the guy punched me really put some stuff on it--I mean for a second I's in the octopus room--everything lit up inside all flickery and radioactive--the bugs crawlin' all over me.

Benny the Antichrist, Page 126

Everything hurt. It was real. Finally--tonight--somethin' was real. He done me a big favour.

MARAN: Dwayne, you sound like you're still concussed. I'm coming over.

DWAYNE: Now you just set tight, darlin'--I been jumped on s'much s'I can take for one night, an' I got all the company I need. I'mon' talk to somebody who understands--me an' Mr. Glock gonna have a conversation. We gon' talk about Spain.

MARAN: Oh, Jesus--what is it about Spain? Dwayne, listen to me. Put the gun away. Don't do anything stupid.

DWAYNE: Lovebucket, you ever noticed what it is I do? I get wrapped up in sticky tape and weird pieces of plastic. I cover it all over with ugly clothes got big numbers on 'em and a hat that makes me look like some kinda giant termite. Then I take out after a cockamamie-shaped ball and mash other guys when they get too close. Stupid works for me. I swallowed so much stupid shit tonight, one more li'l piece of lead won't make no nevermind.

MARAN: Dwayne! I'm sorry--I didn't mean stupid. Look--please-- talk to me. Tell me about Spain. Don't do anything till I get there, OK?

DWAYNE: **GODDAMMIT, MARAN--YOU STAY PUT!** I got a belly-full of bein' fucked over--you think my brains is all between my legs?

MARAN: I never realized that making love to me was such a chore.

DWAYNE: Aw, you know that ain't it. Sometimes I think that's the only thing we got right. You know what I been thinking about, ever since I got got up from the dinner table and left Lucille and Tim's place--what I can't get out of my mind?

MARAN: No, what?

Benny the Antichrist, Page 127

DWAYNE: Neutrinos. Fucking neutrinos--ain't that a bitch? Guess I'm just the dumbass peckerwood jock your sister thinks I am. Alls I got on my mind is these little subatomic particles that ain't hardly there. Got no charge, no force. Been around since the Big Bang and ain't done jackshit, except hiss on the phonelines, a little. Every second, every day, these little suckers is zipping through us, shooting clear through the earth, through the universe. Like we wasn't even there. Like none of it matters. You know, they set up labs in salt mines. Way down, miles deep in the earth. Looking for neutrinos come flying through from other stars like you and I stroll on down to the 7-11. Or over to Europe, anyway.

MARAN: OK--look--I'm staying right here. Can I ask you, though--

DWAYNE: Of course it's fucked up. The hell good is a neutrino anyway?

MARAN: Just what I was thinking--

DWAYNE: Can't do squat with 'em--they ain't good for power or nothing.

MARAN: -Right--

DWAYNE Except for one little thing, one tiny chance: They might be the secret of the universe. Might be God, calling us home.

MARAN: Dwayne, are you sure you're all right?

DWAYNE: Yeah, crazy talk. Shit, I ought to let you get some shut-eye.

MARAN: You know I can't sleep while you've got that horrible pistol out.

DWAYNE: Now that's no way to talk. Mr. Glock's a handsome fellah. He jes' wanna look after my best interests. You know: Take care of your gun and it'll take care of you.

MARAN: And have you been?

Benny the Antichrist, Page 128

DWAYNE: Have I what?

MARAN: Have you been taking care of your gun? Since the last time you were at the target range, have you cleaned it really well?

DWAYNE: Y'know, I do b'lieve you're right, darlin'. I need to break this sucker down an' give it some serious maintenance.

MARAN: OK, Dwayne--listen to me. Take the clip out first. Is there a bullet in the changer?

DWAYNE: Chamber.

MARAN: Whatever--have you got all the bullets out?

DWAYNE: Yes, sugar--*(in staticky astronaut voice)* We have disarmed the projectile launcher.

MARAN: You remember telling me about your father drilling you on the right way to clean a gun?

DWAYNE: Daddy always said you didn't know your gun proper till you could clean it blindfolded.

MARAN: I don't think you're up to it.

DWAYNE: Say what?

MARAN: I don't think you know your gun that well.

DWAYNE: What I don't know about this gun don't amount to a hill of beans.

MARAN: Then do it. Get your cleaning kit, put on a blindfold and show me.

DWAYNE: Lady, you got yourself a deal. Show you... *(Looks for his cleaning kit.)* Here it is.

MARAN: Now the blindfold.

DWAYNE: Right... *(Looks around. Finally sees a bra on the nightstand. Ties it over his eyes.)* Smells nice.

MARAN: What?

DWAYNE: Nothin'. *(Gropes his way back to the kitchen table.)* Now you

Benny the Antichrist, Page 129

gon' see some serious firearm maintenance... *(Begins cleaning the pistol.)* Sometimes I think I should go back to Spain again, you know? Or Africa, or something.

MARAN: Look--I give up. I don't know what you want, Dwayne. Whenever you start going on about Spain, all I know is that you won't tell me about it--

DWAYNE: You wouldn't understand.

MARAN: Fine. Tell yourself that, then, if it makes you feel better. Poor little Dwayne--no one understands him.

DWAYNE: You're always lightin' into me 'cause I can't guess what's on your mind. Well, sensitivity this, since you know all about it.

MARAN: All I know is something really hurt you tonight--

DWAYNE: Hurt? This ain't hurt. Hurt is being crumpled up against a truck fender, shakin' off the wim-wams, watchin' a fist full of keys comin' at your eyes--

MARAN: Oh God--don't tell me any more about it. Dammit, when are you going learn to shut up and walk away?

DWAYNE: Yeah, well, that's easy for you to say--barfighters don't look at you like some kind of trophy head. This ain't comin' out right. I just wanted--about tonight and your family and all--

MARAN: I realize you weren't comfortable there. But you can't just stomp out every time the situation's not to your liking. You really left me in the lurch.

DWAYNE: Yeah, I'm sorry 'bout that, darlin'. It's just, with your sister watching me like I was gonna hork up a gob of Red Man on her broadloom--look, I just wanted to say I shouldn't't've let Lucy get to me like that. Her and her husband.

MARAN: Now you just hold it right there. Tim never said a nasty thing to you all evening.

Benny the Antichrist, Page 130

DWAYNE: Oh yeah, that's right, ol' Timothy was just as sweet as pie to me, wasn't he? Keeping my glass filled and telling all those little stories about his Indian band clients, out there on the Rez. They're "admirably direct" and they're "differently enculturated"--"Cree people call a spade a spade or sometime just *[Cree accent]* 'a fucking shovel'"-- and mostly they're just dumb old Redskins. Except he won't say that. Oh, no.

MARAN: Can't anyone be nice to you without you twisting it? Tim was doing something we in Canada call "making conversation" and that's all.

DWAYNE: Funny, I didn't notice anybody joining in. You spent some time up there, right? I don't hear you telling any stories. Come to think of it, you never talk about that stuff.

MARAN: That wasn't the point. Tim was just trying to put you at ease.

DWAYNE: Jerking my chain is more like. "I guess it gets pretty rough, Dwayne, in the locker room, with everybody on amphetamines and steroids." And Lucy keeps giving me the hairy eyeball, checking to make sure I use the right fork on her weird little horse doovers and just daring me to tell a coon joke. You think I don't notice stuff like that?

MARAN: Well, you didn't need to mouth off about the trial.

DWAYNE: Oh, yeah? Well, let me ask you something--who brought that up? Wasn't me.

MARAN: I don't care who brought it up--you didn't have to make such a big thing about it.

DWAYNE: Oh, like your big sister and her mushmouth husband can rag me all night about being Southern and football and engineering and all. And I can't say I think the sumbitch is guilty?

Benny the Antichrist, Page 131

MARAN: Let me ask you something, Dwayne. Would you get so mad about it if he were white?

DWAYNE: Black. White. Don't make no never mind. He's guilty, is all.

MARAN: You just know this, eh?

DWAYNE: Yeah, and I'll say it again. Just because being black used to get you hung, don't mean it should automatically get you off now.

MARAN: He's not getting off because he's black. He's getting off because he's rich.

DWAYNE: OK, so rich people walk. And the cops were dirty and slackass. You think we'd be talking like this if he were some down home redneck, no matter how rich, and he done a black woman?

MARAN: I don't know. Does it matter?

DWAYNE: *(Finishes cleaning the pistol. Takes the bra-blindfold off.)* I should have told your sister I met him once.

MARAN: You did?

DWAYNE: That's right, at one of those sports banquets. Made a speech--sounded whiter than I do. And on the bus back home, I'm sitting behind Jamal Berry, guy who plays half for the Lions now? He's talking to the quarterback, Micheal Washington. And they was saying "Man, thass one oreo got no time for the brothers. He walk white, talk white, fuck white. And he signifyin' 'bout 'racial harmony'? Shit. Trust him far's I throw a fit."

MARAN: So now he's guilty because, according to two guys you overheard on a bus, he's not black enough?

DWAYNE: No, I'm just saying: This is the dude your sister is ready to go to war for, is all. Guy who don't even back up his own people. I ever tell you how I really got hurt the first time?

MARAN: Look--Dwayne--I wish we could have talked like this a

Benny the Antichrist, Page 132

long time ago--but I do want to know. But there's one thing you've got to tell me first. Do you really have your gun there?

DWAYNE: Yes, sugar, I do have my gun in my hand. Scout's honour.

MARAN: I'll make you a deal. You're at your kitchen table?

DWAYNE: That's right.

MARAN: Here's the deal: Put your gun away--far away--and I'll try as hard as I can to listen to what you've got to say. How does that sound?

DWAYNE: You ain't gonna jump in every three words with that sensitivity shit?

MARAN: I'll try to keep the sensitivity shit to a minimum. Deal?

DWAYNE: Well, yeah... deal. *(Puts the gun across the table, but within reach.)*

MARAN: But you've got to tell me everything. Promise?

DWAYNE: Promise.

MARAN: OK, now what about when you were hurt?

DWAYNE: Huh? Oh, yeah... well, this was before I went to Europe or transferred over here. Tight end for Pennsylvania. Near the end of the season and we're all banged up. Playing Kansas State. And they're rough, real rough, and big. One their boys got him four sacks that game. Brother called Sunbeam Neville, 'cause he turned so many guys to toast. Went about 290, quick as a cat and bugfuck on 'roids and speed. Talkin' a blue jag all through the game, "killyouhonkymuhfuhfuckyouupwhiteboyfaggot" staring at you with those bloodshot eyes.

We were hung up with five to go on third down and Washington calls a handoff to Jamal Berry. And Berry just can't believe it--he thought they were tight buddies.

Benny the Antichrist, Page 133

"Brother, you crazy? That's Sunbeam out there."

And Washington: "I don't care. You takes your hits, like everybody else."

So that's what we do. Berry comes up the centre like spit on a griddle. Except I guess somebody sideswipes him and, funny thing, the ball pops up. Towards me. I catch his eye and I know he won't go for it, even though he's closer. In a split second. I can see Sunbeam coming and I could let it go. But I jump for it. You got any idea how hard you gotta be hit to crack your spine **and** break your pelvis? Plus tear up my knee real good...

MARAN: Oh my God...

DWAYNE: Yeah. I's on crutches for six months. Old Jamal made All Pro this year, top of a four million dollar contract. Sunbeam didn't make out too well, though.

MARAN: What happened to Sunbeam?

DWAYNE: Well, he was off steroids when he came to see me in physio. He was lookin' real thin and peakéd. "Hey Sunbeam." "Hell, Dwayne, call me Otis. How ya doin'?" "Not too shabby. Ah'mon lay a whippin' on yo' butt any day now." "Well, you gets yo' chance day after tomorrow. I'm checkin' in here." "Nothing too bad, I hope." "Naw, jes' a li'l cancer." "Aw man! Whereabouts?" "Well, the doctors don't know, but they suspicion it down to my lef' ball." "Aw man, Otis, that's harsh." "Yeah... Dwayne?" "What?" "I want you to know I saw what went down when I hit you. You twice the brother Jamal Berry ever gon' be, you cracker motherfucker"

He's on radiation therapy two days later. That's rich--I mean that kills me. Why's he in there? Could it be somethin' to do with all the steroids and speed and growth hormones and coke and protein supplements and I don't know what all kind of shit he put in his

Benny the Antichrist, Page 134

body? And now they're tryin' to fix him. How? They're firin' more shit, subatomic shit into him. Gamma rays, mostly--statistically. But there's bound to be other weird shit--pions, negatrons, neutrinos--that they're shootin' into his guts, into his balls.

MARAN: How could he do that to his body? How could anyone swallow all that poison because someone somewhere says it might make them a little bigger and faster?

DWAYNE: Huh. While you're talkin' to me, what's your other hand doin'?

MARAN: What? This isn't making me hot, if that's what you're thinking.

DWAYNE: No, I mean it's down there playin' with that locket, the gold one you keep on a silver chain between your breasts, ain't it? The one your great-grandma gave your great-granddaddy with her picture in it and a lock of her hair inside. The one you told me was made in Cracow in 1854 and you found hangin' on the backyard apple tree for your twelfth birthday. 'Spose they had an apple tree in the Projects where Sunbeam grew up?

MARAN: God. But that's still too high a price.

DWAYNE: Yeah, I guess... You know those scars on my shoulders? 'Roids give you some real killer acne.

MARAN: Don't tell me you--you're off them now? Please tell me you are.

DWAYNE: Oh, yeah, long time ago. All I had to do was think about Sunbeam. Had a poster on his ward wall--beefcake from some charity calendar. It was him, a year before--lined up and set, in nothing but a jockstrap. I still got it somewhere. Looks like he could rip up an oak tree 'thout breakin' a sweat. He's down to 90 pounds when he died--like something from Bangladesh. Thing was, he did

Benny the Antichrist, Page 135

his job and I come through for a guy called me white trash to my face. Because, believe it or not, soon as he put that jersey on, he was my people. Tell your sister that.

MARAN: You know, I've been having the strangest sense of deja vu about this whole conversation.

DWAYNE: Don't see how. I ain't never told you this stuff before.

MARAN: That's exactly it. You've got a bottle beside you, right?

DWAYNE: You got that first time. In vino fuckin' veritas. I'm on the Jim Beam Bullshit Buster.

MARAN: It's like--I'd come home for lunch in the 11th grade. I remember I was in a hurry--I had ringette practice first period that afternoon. Mother was away at one of her charity conferences--in Barbados, I think this one was. The housekeeper gave me a strange look as I came in--like I'd done something--or was supposed to. And there was my father, drinking, at the head of the dining room table, in the middle of the day.

DWAYNE: I ain't nothin' like your Daddy.

MARAN: He didn't smile or even move when I saw him. Just took another drink and started talking. Later on, I found out he'd gone through most of a bottle of Scotch before I got there. But he sounded completely steady.

DWAYNE: Yeah? What'd he say?

MARAN: He said the firm was in trouble. He'd made some bad investments and the government was suing them over something else. He said Mother was in New York, having an affair with a client he couldn't afford to lose. It wasn't her first, he said, and he'd had them too. All of it like he was analyzing a stock prospectus. And the worst of it wasn't that he never broke down--I don't know what I would have done if he'd cried or something--it was the tone. He

Benny the Antichrist, Page 136

talked to me like you push secrets at someone your own age--not: "here's something you need to know," but "I can't believe you didn't know this."

DWAYNE: And did you?

MARAN: I was in a Southern Ontario girls' school, Dwayne. It was like having a thick coat of asbestos, spun soft and fine as lambswool, between us and anything that could hurt. Sometimes girls' parents were divorced. You heard about people getting pregnant or having breakdowns. But it was all at a distance--even if you knew the person, suddenly she was far away and everybody would smile and change the subject.

DWAYNE: So what happened?

MARAN: Nothing happened. In a month he was dead. An aneurism on the golf course. We were well provided for, with the insurance. Mother came back. Or maybe she didn't--it was hard to tell, with all her trips. Lucille--that was her year at Cambridge, but she came back early. She took care of me. So, Dwayne?

DWAYNE: Yeah, baby?

MARAN: Tell me what's on your mind sometimes.

DWAYNE: I'm tryin' to. I was tryin' at your sister's place--but every time I open my mouth, feels like I'm gettin' pinned to the table, my guts spread out and labeled by someone who don't even care what they're lookin' at.

MARAN: Dwayne, when are you going to stop blaming everyone else for your failure to communicate?

DWAYNE: Communication? Ain't none of it Lucy's problem? Or yours?

MARAN: Mine?!

DWAYNE: Yeah, yours. I don't know how many times I heard

about your sister, what a bitch she is, how she try and run your life for you, all that shit. And every time I see you two together, it's always the same, Mutual Admiration Society World Headquarters. Both of you, lovey-dovey till my teeth hurt. Soon as we leave, I get to hear about how you can't stand this and she make you so mad about that, etc., etc. And the next breath, **the next breath**, you're telling me "Men are so emotionally constipated. So closed off. Women are so much more open and honest." I mean, who's fooling who?

MARAN: Dwayne, look. It's late--I mean it's early. Did you really call me up just to yell at me and take my words out of context?

DWAYNE: Oh, I don't understand, huh? Just this big, dumb jock-- how could I comprehend anything so sub-till like that?

MARAN: That's not what I meant and you know it.

DWAYNE: Oh it ain't, huh? Tell me, sugar, what was it that you were trying to convey? Words of one syllable, please--I'm trying to get it through my thick, cracker skull.

MARAN: I think I've had enough of this.

DWAYNE: Fine. Hang up, then. That's what you always do when things get too close to home, ain't it? I'll come crawling back on my belly sooner or later...

MARAN: Dwayne--

DWAYNE: Or maybe I won't, this time... And while you're studying on that, let me ask you--you gonna pile into your sister like you jump on me? About being insensitive and rude and all?

MARAN: OK, look. Obviously Lucy and I have some issues to work out. But we'll do it in our own way and--

DWAYNE: I guess all that means no, huh? She been shitting on me for months and you for years--don't tell me she hasn't--and you just got to shut up and take your ration. And me too, I guess.

Benny the Antichrist, Page 138

MARAN: I don't have time for this.

DWAYNE: I know, you're right. And you know something? I don't have time for it neither. So let's just drop it, OK? Don't none of it make any difference, anyhow.

MARAN: Fine... What do you mean? Drop what?

DWAYNE: The whole thing. All the fighting, misunderstanding, all this shit. Let's just leave off, the whole ball of wax, huh? Because--I tell you true--communication just a pile of horseshit anyway. It's all just fucking neutrinos, whistling through without ever doing nothing.

MARAN: So that's what this is all about. You want to break up, so you call me up and pick a fight. Great.

DWAYNE: Aw, that ain't--

MARAN: Do it late at night, when my defenses are down. Saves the cost of a last meal.

DWAYNE: Maran, I'm sorry, but I can't--

MARAN: You've pulled some pretty nasty stuff on me, Dwayne, but this is the lowest--

DWAYNE: You think this is easy on me? Day in, day out, that's all I hear about--how I did this and I did that. You got some kind of license in your purse, says you the only one gets hurt?

MARAN: **NOW** he talks about his feelings! Just before he ditches me, I get to find out that Dwayne Fitzwilliams is not made of stone!

DWAYNE: Oh, yeah, like I'm supposed to run and cry on your shoulder. I hear you and your girlfriends talking, when they over. That little Marcie? How come she ditched her last boyfriend?

MARAN: Charly? He didn't last long enough to make an impression.

DWAYNE: No? Well, I remember--he was a wimp. According to her. And Colleen and Barry--same story. You remember the night we met?

Benny the Antichrist, Page 139

MARAN: Of course I remember.

DWAYNE: Yeah, that party after the game. Over at Phi Epsilon house. I's doing all right that night--50 yards and some good blocks. Plus I aced a test in microwave that morning. You were with Colleen and Marcie, doin' your little anthropology study--"Observe the natives in their quaint tribal activities."

MARAN: Oh, spare me. Dwayne, we were just nervous. Do you have any idea how much nerve it takes for a woman to walk into a crowd of big, strange men, all of them getting rowdy and drunk?

DWAYNE: If we make you so jittery, why weren't you over there with Tim an' them, at the Faculty Club?

MARAN: I don't know, Dwayne--why don't you hang around with the women's rugby team?

DWAYNE: Goddam! You are a pisser. I thought of breakin' off--I don't know--half a dozen times--an' every time what stops me--that Maran--she's a pisser.

MARAN: Thank you, Dwayne. You're a pisser too.

DWAYNE: So anyway, at the party: Marcie made a beeline for Levon Phillips, the cornerback. Funny, none of the spades that girl hooks up with turn out to be wimps--they just dump her when something better comes along. Colleen gets into it hot and heavy with one of the linebackers. She likes 'em big, Colleen. And you, well I be dipped in shit, but you couldn't have cared less for me. I'm trying to make nice till my face hurts and your eyes just going like pinballs, all over the room. So you know what I did? I walked off into the kitchen. You maybe heard a little bump out there. You remember that?

MARAN: Maybe I do, maybe I don't. What's this got to do with anything?

Benny the Antichrist, Page 140

DWAYNE: That was me, smacking my knuckles against the edge of the kitchen counter. Get a little blood on them. On the right hand, you remember?

MARAN: Come to think of it, I do remember thinking you must've done something awfully clumsy in there...

DWAYNE: That's right. Then I walked back into the livingroom to say goodnight. Wave goodbye and, what do you know, you notice that my poor hand's bleeding. "Aw, I musta reopened that. Shee, it ain't nothin'--I'll just put a bandaid on it when I get home."

MARAN: "Oh, no, no, let me see that. I've got some mercurochrome in my apartment. You don't want an infection, do you?"

DWAYNE: "Aw, don't put yourself to any trouble..."

MARAN: "Now you just come with me."

DWAYNE: "Well, if you say so."

MARAN: I can't believe I'm hearing this. You really astound me, Dwayne. Every time I think: Well, that's it--he can't do anything worse--

DWAYNE: That's right, I suckered you into it.

MARAN: And such a smooth move, too. You must be really delighted with yourself.

DWAYNE: No, I ain't proud. But the point is: You should have seen your face when I give you that ol' paw of mine, all tore up and leaking blood. You looked like you was gonna lick it clean, right then and there.

MARAN: You're disgusting. It is so like you to take basic human tenderness and twist it so--

DWAYNE: Oh I'm disgusting, huh? Let me ask you, when's the last time we had a really great fuck? Last week's practice, when I took the

Benny the Antichrist, Page 141

cleats in the face, wasn't it? And before that, the Waterloo game, where I had a separated shoulder? Shit, you damn near killed me. Seem ever time I get hurt, y'all want to jump my bones bad. Then rub my back and mother me, 'cause I'm such a little boy, even if I am a big, strong, peckerwood lunk.

MARAN: You know, Dwayne, it seems to me that most of our discussions of your feelings come down to you getting your rocks off or you hitting someone. Have you got any idea why that might be?

DWAYNE: Is that so? Some "feelings" is more equal than others, I guess. I'm supposed to go on about those other feelings, those ones about being scared and fretful, 'cause that's mature, according to you. Like I was Phil Donahue or something. Well, guess what? I may not be too smart, or too sensitive, but I got one thing figured: If I ever carried on like that I'd see the back of you so quick it'd make my head spin.

MARAN: How would you know? You've never tried it.

DWAYNE: Oh, yeah, you talk now. You know, I thought it was bad there in Spain, everybody looking at us like we were too stupid to tie our shoes. Just big, dumb American jocks--laugh at 'em when you don't spit on 'em. But I been back for a while and you know what? Ain't no different here. Lucy and Timothy--they look at me and all they see is trash. No matter what I say, don't nothing change. It's just like Madrid.... Aw, fuck it. I do go on, don't I?

MARAN: You sure do. Can we talk about this--

DWAYNE: Listen, I'll let you get some sleep, OK? I'll drop your books and stuff off tomorrow.

MARAN: Dwayne, don't do it this way. Please, let's talk about it.

DWAYNE: It just isn't working out, is all.

MARAN: Goddammit, Dwayne, every time something goes wrong--

Benny the Antichrist, Page 142

DWAYNE: Aw, Maran--

MARAN: -you're just so willing to toss your hands up--

DWAYNE: -now don't--

MARAN: -in the air and walk away--

DWAYNE: -c'mon--

MARAN: -and, Goddammit, please don't leave me, Dwayne.

DWAYNE: -now, sugar--

MARAN: Tell me what happened to you, why don't you?

DWAYNE: -it's--

MARAN: You're always hinting around, but when I ask you about it-
-

DWAYNE: I'll talk to you sometime, OK?

MARAN: -you pull back and will you finally tell me what happened--

DWAYNE: Goodb--

MARAN: -to you in Spain?

DWAYNE: Aw, no, honey, it's too late and--

MARAN: Please, Dwayne?

DWAYNE: ... You sure you want to hear about this?

MARAN: Just tell me.

DWAYNE: OK, I guess I owe you that... Let me see now: This'd be
a couple of years ago, summer vacation after I got hurt. Four of us
on the team, we decide we're going to head over to Europe. It was
cold in London when we landed, so we deked over there to Spain.
Well, everything was cheap, seemed like, and we stayed for quite a
while in Madrid, till the guys were ready to take off home. The
charter was for tomorrow, so we decide to have a really hellacious
blast that night, bar-hopping.

 Kyle keeps yelling "*Mas coñac!*" and "Root Hog!" It's our fourth bar
and Schmidt, Dougie and him are putting 'em away to last a semester.

Benny the Antichrist, Page 143

I'm keeping up. Say this for Madrid, it's a great place to party late. We're in that mall with the name I always forget. The one that's like three levels of stores and bars and shit. *Paseo* something. Everything from fuckin' A radical discos to tourist traps where some old fruit minces around with a fat mama and everybody yells *olé*.

This place is just a bunch of students and workies swilling red wine. Pop music and people yelling *"Arriba!" "Coño!"*, floor ankle-deep in lottery tickets, the usual crap. The only other foreigner's an English kid talking to this old guy with one arm. He keeps buying *abuelo* drinks and they go on about the workers, *Los Popularos*, Franco, the Lincoln Brigades, shit like that. I don't know why I'm listening, except Dougie's telling us for maybe the fiftieth time that since he got written up in Sports Illustrated, coach can kiss his butt about curfew or he goes straight to the pros. Anyway, I'm taking it in, two dudes knocking themselves out at a foozball table, little kids playing in a corner, soccer game on TV, waiter pouring beer from way up so it makes a big splash. We're the only ones in there without red armbands. Spain, man. Communists got their own bar, right in the middle of town.

MARAN: Dwayne, you know, there's no law that Spanish people have to check to see whether you approve of who runs their bars.

DWAYNE: There you go again. I know that.

MARAN: So why did you make that comment?

DWAYNE: Maran, when you were up on that reserve, didn't you ever see anything and say to yourself, that ain't how we do it at home?

MARAN: Of course I did.

DWAYNE: Well there you go.

MARAN: It's not the same thing at all. What I try to keep in mind is

Benny the Antichrist, Page 144

that learning is a two-way street. You say "Communist" and I can tell you've just shunted those people into a rigid little category. It's so judgmental.

DWAYNE: Is that a fact? Well, it may interest you to know that my family were called Communists.

MARAN: You never told me that.

DWAYNE: Sure. You ever hear of the Portertown massacre?

MARAN: Portertown?

DWAYNE: Well, that ain't surprisin'--hardly anyone has. My great-uncle Chilton was a machinist, organizing for the union in a little mill town in Georgia. Folks makin' ten cents an hour, when the bosses didn't steal it all back. Held a big union rally when it looked like they'd gotten certified. Turned out the bosses had deputized half the peckerwoods in town, filled 'em full of corn licker, give 'em shotguns and turned 'em loose. Twelve people killed, their own neighbours shootin' at 'em. Broke into Chilton's house and killed him. Beat up his son, my uncle Beau, so bad he walks with a cane now. My Daddy had been stayin' with him since Grandpa died. He'd just shipped out with the army or they might have killed him too. Came back to find the deed for the house was gone. Just gone. Somebody else livin' there now.

MARAN: So how can you--

DWAYNE: Hold on now--I never said I agreed with what Chilton done--

MARAN: But--

DWAYNE: -and I never said I didn't.

MARAN: Don't you stand for anything?

DWAYNE: Stand for something? Huh. Your great-grandpa had some garment factories, have I got that right?

Benny the Antichrist, Page 145

MARAN: Yes...

DWAYNE: Which sent your Daddy to law school, which in turn pays your tuition?

MARAN: Well, yes, sure, but--

DWAYNE: Those be Union shops, by any chance?

MARAN: ...I don't know.

DWAYNE: Might be interesting to find out--and while you're at it, see how squeaky-clean and rosy everything was when the union tried to organize in there. When they come to your great-Granddaddy, all them immigrant women working the sewing machines, and said "We want to work eight hours a day, instead of 12 and we want 20 cents an hour", maybe he invited 'em into the mansion for tea and crumpets. Waddya think?

MARAN: Just because people did bad things in the past, it doesn't mean-

DWAYNE: Want to know what happened to old Beau?

MARAN: Why?

DWAYNE: Like I said, he nearly died. Was in the hospital the better part of a year. Come out lookin' 10 years older, my Daddy said. The army wouldn't have him--he was a cripple. Did odd jobs all through the war. Then, after, the GI Bill didn't apply to him, so he couldn't get an education, even though Daddy said he was the brightest of the lot. Turned him mean as a fire ant.

MARAN: That's terrible.

DWAYNE: He's doing all right now. Hired on as a foreman for a big farm in California. Now he manages the whole works. They grow strawberries. Got a son my age, name of Jimmy.

MARAN: So what's--

DWAYNE: Did you know they still have to pick strawberries by

Benny the Antichrist, Page 146

hand? And who does the picking? Illegal immigrants--that's who. Like in that "parfait" your sister made tonight--them strawberries was probably picked by some wetback Beau hired for peanuts and worked like a brother--a real brother, not just some dude whose folks happened to come from Africa--then deported soon's the season was over. My uncle's doin' fine--due to retire any day now with a nice pension, if he don't drink himself to death first. Jimmy won't talk to him. Ashamed of him, for doing the only job he could get. And you know what? Jimmy's right. 'Cause Beau really is trash, doin' what white trash does best: Keepin' the brothers down.

MARAN: Now **that's** harsh. His own father.

DWAYNE: Know what I always hated about English class? The fool things those great authors said. "To know all is to forgive all." Only a rich, numbnuts Yankee could come up with anything so stupid.

MARAN: So life isn't fair--

DWAYNE: I'm just saying--if my great-Uncle Chilton had shot his friends, 'stead of bothering folks to put their necks on the chopping block--maybe you and I'd be talking about Cosmic Consiousness or Male Feminism or some damn thing. Or maybe if your grandpa hadn't brought in the goons and the scabs, we'd be livin' in a trailer, goin' to bingo every night.

MARAN: OK, time out. Let's go back to Spain...

DWAYNE: No, you hold it. How come your family's off limits, huh? Your sister can sneer at me and your brother-in-law can push my buttons like I was a remote control and I can't talk about a few things I noticed. Why is that?

MARAN: You're so damn smart.

DWAYNE: The hell is that supposed to--

MARAN: No, I mean it, Dwayne--I don't know why I keep

forgetting, but you're really smart.

DWAYNE: Well, jeez, I--

MARAN: So let me ask you--why do you let them get to you, eh?
Tim and Lucille and everybody else--all someone's got to do is wave
a little scrap of red and you come charging in. Then they turn aside,
you slam into the wall and they laugh.

DWAYNE: Well, where I come from, you don't invite someone over
to stick your thumb in his eye. And your girl backs you up when
you're gettin' hammered by people who've got no cause.

MARAN: Lucy's my big sister. She thinks she's protecting me.

DWAYNE: Pro--Is that what being a feminist is all about? You burn
my ass down to the ground if I hold the door for you, but Lucy can
shake her rattle and hiss at me all night, 'cause she's protecting you?
Well, you done made a pacifist out of me--I quit. I love you darlin',
but I ain't fightin' you **and** your folks. *(starts to hang up)*

MARAN: Dwayne, wait!

DWAYNE: What?

MARAN: What did you just say?

DWAYNE: You heard what I said.

MARAN: You never said that before.

DWAYNE: Hell--ain't it obvious? You think I'd sit all night wearing
a tie that half-strangles me, eatin' horse doovers that look like trout
flies and taste like weasel puke? Lettin' Lord Carefree stick pins in
me--

MARAN: Tim? Hardly. Tim would kiss up to anyone who'd give him
a crack at tenure right now. He's desperate. Between you and me, I
think Lucille will leave him if he doesn't get it.

DWAYNE: Nobody told me that. And it don't excuse him talkin' to
me like some kind of trained monkey. You know, I grew up on army

bases and army bases are always near some Indian reserve or other. I know some Seminole boys'd straighten out ol' Timothy right quick if he pulled that "differently enculturated" shit out there.

MARAN: Oh they would, eh? Just kinda take him out back and re-educate him, is that what I'm hearing?

DWAYNE: Yeah.

MARAN: Maybe that's what you ought to have done, eh? Punched him out.

DWAYNE: I's thinking of it.

MARAN: That would have been fun, wouldn't it? With Tim being half your size and out of shape, to boot.

DWAYNE: Hey now--listen--

MARAN: No, you listen--if there's one thing that makes me sick, it's when men talk about fighting as a recreational sport, like golf. Or a way to continue a discussion. You want to know about my reserve time? Well, I hung out at the pub there--everybody did, loggers, miners, half the village on any given night--and I saw plenty of fights. And you know the one thing I never saw? Two men the same size going at it, face to face. It was always two on one, bigger on smaller, somebody jumping somebody, gouging, biting, kicking. And Dwayne? Guys who beat on other guys don't draw the line at women and kids. I know that for a fact...

DWAYNE: Aw, Maran. Aw, baby. You never said nothing about that...

MARAN: It's not something I like thinking about.

DWAYNE: What happened? Who was it? Was it--

MARAN: Dwayne, no. **NO!** I'm not ready. And when I am ready, **nothing is going to happen.** No one is going to get beaten up. No one is going to get hurt again.

Benny the Antichrist, Page 149

DWAYNE: I never said I was gonna do that.

MARAN: What were you going to do?

DWAYNE: I don't know--I just--

MARAN: You can't solve this with your fists, Dwayne. Or with a gun.

DWAYNE: Now what did I just say? Did I say I was going to do that?

MARAN: Weren't you thinking it?

DWAYNE: Tell you what--since you're so good at mindreading and all, maybe I should leave you to finish off the story all on your lonesome. Bein' as how you know how this whole thing turns out.

MARAN: Right now, Dwayne, I'm wondering if I even care.

DWAYNE: Do you want to hear what happened or not?

MARAN: ...Yeah, I guess I do.

DWAYNE: You sure?

MARAN: Just get on with it, Dwayne...

DWAYNE: Hmmm... Let's see... Oh yeah, the bar. Anyway, this English kid looks at our blue varsity sweaters, leans over to the old guy, points and says "*Phalangistas Americanos*". I used to go out with a chick taking Spanish history, so I know he's talking about blue being the fascist colour and it's not a good thing in here. Little faggot can see our team letters but he's gotta shoot his mouth off.

Somebody repeats it "Phalangistas" "Phalangistas" and all of the sudden you can't hear nothing but the jukebox changing records and the TV announcer. All these Spaniards looking at us real mean and I see this beaner beside us reach into his jacket. Schmidt drops him with a forearm. Kyle smashes a bottle--"Get ready to rock and roll, man", the air sparkling around his fist.

Then the bartender sticks a sawed-off shotgun up under my chin.

Benny the Antichrist, Page 150

I'm between Kyle and the bar, so he can see it's one shot for me and the next will be coming his way. Even a nose tackle don't argue with that. We're all frozen: I can see Kyle's fist start to bleed where he cut it. The creep on the floor is making little retching noises. The barrel is cold, real cold. Must have kept it next to the beer, is all I can think. The bartender catches my eye. "*Vamos.*" He nods at the door, but he keeps that gun where it is.

We back off. The bartender wipes his forehead with a big dirty kerchief, but he keeps us covered. Him and a few customers follow us and make sure we get our butts out the mall. He's got the gun wrapped up in his apron, which he's carrying loose, like he just took it off. It's something he's done before. People are pointing at us and laughing. Even a couple of rent-a-cops watch us, but they don't give a shit. When the bar guys are satisfied, they turn around and head back, giving it plenty of walking Spanish. The rent-a-cops stroll up and watch us from behind the door. Everybody whistles, calls us *maricones* and shit.

The guys just go pig. "I'm goin' back in there and kickin' me some dago butt!" "Fuckin' A, man! Let's do it!" "Let's fuckin' get some!" "Show those greasers, if it's the last thing I do!" and it takes me a long time to straighten them out: "Walk through that door, and it **will** be the last thing you ever do." "You pussyin' out on us, Dwayne?" "Fuck you--you know I'd be the first one back in there, if we had a chance." "So what's your problem, man?" "We do a blindside rush on that barkeep, we'll have his gun before the spics know what hit 'em!" "Look you guys, I know *hombres malos* when I see 'em. They're just waitin' for us, man. We wouldn't get halfway through the door without they'd be on us like mean on a mink." "Fuck, Dwayne! They're nothing!" "Yeah, well, that nothing had at

Benny the Antichrist, Page 151

least one shotgun. You ever seen a crowd of beaners without a few knives?" "Aw, man!" "C'mon, Dwayne!" "Tell you what we'll do, you guys. Let's go on down to the Plaza Major for a council of war. Then, when these guys are juiced up and forgetful, we can make our move. What do you say, Kyle? Schmidt?" "Aw..." C'mon, dudes... Y'know, I got me a strong suspicion that ol' W-Kilroy gonna do some international brain-scramblin', down at the magic phone tonight..." "Whoo-wee! W-Kilroy!" "Yeah! Kilroy gon' fry some sucker's mind!" "Taxi!"

MARAN: Now, wait a minute. Let me see if I'm getting this straight here: Dwayne Fitzwilliams, the fastest fists in Georgia, walks away from a fight?

DWAYNE: Didn't say I walked away. Postponed is all.

MARAN: And did you go back?

DWAYNE: Let me ask you something, little Miss High and Mighty. You remember the night you done your last exam, last term? We went out to celebrate?

MARAN: Um, yeah. Vaguely.

DWAYNE: I'm not surprised. You drank more'n I ever seen you do before, or since. You and Colleen were good and juiced.

MARAN: Don't remind me.

DWAYNE: Oh, this won't take long. On the way back, them bikers started talkin' trash to you, 'long C Avenue there? Five of 'em?

MARAN: God, they were horrible.

DWAYNE: Seem to me you and Colleen found 'em mighty droll at the time. Pitiful, even, considerin' how much lip you give 'em. I guess you figured you could take 'em easy, what with havin' the advantage of a post-secondary education and all. And a redneck bodyguard.

MARAN: OK, you've made your point.

Benny the Antichrist, Page 152

DWAYNE: Who hustled you up to that apartment block and got you buzzed in, when they cut us off at the corner, huh? Made you two wait 10 minutes and went out to make sure they was gone?

MARAN: OK, OK. So why tell me about this now? It's been--what?--two months? Why do you let these things wait?

DWAYNE: As I recall, you were gully-low the next day. Didn't seem right to rag on you when you felt so hangdog. And then you went off to your uncle's place in Belize for the holidays and it never come up till now.

MARAN: Yeah... Dwayne?

DWAYNE: Yes, darlin'?

MARAN: Thank you, sweetheart.

DWAYNE: No trouble.

MARAN: So why don't you come over, eh? You could clear your head and I'd rub your shoulders when you got here--

DWAYNE: Sugarlump, I'd love to, but I'm so fucked up right now, if anybody looked at me sideways I'd kick his teeth in.

MARAN: Then I'll come over there--

DWAYNE: Baby, baby--that just ain't gonna get it. Oh, it'd start out fine--ten minutes after the door closed you'd have your sweet ankles behind my head and we'd kiss and howl and grind all night. An' a couple weeks later I'd beat the shit out of some poor slob who got on my nerves. I got this murderin' sad inside me and the only way it's comin' out is if I tell you this stupid, sorry-ass story. I don't know what else I can do.

MARAN: Tell me your story, babe. But first, can I ask you something?

DWAYNE: What?

MARAN: What's a girl have to do to get a drink around here?

Benny the Antichrist, Page 153

DWAYNE: Well, pull up a stool. Plenty of room at the bar. What're you having?

MARAN: Looks like it's *(sound of a cupboard opening)* gin and... *(refrigerator opening)* diet rootbeer *(bottles being poured)*.

DWAYNE: Yech. You tougher than I am, darlin'.

MARAN: Don't you ever forget it. Now keep on with your story, Mister. And don't leave nothing out.

DWAYNE: Let's see... Oh, yeah, just after the bar... I grab us a cab and we head down to *Plaza Mayor*. The guys're singin' the team song and banging out the rhythm all the way there, so I 'spect the cabbie was glad to be shed of us. By this time we're totally polluted on that sweet Spanish brandy. This magic phone's in one of them twisty little alleys just off the Plaza. Most of Madrid is like Milwaukee with Spanish signs, just gray highrises, pavement and gridlock. Down here, though, you got all these shifty cobbled walkways with little barred-in windows looking down on you from big old stone walls. Sniper posts. Like the whole city tries to sell you on setting up a McDonald's or Dunkin' Donuts franchise. But come to where the important stuff goes down, and feels like there's always some historic dude covering you with a musket or crossbow or something. Not to mention all the army and Guardia Civil hangin' around with machine guns, givin' you the hairy eyeball.

Nothing really magic about the phones, it's just what they call them. Spain's got a real primitive telephone system and it's super easy to jimmy a pay-phone so you can call any place in the world, for free. You've just got to keep an eye out for the cops. Some Dutch hippie was telling me, though, that the oldest magic phone was right across from the police academy. You got to be a cop to use it. Goes to show you. Spain.

Benny the Antichrist, Page 154

So I fixed us up one, first night we were here. Three years of electrical engineering, but I could have done it with what I knew from high school shops. I get a bang out of it - lines that haven't had any serious work done on them since fucking Alexander Graham Bell and you're tapping into this entire satellite system, this totally cutting edge stuff thousands of miles up there handling a zillion messages a second, maybe rerouting your call to Kuala Lumpur or whatever through undersea cable where it goes to microwave relay and back to satellite again and this could all happen just while you say hello. With a bit of the old know-how, we've got it for free. Any time I want I can come out of the wild blue yonder at some nerk in Nairobi or Tierra del Fuego. And all the time I'm talking, laying a trip on some dude, there's a little satellite, stuffed with microcircuits, orbiting way over this sucker's head, turning my words into radiation. They're beaming down there in Thailand or Sweden, they're getting amplified and coded and decoded, they're bouncing off and penetrating shit, they're filling the air and shooting back off into space. Heavy duty.

The other guys mostly call their families and girls. But my Mom took off a long time before I remember. Every so often the old man starts getting sloppy and whips out some old snaps. *(raspy, drunken Southern voice)* "This here's your Mama, boy, jes' so's you know. Ain't she pretty? Smart, too. I wan' you to know that I loved her truly, the whore." But I never recognize her or nothing. Shit, I barely recognize him, looking so young and stupid, arm around some blonde broad. He says I take after her. I guess that's cause I'm gone most of the time. Anyway, I've got no particular reason to call him even if I could remember which Noncoms' Club he'd be getting shitfaced in.

And it'll be a cold day in Hell before I call Kimberly again.

Benny the Antichrist, Page 155

Thousands of miles between us and she wants to start a fight. I'm standing there, so fucking lonely I'm actually getting tears in my eyes hearing that little silvery voice that just seems to sashay down my spine and I'm seeing her right in front of me with that dark red hair spilling down over her shoulders and that skin all buttermilky and those baby pink nipples that come up so fast and those round thighs and those green eyes that made me catch my breath the first time I saw them.

MARAN: My, that was graphic. So Kimberly is gorgeous, eh?

DWAYNE: Oh hell, baby, not near as good-looking as you.

MARAN: Anything else you want to talk about, Dwayne? Have you been making phone calls to Tennessee lately?

DWAYNE: Aw, come on, sugar, don't be like that. Swear to God, Maran, that was over before I ever met you.

MARAN: I don't know, Dwayne. It all fits a certain pattern.

DWAYNE: Aw, goddammit, not that again. Now look. Nothing happened there, with Charlene. You hear me? Nothing.

MARAN: I wonder if Charlene feels that way. It looked like something to me...

DWAYNE: You want to hear my side, for once? Just listen?

MARAN: Why not? As long as I've got you talking, I might as well hear it.

DWAYNE: OK, Old Charlene, she was all drunked up and she wanted to cry on someone's shoulder, is all. And she was feeling so bad, she didn't care who. 'Cause that girl was lovestruck.

MARAN: Charlene always did wear her heart on her sleeve. Who was she stuck on this time?

DWAYNE: Yeah, who? Tell you what, though, it wasn't me.

MARAN: OK, just for the sake of discussion, let's say that little Miss

Benny the Antichrist, Page 156

Roundheels had fallen for someone she hadn't already boinked. Are you going to keep me in suspense?

DWAYNE: You really want to know?

MARAN: Yes, Dwayne, I really want to know.

DWAYNE: You, that's who.

MARAN: Me?!

DWAYNE: Yeah, you. Oh, I don't deny she come on to me, a little, but her heart wasn't in it. It was you she talked about:

CHARLENE: "Oh, Dwayne, I hope you realize how lucky you are to have a girl like Maran. So smart and beautiful. And sweet. Maran's so sweet, don't you think?"

DWAYNE: I was just her way of getting close to you. And that's the truth.

MARAN: That's ridiculous! Charlene couldn't even look me in the eye, even before I caught you two. And she quit the day after.

DWAYNE: Shit, I'm telling you why she left!

MARAN: But--oh, **now** I see... Nice try, Dwayne. Really, good recovery. You not only confuse me a little, you come out of this looking like a humanitarian. Good one.

DWAYNE: Oh, is that what you think? Well, you are one hundred percent correct. Us Southern boys--we'd fuck a snake, if we could. Poor little Charlene, crying into my arms, so drunk she don't know what she's telling me. Well of course I whipped out the old Georgia Express and put it to her, just to kind of settle her down, like. Fuckin' A.

MARAN: Alright, maybe that was uncalled for. It's just... I guess I'm having a little trouble digesting all this...

DWAYNE: You can believe anything you like. I'm through with it.

MARAN: Are you sure you're telling me everything?

Benny the Antichrist, Page 157

DWAYNE: Sugar, that's one thing you are just going to have to wonder about.

MARAN: Did Charlene-

DWAYNE: Nuh-uh. Not another word out of me.

MARAN: You can't just drop this on me and expect-

DWAYNE: I told you everything I'm gonna tell you.

MARAN: Well, it's a lot to think about. Considering the source... *[a long pause]* OK, so what did you talk to Kimberly about?

DWAYNE: Oh yeah, I'm talking to Kimberly, two nights before all this happened? Getting all knotted up, like usual. Some things never change, huh? And she goes on and on and it's this and that and

KIMBERLY: Dwayne, I declare, but you can be so insensitive.

DWAYNE: Aw, Kim--

KIMBERLY: Dwayne, honey, I think we need to explore new options.

DWAYNE: Now listen here--

KIMBERLY: Dwayne, if you're going to commence to carry on that way, I can't see myself continuing to wear your ring.

DWAYNE: I can barely keep from tearing my hair out, she gets me so mad... Of course, she'd tell you I started it. Whatever... So now, what I was doing, I just called up suckers in Samoa or Cairo or some fucking place, whip down on them like a ghost from the sky on the magic phone. W-Kilroy, that's my handle. Most of the time you don't get nothing, but you just keep trying. Night before, I had this doink in Argentina convinced I was a tax-collector after his ass. I fed this poor beaner line after line, got him just about shitting his pants. Then I says "Congratulations, you've just been had by W-Kilroy," and hung up. In Spanish, of course. Can't have this poor guy jumping at his shadow for the rest of his life.

Benny the Antichrist, Page 158

So when we get to the phone, for once nobody's there. Usually people find out about them in about two minutes and you got a line round the block.

Dougie goes first. See, the way we work it is one of us makes the call and the rest sort of surround the booth. Persuade people from butting in. They'll try it if you let them. They see you're from the States and they think you don't know dick-all. Night before last I had some geezer rapping his cane on the door, till Kyle gives him one of his looks. He hobbles away, then turns around yelling, some dialect I can't make head or tail of, even though I learned a lot of weird Spanish from the ten years the old man was stationed in Guatemala. I don't know, maybe he thinks that's his personal phone. Maybe it is. Nothing would surprise me about this place.

We got nothing better on--the hostel is closed for the night. It just rained a little earlier and the air is fresh and warm. We've got a couple of bottles of *coñac* for company. So Schmidt reaches into his gym bag and takes out the football and we're heaving it around, little game of four corner under the moon.

The guys are taking their time, shooting the shit, even though they'll all be back in Pennsylvania tomorrow night. Three weeks they've done Spain, drunk a bunch of sangria and seen a bullfight. Monday morning they'll be in the back of the lecture hall, trying to read the playbook while some dried up old fruit rattles on about Shakespeare.

Not me. What have I got to go back there for? With my injury, I'm off the squad and I was only backup anyway. I've had it up to here with Kimberly and her bitching. She wants to break up long distance? Fine. Find another sucker for a fiance. I'm doing OK in school, real good if you don't count English. All fours in theory and practice. Show me a circuit board, man, and watch me go to town.

Benny the Antichrist, Page 159

But I've had it with university for the time being. Figure I'll stick around here and get some experience under my belt, like the old man is always saying. Though all he ever seems to put down there is sour mash. "Pour me a drink. And don't you give me that high and mighty look, goddammit. Hit ever occur to you, who's puttin' you through school?" "Well, Daddy, seems to me I'm on scholarship." "You think you're so smart, you li'l pissant. Just like your Mama, always after me to suck up for a promotion. Master Sergeant wan't good enough for her--hit had to be an officer or nothin'. And what then? You tell me that, huh? "I don't know, Daddy." "Yeah, some things you still **don't** know, after years of givin' me a hand full of gimme and a mouth full of much obliged. I'll tell you what then--that bitch wouldn't be happy till I was Chief of Staff. I told her--I don't never wanna be no candyass lieutenant or no chicken colonel, but--" "Aw, that's just crap." "What did you say, boy?" "You heard me--crap. Billy Thompson showed me the records. You been thrown out of Officer Training School twice for drunkenness." "You li'l shit. I'll learn you to give me some respect!" (*Dwayne picks up a bottle, smashes it and acts out a fight, which ends with him looking down at the floor.*) "That's it, old man! You and me are quits!" "Son, don't--" "Fuck off and die!" (*He turns away.*)

MARAN: Jesus.

DWAYNE: I worked on losing that Georgia accent, man. Nobody's ever going to call me a stupid you-all.

So now, I'm thinking maybe I'll head out to the coast, see if I can get a gig on one of those pirate stations. I hear they can always use a good engineer.

I sure was missing Kimberly, though.

Once Dougie gets on the phone we put the football away. Nobody

Benny the Antichrist, Page 160

feels much like talking. It's one of those summer nights, air soft and moist like baby breath. You can't hear crickets, like at home, but it's nice. Not a cloud in the sky. I'm looking at the stars, thinking about space. If you know what to look for you can see satellites, sometimes. Just real faint, but they go straight across, through all the silence and the planets and stars. Nothing gets in their way.

Then this fat, old drunk comes waddling up. He stinks a block away, garlic, dirt and tobacco sweat. Sees us waiting and for a minute it looks like he's going to be a good guy and wait his turn. Mannerly. One thing I'll say for the Spanish, they know their p's and q's. But this guy's really loaded and he decides he don't have to wait for us. He cuts loose on us in some accent I can't place, all z's and nasty gutturals, even though I heard a lot of weird Spanish from when my old man was stationed down in Guatemala. "One side, you gringo hoodlums! Can't a gentleman telephone his own daughter, without contending with a mob of rude, ignorant foreigners?" Dougie cuts a big one and tosses an empty bottle so it smashes on the cobblestones, close to the guy's feet. For someone whose Spanish is hardly up to ordering a taco, the dude can pick his spots. It don't faze the old guy, though: "Thugs like you stink up my home with your dirty money, ruining good girls reputations--"

I'm trying to calm the old guy down, all *por favores* and *con perdones*, but when he gets to the part about ruining reputations, I finally catch his eye and point up. He looks and I sucker-punch him in the gut. That stupid beret of his goes flying and he crumples like a soggy lunch bag.

MARAN: Dwayne!

DWAYNE: Look, I'm tellin' you what happened. Do you want to know, or not?

Benny the Antichrist, Page 161

MARAN: I'm not so sure.

DWAYNE: You're the one who's always going on about tellin' each other things. And then when I do--

MARAN: I didn't think you were going to tell me about hitting old people!

DWAYNE: You never done nothin' you're ashamed of?

MARAN: Of course I have, but--

DWAYNE: How come I never get to hear about it? All this confessin'--I guess it's a one-way street, huh?

MARAN: Well, let me ask you, since I'm not supposed to be making assumptions: **Are** you ashamed of hitting him?

DWAYNE: Honey, most days I'm ashamed of every breath I take...

MARAN: It's just... I'm trying to understand...

DWAYNE: What's to understand? I ever tell you about Schmidt?

MARAN: What's that got to do with--

DWAYNE: Schmidt was defensive team captain, even though everyone knew he'd never make the pro cut. Too small for his position, really, and too slow. He read plays well enough, but what Schmidt really had was heart. He just never stopped coming. Dog it with Schmidt, or do something cute and he'd hurt you. Didn't matter which side you were on, didn't matter if it was practice or game, he'd blindside you or clothesline you or leg whip you. Dirtiest, sneakiest player I ever saw, but he kept everyone honest. You had to play straight up and hard with Schmidt. Got so whenever somebody got hurt doin' something stupid, or burned 'cause they were doggin' it, even if he was nowhere near the play or even on the field, we'd say "Schmidt happens." Fuck up--Schmidt happens. Bad luck--you musta been doin'something--Schmidt happens. I was just the Schmidt comin' to that old man that night.

Benny the Antichrist, Page 162

MARAN: So it was out of your hands, eh? None of your responsibility...

DWAYNE: I never said that.

MARAN: Oh come on Dwayne, that's as much as what you did say... You know what bothers me, more than hearing about you sucker-punching people and being a general asshole abroad? I just want to know where it ends. Can you tell me that?

DWAYNE: Maran, have I ever raised my hand against you? Even when we've both been mad enough to spit? Have I?

MARAN: No, you never have or I'd be gone in an instant. It's not that... Tell me, where's Schmidt these days?

DWAYNE: Last I heard, he was doin' real well for himself in the oil business. Management.

MARAN: Why am I not surprised? Look Dwayne, much as I hate to say it, you're right sometimes. Lucy dumps on you. I get on your case, without thinking. People look at you and figure you're not worth talking to. And sometimes you have to defend yourself, the only way you know how, because no one else is going to. And it's not always pretty.

DWAYNE: That's what I'm--

MARAN: But you know what I see, when I look around at people taking over companies and throwing everyone out of work, people who want to pay me 60 cents on a man's dollar, people who send out armies to rape women as a matter of policy? Guys like you. Guys who figure they can never catch a break with everyone doing them dirt, with smartasses like me, so why even try being civilized? And every one of you, knotted up with pain, staggering under pressure coming down from above, coming at them from all sides and who jacks it up, all that pressure? Guys like you.

Benny the Antichrist, Page 163

DWAYNE: You got it all figured out, huh? Just us guys, fuckin' everything up...

MARAN: Of course women aren't innocent. We have to live in the world too. But we know something guys like you never seem to figure out--we know how to live with things we can't hit and we can't run from. We learn because we have to.

DWAYNE: Well, that's all fine and dandy--

MARAN: It's more than that--it's the only way this shit is ever going to stop, Dwayne. All this fighting and hurting--somebody's got to say "Enough. This is only making things worse." and live with it.

DWAYNE: I don't notice you puttin' up with much. Seems like every day, you're layin' into me for something or other.

MARAN: Women have to make their voices heard. Get used to it.

DWAYNE: Honey, whenever you start talkin' like this, I always want to check the closets and under the bed and stuff.

MARAN: I'm not even going to guess what that means.

DWAYNE: To see if I can find all those other women you claim to be speaking for. But you know, all I ever come up with is one rich girl with nice, expensive teeth and nice, expensive clothes, at a nice, expensive university.

MARAN: You really are a pig sometimes, you know that?

DWAYNE: I gotta say--you talk a good game. Sit and take it from your sister, 'cause she's protectin' you and Sisterhood is Powerful. Take it from your profs, 'cause they're so knowledgeable. Take it from anyone whose skin's darker than yours, 'cause they're oppressed already. And you don't raise your voice and you tell me to express my feelings, the nice feelings anyway, and you got me halfway shamed for wanting to give ol' Timothy what-for. And I just want to know, now that we're **expressin'** everything, what the hell is it you see in

Benny the Antichrist, Page 164

me, you bein' such a saint and all?

MARAN: About Tim, Dwayne, did you ever consider what it must be like to grow up small and unathletic, watching football heroes get all the girls, getting beaten up if one of them didn't like your looks? Put yourself in those shoes, for once. What would you do to a jock if you had him on your turf?

DWAYNE: Well, there's something to that, I guess. But like usual, you haven't answered my question...

MARAN: I never said I was a saint.

DWAYNE: And some of the time you ain't. Sometimes you laugh and you bitch and you get silly. Come down to the hard stuff, though, and all I get out of you is non-stop holiness.

MARAN: You think it's easy, trying to live up to what I want to be? Trying to speak up for myself and watching Lucille stop me with a look, because she knows, she **knows** she's right and watching stupid Timothy play you for a redneck fool and wanting your nose rubbed in it and hating myself for that and hating myself for wanting you to smash his crooked little teeth in and slap my sister silly while you're at it and always after you to tell me things I'm too scared to tell you and hating myself for that, you think it's easy?

DWAYNE: Aw, Maran, honey--

MARAN: Shut up. Tell me about Spain.

DWAYNE: You sure about--

MARAN: Spain. At the phone booth.

DWAYNE: Huh? Right--now where was I? Oh, yeah, the old guy, lying on the ground. He's moaning and I guess I hit him harder than I meant to. I try to help him up and apologize, but he's not having any. He pushes me away when he's halfway up. He's cursing a blue streak, Spanish and something else. Looks like he's getting ready to

Benny the Antichrist, Page 165

spit, but he thinks better of it.

He goes staggering off, still swearing, smelling even worse with a little puke on his shirt. Just rounds a blind corner and disappears.

A minute later, he's back, only this time he's got a couple of *Guardia Civil* in tow. Some days you just can't win for losing.

So Mr. Concerned Father goes through his number again. We're young rowdies threatening Spanish womanhood, assaulting leading citizens and on and on.

All the time he's yammering, I'm watching these two Guardias. I guess I've never really taken a good look at one before. You see the bullfighter hat, the boots and the submachine gun and you just tend to stop right there. But now I notice that their uniforms are really old and they don't fit that well. And these two are young--our age, if that. They look like a couple of tired kids dressed up for Halloween in grubby hand-me-downs. Except no kids should have these eyes. Old eyes, man. Eyes that see everybody else reaching in and getting some till there's practically nothing left. They look at us and our big, dumb American smiles and they're not fooled or on to us. They just don't care. They'd gun us down right here and now for a couple hours of shut-eye and a little better chow at breakfast.

The Leading Citizen gets to the end of his rap, but not before he's pulled in the Blessed Virgin, the Blood of Spain, drugs, murder and pollution. Even Kyle is starting to look a little worried.

These Guardias just stand there, fingering their guns and looking at us and the old man. Finally, one of them nods to the other. "Fuck off, you stupid old Basque," Well, the *Señor* starts screaming at them, calling them *madrileño* queers and I don't know what all else. They let him go on for a while, then one of them gives him a nudge with the gun barrel and he gets the idea. He scuttles off around the corner.

Benny the Antichrist, Page 166

One of the Guardias turns and looks at us again. He shrugs and smiles the kind of smile a cat would give you just before he clawed your arm to the bone. Then he nudges his buddy, who looks asleep on his feet. They amble off. Don't even wait for the golden handshake.

Aw, there ain't no point to this crap. I don't know why I'm wasting your time with this stupid, puppy-shit story. Wavin' a gun around like a macho white trash fool. I should just kill another bottle, take some sleeping pills, go somewheres and tie a plastic bag over my fuckin' moron head.

MARAN: **GODDAMMIT, DWAYNE, DON'T YOU CALL YOURSELF THAT!**

DWAYNE: What?

MARAN: **I SWEAR TO CHRIST, IF YOU SAY YOU'RE STUPID ONE MORE TIME, YOU WON'T HAVE TO KILL YOURSELF--I'LL COME OVER THERE AND DO IT FOR YOU!**

DWAYNE: Huh. Nice try, Maran--but you're going to have to study up on your corn pone. Look--I don't have nothin' more to say here--

MARAN: Dwayne, you remember me talking about about my film prof?

DWAYNE: The one who's so insightful and knowledgeable--

MARAN: He's a fucking idiot.

DWAYNE: Well now, you gave me the impression--

MARAN: This guy knows all there is to know about camera angles and jump cuts and embedded narratives and all that shit. But put him on a set--hell--put him on a crosswalk--and he can't get one foot in front of the other. What's worse is--he manages to screw everybody else up. He can't help it. He went from school to university to

Benny the Antichrist, Page 167

teaching in one shot. If he finds himself in a place without a podium, he panics.

DWAYNE: Now who's bein' harsh? Everybody has places they don't fit in--I came off like hammered shit over at your sister's.

MARAN: They had the knives out already. But this prof--it's worse than that. He doesn't have a body--I mean, he's got a body--but it's just a machine for carrying his head around. Sometimes, when you're playing or in the shower or sleeping, I just look at you. And everything about you--your skin, your muscles--is smarter, more graceful, more you--than my profs, than Tim or Lucille--than anyone I know. And I don't understand why you want to kill that.

DWAYNE: All that shit's cheap. That's just bein' 6'4", 'stead of 5'9", havin' a certain reaction time, hand-to-eye coordination. Plenty of guys work harder, deserve more. My cousin Jimmy--

MARAN: I don't give a rat's ass about him. It's you I care for. Dwayne, honey--I could listen to you, touch you, all my life. And I don't know why you have to get so crazy--so down on yourself and everything else. Tim and Lucille--

DWAYNE: Naw, they're right. It's a joke, baby. I's watchin' you at dinner, laughin' an' carryin' on with your sister over some literary allusion Tim batted over my head. Both of you, got those long necks that shine in the light, that don't nobody have without rubbin' 'em with fine cream that yo' mama gave you, same as her mama give her. An' me, I'm sittin' there tongue-tied, chokin' down food I can't even pronounce. And while you were laughing and didn't notice--I guess-- Lucy give me one of her fishy-eyed looks. And I knew she knew-- why's I even pretending I belonged there?

MARAN: Look, I'm sorry for tonight. I know Lucy comes off as cold. She's had to work like a dog, taking care of me and slaving away at school. She's maybe a bit over-protective. But she's really a decent person, at heart. If you two could just communicate--

DWAYNE: Communicate. Seems like nothin' I do is really communicating--

MARAN: Why are you making such a big thing about this?

DWAYNE: Communication is for you and Timothy and Lucille and everybody in your fucking faculty--

MARAN: It's just a word. Why--

DWAYNE: I did me some communicatin' tonight. You know how they say music is the universal language? Me 'n' them boys in the parking lot had us a sweet little jam session. I's down on one knee, watching that fist comin' for my eyes, the neon lights glitterin' off the keys stickin' out between that drunk's knuckles. I's still shakin' off the first punch, puke clawin' up like a squirrel in a drainpipe, everythin' all catawampus an' lit up like it's burnin', like I could see the tiny particles, the subatomic bullets the universe fires at us day in, day out--that fist was swingin' in like a boom an' I knew it weren't time to **talk** no more--it's time to **LOCK AND LOAD!** I grab that ol' boy's thumb an' twist 'er back till the socket give out an' the bone snap an' I haul myself up--playin' an arpeggio all over him an' the other one was comin' on--an' I let my boy drop--an' the other guy's gettin' ready to kick--an' I look at him--that trailer park trash--Georgia to the fuckin' arctic--we know each other--an' he stops--an' he turns- an' he runs. He didn't have no problem with my accent after all.

MARAN: Oh, Christ, Dwayne. What happened then?

DWAYNE: I came home and phoned you.

MARAN: Well it could have been a lot worse. You could have been really hurt. You could have hurt--you could have killed those men. Instead, you walked away. You got it out of your system.

Benny the Antichrist, Page 169

DWAYNE: It's not somethin' that's **in my system**. It's **me**. It's what I am. Those guys are alive 'cause one was smart enough to run. Sooner or later somebody's not going to get out my way fast enough. Or maybe I'll be just too damn full of murder to let him go. Or my gun'll be too close to hand. Or some stupid thing.

MARAN: At least you recognize that you need help.

DWAYNE: *(mimicking)* "At least you recognize that you need help". What am I 'sposed to do--check into some peckerwood support group? Fitzwilliamses come over on the prison ships--an' we never left. There ain't no other place for us. It's that or the grave--and I know which one I pick.

MARAN: So that's it, eh? Bat my head around like a ping-pong ball-- then shoot yourself anyway--is that right?

DWAYNE: I shouldn't have phoned you. I only did it 'cause I didn't have the stones, right off.

MARAN: But now you do. Now you've got the guts to point that gun at your head like a--what was your phrase?--"macho white trash fool"--and pull the trigger.

DWAYNE: Who fuckin' cares what I say?

MARAN: Nobody you respect, evidently.

DWAYNE: Respect don't enter into it.

MARAN: I guess not--since you don't have enough to keep a promise.

DWAYNE: What promise?

MARAN: Finish your story, Dwayne.

DWAYNE: Aw, that piece of horseshit--that don't go nowhere.

MARAN: Maybe not. But I'm holding you to it. Afterwards you can do what you like--I certainly can't stop you--kill yourself--pick a fight- -go join the fucking circus--but finish the story.

Benny the Antichrist, Page 170

DWAYNE: I don't even remember where I was at.

MARAN: The Guardia Civil had just sent the old man packing and walked away themselves.

DWAYNE: It's the same old dumbass Dwayne crap. It don't mean nothin'.

MARAN: Finish it, Dwayne.

DWAYNE: Goddam it... OK... Well, afterwards, the guys are hooting and hollering, doing high fives and all that shit. I don't know why, but I just have to phone Kimberly. The guys are going "Come in, W-Kil-ROY!" and "Wild, wild, wild W-KIL-roy!" and all that stuff I used to say, but I get them hushed up. There's half a bottle in the booth, but I don't want none just now.

 Her phone is ringing and ringing and I'm hoping that there is just a bit of magic in this phone here, that she's there on the end of all those relays and cables and it's a good connection. After I don't know how many rings the phone gets picked up. My Jesus luck, it's her mother.

K's MOTHER: Hello?

DWAYNE: Hello, Mrs. Michaels, it's Dwayne. Is Kimberly there?

 She takes a long time answering. Kimberly said her mom liked me but who can tell about that kind of stuff? The old man says he loves me when he's halfway between spifflicated and shitfaced. It's done me a world of good, let me tell you. The guys are yelling, "Pussy-whipped" "Izzums wonewy?" Kyle is down on his knees, with his big, stupid hands clasped up in front of his face.

K's MOTHER: Kimberly moved out a little while ago, Dwayne. I'm sorry. DWAYNE: Well. Next time you see her, could you please tell her that I said hi?

K's MOTHER: I'll do that, Dwayne. I hope you're having a good

Benny the Antichrist, Page 171

time over

there.

DWAYNE: Oh yeah, you bet. Just phoned to say that I've got a job here and all. Well, give her my best. Bye, now." I hang up...

WHOOEE! IT'S W-KILROY, WILD, WEIRD AND WONDERFUL ON THE WIRES, COMING AT YOU **DIRECT** FROM SPANISH HARLEM BY WAY OF THE IONOSPHERE AND THE MARIANNAS TRENCH AND HERE TO ASK THE MUSICAL QUESTION: HOW TIGHT IS YO' HEAD SCREWED ON?

The guys are hooting and screaming and trading high and low fives like they're a pack of bloods instead of a few stupid Yankee jocks. I close my eyes, spin around 3 times, and hold the phone way up in the air while I dial. The guys chant the numbers as I pull them out. I hope I get somebody first time. I'll mess with his head till he thinks the taxman, every lawyer in his douchebag little country and God Hisself are on his fucking case. He won't know whether to shit or go blind. *(takes a long swig on the bottle. The phone rings repeatedly, with an odd, old-fashioned sound, like that of a rural party line.)* I'm about to hang up-- *(sound of the phone being picked up on the other end. A small GIRL says greetings tentatively in some Semitic, African or Subcontinental language.)* DWAYNE: Usually when I get through to someone speaking a language I don't know, I whip a bit of CB slang on them, then a little Spanish. Then some pig-Latin and finally just start making the grossest sounds possible and call them names till they hang up. "Scuse me, honey. Is your mother there? Can I talk to her?"

GIRL: *(in her language)* I'm sorry, but I cannot understand what you are saying. Wait here--I will go get someone who can talk to you. *(in English)* You waiting here. *(puts the phone down. We hear her sandals as she*

Benny the Antichrist, Page 172

runs off, flies buzzing, a goat bleating in the distance.)

DWAYNE: She puts the phone down, not on anything, but dangling in midair. I can hear her sandals flop as she runs off. There's a bit of a breeze and the phone keeps bumping against something, scraping on it, rough, like against stucco. Flies buzzing and there's a goat, a little one, sniffing and muttering. The old man told me once about the nanny they kept, name of Wilbur, where he grew up. She was the only thing who flourished on that little speck of dirt farm. Funny, hearing Daddy come up with a word like "flourish". She came up with litter after litter, on nothing but what she could gnaw out of that hard red dirt. Even climbed the silk tree to get at the leaves and new branches, he said.

He took me there once, or where it was. Nothing there now but a trailer park by the river, bitty Travel-alls with sod squares so new you could still see the seams and already they looked half dead. It had just rained, hard, and there was dark red mud slumping out from beneath the jacklegs, trailers leaning all whopperjawed. One had fallen over on its side in a big red puddle like it was bleeding to death. A plane flew overhead and I wondered what it looked like up there, how far the red swollen river stained the ocean, if it ever turned blue. From space the whole of Georgia must have looked like a sucking chest wound.

Me, if I was up there, I wouldn't look down that much. No, I'd be watching the stars, checking out all the colours where there ain't nothing to get in the way. Quasars, planets, galaxies, stars every which colour. The light up there must be some intense, man. I bet you could even see into the ultraviolet and the infrared, up there. There's all kinds of space stuff that don't give out our kind of light at all, maybe more things like that than anything else. Dark matter, they

Benny the Antichrist, Page 173

call it. Maybe it's made out of neutrinos, so many of them that they make a difference, no matter how puny and shiftless they are. If there's as much as they think, it holds the universe together, makes sure it all don't keep flying apart. Everything is gone smash, scattering hell to smithereens, and the whole mess could go on forever, just getting farther and farther away, colder and colder. Sooner or later, though, that old invisible stuff is going to slow it all down, with gravity and all. And then, the stars and planets, it'll all come back, everything will be back just the way it was.

 Dark matter, maybe that's my new handle. 'Course that'll have some turkeys thinking I'm black. Fuck 'em--they can think what they like. *(Sounds of a small crowd coming towards the phone. Somebody picks it up. An OLDER WOMAN's voice, loud and querulous, in the same language as the GIRL:)*

O. WOMAN: Who is this? Is this Dillip? Dillip, it's your mother. My son, when are you coming home?

DWAYNE: Usually, this is my cue to start yelling "Ooga Booga to you too, Liverlips," and shit like that. Maybe I'm tired. All I say is "Excuse me, does someone there speak English?"

O. WOMAN: *(loudly, in her language, over crowd sounds and line static)* Dilip, you have to talk louder. The phone is bad here. Are you well? Can you send us money?

DWAYNE: For some reason I know that they can't hear me so well on their end. I'm sure she's telling me to speak up, even though I'd probably have a hard time understanding her even if I did speak her language, what with them all carrying on. "Is there someone there who can speak English?"

O. WOMAN: *(in her language, angry)* Have you become a rich European, that you will not speak in your own tongue? Very well, I

Benny the Antichrist, Page 174

will ask the foreign lady to talk to you. *(the phone is passed through a number of hands to a YOUNG WOMAN)*

Y. WOMAN: *(Scandinavian accent)* Hello? Dilip, can you hear me?

DWAYNE: Listen, ma'am, there's been a mistake, I'm not--

Y. WOMAN: Dilip, I'm afraid that I can barely make you out. The connection is very bad here. The people were surprised that the phone rung at all. The lines have been down for months. *(As they talk, the line gets more and more staticky)* My name *(static)* -esco worker for the area. The drought here has been *(static)* though I'm sure you've read about it." *(as the YOUNG WOMAN speaks, we hear the OLDER WOMAN talking to someone about her son, Dilip)*

DWAYNE: I can hear the old woman talking off to the side. She's chatting with someone about Dilip, saying something proud and happy. Then she speaks to the woman on the phone, telling her things she wants translated.

Y. WOMAN: "Sayid and Ali have gone to join the rebels. We have not heard from them in a long time. We think the government men may have taken Ali's little *(static)* died and the other is not well, either. Your mother *(static)* worried about him as well. Iqbal is very sick and had to quit school. Hafiz is married and has two little girls. Thank you for the money, but you should write us more often, even though you don't want to speak your own language. Your mother worries about you. Didn't your *(static)* language? The last time she heard from your father he was a guest-worker in Switzerland *(static)* alive? We haven't heard in so long. Why are you so proud? The government men were here three weeks ago. They took Mahmood. They are nothing but robbers. We need more money if Achmed is to *(static)* so proud? Why do you not come home? We need *(a long burst of extreme static)*"

Benny the Antichrist, Page 175

O. WOMAN: *(in her own language)* Dilip, my son, come home. Where is your father? Where are you? Don't forget us Dilip or we will die, Dilip! Why will you not speak to us? I love you, Dilip. Please come home! *(As she speaks the static gets worse and worse, till it cuts her voice off completely)*

DWAYNE: I stood there clenching the phone for I don't know how long. Finally I know that wherever they are, I'll never get them back. Dawn is coming up. Kyle is passed out against the side of the booth, snoring through the gap where his front teeth are missing, plate spit out on his chest. The other two are gone. The brandy still has a pull left in it. I don't want it and go to smash the bottle on the gray cobblestones. Instead, I leave it on the shelf in the booth and started walking towards American Express so I'd be first in line to get my checks cashed...

You still there, Maran?

MARAN: *(entering the the apartment doorway)* I'm here, Dwayne.

DWAYNE: *(gun in one hand, with the other makes a gesture that could either be entreating her to come closer or to stay away)* Well, there ain't much more to tell. I come home, by and by. Least, they tell me it's home. Couldn't prove it by me. My athletic scholarship was finished, but my grades were good, so I transferred over here. And I'm doing fine, they tell me.

Some nights, though, like tonight, it's like I'm not here. Or at least I'm not home--just standing there on that street corner, inside that old, gray city that'd kill me soon as look at me, but don't even care enough to try. I've got a phone in my hand and the signal is going way out where it's icy and bright and there ain't nothing to breathe. Then down in the dark, where the water is so cold and heavy it crushes you to nothing. I've got that phone in my hand and there

Benny the Antichrist, Page 176

ain't nothing but static. They say some of that hiss is the Big Bang, Creation itself, on the line. I don't know. Got nothing to do with me. No voices out there. Or maybe so many voices, can't nobody hear each other. But I've got that phone in my hand and I'm calling you, sugar, hoping you'll pick up and talk to me.

(She goes to him.)

The End

REMOTE CONTROL

Oh, hi! C'mon in, Bev.

Oh, nothing. Harry's out West on business, so I'm just watching some TV. Well, I'm not, not really. Not a real football fan, the way Harry is. But, you know, when he's gone, and I've got the remote, it's a different game. Everything's different, really. That's right, a lot of buttons. More than Harry ever uses, anyway. But you know how he is, had to have the top of the line. And he doesn't even know half the things it'll do.

Well, let's see, what can I show you... There! Have you ever seen that before? Yes, the announcer does sound sort of excited. He's probably never seen the players on both teams get in the same huddle. Well, let's just say it's my rules. I know, butts to die for. You know, I don't know - let's listen in. Now where's that button? I thought so: decorating tips. I guess we'd better let them out of the huddle - some of those boys have back problems. Well, I *like* having them all holding hands - makes them look more friendly.

Now let's see, what else can I show you?

Oh, now here's Harry's big favourite - Baywatch. Of course, he doesn't watch it like - this. You're right - putting parkas on everyone really changes things. Oh, wouldn't you know - Pamela's got hers off first. Now, I remember there was something I did last time Harry got up and made a snack before the show.

Ah, here it is - really gives it a different look, eh? Oh, just a little something that makes silicone glow green. Pam looks like something out of Chernobyl, doesn't she?

Oh, there's that Peter Mansbridge - what a stuffed shirt! I think I'll... You're right - he's a lot more fun when he sounds like Jose

Jimenez. You haven't lived till you've heard Dan Rather and all the rest of them doing Paul Lynde.

Well, I don't know. I mean, I've thought about it, but I wouldn't want to upset Harry. You know, he was a big Pat Robertson fan and when the reverend came out of the closet as a gay necrophiliac, it really got Harry all depressed.

I know, sometimes I fly off the handle.

Oh, look! There's Sylvester Stallone! Here, would you like to try something?

Oh, go ahead!

The End

THE DEEP CREW

Chapter One

You only get one shot, do not miss your chance to blow
This opportunity comes once in a lifetime yo
Mon-E scowled and switched off his cellphone's mp3 player. Like
he needed Eminem reminding him of that, bitching up an already
crappy morning. Involuntarily, he glanced at the screen. Yolanda had
called last night and Lo-Ball this morning. He grimaced and looked
away guiltily. Torn out of his usual cocoon of music, he looked
around, keeping his eyes moving New York fast, not lighting on
trouble. It was the usual morning mob, most of them going to the
sewage disposal plant like him, white and Asian faces pale with
missed sleep, scarved and down-coated against the chill. A knot of
Puerto Ricans shivering in jean jackets or leather. Blacks in every
phase of economics and fashion, Burberried, in rags, expensively
baggy hoodies and one dude in a fluorescent green poncho. A
wizened bag lady in layers of stained, frayed sweaters, chattering
endlessly to God on a busted cellphone. Every second head was gnat
buzzing with an I-Pod or Walkman, swaying with each lurch of the
bus. All of them like him a minute ago, minds anywhere but here, at
six in the foggy gray morning, wheezing and shambling toward a
huge, stinking compound in Jersey.
   The bus was crowded, as usual, but Mon-E had managed to score
himself a window seat by dumb luck. At least one thing was going
right. Winter had everything locked up, but not tight enough, not
nearly tight enough. He stared out at the sleet-gray crush of Sixth
Street traffic and willed everything to cease and desist. Shut up to the
dull stabbing of car horns, phlegmy throat-clearing of engines,

yipping of tires, bag lady yammering, just shut up. Lay off to the weight of a pot-boosted headache swelling behind his eyes, the grinding lock in the small of his back, sick heat in his gut. Stop, please stop to the way Ma looked this morning, the fear when she opened her eyes to a stranger, her son, shaking her shoulder gently.

She'd wet herself again last night. She didn't even smell the pot smoke on his breath and clothes as he cleaned and dried her, then fixed her breakfast. Not that this would have stopped him; stoned in the morning was the only way he'd been able to face the last few weeks. But he almost wished she'd wrinkle her nose and clout him the way she used to, just to know Ma, his Ma, was still somewhere in that stroke-frozen stranger's body.

He stared out the window, eyes unfocused. Usually when he was lucky enough to snag a window he'd visualize passing and shooting angles in the traffic, make all of the Number 81 route a giant, perilous basketball court. Today he just didn't have the energy. He hoped Ma was all right. Mrs Torres from the agency was supposed to be there by nine, but sometimes she was late. Jack and Kelly didn't send enough to afford full time care, which was really what Ma needed. The doctors had held up some hope of a recovery, but so far he hadn't seen any sign of it. She needed more and more attention, just getting through a day.

Eyelids at half-mast, he watched the fog drifting up out of the sewers and drains, letting his gaze wander, idly shaping faces and bodies out of the swirling tendrils of mist. Here the face of a teammate, there a dragon's wing, off in the distance a horseman... and that little cloud pouring out from the vent in a manhole cover seemed to be swirling faster than the others, thickening, hunching... somehow familiar... turning toward him...

Suddenly the mist shrugged itself into a squatting hag, her shriveled face half-hidden in thickets of iron-gray hair. She opened her hard-vacuum eyes and ravenous gape of a mouth. Raised and flexed clawed hands. And sprang straight at him, trailing cold mist.

His back spasmed as Mon-E jerked upright. Impossibly, the naked crone clung to the outside of his sleet-streaked window, scrawny arms straining, gray dugs swaying. She mouthed something at him, face alight with predatory glee. He couldn't move. She drew back a knotted fist...

And dissolved, a knot of smoke in the hard, cold wind.

Benny the Antichrist, Page 181

Abruptly Mon-E was aware of his surroundings again, the bus rumbling and wheezing, the subliminal buzz of earphones, the guy sitting next to him edging away warily, carefully not making eye contact. He exhaled a lungful of gasped air, tried to loosen his back. Looked around, ever so casually.

And there she was again, swathed in grimy, polyester rags, leering at him as she chattered into the busted cell phone. He heard her rasp "Did you think I'd let you go?" as she shoved the phone into her pocket and lurched toward him.

In one panicked moment he recognized her. Just as quickly his mind rejected that knowledge. His bowels turned to water. Like a frightened child, he closed his eyes. Then, furious, forced them open, clenching his fists.

She was gone. The bus had stopped. No longer caring how he looked, he stared wildly about, terrified that she'd be right behind or beside him. And caught a glimpse of a hunched figure, still nattering away on her old phone, just getting off at the back door.

*** *** ***

Reverend Talbot Holcombe tuned out Wilkins, his chief accountant, droning on about construction cost overruns at the Holcombe Judgment Centre and scowled out under heavy white brows at the gray slush and fog-ridden street as the limo inched its way through morning Manhattan traffic. Usually the aftermath of preaching a good sermon in New York relaxed him. It was as if he'd slapped the Whore of Babylon in her red mouth and made her acknowledge her Maker. Like sex without guilt. And the crowds were wonderful, so grateful that someone of his calibre would venture into this cesspool of Evil to save them. Revivals here really got him charged up.

As long as they weeded out any jokers, heathen or atheistic scum who might disrupt the show, of course. Lips pursed, he glanced at Ephraim Paulley, his security chief, slouched across from him. Behind that glassy stare and sardonic smile Paulley was probably asleep; he had that Special Forces trick of snoozing with his eyes open.

Perdition take the man. Nothing seemed to get to him. Everybody else in the car hopped to attention when Holcombe was around, his personal assistant Goodall, Wilkins, Rogers the driver, all on the alert for any danger or way to serve the Reverend. But Paulley dozed like a lizard on a wall, ready to move blindingly fast, but only if

Benny the Antichrist, Page 182

needed. He was good, Holcombe gave him that. But the day the Judgment Militia no longer needed Paulley's military and intel connections, he'd be gone.

Wilkins seemed to have asked something that needed an answer. Stalling, Holcombe asked him to repeat the last part, then interrupted him, saying "Let me give that some thought, Jimmy. I'll get back to you."

He knew he'd have to get the explanation all over again, but didn't really care. He stared back out the window into the mists drifting through the snarl of midtown traffic. He could see them drifting up from the manholes and sewers, in faint, almost subliminal flashes: a wincing face here, a claw there, here a silent, throttled scream, there a darting, bug-mandibled head, the damned and their demon tormentors.

The visions had been coming more and more frequently lately. He'd never told anyone about them. Or rather he had, but everyone thought it was a metaphor when a preacher said "I have had a vision." Something tent-show revivalists were supposed to say for drama's sake. As with so much else, he let them think what they liked. They had no idea, not even Abigail Goodall, who worshipped him. They had no clue what it felt like to stand at the pulpit in front of the lost multitudes, the lonely, the failed, the druggies, the sexually confused and tortured, the vast wounded, wicked human jungle of the City That Never Sleeps and to see the dreams and nightmares that roamed New York every waking moment, flashing in front of your eyes.

He'd felt it coming as he was driven to the stadium, past the Eternally Damned chanting rows of Abortion Simps, the flaunting, jeering drag queens, disloyal heathens and prowling investigative reporters. One of those, a woman cleverly tricked out in a decent church-goer's dress, had even tried to ask him an on-air question about Moab Ndele before Ephraim Paulley got to her.

None of them or their pathetic sinfulness mattered. To the roiling energy of the faithful, they were chaff in a great wind. Perhaps they even helped. Maybe they were the tiny but relentless scratch of doubt that brought forth the mighty, cleansing rage of the Believers.

He could feel it stirring even before he started to speak, while the gospel choir shouted and strutted through a punched-up version of "Onward Christian Soldiers".

Benny the Antichrist, Page 183

Every city's crowds had their own rhythm and temperament. Houston was quick to take a cue, but easily distracted and bored. Detroit was slow to coalesce but bloody-minded and intense. This was a real New York congregation, fast, erratic, hard to rein in, but sizzling with rage and loneliness. He could feel that energy put the fire in his feet, making him dance across the stage, light on his feet for such a big man. His voice thundered and broke just right. He could see the apparition stirring in little blue ectoplasmic flickers, formless just yet but growing in power, bleeding from the sweating foreheads of the mass, as New York raised its voice and thundered back at him, swooned in his hands, made itself his.

He had almost reached the climax, cueing the organ's slow, ponderous arpeggio, laden with doomy subsonics, while intoning "the infinite might, majesty, and terror of the omnipotent God shall be magnified upon them", when it came as if suddenly rounding a hidden corner, a mighty Angel with eyes of flame, towering over the top bleachers of the stadium and carrying a great sword.

He gazed up, smiling, speechless for once, not knowing if anyone in the audience could see the apparition and not caring. I have brought it on, he thought, the Terrible Judgment can begin and all the whores, the intellectuals and the unbelievers, all the pill-poppers and the liberals will be swept from this earth. He clenched his fist and the Angel raised its sword...

Then faded away, as if it had never been.

Somehow he finished the sermon, anticlimactically. The audience was tolerant and they hardly seemed to care. Their cheerfulness was ashes in his mouth. A moment ago he had felt them rise to his will, a mass clenched in a mighty fist. Now they were a slack-jawed bunch of sinners who'd sat through an evening's entertainment, had their vanities and fears tickled and were thinking about getting something to eat.

He had cut the autograph session and interviews afterwards short, saying he needed to do some private praying for a great cause, and returned to the hotel in a black mood. Sensing his displeasure, his entourage had been hushed then and today, not one of them wanting to risk his wrath. He'd barely noticed. Close, he had been so close. He could almost taste it--Judgment Day, the reckoning for the sinners and freethinkers of this wicked world--and it was his to bring to them. And where else should it begin but here, in the city that made

Benny the Antichrist, Page 184

Babylon look like a playground? And when, if not now? The signs were right and the Day of Days should be here, had to be here...

Even now he could feel it stirring in the very stones of this place. So near, yet out of reach... He stared out the window, biting his lip, straining for tantalizing glimpses of the Day of Wrath. He needed a sign that he, Talbot Holcombe, was to be the Instrument of the Great Cleansing. "For am I not thy worthy servant, O Lord?" he murmured.

Abruptly it appeared before him, above the honking, exhaust-fogged lines of traffic stretching from here to the airport: a great fist dangling a monstrous pair of balancing scales. It was so huge he had to bend down and tilt his head to see the top of it from the car window. He could see the sun glowing on the knuckles above the clouds. It blotted out the skyscrapers. In one brass bowl was the world. In the other, the flames surrounding something he couldn't make out, a coiling shadow with a red gleam of eyes... and then it blew away, like a cloud scattered by the wind out of the South.

But when Holcombe looked at the American flag on the limo's aerial he saw the wind was coming from the North.

He felt a tap on his shoulder and, startled, drew back from the window, still gaping vacantly. Paulley was looking at him knowingly and Holcombe suddenly realized the man knew or had guessed about his visions. Paulley held an envelope extended toward him. "Rev, I got a letter you might want to read," he said.

The Deep Crew
Chapter Two

Mon-E still wasn't feeling right when Eustace Bearclaws and a couple of other Deep Guys came for him that morning. He was trying to put his vision out of his mind, shying away from what it might mean. Carlson and he were mopping out one of the upper filter rooms, taking it slow. He had the phone cranked up on Run DMC and was grunting along with the rap, putting his own voice into those tough rhymes, juking on either side of the broom like Allan Iverson on a crossover dribble. He liked getting up here. It didn't smell so bad and his back didn't hurt so much when he was wasted. On breaks you could stand out on the fire escape and watch the sun set on Manhattan. He was going over a favorite memory, sinking the winning 3-pointer against Vanderbilt in the semifinal, when Carlson tapped him on the shoulder.

Carlson had a steady line of passable dope, the only reason Mon-E put up with him. Otherwise, he was a snotty Poli-Sci major from Rutgers who'd just read Leo Strauss and thought his mission in life was lecturing everybody about what Plato Really Meant. That, and to remind Mon-E that he Wasn't In Staten Island Any More. Carlson seemed to think he was somebody's inside source, a guy with juice, a Rabbi, instead of a chubby wonk hired a full two months before. "Walk This Way" was on and Mon-E wasn't letting nobody step on that. He had his head down, doing a Phillie shuffle when someone reached down and turned the disk off.

He spun, fists up. "Hey, yo! The fuck you think you messin' wit?" Behind Carlson, Bearclaws loomed like a boulder you could beat all day and never make a dent. Testosteroni stood off to one side, looking Mon-E over like a bad piece of meat. Ka-Chang was puffing away on one of his rollies, like always. He had his arm over Carlson's shoulder, leading him out the door, talking too low to hear over the filtration system's hiss and roar. Carlson's mouth opened, then

Benny the Antichrist, Page 186

slammed shut. He seemed to crumple in on himself, but not before a stabbing, envious glance at Mon-E.

Mon-E wondered why nobody ever got on Ka-Chang's case. Smoking wasn't allowed on government property. Everybody knew that. He even mentioned it to Lipinski, the foreman, once, just to see what kind of reaction he got. Lipinski looked uncomfortable and muttered something about the Deep Crew before hurrying off.

"Hey Eemie." said Testosteroni, "Sorry to rain on your private Rave and all, but we got something to ask you."

No one was allowed to call him Eemie but his Dad, which now meant no one. Mon-E looked the old greaser over, eyes travelling down the gray-streaked DA, purple silk shirt billowing over his windy gut above faded dungarees to his snakeskin half-boots. Where did you even get those now? He waited, filing it away.

"Thing is," Bearclaws said in his soft, raspy voice, "your dad, he… We all thought you should have the chance to join the Deep Guys. If you want. Nobody'll think less of you, you pass it up.

Since he was Eemie, then Eamon, then Mon-E, he'd been hearing about the Deep Crew, but always indirectly, things Mom muttered when she thought he wasn't listening or hissed late at night when she thought they were sleeping. Nervous jokes in the Union Hall or at family gatherings. He asked his Dad about it a couple of times but the old man put him off, saying he'd tell him when he was old enough. It was his older brother Kelly, home on compassionate leave when Dad was hooked up to the respirator and morphine drip, who finally gave him the 411. They'd killed most of a fifth of Jameson's when Mon-E casually mentioned that all the Deep Guys had been up there in the last two days. He watched his brother's face while he said this. Kelly snorted. "Listen, Eamon," he said, pouring another round. "All that Deep shit, it's all a buncha old workies who put way too much time in at a sewage plant and told each other a lot of fucked-up lies. End of story."

So his first inclination was to blow these guys off. He had his crew and he was only planning to be here long enough long enough to make a stake and get healthy for hoops. Dive deeper into this shithole, no thank you. It was bad enough he spent most of his time on the main level, where the stench of New York's bowels nearly knocked you flat every time you clocked in.

Benny the Antichrist, Page 187

Testosteroni said "This ain't our guy, Claws, even if he is Mick of Time's kid. He's just a gimpy little Wigger who don't wanna do nothing but get fried and pretend he's some kind of NBA star."

"Aw, give him a chance," said Ka-Chang. He had quick hands and he'd gotten one of Mon-E's discs out of his shoulder pack unnoticed. "Kurtis Blow: The kid's got a feel for tradition."

"Some tradition. And anyway, it ain't even his tradition."

"You should talk, Himmelfarb…"

"Keep ridin' me, Seth, just keep ridin' me…"

"Thing of it is," said Bearclaws, "You prolly heard a bunch of stuff, one way or the other, 'bout the Deep Guys. Lotta guys think it's all garbage. Sometimes I do too. But we thought we'd give you the chance.."

Just then Lipinski strode into the room, nearly tripping over Mon-E's mop pail in his rush. "Don't you guys ever give up?" he asked, staring up at Bearclaws uneasily. "Coughlin, no matter what these guys told you, you don't have to go with them. Just do your job and you gotta place here next summer, if you want it."

As soon as Lipinski said that, Eamon had a cold vision of his life, dancing gimpily with a mop in one hand to rap nobody listened to any more. He had to get out before that. But he had to stay here, at least for now, til he figured out if he could hack school without an athletic scholarship. If they'd take him. Besides, mortgage was due. It was time to bust a move, even it might be the wrong move.

"Yo, Claws man, you got a benefits package?"

Testosteroni smirked. "Kid hardly knows enough to wipe himself and he wants benefits."

"Why not?" asked Ka-Chang. "You and me, we'd been smart enough to ask when we was his age, maybe we coulda retired by now."

Bearclaws smiled, which was both scary and reassuring. "You really worried about benefits, Eamon?"

Mon-E grinned back at him, not giving up anything, but not too serious either.

"Yeah, Eamon, we've got a benefit package. And the first one is…" motioning Mon-E closer and bending down like a saguaro about to tell you a secret, "down there it don't stink like this."

By this time Lipinski had had enough. "All right, back to work, all of you. That especially means you, Bearclaws. Jesus, I ought to write you up."

Benny the Antichrist, Page 188

Ka-Chang glanced at him. "So what do you say, Mon-E? Wanna give the Bath a try?"

"Coughlin, if you know what's good for you, you'll stay right here. These guys are nothing but bullshit artists. You'll end up half-nuts, with a bone through your nose."

"Lipinski, you're fuckin' with the Deep Crew," said Bearclaws in that soft rasp. "Heap bad medicine."

*　*　*

It didn't look like much, just another government-green painted door, behind some pipes off to the side in a small, nondescript dark brick building on the river side of the compound. They called it the entrance to the Bath. Mon-E had heard Dad call it that once or twice too and never understood it. He'd often came home sweaty, when he did come home, his clothes musty with a strange ozone-y tang, gritty with oily, yellow dust.

Behind the door was a concrete landing and what looked a couple of miles of stairwell stretching down past where he could see. The lights seemed to flicker down there. There was a freight elevator with a couple of guys he didn't know coming out, but for some reason Bearclaws and the others headed for the stairs. Ka-Chang caught his glance. "Rite of passage," he said, like that explained anything.

All the way down, the guys did nothing but talk politics. Some of it was names he recognized, the mayor, the president, this or that commissioner. But there was a lot of stuff about which he had no clue. They had their shorts in a twist about something happening in Tajikistan, wherever that was. Testosteroni had some big opinion about a crime bill, what the Supreme Court was doing and how that was interacting with the budget, or something like that.

His old man and lady used to get into it, both of them registered Democrats and following ward politics, national politics, whatever. She was even shop steward at the factory, before she took sick. He remembered them sitting on the back stoop of a summer night, drinking ginger ale shandy, arguing this or that about the governor or the party or something, Mary Ellen McInearny laughing and giving as good as she got from her husband, Mick "O.T." Coughlin.

Mon-E stayed out of that shit. He was a player. Citizens got knotted about suckers on a ballot, but all he cared for was presidents in his wallet.

Every ten flights or so, the old guys would stop and take a breather and Mon-E would look around. He tried to be casual about

Benny the Antichrist, Page 189

it, keeping his face neutral so they couldn't tell how much the stairs were making his back ache. The doctors said he'd never play competitive b-ball again, but what did they know? Any day now, they'd come up with an operation that would put him back on the hardwood. He did a little stutter-step that sent a twinge right down to his toes. He winced and caught Testosteroni smirking at him. He glared back and looked away.

Most of the shaft had featureless concrete walls with the occasional steel door, but the pipes were different from the ones above, older, twistier. Some of them looked handmade. Others seemed so corroded it was hard to see what good they'd be, but they had been lovingly patched, relined and supported. They had strange looking symbols painted on them and valves and linkages that didn't seem to be there for any normal plumbing reason. On the sixth stop, or maybe the seventh, he realized that the somewhere along the way the concrete walls had given way to stone. Weird.

At least Bearclaws was right. It didn't smell like shit. What it did smell like he didn't know. Kind of like Dad when he came home late, but stronger, more complicated than dust. Incense, maybe, but different from the stuff they used in church. Sweat, the kind of funk sweat you got off a guy late in a fight when you both knew you had him beat. And something else, kind of sweet and strange... Bearclaws caught him wrinkling his nose once and gave him a hatchet-faced grin. It was like he'd passed some sort of test.

Then he tripped. Coming down the pipes got denser and more convoluted, went off at angles, even running along the sides of the stair well, like clinging vines. He could have sworn one of them struck at his foot like a snake. Ka-Chang caught him just before he bashed his head on the rail. Testosteroni looked back. "Watch your Irish ass, Eemie. You ain't in Staten no more."

That was just about enough. He vaulted over the well, from his flight to the next one lower, so he was two steps over Testosteroni. The pain when he landed shot up his spine like a jagged blade, but he didn't care. He grabbed the old greaser's shoulder and yanked him around. "Hey, Testosteroni or Himmelfarb or whatever the fuck your name is, all right? Every day I catch the bus, then the subway, then the bus again, with all the freaks and the uptown Eurotrash, all the Hermanos and Brooklyn humps like you. You think I need some decrepit fuckwit telling me I'm not in Staten no more? Guess again, dipstick. And the name is Mon-E to my friends and Eamon to you. Call me Eemie again an' I'm a fuck you up."

"Well, well," Testosteroni grinned, "sawed-off little Wigger's got a pair on him. Relax, Sunny Jim, I'm just yankin' your chain." He nodded to Bearclaws. "He's mean enough, anyway."

Just then a roaring came out of the hole. The men started, then listened intently, crowding around the stairwell. It didn't really sound like anything mechanical or electronic, more like a rhythmic animal bellow, with subsonics that set your bones aching.

"A lot of people scared and mad," Bearclaws said.

"And a few dead," added Ka-Chang.

"Something old uncovered, too." Testosteroni chimed in. "Ever notice how nothing gets Albie goin' like the old stuff?"

"It's the carrion smell."

As if by pre-arranged signal, Bearclaws swung his leg over the banister and grabbed onto a smooth pole in the stairwell centre that somehow Mon-E had never noticed. He nodded to Mon-E, said "You next," and slid down with an agility remarkable in a man half his size.

Mon-E didn't have to look over at Testosteroni to figure he had a challenging leer on his ugly puss. Ka-Chang ground out his rollie and got ready to brace him, but Mon-E nodded him off. He jumped up on the rail-always had good hops for a paddy-boy, they said. It hurt his back, but he kept his face still. Then he grabbed on, locked his legs and slid. He turned his head so they couldn't see his eyes were closed.

The Deep Crew
Chapter Three

How far he slid , he didn't know. It seemed like miles. The roaring didn't fade exactly, but somehow he seemed to get inside of it and the darkness, swimming in them rather than being pressed under them. The other guys' voices floated to him out of the blackness, often from far away, sometimes as if they were right beside him, talking shop peppered with names he knew and some he didn't: Jimmy-no-Jimmy, Rajiv, Big Belinda, Otto, Pearly June, Even Steven, Miguelito, The Other Igor, Captain Cheerful, Weasel Marie, Akbar the Plug. It was as if the names were an incantation, easing and prying him into some different here and now…

His body was loose but charged, limber, and his back had forgotten to be a nagging tyrant, punishing every step and turn. Somehow his hands were open, waist-high and he was loping when the basketball hit them, a bounce pass, hard and perfect. Spotlights followed his effortless pivot, dancing off the blond wood floor, sweat-slick team jerseys, the ref's whistle, the Plexiglas backboard and steel hoop. The crowd roared his name and he head-faked his man off his feet, dribbling right to left between his legs to shake the Vanderbilt power forward who tried to help out. The center waited for him, arms aloft, a great shadow in black and tan, between him and the basket. He leaped, every muscle commanding UP. The earth let him go and he soared, without thought or effort. At his zenith for a timeless moment, he saw it all, the dark orange pebbled ball whirling on the tip of his finger, his da and ma, young, whole, full of juice, laughing and waving their green banners in the faces of the drawn-faced, black and tan clad hordes. He caught sight of his reflection in the Plexiglas backboard, tall, square chinned, his muscles rippling, thick blond hair waving above his clear-skinned brow. Down below were his teammates and enemies, faces frozen in wordless prayer or curse. The O's of their mouths reminded him of something. He turned, casually, to the basket, his ball arm arcing down, gathering speed…

And was wrenched sickeningly out at the shoulder when something cannoned into his lumbar vertebrae, bursting them like soggy, rotten fruit. The floor swatted him like a great, peeved animal. He found himself twisted, mouth fouled with vomit and blood. When he could focus he found his hands, huge and bloodless, lying at odd angles in front of his eyes. He tried to lift them and groaned as they melted away in a plume of foul, gray blue smoke. Somehow, agonizingly, he heaved himself to a sitting position, He saw it all vanishing, the gym, the teams, all it of melting and collapsing in a dirty, choking fog, his ma and da shrinking and wrinkling, his own body bleeding away in vapor. None of it was real, he thought.

Then he felt himself grabbed and spun roughly, sending a jagged spike of pain up his spine. Above him stood a gloating dwarf with his own face, his thin red hair, nose pushed to one side, pale, acne-pitted skin, watery blue eye winking at him, bouncing the ball with chimpanzee clumsiness. The dwarf hobbled back and forth, obscenely parodying his game moves. Eamon struggled to keep the dwarf in sight, but the little man suddenly darted to one side. He felt another kick to his back, this one ripping right through him and the world went red, then black. He went numb, mercifully. Finally he risked opening his eyes…

…to find himself standing in an office that looked small because it was crowded with shelves and filing cabinets, standing in front of a scarred oak desk, while Bearclaws rummaged through the drawers on the other side. "Have a seat there, Eamon." He indicated a dusty green, government-issue leatherbacked chair. On and above his desk were pictures of him shaking hands or standing beside various dignitaries, a couple of mayors and senators, the governor and a lot Mon-E didn't recognize. Not all of them looked happy to be there. Some wore strange clothing and hats. "Thought you'd gone to sleep or something."

Mon-E sat down before he fell down. Somehow all the questions he had were packed together so tight he couldn't speak. He could still hear that roaring, the audible sound faint through the office walls, but the subsonics were like somebody jabbing him in his herniated disc. There was a barbed trident leaning up against one of the filing cabinets. As he watched, green sparks jumped from one tine to the other. He shook his head.

Benny the Antichrist, Page 193

Bearclaws found what he was looking for. It looked like the usual stack of papers you had to go through to get a government job, except a few of them were on strange, yellowish paper and looked like they'd been handwritten. He tossed them across the desk. "Look them over there, Eamon, before you sign. There's some kind of special provisions there, so make sure you ask me about anything that you don't understand. Hey, listen, that's going to take you a while. You want a cup of coffee? Cafeteria's two doors down, your left. Here's ten. Bring me a double double 'n'a cinnamon bun. Get a bun for yourself, you want."

Mon-E stood up, then sat down again. "Yo Bearclaws, what the hell is this place?"

Bearclaws's grin was a sudden fissure splitting a rock slab. "You know, Mon-E, I was beginning to think you were too cool to ever ask. It's just another part of the sewage treatment plant. Kinda." He reached up for something on one of the top shelves. When he laid it on the desk, Mon-E could see it was scale model of a collection of rooms, one big one and a bunch of smaller, with various tanks and platforms and odd-looking machinery, shot through and ringed round in a maze of pipes.

"What's the big deal, then?"

"You wanna open that blind," he pointed to a dark green piece of canvas over Mon-E's shoulder, "and I'll show you."

The blind was on stiff, new springs that seemed as though they'd barely been used. Underneath was a dark blanket tacked over something. "That too," said Bearclaws.

When he got the blanket off he was looking out a large picture window over the Hudson to Manhattan. They looked closer than they usually did from the sewage plant. "Hey, wait a minute," he said, frowning at Bearclaws. "We must be miles underground here."

"Round here, in the Bathostratum, distance and direction are kind of, um, subjective."

"Subjective, huh? So, OK, we're lookin' at New York. So what?" He glanced back, then really stared at the window. There was something off about the view but he couldn't figure out what. It was a cloudy day. He could see a garbage scow and edge of the Statue of Liberty. Traffic on the bridge looked light.

"Eamon, you ever stop to think just how many people are in all of those skyscrapers? And how many down on the sidewalks and streets below? And in the subways and the sewers and comin' in for the

Benny the Antichrist, Page 194

night shift and arriving from La Guardia or on the turnpike. And all of them wanting a thousand things and scared of a million things and dreaming and scheming and schmoozing and getting stoned. Sitting on committees while they're wondering how're the kids, is the wife having an affair, should I go out with that guy in Accounting tonight. Or putting in hours in sweatshops, while their backs ache and their bellies rumble and they have to tell themselves stories in their own languages just to get through another day.

"D'ja ever ask yourself, where does it all go? When a crackhead whore scores a pipe, all the crawling misery she was feeling just a minute ago, what happens to that? When some artist makes something she's always wanted to make, without knowing it, what becomes of that feeling? When some stockbroker yuppie scores big, when an old lady in the subway sees a shadow behind her at night, when everybody jumps up and cheers in Yankee Stadium, when we're all of us sleeping and dreaming, or not sleeping and fuckin' or sweatin' out the shakes, what happens to all that fear, rage, happiness, all that stuff? What happens? It ends up here, is what." He waved at the scale model on the edge of the desk. It must have had a hidden switch somewhere, because it seemed to have little things moving in it. It was hard to focus on.

"Yo, you're tellin' me feelings are like real stuff, that you can put in a pipe, like water or shit? That's fucked up." There was definitely something weird about the window. For one thing the perspective seemed to have changed, ever so slightly, since the last time he looked at it. And there was something about the bridge....

"Fucked up or not, that's the way it is here."

"How come you can't see them or smell them or nothing?"

"Work here long enough and you do see them. Some people do it, even on the outside." Bearclaws looked at him closely. "You know, Eamon, I'm pretty sure you know exactly what I mean."

Mon-E definitely wasn't going into what happened this morning, not here, not now. He grinned, weakly. "So, like, you Deep Guys can read minds and the future and shit? That's ill." He hummed a lame impression of some creepy theremin music and wiggled his hands on either side of his face.

"Naw, seeing it ain't the same as knowing what it means. And ya don't see them that often, up above. Mostly, people are pretty good containers. But when you got stacks and stacks of people, and money and fear and politics—

Benny the Antichrist, Page 195

Just then someone rapped on the door and Bearclaws yelled "Yeah?"

Ka Chang pushed the door open. He was standing at the top of a flight of steel stairs with a small, short-haired, hard-looking woman Mon-E recognized from the funeral as Weasel Marie. Ka-Chang had on coveralls, but Marie was dressed for the street, plaid shirt, black straight-leg jeans, Doc Martens. Standard downtown dyke uniform, but for the halberd she had leaning on her shoulder. Behind them, Mon-E could see down into a vast space, filled with tanks and pipes. A small knot of people stood around one of the largest tanks, talking, taking readings, opening and closing valves. Out of the corner of his eye he thought he saw vague shapes flicker down a pipe.

Ka Chang said "Shift change coming up, boss and Marie's already into heavy overtime. She's gotta go."

"You really gotta, Marie?"

"I hate to leave y'all short-handed," Marie drawled in a Texas contralto, "but my sister's poorly and I need to see to her and her li'l girl."

"Yeah, yeah, you're right. You take care, Weasel."

"Will do, 'Claws. Say, aren't you Mick of Time's boy?"

"How come everybody calls him that? I thought he was OT 'cause of all the overtime he put in."

"Maybe later, he was. He was OT because he saved our butts. You might even see where he did it. You're the right size, anyway. And you look like you know the Count."

"Count who?"

"The Count of your steps. It's--Aw, shit," she muttered, looking at her watch, "I got to skeedaddle. I forgot I need to get my niece to daycare. Y'all have yourself a nice day now, Eamon. Don't let yourself get spooked and you should do finc..."

"Who've we got to go inside?" Bearclaws asked Ka Chang, as Marie strode away.

"Well, Pearly June & Testy, of course..."

"I mean for lead hand."

"Just Even Steven."

"Jeez, he's way overdue for rotation. Ain't Akbar back yet?"

"Still down with the flu."

"What about Captain Cheerful?"

"Last anyone heard, Jerry'd been drunk since Friday and wasn't showin' any signs of slowin' down."

"Damn it. Well, tell Steve to be ready to suit up. I got a feeling this is a bad one, the way Albie's carrying on. Listen, Eamon, you sit down and read those papers and I'll get the coffee. Way things are going, you might see some action on your first shift."

While Bearclaws was out Mon-E started reading the contract, which was phrased in Latinate legalese and kept referring to "the postulant". He asked Bearclaws about that when he got back with the coffee.

"The postulant is you, Eamon."

"Why come they don't be sayin' so?"

Bearclaws sighed. "Lookit, Eamon, not that it's my business, but I happen to know you went to Sacred Heart Collegiate, for which your Dad shelled out ten thousand beans a year. Any black kids you're likely to know had to learn that ghetto stuff from MTV, same as you, OK? So the gangbanger stuff, on you it's old already. Why come they don't be saying so because around here you aren't on full till you've been through your first backup. Some make it, some don't. Till we know, you're just a postulant.

"And what did Weasel Marie mean by the Count of your steps?"

"We'll get to that later. What you need to know, for now, is this: You can't tell anyone about this. You really can't. Not that you'd ever want to, 'cause they'd think you were nuts. Other than that, you start at 97 cents an hour over and above what you're making now, plus 50 for nights and evenings. Full medical and dental. Sound good?"

"Sure."

"OK, sign here… and here… here too. Now where did I put that…" Bearclaws groped in his desk, setting various items out while he searched for something. One was a jar full of cloudy, scummed-over water labeled Ganges. Another was a singed bundle of grass. "Here we go…" He pulled out a squat metal thermos and unscrewed it, dipping in a stick Eamon only recognized as an aspergillum when the splash of holy water hit his face as Bearclaws muttered something that really didn't sound like Latin. All of the sudden his jaw cramped up, but loosened immediately when he swallowed.

Just then the rhythmic roaring started again, louder than ever. There was something piteous, but ferocious, in the sound, like the dying screams of an ogre. Bearclaws listened intently. He shook his head. "Albie's startin' to repeat himself." He pointed to an old fridge in the corner, stacked high with files on top and with what looked

Benny the Antichrist, Page 197

golden Sanskrit letters painted in chipped paint on the door. "There's a package from the deli in there, kid. You want to bring it out?"

When Eamon had fetched out a large, kraft paper-wrapped bundle out from behind various lunch bags and a watermelon turning into a science project, Bearclaws looked up from his paperwork and nodded. "You see that tank, the great big blue one?" Nodding out the shopfloor window. "Yeah? Hang a right there and take this to Albie. He'll need to get to know you before you work here. Oh, and cover up the window."

The window looked fine now. Eamon had a vague recollection of an old-looking bridge being somewhere it shouldn't have been, but he decided he must have been confused. This had been a really freaky day.

"Hey Bearclaws, how come you don't leave it uncovered? It lets in the light and it looks, you know, nice."

"Nice, huh? Mon-E, take a look, down there in the water. What do you see?"

"There's, like, a sailing ship. They havin' a regatta or something?"

"That ain't a yacht. That's… Well, what do you know? You got lucky, your first day. Maybe. When you see the Half Moon, something's gonna happen."

"Henry Hudson's ship? Cool."

"You know, Eamon, you're full of surprises. I never would have figured you for someone who stayed awake in History class. Sometimes it's birchbark canoes, sometimes old clippers and steamers. Sometimes it's all mixed up. One guy swears he saw Betty Boop and King Kong. Lotta times there's nothin' out there or things I don't have any names for. Now take a look at all the buildings. Off to the left there. You see those two?"

"Those two? They're… oh, Jesus."

"Twenty years ago someone saw the planes hit. He didn't think much of it, because a lot of things you see there don't happen. Since it did happen nobody wants to look at them any more."

The Deep Crew
Chapter Four

When he turned right at the blue tank, someone called out to him. It was Ka-Chang. He was seated at a small desk on a platform near the top of the sky blue tank, filling out some kind of form. He wore industrial strength earphones he pulled off as Mon-E climbed the steel stairs. "About time Claws sent you over. I was beginning to think he'd let Albie howl all night." Nodding toward the package. "He likes it better when you unwrap it."

The package proved to be a head-sized mass of chopped liver. Ka-Chang sniffed it critically. "Startin' to go, just the way he likes it. OK, Eamon, let's get you checked out." He spun the wheel of a massive steel vault door set in the side of the tank. It swung slowly ajar, then suddenly crashed open as a huge, scaly snout jabbed out, opened a vast mouth full of six inch teeth and loosed a roar that was like being punched in the kidneys. The alligator was a dull white, with an oak trunk throat that filled the doorway. He must have been a lot smaller when they got him in there, Mon-E thought. Baleful red eyes fixed on him.

"Throw him the liver."

Albie snagged the nervously overthrown toss: a shortstop pulling in a pop fly. He inhaled the liver, then jerked back into the darkness like a mouse streaking into his hole. A thunderous splash spattered them both from the knees up.

A huge sigh seemed to rush through the room, as if the abrupt quiet had hoisted a weight off everything. Talk radio jabbered thinly somewhere. Beneath them a pump shuddered to life and Mon-E realized this was the first time he'd heard anything actually hydraulic in the Bathostratum.

Ka-Chang stepped through the doorway, into the darkness. He turned to Mon-E. "C'mon in. He isn't hungry now." He winked. "Well, not very."

"You're sure about that?"

Benny the Antichrist, Page 199

"Would I be in here if I wasn't?"

"Aw, man…"

"Part of the job, Eamon. Step in. Your dad did."

"OK, but this sucks…"

Once the door was closed and his eyes adjusted, Eamon saw that he and Ka-Chang were standing on an O-shaped grillwork platform six feet over a deep, dark pool. Down below, Albie ponderously looped the loop, over and over, great tail churning, desk-sized head occasionally slapping the surface with a meaty whack. He glowed faintly, greenish white. The air smelled oddly fresh and ozone-y, like the time Dad took them up to Cape Cod.

"So what's supposed to happen now?" he whispered.

In a normal voice, Ka-Chang answered, "That's up to Albie." That didn't sound good, Mon-E thought, but Ka-Chang seemed unconcerned, expertly rolling a cig and lighting up as he put one foot up on the low railing. "He's doing his Chopped Liver Boogie right now. It'll take him a few minutes to focus."

"I thought albino alligators in the sewer were one of those urban myths."

"Eamon, you saw the window, right? Bearclaws always shows new guys the window. What do you think we deal with in here? Of course he's an urban myth.

"Thing about myths is this: People believe 'em. Explain 'em away with logic, make fun of them, do any goddam thing you want. It doesn't matter. People believe them, till they're ready to believe something else. And that's what we're here to deal with."

"So you keep all the weird shit people believe in down here?"

"Naw, we don't keep it or we'd be all the way backed up in no time and the whole city'd be going crazy. Well, crazier, anyway. We're talkin' New York, after all. What we try to do is detoxify it, break it down and send the energy back where it'll do some good."

"If you don't keep it around, what're you guys doing with an albino alligator?"

"Some things it's better to make your peace with. For some reason, the idea of gators in the sewer is something New Yorkers really like. My theory is you've gotta be so cutthroat, so pushy just to get by here, everybody's sure they're going to be bitten in the ass by something or someone they flushed down the toilet. Whatever. Anyway, in the old days, they'd get alligators here like conventioneers from Milwaukee. Thousands of 'em and not half dangerous, neither.

Benny the Antichrist, Page 200

So finally somebody gets the idea, why not consolidate? Instead of a buncha mean little fuckers crawling out the pipes every time you turn around, put that energy in, like, a psychic capacitor and make one king-hell bull gator. That's Albie. He's worked out good, all things considered. Uh oh, here we go."

Eamon glanced down, noticing for the first time that the tank was shallower on the edges than the middle. Before he could figure out what this meant, the pool erupted as Albie thunderously launched himself out of the water, planting a massive, scaly foot on either side of him. Metal groaned as the platform tilted under the reptile's weight. He barely caught himself with a foot on the lowest rail before he smacked right into the dripping, massive head. He was trapped, face inches from a yard of white, snaggletoothed jaw. He could see faint concentric rings in each hand-sized scale. Like growth rings on a stump, he thought ludicrously.

"Just keep still," Ka-Chang ordered, unnecessarily. "He just wants to check you out. He ain't ate anybody yet. Well, one guy, but he had it coming."

Albie did seem to be inquisitive. The alligator sniffed Eamon over thoroughly, the breath on the indraw so powerful he could feel it pulling the small hairs on the back of his hands, paying particular attention to armpits and crotch. It was like being investigated by a gigantic, not-unfriendly, but business-like dog, but for the red, slanted eyes. It was hard to look at those eyes and even harder to look away. They beamed with ancient, predatory hilarity.

At length Albie seemed to decide something. He drew his head back, the skin of his throat bunching in thick folds, like a heron about to spear a frog. Slowly the great jaws gaped open. His breath was the stench of a mass grave. Eamon closed his eyes. Into your hands, O Lord, I commend my spirit...

He shuddered when the cold, smooth tongue brushed his face, daintily tickling his ear. He opened his eyes just as Albie bellowed, a seismic roar that felt like it would crack his skull. The giant toppled back into the pool, soaking and deafening him with the impact.

Ka-Chang shouldered open the heavy vault door, dragging Eamon out by main force and heaving him onto a chair in front of the desk. Eamon was dazed, as if he'd been worked over with a sap, bruised in places he'd never known he had. His fingers closed nervelessly round the bottle Ka-Chang shoved in his hand. He took a gulp and nearly retched up his lunch. Straight red pepper vodka, like fire down his throat. His eyes watered as his chest was wracked by deep, rasping coughs. Down in the tank, the gator roared, over and over, a rhythm of slow, heavy blows.

When he could finally sit up straight, he glared at Ka-Chang lounging behind the desk, who shrugged. "Sorry, kid. You were in the tank a long time and Albie sucks the juice right out of people. Had to put you right in a hurry. OK, let's get some coffee and lunch and you can change into some dry clothes. We don't have to listen to Albie all night to figure out there's something new in the mix."

"Can't you just give him some more chopped liver?"

"Well, thing is, Albie don't really eat all that much. He remembers eating, but that's not what keeps him going. The liver is mostly ritual."

They were halfway down the steel stairs when they were intercepted by a tall, Middle Eastern-looking man with a heavy mustache. "Bearclaws said to tell you we're way over the limit. All the floor staff are on standby."

"I figured," Ka-Chang groaned, resignedly, nodding at a pipe valve which slowly leaked something blue and luminous. When Mon-E glanced that way, the puddle seemed to be forming itself into an old-fashioned woman's lace-up shoe. He rubbed his eyes and it was only a puddle, Another glance and it was a shoe again, this time with the beginnings of a stockinged leg coming out of it. "Shit," Ka-Chang said, "and me with Knicks tickets, too."

"Knicks? I'll buy them off you, you want."

"Thanks, Haddad. Hey, meet Eamon, our new guy. He just met Albie."

"Yeah, he's got that wet, shell-shocked look. How'd it go, postulant?"

With an effort, Eamon pulled his attention away from the blue, glowing substance, which was now undeniably a woman's leg, rapidly becoming swathed in petticoats and an ankle-length skirt. He suddenly realized he had no idea of how it had gone.

Ka-Chang rescued him. "Guess who got licked?"

"Licked, huh?" Haddad gave a low whistle. "That hasn't happened in a long time."

"Not since his Dad."

"I thought you looked familiar. Hey, I saw that championship game you played against Vanderbilt. Too bad that punk fouled you at the end. You'd've won, otherwise. That jerk shouldn't ever be allowed to play again, what he done to your career."

Pain lanced through the small of Eamon's back, into his head, legs and arms, as if he were nothing but a circuit of agony. Just managing to grab a steel pillar before he fell, he was violently sick. The world went gray and dim. He was vaguely conscious of being lifted up before his eyes rolled up in their sockets and everything went away.

* * *

He woke to find himself lying on a cot in a dimly lit room. A woman's cigarette baritone said "He's awake." Then, "Here you go, honey." Looking worried, Ka-Chang helped him sit up and a redhaired, scarfaced woman pressed a glass into his hand.

Warily, he took a sip. It was just water. Suddenly, he was enormously thirsty. He started to gulp it down, but the woman gently drew the glass away. "Easy, guy. We don't want you to choke, on top of everything."

As he slowly drained the glass, he realized he was in his skivvies, lying under a thick comforter. His back still hurt, but he was warm and dry. The woman watched him as he drank. She seemed to be in her fifties, with big red hair going white at the edges. A thick scar crossed her face diagonally, from her left temple to her right jaw. She stood to pour him another and he realized she had to be at least 6'2".

Ka-Chang cleared his throat. "So what was it that never happened, Mon-E?"

"What?"

"That's what you've been saying for the last ten minutes: It never happened, it never happened. It seemed like a big deal to you."

"Oh, the game that guy, Haddad, was talking about. Ka-Chang, we won that game. Nobody fouled me before I shot. I hurt my back a few weeks later, in practice. Only…"

"Only?"

"Only when we were coming down here and I was sliding on that pipe… or whatever it was that was happening… I had this dream. And it was so real and everything happened just like Haddad said. And here he goes and says he saw that game I only just now dreamed about. What the hell is this place anyway?"

"Eamon, you deserve some answers. But first you need to get dressed and—you got a fresh pot on, Belinda?"

"Comin' up," Belinda affirmed.

"So put these on," he tossed over some dark green coveralls, clean and pressed, "and we'll have a cup of joe and talk things over."

It was short, though painful, limping walk down a hall to the small cafeteria, which was deserted but for the three of them. He sat gingerly down at a formica-topped table and Big Belinda poured them all mugs of the most delicious-smelling coffee he had ever had. He forced himself to slow down enough to put some cream from a thick, green earthenware pitcher and took a sip. If possible, it tasted even better than it smelled. He sighed as warmth billowed in a slow wave through his body and suddenly realized that this was the first time he'd relaxed since sweeping out the filter room with Carlson, an age ago in a different world.

Ka-Chang sipped his black and smiled. "Superb, as always, Belinda. And would I be right in thinking you've got a batch of cinnamon buns in the oven?"

"They'll be ready in two minutes."

"My day is already better. Now, Eamon, how does a guy you've just met come to think he saw something happen in a dream you just had? By the way, poor Haddad feels terrible about this. Everybody here knows he's a triple Smith and makes allowances. He just forgot that having a dad in the Bath doesn't make you any less of a new guy."

"Jeez, there you go again. Every time anyone here opens their mouth, they say something that doesn't make sense. What's that mean, a triple Smith?"

"First things first. Here's the deal: Up on the surface, you got your Cause and you got your Effect. They're connected but it's like one of those ballroom dances they put you through in Sacred Heart. Hands above the waist and the teacher better be able to get one of those little rulers between them. Cause leads, Effect follows, every single time, cha cha cha. You with me?"

"Yeah, OK, so?"

"Down in the Bath, short for Bathostratum, deep layer, you got things that might be Cause or Effect, depending, and they do the dirty boogie, when they aren't tangoing or breakdancing. So down here, when you have what we call a Going Under Dream, which is what happened with you, there's a chance somebody, especially a Smith, will pick up on it. If it's powerful enough, there's a chance it happens, for real, up there."

"Wait a minute. Because I dreamed it down here, you mean I actually might have lost that game? That's crazy. That can't be right!"

"It happens. Sometimes. It's hard to say."

"But thousands of people saw us win. The guys on the team know we won."

"And down here you ran into a guy who remembers you losing, just the way you dreamed it. Who's to say everyone doesn't remember it like that now? Maybe it was supposed to be like that, all along."

"That's totally crazy. And this could all be happening because this Smith guy said so? No way can this be happening. It isn't fair. And anyway, I thought you said his name was Haddad."

"Haddad means smith, in Arabic. Listen, you hungry? This is gonna take a while and we might as well get some lunch, huh?"

It came to him that not only was he ravenously hungry, but that somehow his back didn't hurt, for the first time in a long time. "Sure."

Eamon had just tucked into the best Reuben he'd ever had in his life, when Ka-Chang resumed his explanation. "OK, the Smiths. Mon-E, where do you think we are?"

This didn't seem to be a rhetorical question. He waited while Eamon swallowed his mouthful and took a bite of crisp, sour dill pickle.

"We're down in the Deep Level or whatever you call it."

"We are? Down where? How many stairs did we go down? How long did you slide on that fireman's pole? Is there really any reason to put sewage disposal, any kind of sewage disposal, down deeper than the deepest mine?"

"Well, it's like Bearclaws said, it's subjective."

"There you go. Before we got out of the main tank room, I saw you watching a leak from one of the pipes. What'd you see?"

"Nothing."

"Didn't look like nothing, the way you kept peeking at it."

"OK, it looked… it kind of looked like part of a ghost. Or something. It was hard to see."

"It's not so hard to see now. I can guarantee you that. What'd it look like?"

"Kind of like a lady's leg in old fashioned clothes."

Ka-Chang glanced at Belinda, who was cleaning the grill. She nodded.

Benny the Antichrist, Page 205

"Belinda's been telling all the new guys for months to get ready for this. They demolished an old mansion in the west eighties to put up some yuppie stack. Nothing much for us, no murders or major mojo hanging on there. Maybe a few opiated, turn-of-the-century ghosts, but they're kind of fun, compared to some of the stuff we get here. But the grounds, that's another story. Turns out there's a whole, undocumented slaves' graveyard on the grounds. The builders tried to keep it quiet, which made it worse. I hate unhallowed grave stuff. That shit just keeps on comin' and hangs around forever."

Mon-E looked questioningly at Belinda. She winked, which wrinkled her scar unsettlingly. He looked away.

Ka-Chang said, "Belinda's a Smith. In fact she's The Smith."

Belinda said "Was, Seth, was. Now I'm just the lady who runs the lunchroom."

"See, Eamon, all that stuff out there, the pipes, the tanks, the gauges, the Smiths make it for us. Right down here, in the workshops, and it don't look anything to them like what it looks like to us. Fixing it to look like normal gear is to make it possible for working stiffs like you and me to deal with this shit. Cause believe you me, if you had to deal with all the pure psychic energy running through here, even when it's quiet, you'd go crazy as, well, a Smith." Belinda stuck her tongue out at him. Then she cut off a couple of warm cinnamon buns, sliced them in half, buttered them generously and set them down in front of them.

Biting into the fragrant, golden sweetness, Eamon realized he felt as good as he had in a long, long time. These people might be bugfuck crazy, but they eat like kings, he thought.

"OK," he allowed, his mouth still half full of cinnamon bun, "so, there's like these Smiths. How can anyone be a triple Smith?"

"Well, some people work as Smiths, which by the way is the world's most popular name, because everyone in the village knew that the smith was the Man, day-to-day magic-wise. The old guys used to say smiths and shamans were hatched in the same nest. Their names can be whatever, as long as they got the talent for it. But it seems to work better if their name is Smith, or something equivalent. Don't ask me why, it just does. That's why we got Schmidts, Herreras, Forgerons, Kovalevs and every other jeezly kind of Smith working here. So someone who works as a Smith and his name's Smith, that's a double Smith. A guy like Haddad, whose Mom was named Kovacs, or Smith in Hungarian, he's a triple Smith. And Belinda's parents

Benny the Antichrist, Page 206

were both Smiths and she married a guy named Smith. She's our one quadruple Smith. You don't want to mess with her."

Belinda lit up a smoke. "Kid, you don't want to think about all this stuff too much at once, is my advice to you. In fact, maybe don't think about it at all. I can see your eyes spinnin' and you're thinking what the hell kind of nuthouse have I gotten myself into? And truth to tell, this all might be crazy and definitely might not be for you. Just 'cause your old man worked here doesn't mean you got to. Because if you stick around here, I can tell you it's going to get weirder. You'll be hearin' about how some war in some ungodly place you never heard of is going to play merry hell with tank three and how this or that economic policy will max out capacity in the grief pipes. You'll find yourself takin' courses in sociology or physics, just to keep up. It never ends, this stuff."

"Hey Belinda," Ka-Chang smiled, "remember that theoretical physicist guy we had down here? Igor's nephew? Man, that guy used to follow us around all day, askin' questions, writing down everything in equations and symbols. When we told him Miguelito and the others had a band, Quark and the Quantum Mechanics, I thought he was going to have a ratch." He glanced over at Eamon, who looked back, blankly. "I guess you had to be there. Finally we gave him a look in one of the main pipes. Bad idea, but he begged us for it. I hear he's makin' sandals at some commune in Oregon, now. Doesn't ever want to come back to the Apple, since he recovered. More or less."

"You guys, you guys are such a… You see, Eamon, what a bunch of humps these guys are? And they're dealin' with the deadliest shit. Nuclear waste is play-doh, compared to what goes through here. All that grief, rage, greed, nightmares, if it ever got out, well, everyone on the surface would have killed everyone else and themselves before you could even tell what happened. It's not for everyone, this job. Maybe what you want to do is get dressed, right now, in your civvies and go live your life. You don't need all this stuff."

Eamon asked "If I go, will that dream be true? That I lost? That my back'll be out forever? That there's some kind of bloodsucker ghost after me who looks like my Mom?"

"Whoa, kid, where's all this other stuff coming from?" Ka-Chang asked. Belinda stared at him, her eyes suddenly clinical, appraising.

"When I was coming here this morning--"

Benny the Antichrist, Page 207

Ka-Chang held a hand up. "Whatever. I mean, not whatever, but... Look, Eamon, this is important stuff, really important. But I ain't the guy you should be talking to.

"But this happened here, right? Some of it, anyway. Can I fix it here?"

Just then the door banged open and Testosteroni strode in. He was breathing hard, as if he had run a long way. "Sorry, you guys, but Bearclaws says he needs Ka-Chang on the floor now. Even Steven is down and we need backup."

Ka-Chang stood. "How bad's Steve?"

"They don't know yet. It's dicey. A suicide bomber got to the Israeli Prime Minister, they've got Trenton quarantined with a new strain of bubonic plague and the President's brother's been arrested for fraud and arson. It came down together before he could get out of the way. The pipes are shaking with it. We may have to do a dump."

Ka-Chang turned to go, then glanced back at Eamon. "Crunch time, Mon-E. Belinda here can take you back topside, no hard feelings. Or you can stay and deal with some of the worst shit imaginable. It's up to you."

"All I want to know is, can I fix it, if I stay here?"

Ka-Chang sighed. "I dunno, Eamon. I don't know. There's a chance, maybe. But--"

Belinda broke in. "Nothing comes free here, Eamon. And nothing happens just like you expect it to. You got issues, probably more issues than you or anybody else knows. Up there you can do what people do, work things out, learn to live with them. In the Bath, it may be there's nothing you can do about them except make them a whole lot worse. You maybe don't think that's possible right now, but I'm telling you the God's Own Truth. This place can make things a lot worse for you."

"But I can change what I saw, right?

Her mouth worked, then she shrugged. "Yeah. Maybe."

"Then I'm in."

Testosteroni said. "OK, let's hit it. I got a feeling the Gods are going to be riding tonight."

The Deep Crew
Chapter Five

As the jetliner's engines shrilled upward and its wheels started their heavy roll down the tarmac, amid the clutched armrests, gritted teeth and muttered prayers, one passenger eased back into her seat. At last, Rachel thought, I can't turn back now.

The pounding in her head was gone, for the first time in months, though it would soon be back. Carefully thinking of nothing in particular, she scanned her fellow passengers' emanations with the complacent, sidelong gaze of a practiced Smith. Most were dense, formless nimbi of excitement and fear. A few had coalesced into images. As the plane shook while wings and flaps grabbed air and hoisted themselves up the cabin was filled with dim shapes of fire and wreckage, slowly fading as the wheels left the tarmac and they gained altitude. For a moment she saw huge, swelling, rising beams she recognized as the elation of flight, both from Big Belinda's lectures and from glimpsing them as her ex-roommate Tilly slept and dreamed. Then they were quickly overlaid and supplanted by others. A ghostly, impossibly curvy stewardess in a tight minidress sashayed down up and down the aisles, ignoring and sometimes passing right through the tired-looking flight attendants in their businesslike pantsuits. The area around the restroom was a cloud of lust and anxiety, flickering with glints of sex and sickness. Though they had faded, every so often the cabin burst into ectoplasmic flames and wreckage, fitfully dying down, only to peak unpredictably. Dark figures lurked in impossible corners of someone's fantasized plane.

She was startled to find a shadow around herself. Something enveloping, covering her head right down to her feet. Strange. Men usually mentally stripped clothes off her, especially above the waist. Abruptly she realized her dark features and hair, covered by a sunglasses and a scarf, had spooked someone. They were uneasily daydreaming her into a Muslim woman's garb, a burka or chador.

She tried to remember the story about the suicide bomber who'd gotten to the Israeli Prime Minister. What was the woman's name? It didn't really matter, of course. Here and now, she, Rachel Seppanen, Minnesota Bible school nerd, oboe player and sewage treatment worker, was an Avatar of Terror.

If only you knew, she thought, if only you knew. I'm trying to save you all from people who steal your dreams, who stand in the way of God's Work. Then suddenly she felt ashamed by her unearned assumption of superiority, by the hubris of her psychic voyeurism. How had it come to this, that she'd find herself flying among ghosts and nightmares, desperately trying to stop a dark underground coven, some of whom sincerely thought they were keeping the world from tearing itself to pieces?

Hard to say where it all started. Growing up in Minneapolis, she'd always felt like an outsider, a dark-haired, swarthy impostor among all the blond Scandinavians in her suburban school. It didn't help that she was adopted, although her mother often said Rachel made things harder than they needed to be. The Seppanens were a very cool couple, both academics. He taught European History, she Comparative Literature. Eero and Imogen were heavily involved in various committees and boards, for the university, various arts groups and political causes. They lived on a rambling acreage in a bohemian, wooded suburb by the river.

Rachel was their only child. When she outgrew daycare, she spent long hours alone in the geodesic dome that had served as the family home while their split-level A-frame was being built, and which she commandeered as her summer bedroom. Sometimes she didn't see either one of them for a few days, while they cycled through faculty meetings, opera and ballet board meetings, planning sessions for protests against the war, polluting developers, discriminatory government policies and a host of others.

Rachel liked fixing things, or just taking them apart and putting them back together. Her room was full of neatly shelved and labeled clocks, radios and appliances in various states of disassembly. At age eight, she'd taught herself to program a neighbor's cast-off computer and was the family's IT resource, sometimes fielding a number of calls a day, especially from Eero, who tended to panic when his screen didn't show him exactly what he expected.

Rachel's abilities excited both admiration and puzzled concern in her mother, who had never been sure what to make of the darkly

Benny the Antichrist, Page 210

intense, literal-minded little girl who watched her parents' feverish busy-ness and socializing with apparently limitless self-containment and equanimity. Imogen was relieved when Rachel showed musical aptitude. Artistic temperament was something she could understand, though secretly she wished Rachel had chosen something like her instrument, piano, or her father's violin, mainstream instruments with large solo repertoires. Oboists were oddballs and yet the ultimate ensemble players.

Rachel wasn't popular in school but she wasn't a victim either. She baffled teenaged piranha packs with a mixture of apparent unconcern for their definitions of status and sudden, wicked jokes. A trio of particularly spiteful girls abruptly quit harassing her when she whipped a realistic-looking rubber snake at their leader, causing the girl to lose bladder control, then emptied a rubber syringe of ammonia in their faces. She got sent home from school that day, but was a hero the next, something she accepted with the same seeming nonchalance as the former scorn.

She always had an eccentric, brainy girl as a best friend. For the last three years it was Cynthia, a Chinese-Chicano prodigy who wrote erudite, gloomy poetry and was so shy her nickname was Shadow.

Then came puberty and everything came unglued. She finished grade seven in June as a barely-noticed little girl who effortlessly got good grades. She started grade eight in September as a zit-faced teenager with almost comically large breasts, attended and harassed by a hovering swarm of boys her age and older. As if that weren't enough, Cynthia was killed shortly into the school year by a hit-and-run driver. Rachel's grades plummetted and she retreated to her geodesic lair for days on end, ignoring school, meals, the boys who called her teen line and everything but her computer.

When Imogen and Eero finally realized what was happening and cancelled their various meetings and appointments long enough to almost physically drag her out of her room, they found a different Rachel. This Rachel was clearly aware that Imogen's hectic social pace was coordinated by the dictates of her latest intra-faculty affair and that Eero's breezy manner and dry wit masked an inner numbness. This Rachel was obsessed with finding her birth mother. This Rachel was a regular on Christian chatlines, had joined a prayer group and demanded a transfer to Elizabeth Addams, a local evangelical-run girls school.

The girls in her class there weren't really any nicer, but they tended to have large dollops of guilt that checked their worst excesses. And the sheer amount of homework their teachers piled on, plus the fact that they were expected to volunteer many hours to New Jerusalem Tabernacle, the parent church, didn't leave much time for teenage feuding and ostracism. After an initial adjustment period, she seemed to recover her equilibrium. Her grades shot back up and she started getting the same kind of report card comments she'd gotten previously, reserved praise from teachers who recognized her brains and work ethic, but couldn't figure out this intense, self-possessed, stubborn girl.

Had one of these older women managed to get Rachel to open up, she would have found a soul in a maelstrom, angered by her own and others slightest lapses from stern ideals, tormented by her bottled rage and imperfect belief. In her dreams her mother shone among distant, glowing clouds, stretching forth a healing, nurturing hand like Mary Magdalen. In reality the state adoption agency would tell her absolutely nothing about the woman.

In grade eleven, which she had skipped to from grade nine, she managed, by dint of trash-sorting for passwords, online misrepresentation and intense hacking, to uncover the fact that her mother's last name was Darbinian, that she might be at least partly Armenian. It was a tiny bit of data, but it kept her going. She combed the web with ever more sophisticated and wilder searches for Darbinians, in Minnesota and elsewhere. She gathered her own extensive databases out of the Mormon genealogical library. She used a graphics program to project her own face as it would be when she was 30, 40, 50. She found herself staring at any woman who had her own thick, arched brows, broad cheekbones and wide mouth. She read everything she could on Armenia and its tragic history. Her pastor even felt compelled to give her a serious warning over doctrinal errors she had absorbed through her research into the Armenian Orthodox Church.

Then a letter came in the mail and her world collapsed again. In painful, arthritic handwriting Mrs Gladys Gowan apologized for not contacting her sooner, but she was writing now in response to an ad Rachel had placed in the personal section of the Los Angeles Times two years ago. Her daughter Enid, a hard-drinking wildcat she described as "trouble from the get-go", had eloped with a merchant seaman named Rafi Darbinian. It had lasted for five months, when he

Benny the Antichrist, Page 212

signed on for a two-year stint in the Persian Gulf and told her it was over. All she had to show was a diamond with six payments still owing, an erratic string of support cheques and a pregnancy.

Enid, a spectacularly endowed but hard-faced brunette in the pictures Mrs Gowan sent her, had supported herself as a stripper, among other things, til she started to show. The closest she had ever come to being maternal was inexplicably not having an abortion, staying off alcohol through her pregnancy and a tearful, drunken call home after the birth. After that she signed up with exotic dancers agency that booked the Asian circuit. She died in a detox in Guam.

Unbidden, the shadow loomed over her, dark as she was, but taller, slimmer, a figure pieced together from the few scrapbook pictures Gladys had brought to show her, standing hipshot, eyes distant, challenging, a cigarette dangling from a long-nailed hand. Waiting. Soon, Rachel said to her, soon I will come to you or bring you to me. Soon we will be at play in the Fields of the Lord. Her mother's ghost turned and faded to that not-color Rachel had never been able to find words for, flickered and was gone. For now.

The cabin lights flickered slightly as the plane hit some turbulence, a Nor'wester whistling down from Canada. A couple of small screams when a few of the oxygen masks popped free and dangled, swaying in the cramped space like some predator's snares. The captain's voice buzzed through the intercom, his studied nonchalance calming only the most credulous. The flight attendants put all their energies into soothing the hysterical and getting the recalcitrant and blase to return their seats to the upright position, as if disaster could be averted by proper posture, and among these clenched and sweating strangers, the spectres of their lusts and terrors, in the trembling chamber thousands of feet above the earth, Rachel relaxed and drifted into her first sound sleep in months.

The Deep Crew
Chapter Six

Back on the floor, a small knot of people surrounded Even Steven, a black man in his early forties sitting propped against one of the tanks. He had a puncher's face, flattened and thick with scar tissue, like a stone worn smooth in a stream. His eyes were open, but his complexion was gray. He was talking in low tones with Bearclaws, who squatted beside him. Two men rolled in a wheelchair. They put him on with a fireman's lift. Several Deep Crew members touched his shoulder gently as he was wheeled away.

His eyes didn't seem to focus right.

"At least he don't have the blue crawlies," Ka-Chang said.

"What's that?" said Eamon.

"When you've got ectoplasm crawling over you so people can see it. The thing with this stuff is the more concentrated it gets, the more it tries to form itself into a geist. You see someone with that and you're not sure what you've got. Could be he's crazy. Or something else entirely. Mostly something you don't want to know about."

"What's a geist?"

"A geist is a dream, a dream of something we're all afraid of or desperately want. We've all got it in us. It moves between us and everyone we meet. It has to, or we don't make sense to each other. But if you ever see a guy get a blast of it and it sticks, look out. You never know what it'll do to him. Might burn him out and you, too, if you let him get hold of you. Or maybe he'll kill you while he's a God's horse."

"Yo, every time I think I'm down with what you guys are talkin' about, somebody trots out another piece of gobbledygook. What's—"

"OK. Heads up, people," Bearclaws said. "Steve said he never saw what hit him, but it felt like an explosion, which jibes with the news we've been hearing out of Israel. We're expecting the Bomber--"

There was a chorus of groans.

"--maybe with some complications, due to that plague news, though I think, I hope, it's too soon for a synthesis. Let's get it before it goes too actual on us. Steve thinks he managed to flush out the secondary before he got hit and so far the gauges back him up. So what we're gonna do is try and give the main tank time to clear on its own and run everything through the secondary. That'll mean a lot more pressure than usual, but let's try to keep leaks to a minimum. I don't want any fully reified nightmares. There's already ghosts around, as you know. I know some of you think they deserve gentle treatment and normally I might agree. Right now, though, the pipes are crawlin' with plasm and it's gonna get worse.

"We're into full crew overtime, as of now. I want every qualified hand on the floor toting a de-charger and grenades, including Smiths." A wave of grumbling started in one corner of the room and stopped when Bearclaws aimed a thundercloud glower that way. "You guys knew this might happen when you signed up. If you didn't, you never read your contract. You see one of them slave ghosts, I don't care if it looks like your dear old grannie, you zap it and move on. Got it?" A reluctant chorus of assent answered. "All right, grab your weapons and take up stations. If you don't know where you're stationed, talk to me or Hererra. Let's go."

The crowd moved off. Bearclaws stood among the stream, answering questions and giving orders as they passed him by. As the crowd thinned, he glanced over at Mon-E. "Kid, this ain't no place for a new guy. You go on home, enjoy your weekend and we'll see if we can fit in some training time Monday."

"I already told Ka-Chang I'd stay."

"That's fine, Eamon. Except you don't tell Ka-Chang, I tell you. We've got a major situation here and nobody's got the time to be looking out for you. Sorry, but that's the way it is. You can go back on your regular shift until we call you."

Testosteroni said "Claws, can I talk to you?" He nodded toward the office.

"OK, but make it fast." They walked off, talking in low tones.

Mon-E stared out at the shop floor, hardly seeing grim-faced Deep Guys coming back from their lockers wearing rubber boots, toting spears, tridents, axes, swords and plain rubber batons, all of them sparking and glowing green or sometimes blue. His thoughts were tangled, chaotic. He saw himself in his dream, tall, beautiful, impossibly strong and graceful, his back whole and well. Maybe, he thought.

Testosteroni and Bearclaws were back. Testosteroni shook his head and shrugged. Bearclaws said "Hersch told me about your Going Under Dream. Eamon, you maybe got a tough break, but we can't do anything about it now. You're still going to have to tough it out. Anyway, there's a chance it never happened up there. Haddad's a triple Smith, after all. Those guys jump at their shadows all the time."

"But—"

The explosion slammed Eamon into a wall. A man fell from atop a big tank, sloppily battering into pipes and valves as he dropped, hitting the floor with a muffled thud. He was flattened to a scrap of blood-soaked sponge. Silence for an infinitesimal, breath-caught moment. Then a woman screamed "Teddy!" and Albie began to roar. Bearclaws yelled "Everyone down!", and hauled Eamon down from where he stood, stunned.

Seconds stretched out as the crew scattered, hid, cowered, eyes straining for threatening shadows. Bearclaws rolled under the round belly of a tank, manhandling Eamon along with him like a wrestler reversing an opponent. "Stay down," he whispered. Then he pulled out a cell phone, rapidly punching in a four number code. From another corner of the room came an answering twitter. Bearclaws whispered, "Everybody OK there, Miguelito?

Eamon couldn't hear the answer. Bearclaws frowned and said "All right, look. We can't stay pinned here. No I don't know where it is. Prolly on the catwalk, if it's still material. Who's closest to the light switches?

"Good. OK, pass the word. Everybody with an ecto-grenade, get ready to toss it. On the count of ten, I'm gonna try to reach Teddy. You run and hit those lights." While he counted, he passed a small, silvery ball with a black button to Eamon, mimed pressing the button and tossing it up in the air.

At ten a volley of silver grenades went up. Eamon had his hands over his ears, but all he heard was a series of dull clicks. Bearclaws scuttled over to the fallen man, grabbed him and dove to cover in the same motion.

He nearly made it when the something dark darted at him from between two tanks, almost too fast to see.

The explosion blew the lights out.

Benny the Antichrist, Page 216

In the black above him, Eamon saw a glowing blue figure in a keffiyah and dark glasses, standing on top of a tank, backing slowly away. It was fumbling under its robes. Before it moved another step, several grenades rained on it, clicking almost at the same time. The Bomber dissolved like a puff of smoke in a hard gust.

He heard something thudding its way down above him. He raised his arms and managed to catch it before it hit the floor, more by luck than design, before he consciously registered it as a body.

The lights went up. Eamon saw he was holding a young man with a nose ring and purple dyed hair, sprawled limply in his arms. The man's eyes were glazed and one pupil was bigger than the other.

A diminutive, grayhaired Latino ran to Bearclaws and Teddy, who were slumped against a pillar. He waved a small sensor around them, tracing their shapes about an inch away, watching its digital display intently. He said something and nodded to two men with a stretcher, who carried first Bearclaws, then Teddy away. Bearclaws groaned when they lifted him. Teddy was silent.

The Latino hurried over Eamon and his burden. He said "Madre de Dios, it's Vince." and started to repeat the scanning procedure. He didn't offer any help with the young man and seemed careful not to touch him or Eamon.

"You wanna tell me what the fuck you're doing instead of helping this guy and me?" Gun-toting ghosts and magic alligators be damned, Mon-E was sick of people treating him like a chump. The stretcher medics had come back while he was scanned. No one answered him. Two guys in the crew watched him carefully, both of them ready with sparking rubber batons.

Finally the Latino said "They're clean," and the medics gently took Vince out of his arms. Vince looked impossibly small and boyish, slung between them. One of them checked his wrist for a pulse, shook his head and Eamon realized the boy wasn't breathing. The medic pushed the dull eyes closed. They picked him up and walked off, in no hurry now.

"What the hell are they doing? Aren't they even going to try and revive him? Don't any of you fuckers know artificial respiration here?"

"There wouldn't be any point, son," said the Latino. "When a God rides someone that hard, they're cooked inside."

"Don't any of you assholes ever talk straight? All I saw was a ghost guy on the catwalk. Vince wasn't even around."

Benny the Antichrist, Page 217

The Latino took his time answering. From somewhere in his coveralls he produced a hip flask. He took a healthy swig, then wiped it and offered it to Eamon. Eamon glared it away and the Latino shrugged. While he waited for an answer, someone nudged him from behind. It was a young guy in a yarmulke and sidelocks, carrying a ball and chain mace. When Eamon stepped aside, Yarmulke flicked the ball with a practiced movement under the belly of the suspended tank Bearclaws had used for cover. There was a sizzling spark and suddenly the air felt colder. Yarmulke muttered something and moved on. All around, Eamon saw, Deep Crew people were doing the same, prodding hidden spaces with sparking weapons. Over to the left someone was spot-welding one of the pipes.

"You must be Mick's boy," said the Latino. "I'm Miguelito Hererra, Acting Head Smith. Your dad and I go way back. Look, son, I don't have much time, so I'll give you the short version. What we're dealing with here is people's fears, their hatreds, their hopes, their joys. When it leaks out under pressure, it wants to take a form, usually a mythical figure, because those forms are generalized and available. New York's the largest concentration of Jews and Arabs outside of Jerusalem. We've been seeing this Suicide Bomber joker more and more around here since the second Intifada."

"But what's that got to do with Vince?"

"The Bomber rode him, made him an Avatar."

"But the explosions--"

"Look, Eamon, you've got questions, but now isn't the time. I've got one guy dead, three men hurt, including the shift foreman. You can't help here and I can't spare anyone to take care of you. We've got to get you to Bearclaws's office and up to the world."

"But they said--I had a Going Under Dream."

Before Miguelito could reply, a stocky black woman with ashy dreadlocks called him over. She was lying face-up on a car mechanic's creeper, her legs under a huge red tank that seemed to be subtly changing shape as she made adjustments to a small control panel on its side. They had a quiet conversation, involving a lot of hand motions. Miguelito's eyes flicked toward Eamon and she nodded. She scooted out into the aisle, rose smoothly to her feet with a back somersault and flipped the creeper up with her foot like skateboarder, tucking it under her arm. She followed a few paces back as Miguelito walked towards Eamon.

Benny the Antichrist, Page 218

"I heard about your dream, Eamon. I'm sorry, and I really mean that, but the only thing I can tell you is hang in there. It may never have happened, up above. Rasheeda here will take you back to Claws's office."

"Can't I just--"

"No buts, Eamon. Go." Miguelito turned and walked down the aisle and around a corner.

The Deep Crew
Chapter Seven

Standing in the walnut-and-marble-lined private elevator going up the top floor of the Holcombe Judgment Center, Rachel suddenly wished she could just go somewhere and play her oboe.

Maybe if her music hadn't left her, if she could just sit down and noodle with a bit of Mozart or Ellington none of this would have happened. She'd never have gotten a job with the Deep Crew, never written a letter.

The doors hissed open and Krissi, the tall, sleek, blonde staffer who had met her at the airport, stepped out, smiling graciously.

"The Reverend is so looking forward to greeting you personally," she bubbled. She looked vaguely familiar, Rachel thought. Maybe a spokesperson for the Judgment Crusade?

As she followed, Rachel saw a long, paneled, purple-carpeted hallway lined with paintings and framed photographs. The sheer number of images was a shocking contrast to the clean austerity of the rest of the Judgment Center and the evangelical churches Rachel had seen. The paintings, mostly in ornate golden frames, were a mixture of styles, many of them the grimmer Biblical stories, the Fall, the destruction of Sodom and Gomorrah, the harrowing of Hell.

Others were portraits of Talbot Holcombe at various stages of his career. There was the star quarterback winding up for a long pass with a plainly discernable angel looking over his shoulder from the stands. The handsome young minister surrounded by adoring mothers and babies with a burning abortion clinic in the background. The leonine patriarch in the pulpit, his beseeching arms held wide, lit from above by a glorious beam of light.

The photos were more of the same, but a little more prosaic. Holcombe accepting a medal from the President, Holcombe shaking some general's hand. Holcombe on a dais with a burning-eyed black man in a brilliant kaftan.

Benny the Antichrist, Page 220

Unbidden, some rebellious part of Rachel quietly noted that she stood in a huge, richly appointed edifice whose center was stocked with vainglorious trash. A whited sepulchre. The thought stopped her like a blow to the gut. She blinked, confused, her legs frozen. I could go, she thought. I could just turn around and leave. I could be playing, or at least trying to play, in a rehearsal room in Brooklyn by this evening.

Krissi, misinterpreting Rachel's hesitation, cleared her throat almost musically. "There's a Lady's Room off to the right, if you'd like to freshen up." A pink linen-clad arm showed her the way.

Rachel nodded, not trusting herself to speak, and bit down hard on her unworthy doubts. Judge not, lest ye be judged, she reminded herself. As well as The Road is straight and narrow. But she decided to follow Krissi's suggestion anyway.

The restroom was empty, which was a blessing. Rachel entered a stall and sat down. She felt a need to pray, but strangely she couldn't seem to manage it. Prayer had been the one of the few things that had sustained her since she had joined the Deep Crew and discovered her inability to talk about it.

When they said you couldn't tell anyone about the Deep Crew, they didn't just mean management frowned on loose talk with outsiders. No, when you signed the contract and Bearclaws did the ceremony, you really physically couldn't talk about the Bath to anyone who didn't work there. As you worked your way up things and the spell wore off, they said things changed, but when he first put the whammy on you, you couldn't even talk to a co-worker unless you were both on the job.

She had half a pack of cigarettes in her purse, but lighting up here seemed not just wrong, but sacrilege. The dress she'd bought to come down here, blue raw silk with matching shoes, now made her feel tacky and overdressed. She felt itchy under her pantyhose and her feet were swelling the way they always did before her period. Everything smelled bad and things had the queasy brilliance that told her she had a migraine coming.

Please forgive me, Lord, for I am weak, she thought, dug in her purse and lit up a Pall Mall. Sucking in the dry, edged smoke she felt appalled at herself and much, much better. How had she come to this?

Someone was knocking gently on the stall door.

"Um, Rachel," Krissi said, "are you all right in there?"

Benny the Antichrist, Page 221

Rachel's cigarette had burned down almost to the filter. Krissi could surely smell it. She felt a prickle of annoyance, immediately followed by a stab of guilt. Krissi was just doing her job and doing it more graciously than Rachel had any right to expect. The guide had waited at the airport for a couple of hours before Rachel's storm-delayed flight had finally touched down and had treated her with kindness and courtesy ever since.

Rachel had barely said two words since Krissi had met her at the airport and chauffeured her to the Judgment Center. She wasn't being silent out of surliness or shyness. She was just afraid Bearclaws's mojo would shut her up for days. It had happened to her before when she tried to talk about her job. It was all she had been able to do to write the letter.

Enough. It was time to do what she'd come for or leave. And Krissi deserved better treatment than this. Rachel stood up, flushed the cigarette and unlocked the stall.

"I'm really sorry," she told Krissi. She walked to the sink, turned on the cold water and threw some in her face. "I've been behaving like a bitch. But I'm just afraid that I won't be able to tell him anything."

Krissi opened her mouth to reply, then closed it. She looked Rachel in the eye, considering.

"That's what I thought, too," she said, "after the abortion."

"Krissi, um, I don't know if this is..."

"Forgive me, Sister Rachel, but I have to testify about this. Not too long ago, I would have told you that I knew what you're thinking. You'd be thinking 'Goodie two-shoes blondes like Krissi don't get abortions.' Or maybe you might think 'So Miss Homecoming Queen got a little too eager, did she? And now she's working it out like some celeb doing community service, dressed up in her little Christian Barbie pink outfit, ferrying around visitors in a nice limo she doesn't own or gas up.' Or maybe you didn't think any of those things. I don't know. The truth is I don't know very much.

Rachel caught Krissi's eye and held out the Pall Malls. Krissi's mouth worked, but she shook her head.

"If you were thinking any of those things," she continued, "you'd be right about a lot of them. I grew up rich and spoiled in a big house in Malibu. My family was in The Industry. I was in commercials before I was toilet trained and I knew my agent's name before I said "Daddy".

Benny the Antichrist, Page 222

My friends were pretty much the same, child stars, junior moguls, the future next-big-things. My senior year high school boyfriend Jamal was a star running back at UCLA. He came from South Carolina and he was almost blue-black. I might have hooked up with him to shock my parents, fat chance, but he sure was hot.

"Predictably enough, we got careless. Jamal, bless his heart, wanted to marry me. But I had enough air miles on my Platinum Card for a round trip to Puerto Rico at Spring Break, so that wasn't going to happen. Have you ever been to an upscale abortion clinic? It's nice, very clean and quiet. You can have a pedicure while you're waiting.

"Everything went off without a hitch and I was on the beach next day, doing pina coladas and lines with some friends. I got home a few days later, broke up with Jamal and took up with a venture capitalist who'd been sending me gifts for months. A week after that I landed my first big role, supporting actress in a Movie of the Week and pretty much put the whole thing out of my mind.

"Five days into the shoot we were watching the day's rushes and laughing at some bloopers when I started to choke. Everybody thought I was having an allergic reaction to something we'd ordered in. But really I was having a vision. I'd never had a vision before and didn't know anyone who had. People like me and my friends didn't need them. We had coke or E or acid or anything else you could buy. But this was a vision, a vision of a tiny baby, a girl, tumbling endlessly through cold, thin mist. She was trying to breathe with lungs that wouldn't work and neither would mine. She was freezing to death with no one to hold her in their arms and it felt like I'd never be warm again.

"They rushed me to the hospital, made sure my parents' medical was paid up, shot me full of muscle relaxants and put me in an iron lung, where I lay staring off into space for the better part of a week. At least that's what they told me. I wasn't there for any of it. All I remember is that little girl stretching out her arms to me, drifting farther and farther away.

"And the next thing I recall is waking up and wishing I never had. My mother and father were there, together for the first time in years. They were so happy they were weeping. On the nightstand next to my bed was a huge bouquet of my favorite pink-and-yellow glads in a beautiful crystal vase. What really pissed me off was knowing I wasn't

Benny the Antichrist, Page 223

strong enough to tip it over and use a shard to slit my parents' throats and then my own.

"I tried to kill myself three times in the next two weeks. They sent me to a lovely little clinic in Florida, put a tastefully discreet monitor on my ankle, gassed me up with thorazine, topped off with whatever antipsychotics had caught the shrinks' fancy that week and tried to figure out what to do with me. I was a terrible disappointment to everyone.

"I'd be there still, except that Meredith, one of the girls in my group therapy sessions, was a real bookworm. I wasn't a reader myself, but when we went on field trips she'd compulsively pick up any printed matter that came to hand. She'd come back loaded down with real estate brochures, menus, bus schedules, anything, so long as it had words. She didn't mind people going through her trove once she was done. And sometimes I was bored enough to do that.

"I've still got the handbill that changed everything. Meredith said she found it in the trash." She reached in her purse and brought out a worn flier on faded orange paper, wrapped in a Ziploc bag. It said Second Annual Judgment Crusade and featured a picture of a young Talbot Holcombe, lifting his brawny arms and piercing eyes in a beseeching gesture.

"At first I didn't pay much attention to this. It was just one more piece of the outside world to stare at when I got tired of watching TV. But something kept drawing me back to it, nagging at me. It was that word, Judgment, and how it applied to my baby.

She looked Rachel in the eye. "The baby makes a lot of people, smart people, uncomfortable. I've done my reading on fetal development. I know now and I knew then that what they vacuumed out of me didn't look anything like that little girl, didn't even have a brain stem.

"None of that matters, not even a little bit. That child was a Judgment on me and people like me. She was a sign that even though I had lost my friends, my freedom, even my ability to get through a day undrugged, I still had more I needed to lose. I had to die. I had to die and be reborn, not just in Christ's blood, but my own, in the blood of a world that throws babies away. And only Judgment, Final Judgment, can do that for me, or anyone else.

"The moment I realized this I knew I had to change. I started paying attention to what the psychiatrists were telling me. I figured out what they wanted to hear from me and I let them hear it. I wrote letters to my parents and made sure they saw I was happy when they visited me. When the doctors said they were letting me go, I let them know I was glad, but just a little worried. Could I handle the outside world?

"My mother came to get me. We kissed the air beside each other's cheeks, she gave me a brand-new Platinum Card and we walked out to a rented Porsche. I think she'd convinced herself I was in some kind of a weight-loss spa and was a bit surprised that I didn't have any bags. We were in the passenger lounge at Miami International when she pulled her cell and started wrangling with her agent about some infomercial he wanted her to do. I stood up, smiled, pointed toward the ladies room and walked off. Ten minutes later I'd changed flights from LA to Tucson. I came directly here.

"Or I would have, except it came crashing down on me in the cab ride out here. You'd think after months of thinking about this I'd have realized a few things. But I just then figured out that Judgment was not an abstract, impersonal thing. I finally got that nobody here was going to stand up and applaud because I, Krissi Millington, had a little vision. No, I was going to be held personally to account for myself. How worthless my life was. How cruel and thoughtless. How was the Reverend, how was anybody, going to look at me and not say 'Here's an empty-headed little rich girl who just stole from her own mother, ditched her and ran away to see if Armageddon was a better high than anything she'd popped or snorted so far. What can she possibly have to contribute here?'

"It took me three days to work up the courage to come out to the Center. By that time my parents had tracked me down with a private investigator and they were trying to re-commit me. I haunted the grounds here for another two days, dodging the people from the clinic, until finally someone almost physically dragged me in to see the Reverend.

"And he did what I was afraid of. He Judged me. Judged me truly, but with mercy that fell upon me like the morning dew. The Reverend isn't a hard man, Rachel. He doesn't gloat in the prophesy of the Day of Reckoning. He Judges, just as He Who is to Come shall Judge, but with Judgment comes Healing. Let him heal you, Sister Rachel."

Not trusting herself to speak, Rachel nodded. Krissi smiled, stepped forward and hugged her. She took Rachel's hand and they walked into the hall.

Benny the Antichrist, Page 225

Rachel sighed and closed her eyes. There was such comfort in letting herself be led along the soft-carpeted hall, in her own undemanding darkness, with only the warm pressure of a hand to guide her. No part of her journey here had been easy, but this was as close as it was going to be. Don't think about it, she told herself, you're almost there. She reached into her purse to reassure herself that the mini-cassette recorder was still there.

They stopped and she felt Krissi step forward. Another pause. Then a door slid open in front of them and they stepped into a space that smelled faintly floral and had Christian pop music playing softly in the background. "Marcia," Krissi announced, "this is Rachel." She said it in the manner of someone bestowing a precious family heirloom. Rachel sensed the woman in front of them leaning forward, then halting when she saw her closed eyes.

"We're going to send you right in, Rachel" Marcia said in a soft, Midwestern accent, ever so slightly edged with pique and curiosity. "The Reverend asked me to cancel an hour of his appointments just so he could meet you."

Another tiny pause and she said "She's here."

She didn't open her eyes when Krissi led her through the room, hugged her and whispered "Don't worry."

She didn't open her eyes when the door swung open and the familiar rich bass-baritone voice called out "Welcome, Rachel. Please come in," and she stepped into the room.

It wasn't until the door thudded softly closed behind her that she let herself look around her.

In person Talbot Holcombe was even bigger and better looking than he seemed on tv. He had a leading man's rugged, square-jawed face, a brilliantly white smile beneath a sharp nose that had been broken a few times in his football career, deep-set steel blue eyes flashing out from under beetling brows, topped by a wavy silver mane and framed by thick sideburns. He gripped her hand firmly but gently, looking deep into her eyes. There was something quizzical about his gaze.

Of course, she thought, he really doesn't know anything about me. In the last few years she had avoided getting on any church's databases, more through instinct than conscious policy. In her dealings with the Judgment Center, she had signed herself as "R. S.". She'd bought her own ticket down here, only telling Krissi her first name at the airport. Krissi had put down her sign that said "Welcome

R. S.", pulled out a cell phone, speed-dialed and said, "She's come. Her name is Rachel."

A sandy-haired, buzz-cut man watched them from a seat beside Holcombe's massive mahogany desk. Holcombe kept his eyes on her face, but she could feel the other's startlingly dark eyes travelling down her body appraisingly, lingering on her chest and hips. Holcombe's features had taken some wear and tear during his athletic career, but it looked like someone had had tried to kill this fellow, and not just once. A thick scar ran down the left side of his jaw and onto his neck, disappearing beneath his open collar. His nose and jaw had been broken more than a few times. He didn't seem to have a right ear. He leaned back in his chair, almost seeming to doze, but there was something coiled and ready about his slim, broad-shouldered body.

Holcombe's eyes followed hers.

"Rachel, I'd like you to meet my associate, Mr. Paulley. It was he who brought your letter to my attention."

Paulley nodded and smiled unreadably. He made no effort to get up or shake hands.

So they had come to it at last. The letter she had slaved over, that had given her blinding migraines even to plan, that she had broken down, letter by letter, to binary on-off codes, tapped out while thinking of anything but the whole of the message she was writing and using the "1" key on her computer like a telegrapher. She had done it in five, ten minutes at a time, over the course of four hellish days, stopping when the pain got too bad, not daring to check it until the very end.

At work in the Bath she made sure she was punctual, eating her box lunch alone, non-committal whenever anyone tried to chat with her and absolutely terrified that they knew all about her betrayal. She forced herself to watch everything around her, both because she told herself that she'd need to report it one day and as a way of damping her dread at going home to resume work on the letter.

Coming home wasn't a moment of relaxation, just a moment to grab something to eat, steel herself and start tapping it out again, letter by letter, as the pain mounted. And when the computer had reassembled her binary code into letters, words, sentences and printed it out, she held the paper gingerly, as if it might burst into flames, steeling herself for one brief, sidelong scan. She made out a few words and had to drop onto the desk. She didn't make it to the toilet before vomiting painfully, as if someone punched her in the spleen. She had to book off two days at the Deep Level. Even if she'd felt well enough to go, the guilty, sleepless look on her face would have raised questions. When she'd finally managed, keeping her eyes averted, to fold the letter and drop it into a pre-addressed envelope to the Judgment Center, Rachel couldn't get it out of her apartment fast enough. She thought she'd feel better after that. She'd done the right thing. She was sure of it. But she hardly slept for the last three weeks. She tried to blend in at work, tried not to think about where she was, what she'd seen, what she'd done.

She decided after two weeks that Holcombe's people had filed her warning under "N" for Nutbars. She knew she didn't have the strength to try again. If she hadn't finally gotten the Judgment Center's coded answer as she'd requested, in the personal section of the morning Daily News, she'd have quit later that day.

And now she was here, facing Talbot Holcombe and he would want to know why he should believe someone who'd written a letter that described a strange, occult underground on government property, funded with American taxpayers' money. People whose job it was to traffic in ghosts, legends, the nightmares of a city. Government employees who undid God's work with a weird blend of technology and witchcraft.

Holcombe was talking. "--can't tell you what a stir your letter has caused around here, Sister Rachel. The idea of this unclean trafficking in spirits being funded by our own government, it's hard to believe."

She'd worked a long time on that letter, short though it was. She'd had to. When they said you couldn't tell anyone about the Deep Crew, they didn't just mean management frowned on loose talk with outsiders. No, when you signed the contract and Bearclaws did the ceremony, you really physically couldn't talk about the Bath to anyone who didn't work there. As you worked your way up things and the spell wore off, they said things changed, but when he first put the whammy on you, you couldn't even talk to a co-worker unless you were both on the job.

She knew: She'd tried. At first it just seemed odd that when her roommate, Tilly, asked about her job all she could say was "I work in the Jersey City Sewage Plant." It was word-for-word what she'd said when they first discussed sharing an apartment. They'd both been home on a dateless Friday night, in their pajamas, watching "Sleepless in Seattle" and getting loaded on Bailey's. Tilly had just finished

Benny the Antichrist, Page 228

kvetching about her boss in the insurance office where she worked, drooling over a hunky co-worker and dissing a bitchy personal assistant. She was obviously after quid-pro-quo confidences. When she couldn't go any further than the one basic sentence about her job, Tilly first looked offended, then concerned as her roommate sweated and trembled, straining futilely to force more words out. It felt as though she had a closed valve somewhere in herself, holding back a torrent of wonder, bewilderment and fear. She could hear a roaring in her ears. Her vision began to turn blurry and red. Dimly she heard Tilly calling and felt herself being shaken.

When she came to the first thing she saw was Tilly, tears streaming down her face while she waited for the 911 operator to answer. After a cough and a couple of tries, she managed to croak out "I'm all right now."

Tilly helped her sit up on the couch. Rachel had drooled on the pink terrycloth of her pajama top. Tilly looked at her, careful as only the mildly drunk can be, and asked, "Are you sure?"

"I think so. Could you get me some water?"

When she was able to speak more easily, she managed to say, "He said I couldn't talk about the job, but I never thought he meant anything like this..."

"What do you mean, couldn't talk about the job? It's a sewage treatment plant, not a nuclear weapons lab! What's the big deal?"

She shook her head helplessly.

"Who said you couldn't tell?"

She had her lips together for the "B" in Bearclaws when a warning shiver of nausea surged through her. She shook her head and Tilly raised a hand, palm out.

"Don't say anything," Tilly said. "Don't tell me anything, if it's going to make you sick."

But she had to tell someone, she realized. It was as if she'd awakened some part of her that had been numb, frozen since she learned of her mother's death. The things she saw every day, the collective dreams and nightmares of a city and the strange technology she was learning about to control them, it all seemed suspect now, even monstrous. When Tilly moved out the idea stayed with her, growing larger. Someone needed to know.

Going to work on a packed subway car one morning it suddenly came to her that she might as well be among the dead. Every pallid, swaying body was silent, moving only with random jerks and shocks of the wheels on the track. A tiny hissing cacophony swarmed about their heads from the clashing musics of their various radios, I-Pods and cell phones. Their eyes were closed or they stared at nothing. Their dreams, she thought, their dreams have been leached from them. After that she tried to avoid the subway.

She passed a street corner preacher on the way home from work one evening. She was tired, thinking about supper, only paying the wild-haired, sweating man enough attention to navigate around him without making eye contact. But as she drew alongside of him he shouted, "Thou shalt not suffer a witch to live!" That day was when she resolved to write her letter.

Holcombe had said something again. He seemed to be waiting for a response. He must think I'm crazy, she thought. The throbbing in her head was like the barely muffled blows of a sledgehammer. She was going to be sick in a moment.

She reached into her purse and pulled out the mini-cassette recorder. She hoped the re-wind worked the way she'd jiggered and adjusted it to do. Sometimes it went back to factory setting and ran at high speed. Now Holcombe's look had changed from concern to alarm and growing anger. Paulley was up on his feet and moving her way. She waved them back, turned on the machine and spoke. "Kinatas sti. krew yee-ah ra-eeyu, dpots eeb oot vah yee-ath."

Now Holcombe looked thunderstruck, bewildered. Paulley had stopped and was watching her. She pressed the reverse button.

Above the hiss came her voice, strange, phase-shifted, but clear: "They have to be stopped, where I work. It's satanic."

Then she fainted.

The Deep Crew
Chapter Eight

"Hard cheese, Eamon," Rasheeda said in a soft, educated British accent. She shrugged and gave him a rueful smile. Under graying dreadlocks, she had a broad, café au lait face, with laugh lines in the corners of black eyes that looked as though they'd seen everything at least once. "For what it's worth, a lot of what the Smiths say is just so much tosh. Well, not tosh precisely, but potentials that never come to fruition."

When he didn't respond she nodded slightly. "Right. We need to get you back to the World. Hang on and we'll at least take care of a bit of administrative bother on the way." She bustled off in the direction of Bear Claws's office. And reappeared shortly, holding a file folder and two bottles of clear liquid, along with a big, well-worn purse. She thrust the bottle at him. It appeared to be commercial bottled water. "Have some of this," she said.

He frowned. "No thanks."

She smiled and drank some herself. "You're learning, aren't you? But honestly, Eamon, it's just water. This place dehydrates you. You don't think clearly when you're dried out. And I need you up to speed."

He was thirsty. He accepted a bottle and had a drink. While he was at that, Rasheeda tucked the file folder under his arm.

"What's in this?" he asked.

"All the papers for your benefits and the rest of the bureaucratic bumf that Bearclaws didn't subject you to earlier on. The sooner you get started, the faster you'll be covered. You can read it while we walk to the exit. Come on."

She nodded down a long aisle flanked on either side by tanks and machinery. When he hesitated, she frowned and said "Look Eamon, I realize you've had a spot of trouble here. If you're anything like your father, you're the sort of cove who wants to fix matters straightaway. But there's nothing you can do at the moment. Miguelito's made his decision, and believe me, he knows what he's doing. Now let's walk."

Benny the Antichrist, Page 231

Reluctantly, he started with her down the aisle. "Right," she said "Now open your file."

"Couldn't I do this later?"

"The sooner you go through the first steps here, the sooner you'll be a crew member in full standing, if that's what you want. Is that what you want?" She stared at him as they walked, her heavy face still, giving nothing away.

He sighed. Suddenly the day's events seemed to drag down on him. "Sure, I guess. I just need--"

"You need to put everything in perspective, which will take time. The best way to do that is to stop your mind from racing around in circles right now. And in my experience, nothing takes your attention off the unfathomable and ineluctable like paperwork, dry, boring, needlessly complicated paperwork. Open your file, please." Her voice was gentle, but it wasn't a request.

The file folder proved to be full of documents on onion-skin paper, clingy with static electricity. They stuck to his hands and each other, giving him tiny shocks when he tried to arrange and read them. They seemed to be all fine print.

He groaned inwardly. Making sense of contracts and applications always sapped his energy, made him feel foolish and small. Yolanda said that without her, he'd end up signing his own death warrant rather than read it through.

"Let's start with Form AGF-31: Duties of the Appellant."

While they walked down a twisting path through parts of the Bath he hadn't seen before, Eamon managed to locate the form, move it to the top of the pile and smooth it down so he could read it...

... and was dropped into a world both tedious and dizzying, where he clambered and dodged through spiky thickets of convoluted prose and arcane terminology, then suddenly and without warning found himself skirting chasms of unclear referents and unexplained assumptions, only to plunge back into a jungle of bureaucratese. He tried to get through the first sentence five times before he finally managed to keep the thread of it, then had to read it another three to make sure he understood, asking questions of Rasheeda all the while. His irritation level spiked when he found the second as opaque as the first.

"Couldn't they find someone who speaks English to write this stuff?"

"Everyone who works here got through these documents."

Benny the Antichrist, Page 232

"Fine. Gimme a pen and I'll sign them."

"Sure," she said, "but do you know what you're signing?"

"You tell me. What am I signing?"

"Do I look like a tour guide to you, Eamon? Or a kindergarten teacher?" She actually did look a little like one of his grade school teachers, but he didn't think this was a good time to say so. "These are the conditions of your job and benefits. They're not easy to understand. You'll find there many things around here aren't simple to grasp. But you'll have to look at them, assess them as best you can and make choices."

"OK, look. I'm sorry if I came off like a wise-ass. But I'm really tired and--"

"The geists don't care if you're tired. In fact, that's when you really have to be on your guard, when you're getting to the end of a week full of long shifts. Maybe you've been doing some dead tedious chore, and don't kid yourself, we've got plenty of them, like following a Smith around while he mucks about with some calibration or another.

"And you, you lucky newbie, you get to hold his tools, some of which hurt to even be near, wedge yourself into rubbishy corners he doesn't feel like squeezing into, stand for hours while he checks for psychic resonances. And maybe you're doing this while you cover for someone else, because we're short-staffed, as we often are. Not to mention washing up whenever you've a spare moment--something about plasmic emanations attracts dust in unbelievable quantities.

"And your mind is turning over and over because things aren't that great at home, so you've barely been sleeping and you've got a test coming up, on material you need to do this job, and you think you understand about a quarter of it at the most.

"You're an hour past your last break, just counting the minutes till quitting time. Someone taps you on the shoulder. You turn around--

"--and it's not the Mugger, or the Soul Vampire, or any of the other ones they've drilled you on. It's a geist you've never heard of. It's big and you can feel the power coming off it. It might be dangerous. It might be helpful. What do you do?"

"I don't know. Nobody's taught me that."

"But that happens to people who've worked here for thirty years. And the reason they've lasted is that they make an assessment and act on it. Just as you need to do with these papers."

Benny the Antichrist, Page 233

"OK, all right already, I'll read the damn things." Fuming, he turned his attention back to the documents. The language was murky as ever, meandering sentences staggering under the weight of ill-constructed subordinate clauses and unclear referents. Yet without noticing it, Eamon found himself slowly drawn into the gray, nimble obsession of a puzzle-solver. He'd always hated crosswords, sudoku, and any pastime that required him to sit still and think carefully. But now somehow, without quite admitting it to himself, he started tolerating it, then even enjoying it, needing to find the glimmers of meaning hidden within the heaped-up verbiage of the papers, pursuing them with the tenacity of a junkie chasing a high.

As they walked, he asked more and more pointed questions of Rasheeda, comparing her answers with his own interpretations, looking for inconsistencies and building a more complete picture of what the documents represented. Every time he filled one out and signed it he felt a small jolt of triumph.

He jumped when he heard the siren from a distant part of the plant. Suddenly everything seemed brighter, hotter.

"Bollocks," Rasheeda said, and he realized he'd never heard her swear before. "The main tanks are full. Sign the last one and let's get you out--"

Seconds later a klaxon oogahed right behind him and the corridor lights started flashing rhythmically. An alarm bell began hammering above him, sending splinters of pain into his already tender head. He could hear Albie roaring somewhere far away.

"Right," she said, pulling a cell phone out of her purse and punching speed dial. "It's me. Yeah, he's still here. Which tanks has it--as bad as that? How long have we got? Fucking hell. Well, there's no help for it. I'll do what I can." She flipped the phone off.

While she talked, Eamon looked around himself. He'd had a vague notion that he was in part of the Bath he hadn't seen before, but this was different from anything so far. The ceiling in this area was several stories over his head, supported by thick, Gothic-looking pillars. Some pillars were bare, gray stone but many supported a rain forest canopy of pipes and wires in intricate windings and festoons.

Rasheeda reached out and grabbed his hand, turning him to face her with casual strength. "Listen to me very carefully, Eamon. We're in lockdown. I can't get you out yet, but that doesn't give you leave to run around here, trying to solve any of your personal issues. The Bomber has filled up the main tanks and most of the reserves. What

Benny the Antichrist, Page 234

that means is that he could substantiate anywhere and anytime. And since you're the person with the least experience and resistance, odds are it'll be near you. I'd lend you my de-charging wand, but without training and attuning, you'd be more danger to yourself than anything else. And right now grenades would just let him get a fix on you.

"The upshot is that you have to stick close to me, and that means holding my hand."

"You don't need--"

"Don't even think of telling me you can shift for yourself--that's like saying you can handle an avalanche. I'm going to get you to the nearest lift. There's a shelter close by where you can wait for the all clear."

She started walking with him in tow. "We're going up to the next intersection, turning right, then right again. Don't let go of my hand. And keep talking to me--It might be the only thing that gets you through.

"What should I talk about?"

"Any sodding thing that pops into your head. Just so long as--"

A brazen, quavering wail drowned out the rest of her sentence. Sudden, stinging wind blasted him in the face, hot and dusty. Involuntarily, he closed his eyes and felt her draw him near, then move, not out of his arms, but through, as if she were dissolving in the shrieking gusts. He reached for her, briefly felt flesh under cloth-- only to be spun away by the punishing, raking wind. He tried to call her name and collapsed in a spasm of deep, wracking coughs. He felt as if he were being picked up and shaken.

When he opened his eyes, he found himself lying on his belly in a great open space under a huge white sun, blazing through air torpid and dun with dust. His throat was swollen, parched. He hurt everywhere.

Something tugged painfully at his ankle. No matter how much he blinked and squinted, he couldn't bring it into focus. He tried to wipe the dust out of his eyes, but his arm wouldn't move. He shook his head, sending shards of agony through it, gasped and squeezed his eyes shut--

--and opened them again, upon hearing a man's voice. It was a cheerful baritone, with the welcoming air of the host at a backyard barbecue. It came from somewhere to his left, over his shoulder. The syllables it spoke were shaped strangely and he couldn't make out the

Benny the Antichrist, Page 235

sense of them, but he felt that if he listened carefully, he would know what to do.

He felt a breeze, too faint for relief, but at least it seemed to be clearing the air. He was lying, pinned down somehow, on hot, dusty bricks that lined an open, sun-blasted square. All around him people strolled, ran, jostled, yelled, conversed, negotiated and argued. Vendors held up bolts of brilliantly-dyed cloth, handfuls of dates or figs, or tugged passers-by into their shops. A trio of women in dusty black burkas even stepped over him, but no one seemed able to see him.

From somewhere high up a dollop of water sloshed him hard in the face. It was warm, gritty and tasted of soap, but at least it cleared his eyes, once they stopped stinging.   Squinting, he saw he was being held down by innumerable fine, black threads that stretched from the people in the crowd to him. Or rather, through him: He could see how they went right through his skin and into the dusty bricks of the square.

He was hot and thirsty, stitched to the rough bricks, but strangely unhurt, despite his skin being punctured in thousands of places. He wondered why no one was able to see him. He tried to speak, but couldn't make a sound, as if his chest and larynx were paralyzed somehow.

The crowd seemed to be waiting for something, something exciting. There was a festive quality to their voices, but also something yearning and vehement.

A ragged little boy by his shoulder suddenly pointed off toward the muzzy, late afternoon sun and started shrilling something. The crowd fell quiet, then turned and jostled, trying to see, men craning, shouting, women trying to find clear spots to catch a glimpse. The noise grew as whatever it was came into view, men cheering, yelling "Allah Akbar", women ululating. There was a bludgeoning force to the crowd's noise, all out of proportion to their numbers, as if they were just the visible part of roaring army muscling its way into the world by sheer fervor.

Eamon was achingly, stupidly tired. His head hurt and his throt felt parched and swollen. But he knew he had to get up.

Agonizingly slowly at first, he painfully flexed his wrists and ankles, feeling the threads that bound him stretch, then sting as they broke, one by one. He managed to bend his elbows. The crowd was roaring, wailing, ecstatic. Their backs were to him. He gathered

Benny the Antichrist, Page 236

himself, then heaved against the dusty stones of the square, grunting with effort. Whatever they saw was coming closer. He got a knee under himself, arched his back and ripped his way up to standing, bleeding from a thousand pinpricks.

And found himself alone in a bare, wind-blown plaza, the sun like a hot iron on his head and shoulders. There was someone in the distance, walking toward him.

He knew that he didn't want to meet whoever it was. He knew he should run, but it was all he could do to stumble toward the buildings he could dimly see through the glare.

It took forever. His knees were sore and legs wobbly. His skin chafed every time he moved. His t-shirt began to soak through with blood. He could hear faint singing behind him, blown on the wind, a fiery quavered falsetto. Somehow he knew it was a death hymn.

But he finally reached one of the buildings. Leaning against the broiling white stucco, he ran a hand across his brow. It came away dry and dimly he knew that was very bad. He staggered back...

And saw the building had no door. Not even a window at street level. The singing was coming closer. With his last strength he hobbled the length of the building, stumbling over rough cobblestones and around the corner...

To find himself in cool, blessed shade. He could hear a bird calling, low and melodic, in the distance. Leaves rustled in a gentle breeze, somewhere. But best of all, there was a little cafe table, and on it was a bottle of water.

It was cold and he had to choke down the first mouthful through a swollen throat. He managed to control himself and took small sips, pouring a little on his feverish brow. Halfway through, he remembered Rasheeda. He couldn't remember if this was the same brand of bottled water she'd given him. Had she come back?

He seemed to be alone in a little shaded open space, surrounded by narrow two and three storey buildings, some white, some painted in brilliant blues, yellows, greens and pinks, set close together. Through a high-up window, screened by an ornate wrought iron grating, he thought he saw a glint of eyes, but couldn't be sure.

Then everything shifted. Abruptly the hot desert wind blasted the square, which baked in unendurable light. It was as if some terrible force had reached out and turned him and everything around him, into the path of the noonday sun. And into the square strode the Bomber, still singing his death song.

Benny the Antichrist, Page 237

He was olive-skinned and slim, clad in a white robe which showed his suicide vest with every step. His piercing gaze was on Eamon...

Who found himself staring at dark eyes in a burka, a boy in a school uniform, a blond man in dark, monogrammed coveralls, a well groomed looking woman in a blue business suit, the body changing with each step, but each with the same fervent, implacable gaze, as the Bomber strode straight toward him, reaching for something over the heart...

Blast radius, got to get out of the blast radius, was all Eamon could think as he ran. There was a narrow gap onto a little covered, crooked alley at the end of the square and he dodged through that--

--just as the explosion slammed air past him. He stumbled painfully into a rough brick wall, glancing up to see glass and rusty nails embedded in other side of passageway where he'd just been. Dizzy, ears ringing, holding his breath against the dust, he crept back to the alley's opening. Stopped. Nerved himself to peer out at body parts, blood, destruction.

And saw a figure walking toward him through smoke and flames, with the same unhurried, unstoppable stride, the same exultant, ululating hymn echoing off the stones and walls.

Suddenly furious, Eamon bent to snatch a broken cobblestone and hurled it at the figure, all in one motion - And felt time slow to a sludgy crawl, as the Bomber saw the rock, then stared back at him fearlessly, a taunting smile on his face, even as the stone crashed into his forehead. He fell -

And rose up seven-fold, a woman in black purdah, a businessman in blue pinstripes and a keffiyeh, a bearded man in white trousers and Jinnah cap, a schoolgirl in uniform, and three ragged little boys who leaped to their feet and raced toward Eamon, their suicide vests slapping against thin chests as they ran.

Comment

I'm a huge China Mieville fan, largely because of his childish misunderstandings. Now if you're a fantasy aficionado and haven't been living under a rock, this may seem to be a baffling, even dangerous statement. China Mieville is both intimidatingly brilliant and big as a house; he could bury me with erudition or knock my block off with equal facility.

I particularly like the way fantastic devices work in his stories. What gives Mieville`s work resonance is that the irreal principles that apply in his worlds

Benny the Antichrist, Page 238

function along the lines of how a bright, dreamy child would imagine things might go if reality were as cool as it should be. For example, Bas-Lag, the world of *The Scar* and other Mieville stories, is our world on a grander scale, where disjoint historical phenomena, physics and magic coexist and bleed into each other. In *The Scar* there is a modern city, New Crobuzon, at war with a pirate republic, something that only existed on Earth for a very few years in the early eighteenth century. His pirate nation, rather than a tiny, ragtag refuge for buccaneers on one island, is a sprawling, interlinked Armada of ships with a government that provides such services as a library, and has real global clout and long-term plans. One such stratagem is to raise the avanc, an undersea monster several miles long, against its its adversary, an imperialistic oligarchy that calls itself a parliamentary republic, which shares Bas-Lag with nations of the dead and undead, a country whose laws are the stakes of a national gambling tournament, and the Grindylow, a deep-sea race with access to strange technologies and other states of being due to the vast pressures of the Swollen Ocean above them and their proximity to *The Scar*, where the Ghosthead Empire made interstellar landfall, causing a physical and dimensional rift.

So you've got a world dreamed by a politically aware imagination, informed by years of Leftist political analysis and the London School of Economics, steeped in pop culture, comics, fiction and films of horror and sf. What distinguishes Bas-Lag further is that Mieville populates it with self-aware people who have adult motives, passions, weaknesses and ambivalences. They are heroes, turncoats, lovers and cat's paws, all of whom make consequential choices, but are also swept up in history that moves around and through them, whether they will or not.

Without my having consciously planned it, *The Deep Crew* attempts some of the same things Mieville achieves in *The Scar* and his other books. Which is to say, it takes place in a world which is, I hope, very recognizably like ours, to the extent that their history, place names and ambient social scenes are identical, or very close. The only way in which they differ is in a small point of psychology/physics.

Having been probably too coy by half in that last sentence, I also feel bound to issue a caveat for the novel in progress as it stands. I'm a slow writer and the writing came to a point where there were too many issues in my life to finish it at that time. Taking it forward now involves a recalibrated view of the world, if I hope to avoid complete anachronism. When I started the book, I could have confidently asserted that by far the largest part of the American population accepted many of the same things to be true about themselves and their world. They may have had vehement disagreements about what facts mattered, what they meant and what was to be done, but facts were facts.

Benny the Antichrist, Page 239

You and I now are in an utterly different world. As a Canadian, I now find myself sharing a continent with a nation where some thirty percent of the population subscribes to an apocalyptic conspiracy myth, mediated and purveyed, not just by crackpot internet posters, but by media conglomerates, public officials and elected representatives, operating without shame or restraint, and poised to stage a violent coup, trashing democracy and destroying the world order as we know it.

The End

About the Author

Scott Ellis

Scott Ellis has been a door-to-door salesman, professional malingerer, show groom, bonsai lumberjack, phone interviewer, arts scene curmudgeon, peculiarly well-rated credit risk, freelance ontologist and entrance-level maladroit for many years now.

Also by Scott Ellis

Fossil Cove Press presents CRAWLING TO THE MOON, The second collection of stories and vignettes from noted science fiction and fantasy storyteller, Scott Ellis, featuring...

Crawling to the Moon: A tornado, a talking doberman, fate and beauty in a Florida horse show, ca 1971.

System Crash: Sometimes being rich, cool and the boss doesn't pan out all that well...

Sidecar, the path to world peace, through nanotech and alcohol.

The Big Rock Candy Mountain: Two homeless men find themselves in a boxcar with a soldier from a space empire.

Cup of Trembling: A drink means greatness, death or madness. And you have to choose right now.

Dragon Dilemma: A warrior, a princess, a dragon: There are only a few ways this story can go, right? Well, not necessarily....

The New People: What happens when the rich, beautiful and famous have their own dimension?

"Scott Ellis hasa penchant for sophisticated, intelligent themes manifested through realistic, complex characterization. Some of it is light-hearted, much of it makes demands on the reader. Not a book to skip through. Be prepared to think and ponder. Overall, quite a treat to read."
Amazing Stories Magazine

Benny the Antichrist, Page 242